Dave,
I think of
you + high school,
always think of you...
Hope you enjoy my
first novel.
God Bless!
Wes

LOST AND FOUND AGAIN

LOST AND FOUND AGAIN

A Story of God's Grace, Mercy, and Forgiveness

BY WESLEY C. HAYNE

XULON PRESS

Xulon Press
2301 Lucien Way #415
Maitland, FL 32751
407.339.4217
www.xulonpress.com

Printed in the United States of America.

Paperback ISBN-13: 978-1-6322-1461-4
eBook ISBN-13: 978-1-6322-1462-1

Table of Contents

Prologue

*M*any of us live on the fringes of history which we experience from the places we visit, the people we meet and the events we witness. Hanging on to the fringe seldom puts our name in the history books, but we all know when we are watching history being made.

This is a story of a young man and his sister and how they adapt to extreme life experiences. The main characters weave their way through history being reminded of God's Forgiveness, Grace and Mercy.

The story captures one of the most exciting periods in US history, the mid 1800's. Early in life they both show strength in their faith in God, but as life experiences and tragedies occur, Morgan, the young man, questions his faith and escapes his abusive surroundings and reacts to having contracted "Gold Fever." His sister, Sally, retains her faith through thick and thin eventually causing Morgan to reevaluate his having lost his faith. He struggles to regain his faith after seeing and experiencing what can only be a series of miracles.

Some of the events may seem surprising and not believable, but true none the less. The adventures of the old West, romance, good versus evil, provides everyone the opportunity to self-reflect and find who they are in this story.

Very few liberties have been taken regarding the historic facts of their surroundings or the people they meet. For the most part,

Morgan and his sister Sally are the only fictional characters. The majority of characters and circumstances they come across in their journey West are real and historically documented.

They leave their home in Stillwater, Minnesota to travel down the Mississippi to New Orleans, then Houston, San Antonio to Castroville, Texas, where they join a historic wagon train. The people that made up this particular wagon train journeyed the old immigrant trail West to California, circling back and settling in Arizona. The names of the people on that wagon train and a couple of stragglers they picked up on the way, mark many a landmark in Arizona. Sally finds a new life in San Francisco while Morgan makes Prescott, Arizona his home where he finds one dream and loses another.

The discovery of strength through faith and forgiveness can eventually lead anyone to God's grace and a fulfilling life.

Acknowledgements

There are several people that I would like to acknowledge for their support over the last four years. Some of these people may not be aware of the role that they played in the discovery of this story and creating the motivation in me to write this book.

The first and always first to thank is our Lord Jesus. I must give Him credit where credit is due. It was a miracle to watch the words flow across the screen as this piece came together. I know that He had His hand on this.

A very special thank you, wrapped in love, for my wife Linda. She is the one that gave me day to day inspiration by listening as I read each chapter to her as I finished it. Her comments through sixty-two chapters kept me inspired and motivated.

Then there is our family. Jon and Miranda Hayne, Chris and Beci Hayne, Mark and Erin Hayne, Tim and Julie Smith, Wayne and Andrea Brustle, Scott and Jenny Hanson, and Heidi Hanson. Beyond that there are fourteen grandchildren (Ben, Kati, Mathew, Jack, Chase, Blake, Wesley, William, Olivia, Mikalya, Kennah, Tristan, Gabby, and Eydie) in our blended clan. I pray that all of them will constructively find a piece of themselves in this story.

Other people who took an interest, continually asked how I was progressing, along with providing historic information include John and JoAnn Coppage, Ken & Susanne Heintz, Bill & Patty Hoffman, Other friends that inspired me include Craige Thompson, and Brad Haddy. I would like to thank my pastoral friends. Pastor Mark & Judy Bowen, Pastor Jon Anderson, who assisted in the edit and his father Wess Anderson (with our Lord).

A special shout out to my Christian friends who have held me up in prayer from time to time when difficult situations put this project on hold.

I am sure I would have enjoyed meeting and thanking Helen Corbin in person before she passed. She was described by friends as an incredible person. Her accomplishments were vast in many areas of interest. Helen Corbin provided the bolt of creativity for this story while I was reading her book, "The Bible of the Lost Dutchman Gold Mine and Jacob Waltz", for the third time. I came across a piece of history that described a wagon train that left Castroville, Texas for Sacramento, California in 1849. It was hard to believe that one wagon train had so many historic figures to include Jacob Waltz the Dutchman, the Peeples and the Roberts families. A number of these miners regrouped in Yuma in 1863 after the gold in Sacramento ran thin and decided to go into the hostile territory of Northern Arizona. The names of the men (Peeples, Roberts, Walker, Wickenburg, Weaver etc.) are attached to peaks, valleys, and towns as founders. They named the rivers and creeks and were among the first to put their footprint in the Wild West of Arizona. If not for Helen Corbin's incredible piece of literature, I would not have discovered the backdrop for this story.

1

Three Generations

s I walked down the hall that divided the interior of our house, I could hear voices indicating an active conversation was taking place in the front living room. As I got nearer to the archway leading into the living room, I could tell that it was my son Wesley and my dad having a "what was it like...then what happened Grandpa?", storytelling conversation. I stopped just short of entering where I could hear everything but where neither of them would see me. I thought it would be interesting to do a little eaves dropping and see what tale's grandpa was sharing with his grandson this evening. It seemed that he lived to tell his stories. Even though Grandpa was a pastor now, in his early years he was a hellion and he would get carried away with some stories that were entirely inappropriate for children and even some adults. I knew there were numinous parts of my dad's life that he would never disclose of his younger years. I had tried repeatedly to get him to tell me more about some of his adventures but many a time as he would get to an interesting part of the story, it was like he jogged his memory, and at that point his face seemed to get a strange remorseful look. You could tell that he was remembering something painful and private. Something that he had never shared. Then he would snap out of his near trans state and openly change the subject never to return to that particular story. The number of stories that I had heard over the years that got cut off were starting to add up and the thought of never learning the mysteries that were behind these stories, left a gap that prevented me from really knowing who dad was and what made him the man he was. The recollection of historic events continued to increase along with his age. Dad was 68 and even though he seemed in good health we all knew that good health wasn't going to last forever. He was already getting excited about "...his last great adventure!", as he would state it. That was a reference to his death and finally experiencing heaven and learning all the secrets of the Universe and number one, seeing my mother again who passed when I was a newborn. Unfortunately, back here on earth there wouldn't be a source to discover all those historic mysteries of his life. He would take those to the grave. I felt that was, in fact, the current plan.

Some amount of time had passed as I listened to the story about the wagon train that he traveled with at the time he headed West as a young man. I enjoyed seeing the two of them spending time together. It was great that Wesley not only spent time with Grandpa, but that he enjoyed his stories as much as I did. I didn't want to interfere with their time together, but this story would have to come to an end as it was far past bedtime, even for a Friday night. As much as I enjoyed hearing dad's stories, I was also getting tired of standing in the hallway.

Dad knew how to shut down a story once he saw me standing in the archway to the living room. He knew it was Wesley's bedtime. That usually led to him and I having a little time together since Adella liked to go upstairs and get ready for bed after tucking in Wesley.

Grandpa created a quick ending for the story he was mesmerizing Wesley with by proclaiming bedtime, "Ok, young man, time for bed."

As Wesley turned and reluctantly headed out of the room, Dad watched him leave with a smirk on his face thinking of how fast Wesley was growing up. He reached for his pipe, a larger than usual pipe that was hand carved out of a piece of burl. He would talk about how the burl was from the root of some bush found in Israel. He always enjoyed his pipe while we either had one of our late conversations or he read a little before turning in for the night.

Adella came out of the kitchen and walked up the stairs to see Wesley to bed. I turned around and went back into the living room to share a little time with dad.

Dad was packing tobacco into his pipe, tapping it in so the draw on the pipe would be perfect. There was no special occasion that he would smoke his pipe, rather he would bring it out when he read in the evening. The living room always had the smell of dad's tobacco in it reminding me that he was always close around if he wasn't physically in the room.

Dad had the house built big enough to hold our family of three generations. He had his bedroom on the main floor so he wouldn't have to climb the stairs as he progressed in years. The decision to build was made when he heard that Adella was expecting. He thought it would be good to keep the family together and to do that we needed a larger house. He had a large house built. The cost was never discussed. He always seemed to have enough money when he needed it for whatever emergency would come up although he would never speak of his business affairs. He never acted like he had a lot of money. He never bought lavish items beyond building a large house for the times. At his age it was in doubt he had any ongoing business, but that was a part of his life he kept secret. He would keep repeating that it would be ours when he passed on, whatever that was. He appeared in great health so his death wouldn't be a concern too soon, thankfully.

Aside from the house which by the day's standards was lavish, we lived modestly. My wife Adella and I had been married for 10 years. Dad had performed the ceremony and the three of us lived in a smaller house until he or we built this one when Wesley was born. Mom died from pneumonia when I was a newborn. It must have been devastating to dad. With years of separation from that event, he still teared up when her name was even mentioned. They had a very fulfilling relationship which I was still waiting to know more about. Adella and I met through church. She always spoke of how sad it was to never have gotten to meet my mom. I know she would have loved her. My dad had stated on rare occasion how much Adella has so many of mom's qualities and quirks. Sometimes I look over at dad after Adella has done one of her famous imitations of someone leaving everyone in the room laughing, just to see dad staring at her and smiling, myself knowing he was thinking of Mom.

I often thought that if Mom had lived, she could have told me what she knew about dad's past. Dad never spoke much of his parents. His Sister who lived in San Francisco was much like dad in that she never spoke about their parents. This was just another one of those mysteries, and it never seemed the right time to confront or even mention the subject fearing the emotions that might arise. This just added to the mysteries of dads past as they kept building with unanswered questions. I thought that tonight seemed that it might be a good time to try and approach the subject.

I walked into the living room, over to the fireplace and threw a couple of logs onto the fire, thinking that this conversation might take a while if I was successful. As I sat down in the stuffed chair across from dad, who sat in his favorite chair, he said, "Son, I look at us as a family and can't count the numerous blessings that the good Lord has bestowed on us. We sometimes think that after a tragedy that life is not very forgiving, but it is God thru His grace that is forgiving and helping us through those difficult passages. To sit here and look into your eyes and then Adella's and Wesley's, I feel the love and closeness we share. Son, I am so proud of you in the way that you have become a real man. You have led your family to the Lord. Of course, I would like to think that the influence of my sermons over the years may have also helped even as I try not to be prideful. You need to know that I see most preacher's son's in your position become very rebellious and tend to mess up their lives instead of following in Jesus' footsteps."

I had a pounding in my chest backing over the words...I'm so proud of you. It wasn't often that Dad displayed the emotional side or openly commented in this way. I truly loved this man and how he helped mold my life and especially showing me the Grace of God. From that point of my life I felt I had a basis that I could build from and withstand and go thru whatever life threw at me. Not having mom around for insistence seemed like a tragedy until I thought of spending an eternity with her. I kept forgetting that the time that we spend here on earth is little to nothing compared to the eternity that we have before us.

After reflecting on what dad had said, I could only reply with, "Dad, I have most of what I have and what I have accomplished because of you. You have been the best father a son could ask for."

He immediately corrected me, "Don't you mean earthly father? You really have your heavenly Father to thank more than me."

We could both feel we had better change the subject lest Adella come down from upstairs and find the two of us with tears in our eyes just short of crying out loud.

"Dad, you know what I mean. Now, why this would come up all out of nowhere. You never talk like this. Are you all right? You don't usually spend so much time on family flattery." As we broke the seriousness of the conversation with some light humor. As we both sat their laughing, I asked again, "Are you all right?"

"I'm fine son. In fact, I am better than fine so I just thought I would tell you why I feel so great. Anything wrong with that?"

"Sorry dad, there are times that I just get concerned. You know there is nothing wrong with someone else thinking about your welfare occasionally. You have spent your whole life helping others."

"I would like to think so, but that's not fully correct. But the thought is pleasing." Looking down with that expression of reflecting on the past. Some people call it daydreaming. His look told me it was the past he was recalling as there was a small glint of pain. Somewhere in his past was this mystery that he relived in his thoughts that we knew nothing about. I felt it the perfect time to make a statement.

"Dad, what were you just thinking about a second ago?" staring straight into his eyes for response. I had caught him off guard.

He kind of flashed a quick look at me like being pulled out of a trance and said nonchalantly, "It was nothing son, nothing." Collecting himself and putting a smile on his face, he was back from his memory in time.

"Dad, you know everything about me, naming me before I was even born. It has been years that I have attempted politely to ask you to tell me about your youth, my grandparents, Minnesota, and the hundreds of other questions I have asked over the years. You tell so many stories so carefully avoiding describing my grandparents, or what happened during certain time periods in your life. I've tried to put it together, even tonight as I heard you telling Wesley about what the wagon train was like coming out to the Arizona Territory. Was life all that simple. I have said time after time that you are one of the best story tellers, but you have been avoiding telling stories of the mysteries that remain in the past. I'm a part of this family and part of that past belongs to me. It is part of my heritage, good or bad.

Why won't you open to me, your adult son, about the missing parts of your life?"

The room went quiet. The sound of fire seemed to grow louder all of sudden over the silence of the room. I could almost hear the tobacco in his pipe crackle as he drew in and then slowly exhaled a massive amount of smoke so slowly it was as if he was experiencing his last breath. The familiar smell of his special blend of Dutch tobacco filling the room. Again, he looked down and started to enter the historic archives of his mind. I was trying so hard to get any kind of response, yet I didn't want to see him go back into that place if it was painful, but I wanted so badly to get even a glimpse of that archive. It was like a room in the library that was locked, and no one was allowed to go in to explore its treasure.

"Dad!" I spoke louder and sharper. "Dad, what is it that you think about when you seem to go into thought when the past is questioned. I can respect and understand if there is something that you prefer not to be exposed, but you never even say that. You just politely change the subject. Is it that bad? I assume if it were good, the blanks would be filled to blend into one of your current stories."

"Son. Son. I…I haven't' always been a pastor and a lot of those years have events that I am not proud of. The pain and anger of my youth subsided many years ago, and I have learned to forgive many people that hurt me, but I have always had a problem forgiving myself for many of my actions. That will be up to God. Even though the intense pain is gone and forgiven, the memory is still there. You know me as you have grown up with me, but

I have had to ask forgiveness for things I've done in my life that would bring before you a person you don't know and never did."

"For me son, to start to explain what I have done over the course of my early life could develop into more pain as I would have to observe you seeing in me the worst of what God has forgiven me for. Those events in my memory are only bearable today knowing that someday I can die with a smile and that my Lord has forgiven me. However, if you truly wish to know and insist on knowing I guess you are of age to handle it. It might be time to get this all of my chest by sharing as well. I will agree to tell you as long as you agree not to tell the grandchildren until after I'm gone. And... after they have a clear understanding of God's grace and forgiveness. If you promise me this, we will have that talk. But it is too late tonight to expect me to gather up those thoughts. We will start tomorrow night. I love you son."

With that I stood up kissed his cheek like I did when I was a kid, "Goodnight Dad, love you too."

Starting up the stairs, I looked thru into where dad was reaching for his pipe again with a stern look on his face and thought about what to expect tomorrow night when the mysteries would start to unfold.

2

Growing Up In Stillwater

It was a little stressful thinking about fulfilling my son's curiosity of knowing what I have done during those long blank periods of my life. I wish at times that I might claim loss of memory, although that hadn't started yet. Then again, I could refrain from telling any stories that would start a chronology of dating exposing these periods of time that begged the question, "What happened right after that?". What happened over the next ten years or the two or three years between this and that? I was having a hard time thinking about tomorrow night and prayed that the good Lord would give me the answers.

I had smoked through my bowl of tobacco while in thought but now with the fire still burning with a soft glow and everyone in bed, I closed my eyes to enjoy a moment of solitude. These were the best of times with the family safely in bed upstairs. My thoughts drifted toward how different it was in my youth and how I would explain it in the forthcoming evening.

Some of my first thoughts as far back as I can remember were that of my mother and father screaming at each other. As far back as I can remember. Wow! What a first memory. My dad had immigrated from Germany as a child and had met my mom in Minnesota where they got married. I wish that was the end of the story, but I knew my son was going to press me for more. Once this door opened, he wasn't going to let it close until he closed it with his own satisfaction no matter how long it took.

My dad was a pastor and being a son of a preacher, I was expected to be perfect. By the time I hit my teens I was already labeled a "problem child" … "possessed and driven by the devil himself" my dad would say. The pressure of always thinking that I had to be the perfect one was a burden that quickly changed and molded my personality into a non-desirable person. It was as if my folks thought they were raising Jesus Christ himself. I knew I had to get out of that environment before I did something I would really regret, not that I hadn't already. But something far more sinister.

Minnesota wasn't the easiest place to grow up. We lived in a town called Stillwater. We had moved when I was little from St. Paul, Minnesota. Stillwater was on the St. Croix river which seemed to lay in wait to sweep away a child or two every year when it flooded in the Spring. This had been one of the first places settled in Minnesota. The area was mostly populated by people of German and Scandinavian decent. The area was beautiful with trees, which created a number of jobs cutting and working at the sawmill. Lumber was in big demand as the area to include both St. Paul and Stillwater were in rapid growth. The woods were thick with hardwoods. I was told that originally the hardwood forests covered the entire Midwest. The hardwoods as they call them were the assorted oaks, maple and then the softer pines. They were all choice for building. At the same time the land was being cleared for farming and grazing. Stillwater was created and known as a lumber town.

I guess the people that I remember for the most part from my youth were ok. There were a few good friends among my many school mates, the others made my life a living hell.

There was always this group of guys that thought they were a gang and they were always daring each other to pick on someone, usually smaller kids that they found easy to push around. I was one of those kids. It didn't seem to matter what grade; school seemed the same as one year followed the next. I went to school until I was 16. For the first five of the ten years, I went to school I was badgered by this so-called gang of older boys. Their leader was a boy name Jay, Jay Hollander. He seemed like a nice kid when you first met him but for some reason, he seemed to think that his purpose in life was to torment me.

At first it was just a push and shove while making his friends laugh at me. As one thing after another happened, I started to build these feelings deep inside. Some nights I would lay in bed and think about what I would like to see happen or do to him. At the same time, I was being preached to, told to forgive my enemies by my dad who I was starting to see as a weak image of a man because he would repeat what it says in the Bible about turning the other cheek. I don't know where he left his common sense, but in the world around us if someone hit you, you only had one choice. As a man, you didn't give consideration whether you won or lost. You had to hit back.

One day when I was around twelve years old, I was coming out of the school and just as I reached the half dozen steps leading down in front of me, Jay stepped out of nowhere and pushed me. I ended up landing against the edge of the bottom step. As I put my arm out to protect and catch myself it hit the edge of the bottom step, and with my weight behind it I heard a muffled crack as I continued to roll into the dirt, my books flying all over.

It was incredible pain when I attempted to move in any direction. I was on my back looking up at Jay and his friends laughing hysterically as I laid in the dirt with what I didn't know at that moment was a broken arm. My thoughts turned to pure evil. At that moment, I had so much hate in my veins that I nearly forgot about my arm, that is until I tried to get up and my arm didn't come with me. I had to use my left arm to hold my broken right arm because the bone, the only bone that's in my bicep that held my arm together had been broken through.

Any movement or attempt was far too painful to hold back the screaming and the tears. The girls started screaming when I did, and it didn't take long to get the teachers attention and in moments she was leaning over me. At the same time, she sent a couple of the girls to run and find my mom or dad.

As I looked up at Miss Templeton, my teacher I couldn't help but notice Jay trying to cover his snickering and the smile he had on his face. When Miss Templeton asked what happened it seemed that even though everyone knew what had happened no one seemed to see if I tripped or was pushed.

I think she knew exactly what happened, but to the last kid, not a single one told her that they saw Jay push me off the top of the stairs. They knew that if they did, they would be next. It would either be the steps or a mud bath if puddles were around to push someone in to get them all wet and dirty just before school. I saw many of their so-called power pranks that no one including myself ever snitched on.

It wasn't long before my dad showed up and wanted to know..." what have you done now." He would turn this into God punishing me for not listening to him, not doing a chore, or teasing my sister.

When I think about the family I always think of my sister. Good thoughts that help when tragic thoughts seem to domi-nate my mind. Many of my quiet moments reflect on memories of my sister. Maybe the one close friend I felt I had was Sally. Even though we would tease each other frequently it was all part of our fun. We shared a lot of time in our younger years playing together. I think there was a stigma attached to the preacher's kids that had kept most other kids at bay. I think back and wonder if some families figured their kids playing with us might divulge some family secrets that they wouldn't want the only preacher in town knowing. Anyway, we spent more time together than we did with other kids in town.

I was two years older than my Sister and I took it upon myself to protect her. Even though we were only two years apart, I towered nearly a foot in height over her by our early teen years. One of our favorite activities was sneaking off to go fishing in the River. It was always fun to scare her, telling her about the monsters in the deep water. Every so often I would yell, "Look, a monster! It came right up where I could see it. Didn't you see it?" I would point to some swirls in the water that she would imagine were being created by this monster. "I'll protect you. I would never let anything happen to you." As she would hide behind me peeking around into the water.

There were some big fish in the river. I had seen one monster when a local merchant displayed it in his front window for a couple of days. They called it a Sturgeon. They said it weighed 61 pounds. It looked like it was from the age of the dinosaurs. The outside of the fish was covered in a hard, bumpy bone that made it look like a cross between an alligator and a pickerel.

Every so often when we went cat fishing. You would put the bait on the bottom for the catfish to basically suck up and get hooked. Sturgeons ate in the same manner and every so often someone would get lucky and hook one. They were so big that they were seldom caught because the moment they realized they were hooked; they would take off and head straight upriver. When they got to the end of your fishing line, well, snap! And it would all be over.

My Sister and I were fishing one day. We must have been around eleven or twelve years old when my Sister hooked into one of these huge fish. She screamed, "Help me, Its big! Here, you have to take this. Hurry!"

At first, I thought it was funny and then I saw the terror in her eyes. She was genuinely terrified. She was trying to hold her pole, as it slipped from her grip. At the same time, she fell and started to slide into the water. In a last attempt to grab her line she cut her hand as the line she had in her hand around spun thru her grip cutting into the underside of her fingers. "Help! Help! Please!

It all happened so fast. I yelled, "... I'm here, hold on." Dropping my pole and running for my Sister. "I'm here!" as I reached down to pull her up. I noticed that she was up to her waist in the river, grasping at overhanging branches.

I grabbed her arm so hard that she had a bruise for over a week. My grip was like a vice. I couldn't imagine losing my sister, but I found out how quick a strange, out of the ordinary ordeal, can happen that might change your life forever.

Luckily, she was a petite girl and I had continued to tower over her in height as we grew older. I somehow got the strength to not just drag her up and out, but I lifted her straight up by her arm. I was so scared that I forgot to let her down as I backed away from the river's edge. I was literally holding her in the air in shock, her toes barely touching the ground.

"Let me down, it hurts. Your hurting me." As she mixed crying with screams.

Waking out of my shock, I put her down and hugged her. "I didn't mean to hurt you, please I wouldn't hurt you. Are you all right? Talk to me. Are you all right?" blurted out of my mouth.

"I'm ok now. I'm ok. I was so scared... I've never been that scared. Thank you..." As she continued to cry.

The moments that followed seemed to start a bond beyond a brother and sister and best friend. We sat on the ground with her crying in my arms until she finally started to come out of the shock of what had happened. Nothing was said for quite a while, but there was a whole lot of, "what if's" going through both our minds. What if she would have been swept into the river. What if she would have drowned. What if I hadn't of been there? What if I hadn't taken her fishing?

The later comment woke me to a new level of awareness realizing that we now had to go home and explain this mess to our parents. I already knew I was going to get the blame and that this wouldn't have happened if I hadn't' taken her fishing in the first place.

"We better get home and get you cleaned up. I'm so sorry sis."

She gleamed at me, "why are you sorry. You saved my life. What would have happened if you weren't there? Let's go home." As her wet clothes clung to her as she tried to stand up and walk. She was still shaking and weak from her brief struggle.

We gradually collected ourselves on the walk home to the point that we started to inject humor into our conversation and some sarcasm like, "you know I almost had a chance at getting your room." I started and then one line after another came out and soon, we were back to laughing until we reached the front door.

"Well, here goes." I said on entering.

"You got it wrong. You're going to be their hero." replied sis.

As sis walked into the house ahead of me the first thing I heard was my mom yell, "What happened to you? You're getting water on the floor. Get into the bathroom and dry off. I'll bring you some clothes," walking past me to get her clothes I got this disgusted look from my mom. I had guessed right as to how this was going to turn out. I knew what was coming. I just didn't know how bad it would be.

"What's going on in here?" as my dad came out of his den where he was probably in the middle of preparing tomorrows sermon.

"What were you doing? Why is there water on the floor?" as he glared at me, the hero according to my sister.

Mom chimed in, "He got Sally into some kind of trouble and she ruined her clothes and is in the bathroom. Cuts and bruises all over her, in addition to looking like a drowned rat."

"You have some real explaining to do!" as he grabbed my arm with the same grip that I had pulled sis out of the river with. As he dragged me into his den, I could only think about how sis was in the bathroom cleaning up thinking of me as her hero when I was about to receive the wrath of father along with a lecture and punishment of some kind. I had already learned my lessons many, many times as a result of my father and that was that. Life wasn't going to be any fairer today than at any other time!

As my father shoved me into the chair in front of his desk in the den, I knew this was going to be really bad. His anger was building and based on past experiences, it was bad now, but it was going to get a lot worse.

"Dad, I..."

I immediately felt the sting of a slap across my face. He continued to move behind his desk.

"You call me Father. You are not a man yet and you still don't seem to give me the respect I deserve! I don't know why you continually embarrass the family by getting into trouble and always beating or hurting, making your sister cry. What are you? What have you turned into? Are you some kind of animal?"

"Tell me now what happened, and try and be honest about it, or I will bring in your sister to find out what really happened!" glaring with a building hatred.

"I took Sally fishing with me. She hooked into a big fish and in all the excitement she slipped on the bank and fell into the river. I grabbed her and pulled her out. That's what happened." Looking my dad straight in the eye for a calm response.

"You took our daughter down to the river." Speaking very slow and deliberate. An indication that the fuse was lit.

"You took her down to the river?" Haven't we told you not to go down there without one of us with you?"

"Father, all of the kids our age are able to go down to the river... there are..."

I was drowned out with a loud and rising voice. "Shut up! You directly disobeyed us, risk our daughter's life (said as if I wasn't a part of the family) and have the nerve to talk back to me? You need to know your place young man." As he moved around his desk to where I was sitting.

As he raised his hand, I put my arms up to protect myself as I had learned to do in the past from the rain of blows the were about to fall.

His anger would take control as he swung once hitting my arms held over me and then again. His voice was almost lost while I was feeling his blows. "You need to learn a lesson! Who do you think you are? Let my daughter nearly drown? I almost lost her to your evil! How did you ever get born into this family? An embarrassment. You are going to hell young man!"

I often wondered after each incident like this how many folks out there were telling their son that he was going to hell while they landed blow after blow on them. It was even worse, having to take whatever he dished out because he was my father.

"Stop! Stop! Father Stop! ...you don't understand." as sis, having cleaned up and put on dry clothes came running into the room. She grabbed his arm as he was about to deliver another blow. He turned anger in tow and slapped her sending her crashing into a table. The table went over with a crystal lamp and ornate items breaking on the floor.

Sis was laying in amongst the broken glass, bleeding from her hands as she got cuts trying to get up. Then as she screamed, noticing the blood from the cuts she realized her knees where thick with shards of glass also.

These are the thoughts I try not to go back to. When I do, I see sis struggling to get up without me or my dad helping her. The room was thick with hatred, as mom ran in to help sis to her feet.

Again, the first glare was at me. Me? I didn't push her down. I didn't break the ornamentals or lamp. The physical punishment that I received was minor next to the feeling of being convicted of every mishap even though it originated with my dad, yes, dad shoving my sister, hurting an innocent person that just happened to be his beloved daughter.

Now it was the..." look what you made me do" part as mom attended to sis taking her out of the room as dad and I went back to his blow by blow solution to my evil disobedience.

The days that followed were tougher than the beating I took because in some way I began to feel responsible for my sister's wounds. She had her knees and her hands bound up and with additional bruises on her face from dad's arm when he shoved her and mine on her arm and additional scratches on her legs from the gravel on the riverbank she slid down. She was an awful sight. All of her injuries when asked what happened were described as a part of her falling into the river.

At times, I was ready to break down and cry, even as a 12-year-old boy when I would stare at her wounds. I loved my sister so much to see her in such pain. Then being forced to lie as to how she got her cuts and bruises. If the truth be known, our dysfunctional family would not be excepted and if exposed, dad would lose his job if not his career.

These types of events would happen over and over. After each such event, as siblings we knew that we only had each other for comfort and support. After the river incident, with my sister that day thinking I was a hero, then having her thoughts crushed after walking into the house with our mom's comments and later with dad striking her and causing her to get all cut up, she felt that I was the only one that loved her. In turn I was plagued by the fact that as a young teen, I couldn't defend her from my dad. We were both forced to lie about bruises and how we got them. This just made sis and I feel like everything we were being told from the pulpit on Sunday just couldn't be right, especially coming from the person we knew to be an angry soul, if he had a soul at all. Our mother seemed to have a preconceived notation that whatever our dad did, it was done in the name of the Lord. She never stood up to him on our behalf.

As we got older, we found ourselves attempting to be gone from around the house and church as much as possible. It was the only time that we knew we weren't going to get yelled at or punished for something that we didn't even know about.

When I think back to those years, sadness takes over, then anger, then love. I guess I find it better to plan for the future than think of the past. I only get my mind filled with regrets that I can't change the past. Over the years most people I would eventually ask forgiveness from, would pass on. Fewer in heaven than in hell.

My life and that of my sister was very difficult. At the ages of 16 and 17 we would talk about what we wanted to be in life. I worked at a feed store mostly moving and loading inventory. Our supplies started to come in by riverboat as soon as the ice broke up in the Spring. Sis worked at the woman's clothing store which also sold a lot of handmade items from many of the talented women around the countryside.

We were both lucky to have the work, so we didn't have to spend time at home or around the church. We kept wanting to believe that dad was mellowing out a little and with time he would be the type of father we held out hope for.

We grew up quickly and soon I was looking down on him. At 17 my appearance had changed. In addition to growing tall, I had also gotten very strong over the last couple of years lifting feed bags at 50 to 100 pounds each. I had grown and developed an intimidating physic. My bullies from the past that were still around town would always say hi and ask how things were going. They were smart enough now not to mess with me. I still had past thoughts that made it real tempting to get a little payback except they had probably forgot what they did to me back when.

Sis had changed even more. By 16 she had become a woman. At least in appearance. She was still delicate and petite. Due to our family situation, she had been extremely sheltered from the real world. Even growing up in Stillwater left one sheltered. Despite her innocence, she blossomed. She had curves that even amazed me at times as I would remind myself that she is my sister. She had every guy in Stillwater looking at her and trying to get her attention. I must admit that a couple of times, I felt very protective while quietly telling some guy, I predetermined was not someone that I wanted around my sister, to get lost. They usually left her alone at that point and for those that didn't, I usually had to have a more in-depth discussion with a bit of gentle persuasion thrown in.

It was Spring and the first of the Riverboats had docked. It was always a time to celebrate. The big boats were fun to watch with the Captain high up on in the wheelhouse. Sometimes there would be two or three tied up at a time. It made quite a spectacle. We could see them from our house up on the side of the hill that overlooked the main street of town.

3

Mr. Johnson

The "Minnesota" riverboat built in 1849

The riverboat, Minnesota, was tying up at the dock. Morgan approached Mr. Johnson to see if he could skip out for a break from the store to run down and join a growing number of towns people. It was a big event, with everyone mixing and talking as a large number of men showed up to help load and unload cargo, especially firewood to keep the big wheel turning to get them back down river.

Mr. Johnson replied, "Morgan, I don't want you to miss out on all of the excitement. Go on now. There is going to be a lot of work to do when they start unloading our cargo. We will need to get it moved up here and inventoried."

Morgan ran out the door and joined the wave of men and women walking toward the dock. People were saying that the Minnesota was shoving off tomorrow downstream to visit river towns all along the Mississippi. Stillwater was on the St. Croix which flowed into the Mississippi creating a waterway all the way to the Gulf of Mexico. Morgan often dreamed about what that kind of trip would be like. The Minnesota was a new riverboat and the ports it was about to experience would be among its first.

It was finally time to get back to work. Mr. Johnson, Morgan's boss asked, "So you like those big paddle boats? Wish you were on one? I used to dream like that when I was a kid. Now I wonder as I read the labels, where our goods come from and what those places must be like. Probably as close as I'll get to them is my imagination."

Morgan was always quiet around Mr. Johnson. He was a good boss. He was considerate and never asked him to do more than what he knew he could do. He treated Morgan with respect and not like an unruly little kid. As Morgan was looking toward the harbor he asked, "Mr. Johnson, have you ever thought about leaving Stillwater? You don't think about heading West? All that talk about gold. I read about it all of the time."

Mr. Johnson replied, "I doubt that gold is just lying on the ground for everyone to pick up. Plus, why would I leave this place. I love the store, meeting people, and know the community which makes life seem worth living."

"Let me ask you a question boy? What would you do if you found all that gold and had all the money you ever wanted?" Mr. Johnson smiled and would wait until Morgan responded to his question. When Morgan did reply he added, "There are more important things than money. Wealth comes in many forms."

Morgan enjoyed their conversations which over time pulled him out of a lot of his shyness. The thought of having all that gold. What would he do?

"That's simple Mr. Johnson. I would buy a ranch out west and raise cattle. I would buy Sis a large house in whatever town we settled in so she would be able to make friends and enjoy her neighbors."

"Well, well. Sounds nice. You really do look after your sister don't you. But you left out a couple of people, didn't you?" as he chuckled.

Morgan looked at him a bit confused, still thinking of the gold and Sis having a big house and friends to enjoy.

"What about your Mom and Dad? Let's not be selfish now." Spoken as he continued to chuckle and thought he was being funny until Morgan's silence and the look on his face brought the hint of humor to a halt.

Everyone in town thought that the preacher's family was perfect. From the outside looking in, the whole town saw a model Christian family. They didn't understand Morgan's true feelings or why the family didn't mix with people like normal people. He knew that the day would come that Sis and himself had talked about. That would be the day they would leave Stillwater and never look back.

Even though the store was very busy on a Saturday, it seemed that Morgan was lost in silence and Mr. Johnson noticed the change. He could sense that something was very wrong. The young man had a sinister expression on his face. For the first time, as he looked into Morgan's face, he saw a glimpse of hatred. He could see the truly deep set hate he had for someone or something. When Morgan turned his head to directly face him, he tried to lighten up, but it was too late. Mr. Johnson had read his expression and the questions where forthcoming.

"Morgan, Morgan, why don't you talk to me. I think we need to have a conversation. Tell you what. Let's get this day behind us, since it is our busiest day of the week and nearly over. Then we will go over to Sally's diner for a desert and talk about your future. Now... let's get this new inventory on the shelves. Ok?"

He patted Morgan on the back and headed over to the register to check out a customer. Morgan had a warm feeling. Here was someone other than Sis that might be willing to try and understand him. Maybe he could share his thoughts and secrets with him. He felt he could confide in Mr. Johnson.

In many ways, Mr. Johnson treated Morgan like a son. In the way that Morgan thought a father should treat his son. Just the way he called him "son" which was just a figure of speech had more of a literal meaning to him. He mentioned that he and his wife never had children. They always wanted to but couldn't for some reason. It seemed that my presence may have helped fill that void a little, from time to time.

The sun was still bright but slowly going over the hill when Mr. Johnson said, "Let's wrap it up for today. Tuck away those boxes and get the items on the front walk brought in. We will lock up and head over to Sally's. You just tell your folks I was treating you to dinner and a dessert for the hard day you put in."

Morgan replied, "Well that would just be my father. My mom went to visit her sister and won't be back until tomorrow evening. My sister prepares dinner when my mom is gone, so dad is well taken care of. I really appreciate this Mr. Johnson. Thank you."

"My pleasure son. You deserved something special for the work you put in today. I always look forward to Saturdays. Even though it is a long day, it is always fun to catch up with friends that come in from the surrounding area to get their supplies for the week."

As they entered Sally's, one person after another said hi. If they weren't just off the boat, they already knew the local merchant and the preacher's son. Morgan felt privileged to be invited, and to sit with Mr. Johnson. Somehow this seemed like how things should be. At home, he would hear, "... Sally's? No sense paying someone else to fix your food," mom would always say. The only time we ate out was when a member of the congregation invited the entire family over for dinner. Otherwise, Sally and Morgan always wondered what it was like to eat at a real restaurant and Sally's was known to have the best food of any restaurant around.

Sally, the owner yelled over, "Mr. Johnson, just look at that strapping young man you have with you. How are you Morgan?" Like everyone else she knew who the preacher's son was. With everyone turning a head to see who she was yelling across the room at, I kind of half waved my hand and let Mr. Johnson take the lead as Sally pointed over to a table near the front windows.

The smell of baked goods, coffee, assorted specials of the day filled the air. It was a pleasant change from walking into the kitchen at home. Morgan almost forgot about everything else on his mind. Like in a daze he observed the other people talking and laughing as they enjoyed each other's company.

We had just ordered when Mr. Johnson spoke out asking, "Do you want to tell me what is going on in your life.? Sometimes it helps to talk about your problems with someone that will help you think and that won't tell anyone or make fun of you."

With a shy response Morgan spoke, "I think all the time about leaving Stillwater, and heading West, but I wouldn't know anyone, have any money or even a horse to try it. I think about how it would be to live like you do I guess." Looking down because the last part of my statement seemed personal.

"Son, I have a good life and I enjoy what I do. It took some time for me to discover what that was. I didn't dream about being a merchant or having my own store growing up. I had all sorts of crazy dreams. I fell into what I liked rather than having achieved my plan."

Mr. Johnson had a penetrating look as he stared at Morgan and said, "If I were to guess, I'd say you are not running to something as much as you are running away from something? Do you want to tell me what your trying to run from son?"

Every time he said "son" it sounded like it came from someone more like the father that Morgan wished he had, rather ending up with the one he got. He often thought that God enjoyed making his life miserable if indeed there was a God. He found it hard believing what his dad said. His dad without knowing, was a "do as I say, not as I do" type of guy. Morgan had heard that phrase in school and never forgot it having immediately pinned it appropriately on his dad.

With the question from Mr. Johnson still ringing in his head Morgan answered, "My family. Well, not my Sister but my mom and dad." There. I had finally told someone, as if they could figure out the rest.

At that moment, their food came, interrupted with the smell of the Saturday night special. Morgan's mom and Sis were great cooks, but this was something very special to him. In front of him was steak, potatoes and corn. Everything looked upsized, far more than the portions he had at home. At home, he seldom had gravy. This was a treat and tonight he was enjoying experiencing it to the max.

"I know it looks pretty but it's meant to be eaten. Best to stop staring and start eating before it gets cold." As Mr. Johnson laughed. He was enjoying Morgan's reaction, but at the same time thinking over what he had just said about his family. Mr. Johnson seemed to have incredible insight.

The closer they got to finishing their meal the nearer they were getting to the questions that Morgan knew were going to come flowing out of Mr. Johnson. Morgan was afraid of what he was going to say in answering the questions. Then again, he was finally ready for all of this he had held secret for so long, to come out in the open. Well...at least share it with Mr. Johnson.

"Son, I truly enjoy watching someone eat that enjoys their food. I don't have to even ask you if that was good. Now we are going to have some of Sally's bread pudding. They say it comes from an old German recipe. Best bread pudding I ever ate. Do you know that sometimes when business is slow in the middle of the day, I'll sneak out the back of the store and over the Sally's just for a bowl of her bread pudding?"

Now they were both laughing, and Morgan was feeling not only special but truly comfortable with Mr. Johnson.

"Now if you don't mind, I would like you to feel that you can trust me to share your problems. I speak with my closest friends when I have a problem and it always seems to feel better. A lot of times I get their advice, sometimes solving those problems. They just go away. Talk to me son." And he looked at Morgan with a compassionate look that made him feel he really could trust Mr. Johnson.

"I don't' know how to say it because no one would believe it, but I hate the way that my dad treats me and especially my sister. My dad is a monster and my mom seems to agree with his pun-ishment and yet can't stand to watch us get beat so she always leaves the room. "as Morgan looked down hardly believing he just shared that with someone other than Sis.

Mr. Johnson was quiet. Maybe he was trying to figure out if Morgan was telling the truth or not.

"So, what have you done that you deserve this discipline? It must be pretty bad? Are you willing to share that with me?"

"Mr. Johnson, no one in town really knows the kind of person my dad is. I take the blame for everything that happens no matter whether I even know about it or not. But worse, I hate him for the way he treats Sis. When he hits her, or slaps her, I just want to kill him." Just thinking about it and saying that, brought such anger into Morgan's voice as he straightened up from having been slouching at the table. This time when Mr. Johnson looked at him, he was terrified in seeing a person with easily enough hatred in his eyes to possibly kill. Easily. He hadn't expected this.

Morgan was so engrossed in his thoughts, experiencing the hate of the moment and envisioning his dad striking his sister, that he was totally unaware of how Mr. Johnson was just staring at him. That's when the waitress brought the bread pudding. Placing it on the table as she said, "You enjoy this now!"

She didn't wait for a response. Even she noticed that there was some uncomfortable, deep conversation going on at the table. She left quickly and quietly.

"Son, son... listen to me please. I know this is easy for me to say and hard for you to swallow but no one should have that much pent up hate in them. Maybe you don't mean to use the word hate. Hate is a word I try never to use. It's usually followed by regret."

"Sir, I know what hate is and I hold the purest form of it toward my dad. There are many times in the last couple of years especially, that I have been brought to the brink of simply wanting to kill him. I think about it so often that I know I must leave before something horrible happens. If it did, I would have no regrets. Do you hear me Mr. Johnson...no regrets!"

Mr. Johnson had opened up a whole lot more than he had planned for. Morgan seemed devil possessed and the sincerity he spoke with, made him seem more than capable of killing or seriously hurting someone. The incredible amount of hate driving him just might drive it to act out.

"Please stop and think for a moment! Take a deep breath. Here, let's try and enjoy our desert and I'll try and help you talk thru this problem." As Mr. Johnson well understood that this wasn't anything that was going to be discussed and solved over dinner. He understood that Morgan had a tremendous emotional problem that was not going to be easy to address. But he felt it his duty to at least try. He had only seen the good side of him and now he surely wished that was the only side he had right now.

Morgan calmed down and said, "I'm sorry Mr. Johnson. I really didn't mean to let out my emotions that way. You probably think I'm crazy or touched in the head. I just don't like my parents. That's all. "

"Son, I would like to be that special person with a heart to help you. I can see how you treat customers and how you want to protect your sister. You're a good person. Don't let hate consume you. You will soon be old enough to go out on your own and make your way in the world. Maybe explore some of those dreams you have in your head. That's what you should be thinking about. I don't believe your life is here in Stillwater any more than you do," said Mr. Johnson knowing that the best solution would be separation from his primary problem, that of his parents.

Morgan was now enjoying my pudding, and when he had cleared his throat, he looked up and said, "The bigger problem is not me leaving. That I could have done already with a little money, but what would happen to Sis? She needs me to look after her.

I'm big enough physically to finally make a difference in the way my dad treats her. I've told him to leave her alone or he will be dealing with me. The beatings for me have stopped because of my size and strength but he could still shove her around. His fear of me has kept him in check for now."

"I can't leave until I know she will be safe. Maybe she will meet some nice man, get married and then I can follow my dreams" said with a hollow sound knowing that that might take years.

Mr. Johnson and Morgan finished up their desert, Mr. Johnson paid the bill and as they walked outside, he told Morgan that if there was anything he could do to help, that he would always be there for him. Little did he know that he was going to help him in the very near future, leaving Morgan regretful for years to come.

4

Hate vs Love

Morgan headed home which was only a couple of blocks up the street from the main street. The sun had set on the other side of the hill. There was still a little sunlight reflecting across the treetops on the opposite side of the river as I looked back every so often.

Our house was a moderate colonial type house and as he entered his dad spoke from the den, "Where have you been? Up to no good I suppose. I thought your work with Mr. Johnson was done some time ago?"

In reply, "It was. He asked if I would join him for dinner and a dessert at Sally's."

"You let him buy you dinner? Have you no shame? We had dinner here that your sister prepared. You should have come home and ate here instead of begging off our parishioners."

"I wasn't begging. He was rewarding me for the hard work I put in for the day." He couldn't even recognize or acknowledge when I had done something rewarding. All he could do was try and make something negative out of it because it was Morgan. The boy's anger was building.

As I entered the den, he looked up and we faced off eye to eye. I think he saw a little of what Mr. Johnson saw earlier. He looked concerned and to my delight, a little afraid.

"Where is Sis? I should tell her I'm sorry that I wasn't here for dinner."

He raised his voice, "Leave her alone. She was tired and went to bed. Leave her alone. Don't wake her." As he spoke to me his voice softened as he saw the level of my anger rise when he raised his voice to me.

As Morgan went up to his room, He wondered why she would go to bed so early. He noticed that the kitchen wasn't even cleaned up. She always cleaned the kitchen before going to bed. All he could think of was that she wasn't feeling well. Morgan decided he would see how she was in the morning. After all, He had had a long day with a lot of work and the conversation with Mr. Johnson seemed to have stressed him out and taken a toll as much as the day in general took a physical toll. Sleep was a welcome event right about now. Thankfully, he didn't even have time to think. He was so tired that he never remembered his head hitting the pillow. That is until he woke up during the night to some muffled sounds. He was too tired to be concerned. It was probably dad snoring or talking in his sleep which mom said he did every so often.

The next morning, Morgan woke up to the sun blasting its way into his room. His room was on the front of the house as it faced east with a great view of the river. It was Sunday morning, so he had to get up soon and get ready for Church. The window was open, and a slight breeze was blowing in which was unusual since the wind seldom blew in from the East. Somehow, he sensed that this was not going to be the only thing to happen today that would seem unusual. Morgan wasn't ready to go down and face dad again. He was always up tight on mornings before giving his sermon.

The first thing he decided to do was check on Sis. If she wasn't feeling well, he might have an excuse to stay home and watch over her. He would still feel strange about missing church, but Morgan enjoyed being home when dad wasn't around so he could read his books and the paper that feed his desire for the outside world. Especially the articles about what was happening in the Wild, Wild, West.

He slipped his trousers on and as he did there was a growing commotion down by the river. As he looked out of his window that overlooked the river, he noticed a growing crowd of people on the river's edge. At first, he thought it might be a crowd preparing to wave off the riverboat "Minnesota" but it became apparent that they were not interested in the sendoff. They were assembled for some other reason. He didn't know what was going on.

Since there was a couple of hours before church, he thought he would get dressed and run down to see what all the commotion was about. Morgan buttoned up his trousers, quickly tucked in his shirt and ran out to the hallway stopping at Sis's door.

He knocked on the door, then he knocked harder, "Sis, get up, get up, something is going on down at the dock. Do you want to go with me? Sis? Hey, you?" as he now turned the doorknob and opened the door for a peak.

As he moved his head to look around the door edge and into the room to look back toward her bed, he found it empty. He took a couple of steps into her room and noticed that there were spots of blood on the floor. Then he noticed the same on the sheets in her bed. Maybe she had cut herself, after all, it was just a spot or two. But how or what did she cut herself on or with?

He quickly decided the obvious, that she was downstairs and if not, she probably ran down to the see what was going on at the river without him. Her room was next to his facing the river. Her window was open so she must have heard the noise of the crowd and ran down to satisfy her curiosity.

Continuing down the steps and out the front door, Morgan ran the couple of blocks until he was only about a half a block away. Someone noticed him and pointed at him. Then others started to look at Morgan. As he literally ran up to the crowd the conversations, one by one stopped. Kids quietly stared at him. It seemed like the leaves even stopped making noise as they blew in the breeze. He suddenly became aware that everyone, and that meant everyone was looking at him. As he looked back in question without saying anything, eyes would shift and look down rather than contact his. One after another. What was going on? What did he bring to the gathering that was so awful?

As he looked over the crowd, one person caught his eye as he moved forward toward him and that was Mr. Johnson. His hair was messy, and he looked like he had just rolled out of bed. As he came toward Morgan, he began to have a horrible feeling looking at his expression. He didn't know what was wrong, but something was very wrong. Mr. Johnson had wiped the tears from his eyes. As he moved forward, Morgan continued to look around for Sis. With everyone looking at him, he knew she would know what was going on. When Mr. Johnson reached Morgan, he put his arm around him and turned him away from the crowd to speak privately.

"Son, I want you to remember the part of our conversation last night where I said that I'm always here for you. I really meant it. I'm here I'm here."

"Mr. Johnson, please tell me what's going on here and why everyone is looking at me." His gut already knowing that the answer wasn't going to be pleasant.

"Son, a little while ago, just as the sun was breaking, your sister was seen in her night gown walking down to the river."

Having difficulty processing I exclaimed, "In her night gown? Why? Where is she?"

Mr. Johnson now had tears swelling up in his eyes. His grip on Morgan's arm became hard as he held continued to hold his arm, slowly reaching for his other arm. "This is very hard for me to have to tell you."

Morgan's impatience caused a physical reaction as he shrugged the hold Mr. Johnson had on him now and yelled straight into his face, "What is going on! Where is Sis?"

He paled as he said, "She was seen walking right down to the river edge and into the water. She walked in until the water took her away. People say they never heard a word out of her."

Morgan was suddenly dizzy and out of breath. He felt week as he turned, looked and slowly walked thru the crowd to the water's edge. Everyone parted to allow him to walk thru. When he got to the water's edge he just looked out at the river.

So many thoughts were going thru his head that none of them could have been slowed down into audible sounds. He didn't have the words. They wouldn't have come out of his mouth if he did have something to say.

Why? Morgan's thought to himself over and over. "Why would she even think about doing such a thing? She would have spoken to me. If something caused this to happen or was causing her to think of doing such a thing, she would have shared her thoughts with me. I know she would."

The current was strong in the Spring and she was not a good swimmer to be in the river. Immediately, Morgan thought of the time they had gone fishing, and she fell in. He was terrified and went after her with the knowledge that she couldn't swim the river. The currents were so strong they would take you out toward the center of the river. Bodies were often found miles downriver.

"No, no, not Sis. Not Sis." as Morgan lost his strength. If it were not for Mr. Johnson grabbing him, he would have probably fallen face first into the river. He held him, and Morgan held on to him. Morgan would think of that moment with Mr. Johnson having stepped up while everyone else just watched like some stage play was being acted out.

They turned and started to walk away from the crowd.

"I'm so sorry son. I'll go up to the house with you. I doubt your dad knows yet. I'll speak with him. It will be easier that way." He volunteered.

"No, please, thank you Mr. Johnson, I'm ok to do this and I think it is important that it comes from me. Please let me do this." As tears rolled down my cheeks. "You said you would help me in any way. Then help me by letting me break this to my dad, please, please Mr. Johnson."

"Tell you what, I'll wait outside a few minutes just in case you need me to help you talk to him or console him. If you don't come out for me in a five minutes, I'll be on my way home to clean up. I'm sure everyone will assume church is cancelled today and I'll check on you later. Ok?"

"Thank you, Mr. Johnson." Thank you, as Morgan gave him a hug. Mr. Johnson again held Morgan in his arms as if he were a child and for a moment, and he embraced it with all he had in him.

5

Vengence Is Mine

Dad's room, or to stand corrected, fathers' room was in the back of the house. It is unlikely he would have heard the noise coming from the docks and then again it was dead silent at the dock once Morgan had arrived.

Morgan tried to gather his thoughts about Sis over and over to answer one question, why? That simple why? Was this going to be an unknown the rest of life? As he tossed this over in my mind, he went up to his room and peeked out to see if Mr. Johnson was still there. He was just starting to walk away, likely thinking that my dad and me were sharing our emotions over the loss of Sis.

Morgan thought about how short her life was. How ugly it was with his folks and how they should have, or he should have found a way to escape. Then he thought of his mom, who didn't know yet either and how this was going to affect her when she returned. How would it effect dad? Then he was back asking himself why.

As he walked out of his room heading for his dad's room, he once again walked into Sis's room. He was curious if there was anything that might lead him to answer that mysterious... why. Was there a note? Didn't people that did something like that always leave a note?

Again, he noticed the spots of blood on the bed and on the floor. Even though the window was slightly open, there was a musty, strange odor in the room. Then he remembered the muffled sound in the night. There was one of her tops laying under the corner of the bed. When he pulled it out, he saw that it had been torn. There was also a couple very small spattering of blood on it. Then there was the question of why Sis had gone to bed so early. Why? His mind was wrapped around a single word that may never be answered.

Suddenly, as he held her blouse a picture started to form. A picture that began to paint a very ugly and unbelievable story unless you lived in their family where everything was possible in an undaunting way. Morgan started to think about the sound in the night. He kept looking at the ripped blouse he was holding in his hand and looking at the bed.

His anger was building as a picture developed, to proportions that he had never experienced. It was anger, pure unadulterated anger. Then it was guilt for not being there to protect her or figuring out how they could escape before something like this would have happened. Why would he think that the abuse of hitting her and slapping her around was the limit that my dad was capable of. Mom was gone for the night and he had been working all day, tired after arriving home late. He hadn't been aware of the danger his sister was in.

She had acted strangely over the last week. He had meant to ask her what was bothering her and why he was getting the silent treatment, but he was too busy with Mr. Johnson and all the work getting ready for and putting the inventory that arrived into stock to confront her or be aware of what was happening in her life.

He knew now. He just knew. The ugly, horrible dark picture came together as if being painted by one of the masters. It was too horrible to think of. This was a scene although only in his mind that would never go away. This is the thing that Sis didn't tell him. She was so embarrassed that it reached the point that she couldn't even share it with him. It was better to simply walk into the river and drift peacefully away in the dark cold water forever.

Morgan had to act fast. His head was spinning yet weaving a plan at the same time. He remembered that the riverboat was leaving within the hour and he decided that he was going to be on it. But first there was something he had to do that Morgan didn't think he would ever be able to do, but hate can override anything...everything.

It wasn't necessarily hot or even warm in the house, but the sweat was running off his forehead. He quietly snuck downstairs and out to the back shed where he got several lengths of rope and a piece of lumber to use as a club.

As he grasped the chunk of wood in one hand and the rope in the other, he headed back into the house and up to the door of his dad's bedroom. It was early, and he was usually up by now. In the event that he was up but not out of bed he moved very slowly and as quietly as he could to open the door. He had dropped the rope in the hallway and held the club behind his back in case his dad was awake and looked over at him. He got lucky. His dad was fast asleep making small noises as Morgan continued into the room.

He laid in bed facing away from the door. Every little creak that the door made or his feet on the floorboards had Morgan thinking he would wake up and it would be a struggle to subdue him. Instead, he was able to move right up over him in bed. His anger motivated him and at the same time took the conscious reality away and anything to prohibit what he was about to do.

Morgan overloaded with hate started to smile as he raised the piece of oak. It was important to knock him out but not kill him. That would be too easy of a way out for such a piece of pure evil.

Which of the two, Morgan or his dad, had the darkest soul at that moment would have been a tossup, but Morgan wasn't feeling any remorse as the piece of oak met his dad's skull. There was a slight crack and be assured it wasn't the oak. Even with the blow he received, blood starting to flow into his face as he turned, he was not out. Morgan rained another blow remember how his dad had struct him so many times with his fists. It took all the restraint he could muster not to simply mash his skull and be done with it. But again, that would have been to kind.

He laid there unconscious. Breathing shallow, bleeding but alive. He would soon come to, so Morgan was quick to get his work done. He ran out to the hallway and picked up the ropes. Moving back into the bedroom he proceeded to move his non-conscious dad more in a sitting up position in bed against the big wooden headboard. The bed had four large bed posts. Morgan tied the rope around each pedestal and the other to a limb until his dad was tied up spread eagle on the bed.

Then he continued by binding up his mouth so no matter how much he attempted to yell, no one would hear anything. He turned to close the window to make sure he couldn't be heard and then suddenly saw the Bible on the nightstand. As evil begets evil, he had another idea.

Another trip to the shed had Morgan returning this time with a hammer and some large spikes. Before he woke, Morgan took one of his dad's hands at a time nailing his them to the large head-board of the bed. He was intrigued and thought of the story of the cross as he pounded the nails through flesh. How appropriate. He had thought about killing him after he regained consciousness but instead, Morgan simply nailed him up and left a note impli-cating him to his Sister's death, explaining why ...Sis... committed suicide. His days as a preacher were going to be done. Just to add an extra touch to make sure that he wasn't going to get loose and run after Morgan, he took the oak club and gave one heavy swing to the lower section of each leg. He delighted in hearing the bones crack and thinking of the pain his dad would be in when he woke up with two broken legs and his hands nailed to the bed. Morgan doubted he would be grateful that he hadn't killed him. He would experience extreme humiliation, losing his church, daughter deceased, and his son gone. Morgan put himself last in that thought because he felt losing his son wasn't going to matter a great deal to his dad. Morgan continued to think about the enjoyment of his dad going thru months of painful healing, physically, never healing mentally.

With his job completed, he went to his room and dressed in his Sunday best and packed a small bag with some person things including a neckless that his sister had left on her night stand as a memory. Then he ran down to the study where he knew money was kept from the church offerings and where his dad kept some cash and some gold pieces that he didn't trust to the bank with all the robberies that we were hearing of. He scooped up the money into a small sack and put it into his dad's travel bag.

He left the house making sure the front door was locked with a note attached that read "family grieving, come back later." He put on one of his dad's hats and kept his head, down moving behind the houses on his way to the river boat.

On the way to the boat he had one more stop to make. The merchant store on main street. He went down the back way from the house to an alleyway up to the back door. By now there wasn't anyone around, it being Sunday morning and all. There was a key hidden there in case he had arrived early for work, and Mr. Johnson wasn't there yet, he could let himself in. Morgan unlocked the door quietly entering right next to his office area in the rear.

Morgan had been privileged to know where he kept a fair amount of cash from the previously day's receipts. He moved the desk and lifted the floorboard that the foot of the desk always rested on. The previous day had been a long day and there was a considerable amount of cash in the sack in the floor safe if that's what you'd call it.

He was raging with anxiety and yet excited. A strange mixture of emotions that he decided he would sort out later. Right now, he had a lot to do. Morgan felt some real guilt about stealing from Mr. Johnson. He looked over the top of his desk and found a paper and pencil. After he carefully counted the money, he wrote out an IOU to include interest. Then he placed it in Mr. Johnson's empty money sack, putting it back in the hole and moving the desk so he wouldn't know until tomorrow that the money was gone. Morgan was hopefully thinking he would be down the river by a long stretch when Mr. Johnson realized what had happened.

Morgan took a few extra items off the shelf as he started to think about the trip. He had his Church clothes on but not much else to wear. He hadn't decided what yet, but in his mind, he was grabbing a few small things to add to the IOU. He would pay him back when he eventually found a job or better yet, gold out West. That was the plan.

After he carefully locked the door and put the key back, he took off around the back of the final stretch to the boat. As he arrived, looking up at the great Minnesota with its large side wheels, an idea came over him to help disguise himself in case someone fig-ured out that he might have gotten onto the Riverboat.

He stopped for a moment and brushed off his trousers and suit coat. At the same time, he straightened his dad's hat, stood straight, and walked right toward the gangplank. There was a small booth to the side where they were selling tickets. The hat was a final touch that wasn't necessary but helped him look older than he was.

"Where you headed to young man?... quickly correcting himself as he saw Morgan write the name Goodhue (the name of a prominent family from St. Paul). "I meant Mr. Goodhue sir," said the attendant looking away apologetically. Are you by any way related to the Goodhue's that just started up the newspaper in St. Paul? The St. Paul Pioneer?"

Morgan replied with a little arrogance in his voice, "Yes".

He dared not even look behind him for fear that someone in line would recognize him.

The attendant continued, "Where to Mr. Goodhue?"

"I'm headed downriver to St. Louis with my fiancé, so I will need two of your best cabins."

"We have the best sir. Nearly the ships maiden voyage. Everything is new and the cabin suites are magnificent. We especially cater to people of stature like yourself, sir. Please, we are about to shove off. Where are you going?"

Hearing someone behind him acting impatient and not wanting to cause a scene, he quickly repeated, "St. Louis" and he handed Morgan two tickets stating in the process, "We only go as far as Galena sir. 1st class cabins I presume Mr. Goodhue?"

In reply Morgan confirmed, "Of course, Galena... Yes, your best cabins."

He slapped the thirty dollars down on the counter for two tickets on purpose to keep up the arrogance and when he asked Morgan the name for the second cabin, He said, "My fiancé Miss Sally J. Burbank will be occupying the second cabin." The name I chose was well known, very wealthy family that owned riverboats. He looked at me and asked, "Yes sir, Mr. Goodhue".

I said, "My fiancé will be along directly. Could someone show me to our rooms please?"

He jumped and yelled at one of the men aboard to show me to my room, handing me the keys to both rooms.

"We will direct Miss Burbank to her cabin on arrival sir."

Morgan would think of himself from here on as James, James Goodhue. He never looked back as he boarded the Minnesota, amazed at the size, not knowing that this was "almost a maiden voyage" for the ship. His mind was somewhere else. He looked up to see the Captain looking down from his deck house watching the boarding activity. He only wished that it hadn't taken the death of his sister to create the pathway out of Stillwater.

6

The River Adventure

ames was led to the two cabins he had purchased tickets for. The mere fact that he had purchased cabins, which were on the second deck set him apart from deck passengers that were restricted to the first deck. Most did not have rooms and slept on deck in the front of the boat. Anyone he knew would likely be on first deck.

James unlocked his room and entered. It was a very comfortable cabin looking out over the river side of the boat as it was docked. He then went next door to see what the other room was like. It was very similar to the first. He had never been on a riverboat so he didn't know how these cabins would compare to others on the boat. Right now, the only thing he wanted was to get underway and not be discovered. There didn't appear to be any commotion when he approached the boat since everything had settled down from Sis's ordeal a couple of hours ago.

The first thing that James did was to move his items to the room registered to his fiancé. He figured they wouldn't be looking for someone with a fiancé. If they somehow thought he fit a description, they might knock on the door of Mr. Goodhue, but James would be hiding in the fiancé's cabin. He doubted they would bother someone with a name and social stature anyway.

Still the wait, although less than an hour, seemed like forever. Finally, he heard the blast of the Whistle from the wheelhouse. Then he could feel the movement of the boat moving away from the dock. It was going to be with the current the whole way down-river. James never looked at a map to really know where he was headed or what cities were on the way. It really didn't matter much. He had planned on staying in the cabin and going to the end of the line which apparently was Galena, wherever that was. He had taken a couple of books from Mr. Johnson's store about the West and intended to read during the day and go out on deck in the evenings when he was less likely to be noticed.

He felt a bit of a jolt when they engaged the paddle wheel. He almost fell over. After that, the ride was as smooth as could be. It was too bad he couldn't simply walk about and enjoy the trip. There was the smell of the restaurant over the smell of smoke and the river, although the Spring air had a distinct smell of Spring. New beginnings. What concerned him most was the fear that someone from Stillwater might be a passenger and recognize him.

There were a couple of newspapers in addition to the books in his carpetbag. He felt exhausted from the incredible and horrible events of the morning. It was time to settle in and maybe do a little reading. James could only hope that he would never experience another day like this one. Ever. He decided to read this story about gold being discovered in California, but his body told him it was time to lay down and take a nap to regain some of his energy. Surprising how anxiety can drain a person. That was something he would learn to embrace. James had no idea what was in store for him, but it had to be better than what he was leaving.

Not having a watch, James had no idea how long he had slept but he felt drained from a strange dream he had. It was a very short dream where he was underwater, drowning and a hand reached into the water to save him. He woke before he was grabbed or saved. He was almost hyperventilating when he woke.

Once he caught his breath and seemed to relax from what could be called more of a nightmare than a dream, he realized he was on the boat with no place to go. As he laid there another thought came to mind. He remembered again that there was a chance that someone on the boat might recognize him, so he decided he would have to continue to stay in his room. Every so often He would move the curtain and look out the small window at the river. It was too bad that he couldn't look at the manifest to see whether there was anyone on it from Stillwater that might know who he is.

While James was trying to figure out how one would get their hands on the manifest, he heard several loud noises and felt the paddlewheels stop and reverse as he was forced forward falling onto the bed. Men were yelling and again he was lost with something happening and didn't know what. At least this time he knew it couldn't involve him unless someone was boarding the boat looking for him.

Did good ol dad wake up early and get found? Did Mr. Johnson stop by the store and find out he was robbed? Was the sheriff looking at the manifest trying to identify anyone that looked like him? Did dad bleed to death? Did he somehow die? Was he being hunted for murder?

The mind soars when anxiety sets in and he hadn't learned how to befriend it and make it work for him. It always seemed that as much as he tried to avoid anxiety, when it did arrive, it wasn't always bad. He came up with the most creative thoughts, good and bad when the pressure forced him to think. Some people would later call that a quality in a man. To think on one's feet, they would say.

His thoughts were broken with commotion from people moving past his cabin window. Something was creating excitement. He looked out the window but couldn't see what was going on. Whatever it was, it was happening on the other side of the boat. It seemed the boat was in a slight reverse to stabilize and hold its position. He decided to take the risk of being identified and put on his coat and hat. He had to go out and see what all of excitement was about.

James went around the deck scanning as many faces as possible. He didn't recognize anyone and again thought of how nice it would be to see the manifest just to make sure.

It appeared that they had a dingy overboard and were bringing someone to the boat. Why would they stop to pick someone up in this desolate place unless...? unless it was the sheriff? Had the sheriff flagged them over? He never thought to wonder how he would have caught up with the boat in the first place.

At the very moment, the dingy pulled alongside, for the second time in one day he lost my breath. Laying in the bottom of the boat being carefully handed up was Sis!

James lost control and ran to where they were bringing her aboard. He shoved past a few people not caring if anyone recognized him. If it were going to happen, it would be now as he approached her, because everyone on the boat was watching.

As he ran towards Sally, a couple of crew members stopped him until he yelled out, "That's my Sis... fiancé! That's my fiancé!" He could care less if someone on the boat recognized him at this point. He felt that his eyes might be deceiving him, but there was Sally being carefully lifted on board. Was she alive?

The crew members looked at him probably wondering how in the world his fiancé fell overboard and got ahead of the boat. As they quickly looked over to the Captain who had come down to the deck, a nod was given, and they let James pass. He ran over to her side.

"Is she alive? Please tell me she is alive!" He had hardly gotten the words out of his mouth when she choked up some water. Then some more.

"She's alive. Lucky to be alive too. This part of the river is no place to fall overboard. The currents are very bad. She was lucky to get hung up on the shore however she got over there. She must be a strong swimmer but was exhausted once she reached those thickets." Said one of the crew that had been in the rescue boat.

"Please bring her this way to her cabin. Thank you, thank you," as tears started to appear on James's face, due to his sister again, but this time they were tears of happiness.

As they made their way through the hallways to her cabin, it went thru Morgan's mind whether he had been discovered and for that matter had someone recognized his sister. Someone that knew us would put her death in the river this morning together with him and that would be the end of it. Back to Stillwater. This time to the new prison they were building.

Once in the room the Captain, Captain Gray, stayed behind as the crew members that had assisted in getting her to her room left.

"Sir, my crew seemed to have missed her boarding this morning as I show the registry indicates she did not board the Minnesota. Please do attend to your fiancé. When she has recovered, I would like to invite the two of you to join me for dinner. Maybe tomorrow evening in the dining area. Please let an attendant know if there is anything else that we may assisted you with. This is most unfortunate and has never happened on my watch. I will send notice as to time of dining tomorrow night.

James's anxiety had him thinking fast. The first thing he had to do was to help with Sis still choking and coughing up the river an ounce at a time. He kept her on her side slightly facing down toward the bed so she wouldn't choke on the water her body was expelling from her lungs. How could this happen? This was real. She was here. He held her in his hands. This was a real miracle, but the Lord might be his last thought to thank given his recent status.

James had already asked himself repeatedly why God would have allowed his sister to go thru such pain. He was a faithful Christian in his youth. He firmly believed in God. He prayed every night and spoke to God when in trouble or when someone he knew was having a difficult time and they needed prayer. Unfortunately, as his father, a pastor, seemed to become more and more abusive, punishing him in an excessive manner for anything that his dad saw fit to, he lost his faith in the unfairness of it all. The separation grew between himself and his dad. Where was God when he prayed for understanding. His daily walk with Jesus would be conversation after conversation, to no avail.

As his sister lay before him, he wanted to call it a miracle from God that she was alive and well. His loss of faith caused hesitation. A reluctance to give any acknowledgement to a higher being. She looked terrible, but who wouldn't after being in the river drowning for two to three hours. She could have been hung up on that brush for hours before their spotting her and rescuing her. James didn't know how long he had been asleep with the boat moving downriver before they reached her, and he woke up. Truthfully, she looked like a princess to him.

After a short period of time she started to become aware of her surroundings. The room was nice, but he doubted she thought she was in the hereafter. Given the discussions they had had about him losing his faith, she wouldn't have expected him in heaven either. She realized that she was alive. Where? She had pretty much stopped coughing, so James slowly rolled her over facing him.

It was like she couldn't focus as she looked at him. It was really the disbelief that she was alive and second, what was Morgan doing in the picture? Morgan or James was in more disbelief than she was. They were both on the bed staring at each other. Her laying there looking up at him and Morgan sitting on the edge looking down at her.

"How did I get here? How did you get here? Where are we?" as she tried to sit up and look around the room.

"Well, we are on a riverboat headed for St. Louis. I couldn't handle what had happened, or what I thought happened to you, so I was running away. I booked one cabin for a fake fiancé and the other in the name of James Goodhue the man you're engaged to?"

She looked confused, "What do you mean I'm engaged to?"

"When they pulled you out of the river, I claimed that you were my missing fiancé that somehow didn't show up on the passenger log from Stillwater. It is important for us to pretend we are engaged and get as far away from Stillwater as quick as we can. We are not going back. Do you understand?"

With the look of an angel, Sally looked relieved stating, "I understand."

"My cabin is right next to yours. Got that? Don't tell anyone that we are brother and Sister, ok?" as Morgan started to laugh imagining her trying to sort that all out.

"There is one thing I need to say, and I really need you to agree to, trying to get the problems behind us so we can focus on the future."

"What's that?" still puzzled as to his last comments. Riverboat? Fiancé? Engaged to my brother? Sally only hoped she was in a bad dream.

"Listen up. I don't want you to ever speak of our mom and dad and I need you to never speak of the circumstances of our having left Stillwater or better yet that we were ever there. Let's just say we grew up in Duluth." As he waited for her response.

She was awake and alert now and fully understood what Morgan had said. He could tell she was momentarily reflecting on some of the memories.

"Do we have a deal? Duluth! Our parents are dead. Well not really dead, but we will say they are dead. OK with you?" her answer forthcoming.

"Morgan, you don't want to know why I did what I did? "she said. She had no way of knowing how she would start to explain the abuses of her father to the extent that she would rather be dead.

"It's James, not Morgan, and I don't need to know what happened and you don't need to know what I did!" Morgan responded hoping she wasn't going to ask any more questions. It would be so simple to just move forward.

"Love you!" as she put her arms around her brother. A feeling of warmth and safety poured over her as she quietly thanked God under her breath. She whispered for forgiveness for having tried to take her own life and for the opportunity to a second chance.

"Love you Sis!" as the feel of her embrace was the only family Morgan needed, or rather James.

"Remember from here on out you are Sally Burbank and I'm James Goodhue, related to the Goodhue family that own the St. Paul Pioneer Press newspaper. You can't call me Morgan anymore. It's James. Got that? Tomorrow when and wherever we dock, we will see if there is enough time to get to the local merchant and check out some clothes and items for you, since you boarded rather light on luggage," said James gently touching the side of her face still in disbelief.

"You have to be crazy?" as she finally started to laugh. It was great to see her with a smile on her face.

"Were do we get money to buy clothes?" with a questionable look.

"We have money. Ok. Don't ask. That's our agreement." As he tried to laugh and make a serious question funny.

"Do we have enough money to eat because I'm hungry." As Sis smiled in the disbelief of her environment and everything in it.

"I'll go see if I can get something for us. Will you be ok if I leave you alone?" James didn't mean to say that she might try to be suicidal at all, but he knew she took it that way.

"Please trust me. I'll be fine. Can we talk a little more when you get back at least about what we are doing here and where we are going?" Sally was continually sounding more stable and even had a little bit of excitement in her voice like a little kid on a trip not knowing where we were headed but knowing we were going to have some fun.

When he returned with some food from the restaurant, Sis seemed like she had really recovered. She dug right in and ate everything he had brought to the room. James thought she was going to lick the plate. It was then time to have a serious talk about what they were going to do now that their dream to escape Stillwater had been launched. They had to have a plan.

"The first thing we have to do is find out where I can go get you some clothes. You can't leave the room with only your night shirt. Looking at you, you look better in one of my shirts," which he had given her to be decent and dry. "The next thing that we have to do is discuss what we are going to do to find out if there is anyone aboard that might know us. I thought I might just ask the captain if I could look and see if there was anyone on the manifest so you could be around someone you knew as an excuse to see if there is anyone that could recognize us. Then at least we will know who to keep away from. Once we reach St. Louis or Galena, I suspect the city will be large enough that we won't know anyone. I understand that wagon trains form up in St. Louis for the trip out West. What do you think?" looking for her reaction. he didn't have long to wait.

"Do you mean you are thinking of both of us joining a wagon train and head West into the wilderness? Can't we get lost in St. Louis instead of the frontier? Where did you get this plan? I know, from of one of your adventure magazines. People frequently die in the West from gunfights, Indians, sickness, and things like wild animals. I'm sure living it isn't like reading it out of a book. There is a difference big brother. A lot of the real stories of the West have bad endings." Finishing her statement with a look of disbelief.

"Sis. I know that the solution to all our problems is out West. Besides, what would I do for a living in St. Louis. I'm a preacher's son and you're a preacher's daughter. Neither of us has done more than ride a horse or hitch up a wagon team or work at a small store. What would we do? If we go out West, we can get land and raise cattle. Mine for gold. Train horses or open a store. There are all sorts of opportunity. Come on Sis. If we are going to try and live our adventure, then we have to do this."

She looked at James and repeated with a laugh, "You really are crazy. This is following your dream. Your adventure! Not mine. What kind of man would I find? How would I even find one?

"Stop right there! It will be easy for you to find a good man because of the incredible shortage of women" James said smartly.

"Oh. That really sounds encouraging. Are you even listening to yourself or are the words coming out faster than you can think? I want to have a family someday, preferably with a husband that isn't wearing feathers if that's not asking too much in life."

James was about to remind her, and fire back that life didn't seem to be that important to her this morning. Why now? He caught himself knowing that his comment would do some serious damage when they were just starting to get settled in.

"Look Sis, lets enjoy this trip and when we get to St. Louis we will ask around and take one step at a time. Ok?" trying to smile and feel her support. She knew what that all meant. She and her brother were going to experience the last of civilization aboard a boat before riding off into the sunset as they say, to fight Indians and who knows what else.

7

Freedom

The next morning, in the milliseconds before James opened his eyes, he believed that he had a long dream. His Sister... no, no, his dad? The riverboat, Sis? Heading West. All of a sudden, his mind caught up with reality.

His feet hit the floor in a flash and within a couple of seconds it was evident that it wasn't a dream. The strangest day of his life really did happen. His first thought was to run next door and see if Sis was ok. He still wasn't sure how stable she was even though they had found a way to escape the horrible environment they had been in.

"Sis? Sis? Open the door. Its me." As James heard a slight rustling. "Who is me? I don't know a me. Come back later." She responded.

With that he knew that all was well, and she had improved over night and got some of her humor back. As she opened the door to let him in, she asked, "So how is my rich husband to be today?"

James tried to keep up the charade without the acting skills that his sister had. "I'm fine. Look at your hand. Did you lose that big diamond engagement ring I bought you? Too bad. I guess I'll have to get you another. Maybe larger than the last. How's that?

She laughed. "So just how much money do I have to spend Mr. Goodhue?"

James replied, "Enough" as he opened the bundle of bills he was keeping in his pocket. "I had been told that if you travel, learn to keep most of your money hid on yourself. I didn't have a money belt, so I simply keep it in my pockets. I will have to buy a money belt when we, I mean, I go out to buy you some clothes."

But when he looked up at Sis she looked like a ghost. "Where did you get that?"

"Remember. We weren't going to talk about the past. At least not right now. Please Sis. We need to keep looking forward not back."

She knew that he had done something wrong but then again so had she, at least considering her faith, suicide should not have been her way out. So...the best solution was her -brother's suggestion for now and not look back.

James checked with a crew member yesterday knowing that we would be tied up today taking on cargo. They had arrived late the night before. Today he had to get into town, buy decent travel cases for Sis and himself and purchase some clothes so they can walk around outside of their room to include a beautiful dress for dinner. He hadn't forgotten that the Captain had invited them to dine with him.

"Sis, you stay here, and I will go on shore and get you some clothes, a few things so you can go ashore. Then you and I can head out again so you can pick out some things for yourself. Then when we get to a larger city down river you can get whatever else you need. I'll be back and surprise you in a little while. I know we are leaving in about two hours."

James looked very dapper in the one suit he owned, and he figured that he won't have much use for a collection of suits traveling with a wagon train. As he went ashore, he spotted a merchant store not too far down the street. He hurried down to the store so fast that he had to catch his breath as he entered. There was quite a number of people in the store. It immediately reminded him of Mr. Johnson's store creating a tinge of guilt.

James addressed the store owner, "I'm on the riverboat that is going to leave within two hours. I need a change of clothes for my fiancé who had her luggage stolen so she can return here herself and purchase her wardrobe. She and I both need travel luggage also. Hers stolen and mine damaged. Crewman handle passenger luggage in the same manner as throwing feed sacks."

The store owner was very polite, smiled and said, "We can take care of about anything you need sir. Right this way. We will have you fixed up in no time."

The layout for the store and inventory wasn't much different than Mr. Johnsons. James guessed that there was going to be a store like this in every river town they stop in.

The dresses were not fresh from the east coast, but they had some really nice ones with a good enough selection so that when he returned to the store with Sis, she would able to find a very nice one for dinner. After he had everyone's consensus that he had picked some good going ashore clothes for Sis, a fresh dress shirt for himself the rest was easy.

Sis was excited about the casual clothes. James couldn't wait to see her expression when she had her choice of really nice dresses. Then there would be the shoes and whatever else he could spoil her with. It was a ploy to take her mind off of her recent, unpleasant experiences. Tomorrow or the next day, wherever we docked next, she could continue to shop, giving her some kind of purpose in life, however shallow.

James kept looking around in fear of to seeing someone he knew waving at him. What a disaster that would be. He decided that he was going to meet with the Captain once the boat had left the dock for the next leg of their journey.

Knock, knock, knock. "It's me Sis"

This time she unlocked the door quickly. She must have already been on her feet. It was something to watch Sis open the carpet bag he had bought her and took out the casual dress in addition to a couple of hair pins and brushes, socks and a pair of shoes that they said she could return if she didn't like them. At least she wouldn't have to walk back to the store in bare feet.

This was something James was never able to do before, since they never had any money. Dad was more about helping and giving to others than to themselves even on special holidays.

"Oh, ..., I don't know what to say. The dress is beautiful. Socks too? And I love the hair pins and brushes. This must have cost a lot?" as some tears of joy swelled up in her eyes. She turned away to wipe the tears from her eyes before they ran down her checks. Then tears started to run down her cheeks that she couldn't control. As she shook out the simple dress in its full glory, she started to look weak, the tears increasing.

"Did I do something wrong or can someone have that many tears of joy? Sis, it's just a dress. And, you're going to look incredible in it if you don't get it so wet that you'll look like you had just come out of the river again.

"I know this cost too much. I never dreamed of having such a pretty dress. I don't think we should be spending so much money on things like this, although you don't know how much I love it." As she attempted to smile thru her tears.

"Sis don't worry about what things cost. I just want to see you like your old self only happier. Think you can do that for me? Now clean up those tears, you look terrible," feeling pride in taking care of her. She just laughed. She gave James a big hug then pushing him out of the room so she could enjoy trying on her new wardrobe.

It was a fantasy for Sally as they hurried back to the store after she tried on what she had and surprised her with the purchase of some really nice dinner dresses.

"I cannot have you looking anything but aristocratic! This is the act you must play. While you're doing that you might want to enjoy it," said James gazing at his beautiful sister.

Even from the store they heard the whistle blast from the boat, a signal for final boarding. They knew that the boat would be moving within the hour. They settled up at the store and made their way back to the boat.

Back on board, James decided that this would be a good time to move up to the upper deck in hopes that once out on the water, he could get a chance to speak with the Captain or first mate.

As he closed her door to the cabin, he could only think about how different everything was going to be, as long as we weren't recognized. He kept his hat low and tried to blend in as he made his way to the upper deck. It seemed that whenever the boat docked or shoved off nearly everyone found a place on the deck to watch the activity.

As they moved out into the river with a good head of steam, the current still seemed to do most of the work. James assumed the paddlewheel was used more as a drag or break. They were moving along smoothly now.

"Take over Bill, " Captain Gray yelled as he closed the door to the Wheelhouse and walked toward where James had positioned himself hoping he would run into him.

"Ah, Mr. Goodhue, how is your fiancé? The attendant I instructed to check on her said that she was reported doing fine. I'm so glad. Can't have our passengers floating down the river when there is a perfectly good boat to ride on." Stated the Captain hoping some humor might cause me to overlook the seriousness of the mishap. James had other things on my mind. The manifest.

"Captain, I have what may seem a rather unusual request and I was hoping you would indulge me. My fiancé asked me if I had run into anyone aboard that we knew so that she might have friends to visit with. It would make her feel so much more comfortable with some familiarity. I'm sure you understand." As James stood straight and tried to pretend, he was an aristocrat. He was hoping that the Captain wouldn't see through him, his language, the way he wore his hat. He was a commoner and had little experience around or watching anyone rich and important.

"Of course, of course Mr. Goodhue. That makes perfect sense. Follow me and let's see if we can help make her comfortable with some friends. You haven't forgot my invitation to dinner tonight, I hope. "Looking back at me while we entered the wheelhouse.

"Certainly not. She and I are so looking forward to dining at your table" if they knew that there wasn't going to be someone that recognizes them only to start screaming at Sis thinking they have seen a ghost or me as a criminal or both. James reflected that that would rank this day as the second strangest day of his life.

"Here we are", as he reached for the big book with all the passenger's names listed in it.

He pushed it over to James. James was pretending to enjoy the view commenting on the wheelhouse. "Quite a view from up here. Looks beautifully wild out there. "as he quickly started reading names he felt strange as his finger went past James Goodhue and Sally Burbank. There weren't as many passengers as he had thought. He got thru the names and tried to act sad that there wasn't a single person that he recognized, "I know a great number of her friends, so I think I can speak for both of us in that I don't recognize a single sole. I might have thought you had more passengers. At least a couple out of Stillwater."

"Not too many passengers travel up that far in the early Spring. We make the run mostly to deliver goods for the local farmers and merchants." Sounding proud of being one of the first to navigate the Spring waters. "The river in the Spring is tricky with large branches, trees and changes of depth due to the winter run offs or lack thereof."

"Thank you, Captain. Again, we greatly look forward to dining with you this evening" as James covered up a sigh of relief.

"Seven PM shall we say?" the Captain replied with a gentle smile.

"Of course, your too kind", almost skipping down the deck way.

It was time to get back and make sure that Sis hadn't drown in her tears of joy. He held his head up high now, saying hi and tipping his hat to everyone he passed. A perfect gentleman of rank and stature. That was him.

This time he didn't say anything when he knocked on her door. He just knocked and when his Sister answered the door, he remained speechless. There she stood. She had one of her dinner dresses on that he had purchased for her. Her hair was all straightened out except for a small amount of natural curl. She was breathlessly beautiful.

Her face framed by her flowing blond hair, deep blue eyes from her German heritage and the dimples on her face that would dam up the tears before they reached her chin when she was crying. She was a statement of a strong, beautiful, grown woman. James had to admit that over the last year she blossomed in other areas that caused him to remind himself that she was his sister. He knew he would be looking to the ends of the earth for someone with her looks. Especially her smile which made the dimples seem so deep.

"Look, Look at me. I don't hardly believe I'm wearing a dress that mom or I didn't make. A real store-bought dress. It fits really good. What do you think?" as she twirled around stopping to look at me with a big smile.

He hadn't said a word since she opened the door.

"What's the matter, are there people on the boat from Stillwater? There are aren't there? I guess that means we can't go to dinner tonight with the Captain after all. "her smile fading.

"No that's not it! I've just never seen you look so beautiful. Maybe it's the change from yesterday. I started off the day yesterday with you dead and missing, then found you looking dead but alive and pretty dreadful up to now...a princess! I'm going to have to protect you from all of the guys that will be finding excuses to introduce themselves." Said James as Sally started laughing and twirling again. Then she stopped abruptly. "What happened with the Captain?"

"You won't believe this, but he let me go thru the entire manifest. There isn't a single person's name that I could recognize! Can you believe that? Captain Gray also reminded me of our invitation to join him for dinner at his table tonight at 7pm!"

She screamed for joy and sat down on the edge of bed," I think I'm was getting a little dizzy from all the twirling."

"Come on Sis. Let's show you off a little. You need a little fresh air. Let's explore the boat and see how the other half live." As James held his hand out in a gentlemanly fashion to escort the beautiful young lady out the door.

The boat had some seating around the deck areas, and a large area up top near the rear for people to sit and get hypnotized watching the paddle wheel go around. The view was spectacular. As James and his sister came up on the deck area, they found a couple of seats and proceeded to watch the river and small communities go by as they made their way down stream. Several people said hello including one couple that recognized Sis from the water incident and asked how she was doing, exclaiming how dreadful the experience must have been. They chuckled under their breath when the couple walked away. The couple were very genuine and meant well but flashing back on yesterday was like ancient history already. Life was moving on quickly. After James and Sally took a light lunch, they both retired for a nap until near time to get ready for dinner.

8

Dining In Style

As James awoke from his nap, putting his feet over the edge of the bed, he could hear people moving by his window. The activity with passengers heading to the saloons in town or the lounge on board sent a signal that he should check the time and get ready for dinner. As he looked out his guess was confirmed with people moving every which way. The guys, to have a drink and gamble a little, the woman to get their land legs back while checking out some of the store windows. James and Sally didn't have a desire to get off the boat as much as just get out of their rooms. Freedom. They just wanted to feel free to move about and enjoy their evening without fear of being recognized.

James cleaned up and knocked next door to see how Sis was doing. He wanted to walk around the deck a little, view the town from the boat and see the dining area before being seated with the Captain. He was feeling a little anxiety as he knocked on Sally's door.

Sally opened the door and first thing out of her mouth was, "What will we talk about. Where are we going to pretend, we are from? Was it Duluth? I've never been there! Are you listening?" as she dove right over my level of anxiety.

"Hey, hey, this is going to be fun. Just remember Sis, ahh, I mean Sally, my beautiful fiancé, that we don't have to do more than ask questions about the people at the table. If there are questions from the people around the table directed at us, we will just have to make it up as we go. Make it a game. We can play a game amongst ourselves and see who can ask the most questions throughout the evening. That way we won't have to answer any."

"Sis, I guess I better remember not to call you that. Pretend we are in a play and this boat is our stage for now. You always liked to pretend and act in little plays. Here is your chance to really pour it on. Be whatever kind of person you want to be, although I would like something more near the real you than not. We're going to be just fine." stated with all the confidence he could muster hoping some of it stuck to her.

When James came back a short time later to offer her his arm, he could only think that he was going to be envy of the evening with a woman so gorgeous on his arm. As he looked around the decks earlier, he was hoping that the beautiful young ladies came out at night, because they sure weren't out during the day.

Entering the dining area after a walk around the outside deck area they immediately noticed the table that had to been set for the Captain and his guests. They were a bit more comfortable thinking that the guests weren't going to be anyone they knew.

An attendant came over to show them to the Captains table. A waiter was there as fast as we sat down. James ordered some wine for the both of them remembering the wines that Mr. Johnson had on the shelf at one time. He was hoping that Mr. Johnson had good taste in wine so he wouldn't look like he drank for quantity and not quality.

"Sir, would you like to approve the wine?" the waiter said as he poured a finger of wine in my glass. James once again remembered when he had once asked Mr. Johnson about the wine, that he took the time to tell him about how to properly open the wine, taste the wine, pour and drink. James was desperately trying to remember what he had said which at the time seemed like a bunch of silly rituals next to slugging a shot of whiskey or having a sip beer. Even a sarsaparilla went from counter to stomach without ceremony.

"Right" said James as he took the small portion of wine, moved it around in his mouth like he knew what he was doing before swallowing it. It was his first taste of wine. It was dry. For such a small taste he was still trying to get his tongue off the roof of his mouth. It was really dry. He smiled, tried to look intellectual and said, "That's wonderful. You may pour it." As he wondered if the procedure was right? Oh well, he's pouring and a glass or two of this might help before the others arrive.

James looked over at Sally and she looked stunned. Then she started to get this funny expression. He was hoping that she wouldn't burst out laughing. He had no idea what she was thinking. If he were to put it to words, she would be saying, who are you and who are you pretending to be? Nothing James appeared to be doing reminded her of her brother except the looks. Before either of them could comment two additional couples showed up. Before they even got seated the Captain was approaching the table as well.

The Captain spoke first, "So how is everyone? Enjoying your voyage so far?" He seemed to catch himself and had an expression that read, did I really just say that? Everyone immediately looked at Sis with great doubt that she had enjoyed the journey up to this point.

"I'm sorry, that was rather thoughtless," as the Captain tried to walk back his statement.

"That's quite all right. I'm here to enjoy the company and wonderful food. Thank you so much for inviting us." Sis easing any tension created by the Captains statement.

The Captain again took the floor to introduce two couples. "May I present Mr. & Mrs. William Hughes from New Orleans and Mr. and Mrs. Franklin Rockler from St. Louis returning from having visited relatives in Stillwater.

"Allow me to introduce Mr. Goodhue And his fiancé Sally Burbank from Stillwater?" the Captain questioned.

"Sorry, for correction sake, we are both from Duluth, Minnesota. Is anyone familiar with Duluth?" with a slight quiver in his voice that Sis caught right away. James could see her mind working and half expected her to come down with some instant illness that would cause them to have to leave dinner.

With a round of "glad to meet you" comments and no one having any familiarity with Duluth they all sat as the waiter took drink orders. Hard drinks for the men and wine for the women. James started to question if he should have had a good ol bourbon whiskey or simply have waited to see what others ordered. He hoped they didn't think him to be odd in that he drank wine. He was being overly careful, and the evening was taxing on his emotions.

As the evening progressed the people filled the room and the noise level rose. A strange blend of perfume's mixed in the air with the smell of tobacco and liquor. Everyone appeared to be having an enjoyable time.

As the evening went by, conversation and questions went to subjects directed at the Captain, usually brought up by Sally and James. The others not knowing what to say, socially piled on the Captain and he seemed to speak most of the evening. Following the inquisition of the Captain, dinner was served. Dinner was beyond incredible. Sally and James had never experienced such luxury in dining. James declined and decided to retire when the men invited him to go up on deck to enjoy the night air with a cigar.

Sally and James chose to retire. As they went into her cabin and closed the door, they started laughing for what seemed like an eternity. They couldn't stop laughing. Sally was trying to envision James on deck trying to smoke a cigar, or what if he had ordered a shot of Whiskey. He would have no doubt choked on it. What if the others at the table ordered additional shots? They had had the time of their lives and they left the party while they were ahead and yet undiscovered. They had been treated special, especially by the Captain, relieved that they were not likely to file a complaint over Sis somehow going overboard. It was a miracle that no one had asked for Sis to describe exactly how she fell overboard. Instead, they stayed away from the subject like it was too sensitive to discuss.

They had fallen on the bed side by side and laughed until it hurt. James finally catching his breath, got up to head for his own cabin. "Going to be a big shopping day for you tomorrow. At least enough of what you need before we get to St. Louis." Still chuckling he waved at Sis as he went out closing the door behind him.

Back in his room, thinking to himself, he thought about Mr. Johnson and what he would think of him testing a bottle of wine and having dinner with the Captain of a Riverboat. Life was starting to get really interesting. He didn't want this to ever end.

9

A Little Extra Traveling Cash

~≈

James's goal now was to enter a deep sleep, after being stuffed with great food, wine and having had a great time laughing with Sis. He thought he was especially touched from the two plus glasses of wine he had. They both had a little over two glasses so they could finish up the bottle that they had ordered. He could tell it affected Sally although it would have been hard for the others to tell. As he was slowly fading off there was a crash on the side of his cabin wall from the outside. Then he heard something moving around and another crash like someone kicking some of the benches out on the sidewall opposite his cabin. Then it was quiet. Too quiet. He was wide awake now, so he decided to satisfy his curiosity, get dressed and go out and see what had happened?

James got dressed and went out to the hallway that had a door immediately to the outside where the noise had come from. He stepped out and from the side lanterns he saw a reflection of something or someone laying on the deck over a bench that had overturned. He approached with caution until he saw it was a gentleman who he had seen around the boat before. A boastful guy that always had a cigar. There was a cigar burning on the deck which James picked up and pitched over the side. The drunken fool could have put the boat on fire.

He had passed out. It was just after midnight and no one else was on the side deck as James looked around for help. He knelt to check and make sure the man was just drunk and passed out and not injured or dead.

Ya, just drunk. He should know better at which point James's mind started to conger up how the boastful character needed to be taught a lesson. Quickly taking another look around, he reached into the man's pocket and felt a thick money clip. He also felt on the inside of his belt and sure enough there was a slit for cash. James put the stuffed money clip in his pocket and proceeded to pull off the man's belt so he could strip out the cash. He didn't even look at how much money there was. He just stuffed it in his pocket. Then he saw the diamond ring on the man's right hand. If he had to take the finger off to get it he might wake up, plus the mess. Luckily, enough for James and the drunk, it slid off without much effort. Next was a gold watch. That was enough as James looked around to make sure nobody saw him with this drunk. James rolled him back on his side so he wouldn't choke to death if he got sick and quickly went back to his cabin. After locking the door and pulled the curtain over the window, James turned the lamp up slightly so I could see his take for the night.

The watch was gold and had a chain on it alone that was worth a tidy sum. Next was the ring. The first thing he thought of was having the diamond reset when they got to St. Louis for Sis. It would be her engagement ring and something that would always have value if she got in trouble and needed money. Then he opened the money clip and started counting. All denominations. Several hundred dollars. Counting the last as he hurried before someone might notice his light on, with this drunk right outside, was the money belt. Ahhhhhhh. The motherlode!

Folded over and stuffed in the belt all the way around were hundred-dollar bills. Over twenty of them. All he knew was that they needed this a lot more than he did. He shouldn't have gotten drunk. Plus, cigars were bad for you. James put out the light and thought about putting a false bottom in his bag or find someplace to hide this treasure. Then he remembered, that except for the ring and watch it was all cash. He was perceived as being from a rich family. It would carry no suspicion if he had a great deal of money on him. He was expected to, which also meant he had better watch out for thieves. They might try to rob him thinking he had money on himself. No one was to be trusted.

Morning came and James woke up shocked that he had the same dream again about his drowning. It was strange having it just after Sis supposedly drowned and then only moments after waking up from the dream she was found. So, was it him drowning? Who was reaching in to rescue him? Or did it mean something entirely different. It was just a strange dream and he had never had a reoccurring dream. Forgetting about the dream for the moment, it was more important to get up and start the day. He had no idea what to expect.

As the day went on, they found out more about their schedule. The Minnesota only went as far as Galina. From there they would have to board another riverboat. James was concerned, hoping that they would get off the Minnesota before he made any connection with the gentleman, He felt his windfall might be in jeopardy from this man's unconscious state. He didn't know how the gentleman would recognize him in any way, but he just didn't want to take any chances. He chose not to tell Sis anything about having fleeced the drunk the night before.

Once they had docked for the day, Sally had James on deck ready for the gang plank to drop so they could be one of the first off. Sally had her mind set on some body creams, you know, ladies' stuff and some shoes that fit better. James was going to look for a couple of things for himself as well.

With only a couple of real stores in town the shopping was actually over pretty quick, so when they met up, they went to have a bite to eat at a little café that reminded them of Sally's Café back home. James was hoping that not everything was going to remind him of back home. After lunch, they wandered back to the boat to cover another stretch of the adventure down river. As they boarded the first mate yelled, "Hello, enjoy your time ashore? Get a few things?"

"Yes, thank you. The little café is great for anyone on your travels through here that might want a special dessert. More like New York than Midwest." Moving forward with his hand on his Sisters back in a gentlemanly fashion, I could feel her shaking, trying not to belch out in laughter. When we got into the hallway in front of our rooms, she burst out laughing..." New York?"

Joining her in the laughter over the inside joke they arranged to meet up directly after dropping their purchases off in their perspective rooms. They were going to meet up in the lounge to talk about the rest of the trip since they were approaching the end of this leg. Tomorrow they were expected to arrive in Galena. They had no idea where they were going once off the gang plank nor what to expect.

When they docked at Galena, Illinois, they knew they had to say goodbye to the Minnesota and moved their things to a hotel until they found out when and on what boat they could get passage to New Orleans. A somber feeling came over both of them knowing again that this was the end of the line for the Minnesota. It had been a glorious ride. Having been so comfortable aboard the Minnesota. They didn't know what to expect or how they would receive having to change boats.

Galena certainly was an interesting stopping point. The river port was on the Fevre, or Bean River about six miles upriver from its junction with the Mississippi. For someplace that they had never heard of, it seemed to be a growing and active community. For some reason, the riverboats came up from St. Louis for more commercial reasons transferring goods rather than passengers. It was explained to Sally and James that Galina was one the biggest mining areas for lead in the country. As they entered the port there were piles and piles of pig-lead. In fact, the name "Galina" is Latin for sulphide of lead. This was the port that a great part of the ore was shipped out from as well as mining supplies transported in. As James looked at all the lead ore, he fantasized what it would be like looking at a pile of Gold ore. They had heard from the locals that some swamp city called Chicago to the north on the South Shore of Lake Michigan was trying to put in a port to compete. They were having a problem because most of Chicago was around shallow swamp land making it hard to bring in ships of any size. The real expectation was that Galina would continue to outpace Chicago.

It was a beautiful day. They had their bags sent over to the hotel. Waving good-bye to Captain (Richard C.) Gray, they went off to find where the ticket office was to see where the next leg of their trip would take them. Unfortunately, Sally was so drawn from one store to another that they never got to the ticket office. This fast-growing town had some magnificent stores and the homes up on the hill overlooking the main street were very stately. One of the store clerks commented that the town was spreading out on both sides of the river and had over 5000 residents already. Stillwater would never be the size of Galena.

After walking and shopping the town their legs took them back to the hotel. They felt it time for a late lunch before having one last go at the stores on main street.

Sally was having a great time shopping although a couple of times James had to remind her that some of the shoes and dresses, she wanted might be tough to bring along on the trail West. For sure there wasn't likely to be an occasion to wear most of what she had already purchased once we were off the boat. That said she convinced James to buy a real gentleman's suit.

It was going to be a serious adjustment for her to go from the paddleboats with the dresses and little umbrellas to the seat of a covered wagon and the dust from the horses. James had decided that she should enjoy this if for no other reason than to temporarily forget the past. They would face the journey West when they got to the point of leaving civilization. Right now, they were living in luxury and headed South not West.

James was thinking it a good thing that they purchased travel cases that so far could hold all the items that Sally had bought and the few things he bought for himself. Deep down he couldn't wait until he could change into something other than a suit. He didn't know how bankers, and such lived all the time in these outfits.

"I see you did some shopping Miss Burbank", stated the front desk attendant.

"Yes, I believe we may need assistance with a few things that we couldn't manage to carry." Yelled Sally, as the attendant waved over to one of the hotel staff to help us. In the end, they heavily tipped a member of the hotel staff to go to a couple of stores to fetch the rest of their items.

The meal this night was magnificent. The restaurant in the hotel held most of the same people that they had dinner with on the Minnesota, so everyone seemed comfortable conversing back and forth between tables and over drinks.

The evening came to an end, with new clothes, stomachs full and knowing and having good conversation with some of the other passengers, the evening seemed to go by fast, yet with a quiet aura of celebration. They were feeling more and more comfortable that we had truly escaped our past.

They had plenty of money for now, but somehow, James thought about the trip and supplies he had to purchase. How much would it all cost? He needed to know that they had enough to make it to the Gold country. There were many risks had to be considered, including running out of money. He was not as concerned for himself as he was for Sally. He decided, in leu of a budget, they had better enjoy themselves while they could, knowing that both of them would have some serious adjustments to face in a few weeks when heading West.

The day before, they had conversations with a couple of the crewman that worked on the riverboats. The next big stop going south for most riverboats was going to be St. Louis. Although after hearing the stories about New Orleans, they were feeling pulled to board a boat that went all the way to New Orleans and then start working our way West from there instead of launching West from St. Louis.

There was a trail called "The Old Spanish Trail" that they say ran from Jacksonville Florida to San Diego. It spanned the entire width, from coast to coast, of the United States and territories of the new frontiers that were quickly growing from territories to statehood. The Old Spanish Trail went right thru New Orleans, however, they heard that we could instead enjoy the luxury of the riverboats all the way to Galveston/Houston Texas. That's where one could fully equip themselves with wagons, mules, horses, and other supplies for the trip West.

10

Galina, Illinois

The next morning, they were up early, anxious to get to the ticket office and further on their way to New Orleans. There was little chance that word of what happened in Stillwater would catch up with them since there wasn't any faster form of transportation than the river. Even the telegraph wasn't completed the full course of the river or West of the Mississippi. This in mind, James knew they still had to keep moving.

"Morning, how did you sleep?" Admiring her beauty but slightly disturbed how his Sister drew the attention of every man in the restaurant.

"I kind of missed not being rocked to sleep with the motion of the boat or as one of the crew, politely corrected me stating that a boat this size is referred to as a ship. It all seemed kind of silly to her and she wasn't sure he knew the difference." As Sally went on about whether to call a ship a boat or a boat a ship.

James laughed responding, "They call them river boats no matter how big they are. A boat, ship, tub, barge, just so it floats! First thing we need to find out is where they sell tickets, so we know where we are going. I remind you that from what I have read, we do not want to be waiting till fall of next year to make the trip West. A trip like that in the summertime is dangerous just because of the heat. I read that it effects the animals more than the people."

"Ya, that's right. the trip West. That means we have to be leaving in the next month to take advantage of the winter months on the trail." Said sadly with absolutely no enthusiasm at all, Sally was crudely reminded that James was still on a mission. Sally on the other hand was enjoying a life of luxury that they had never experienced and may never see again once they hit the trail. James could understand her reluctance to leave their current surroundings. Sally seemed to demonstrate immunity to "Gold Fever".

After breakfast they asked at the front desk where they could book passage downriver. The desk clerk said, "Down a block on main, next to the bank."

With directions and after asking a couple of kind people where the ticket office was, they found it. As they entered there was a lot of activity. They were starting to realize just how active Galena as a city was.

Stepping up to the ticket masters window James asked, "I would like to book passage for my fiancé and myself to New Orleans. Can you tell me what might be available and when?"

"You're in luck. If you would be ready to leave tomorrow morning, I can get you on the Nominee to Cairo. The Nominee is a fast boat that has taken part in some of the river races. Once you arrive in Cairo, I understand the riverboat, "Big Missouri" will be in from St. Louis next week and you might be able to catch passage on her. She is one if not the biggest and most luxurious riverboats on the Mississippi. You can take her all the way down to New Orleans." Having assumed that they could easily afford luxury passage from our dress and my new Gold Watch displayed on my new vest.

"That would be fine. I would like two cabins, next to each other if possible. The best accommodations you have please," stated James, which brought a broad smile to the agent's face.

"No problem, let's get you signed up and on your way, so you have some time to see our city before you have to leave." As the agent filled out their names and cabin accommodations.

That finished they walked out and decided to go walk along the main street, since Sally wanted to see the rest of the stores knowing they would be leaving first thing tomorrow.

James continued now to remind her that they were headed for St. Louis and the shopping would be incredible there. Sally looked at James in a strange way and asked if we might go into this little café, grab a table by the front window to watch the street traffic and have a cup of coffee. James knew something was up, when Sally suggested coffee over shopping?

There wasn't a sole in the restaurant, so they took the table by the front window which she spotted coming in. They seated themselves as the waitress and owner of the café came to ask their pleasure.

"What can I do for you two on such a beautiful day?" she asked.

"Two coffees please and one of those apple pastries I can see from here and bring my fiancé' a slice of apple pie." Laughing as she said it, knowing James loved apple pie and that it was not appropriate for the lady to order for the man. Sally seemed to get a kick out of that.

"Right away" and the host went to retrieve their morning treats.

"When I stop from all this excitement, shopping and especially shopping, I have to ask you if we have enough money to be doing this. I know we are supposed to act like we are rich, but I know we're not. I also can't help but wonder how you got the money you have and how much do you have? How did you get it?" Sally asking one question after another.

"Whoa, hold your horse's Sis! Your firing questions at me making me feel like I'm under attack, out in the open, and can't hide. You knew we had agreed to not talk about this right away." James replied.

"You knew that isn't good enough and it isn't...right...not anymore. We have been traveling for some time. I don't know if we are running from something, because I know you didn't have any money before you left. And...maybe we can start with why you left? We are alone here and I'm not leaving until you talk to me." Sis's comment ended just as they received their deserts and coffee.

Once the waitress had left and there was no one in earshot, knowing she deserved to know something James began to speak. "Ok, I'll tell you, but you're not going to like what I'm about to say and I don't need you to be judging me for anything. I'm going to take care of both of us and do whatever I need to, to do it. If you start acting upset and start crying, I'm going to get up and leave and never say another word. That's it. Ready?"

Sis was sipping her coffee and was playing with her desert like her appetite had suddenly gone away. She nodded her head in agreement terrified of where this conversation was going to go. Regretting already that she had made demands. She only really wanted to know if there was enough money to pay for the shopping she was doing and still have enough to get out West. Now she realized just how carried away she got. She knew it was time to listen and not speak.

"I have an idea of why you walked into the river that morning." James said, as he saw Sally looking down as she took a deep breath. Her faced turned red and she started hyperventilating. She did not expect this subject to come up. What had she started?

"I'm sorry Sis, but we might as well get this all out before we start on the trail. I want you to know that our dad isn't going to be doing what he did to you to anyone else. When I left, he was tied up on his bed with a note explaining that he had abused you. I also stated in the note, that I could no long stand to be around him knowing what had happened. I stated that it was time to leave."

She slowly looked up at me.

"Sis, it's me, your brother and best friend. You don't have to feel embarrassed that I know. We both know what he was like."

"I really regret...you know... the river. I didn't mean to..."

James cut her off, "Sis, a number of people saw you in your night clothes walk into the river. You weren't very discreet, and I think that what happened at that moment is what you wanted. I don't hold that against you. I understand and am thankful for the miracle of the crew on board finding you washed up along the shore. Let's be grateful that we have each other. Ok?"

She was holding back the tears and hadn't touched her dessert. The waitress could tell that they were in a serious conversation by their actions, so she avoided their table.

"Then tell me where you got the money?" looking at me with bloodshot eyes.

James was happy to tell her since she hadn't asked anymore about him... tying up dad causing him to have to tell her about the nailing. He didn't see any reason that he should need to share that with her.

"I stole the money that dad had in his study and the offering money from the church, what little there was. Then I stopped by Mr. Johnson's store and borrowed some money from him."

"Borrowed?" she questioned.

"Yes borrowed. I intend to pay him back someday with interest." I replied.

"Was he there?" she asked.

"Ok, he wasn't there, and I cleaned out his safe and took a few items from the shop, but I swear I intend to pay him back." Then... well then, I helped a man aboard the Minnesota who was drunk to get off the deck and into a chair for his own safety. During the process, appearing to be very wealthy, I helped myself to his watch and his money belt. I wouldn't have known about the money belt if I wasn't helping him to be more comfortable. That was where I got some serious money." Acting a bit proud until he took another look at Sis.

"You stole all of the money? How could you do that? I don't know what you've turned into. Did I turn you into this?" she started to blame herself for his goings on.

"Sis, we need to survive and now that we only have each other. I'm making sure that we do. We can't go back, so we might as well do our best to go forward. Maybe there is a part of me you don't know, but I intend to get to where we can live our life without thinking about home. Home now is somewhere West waiting for us. Please understand." James closed his comment as soft and pleading as he could.

"Want a warmup on your coffee? Everything ok? You haven't touched your dessert." The waitress avoided eye contact while she topped off our coffee cups.

"Thank you, mam," and we finally started to enjoy our dessert. At least as much as we could.

"Sis, please don't worry about your shopping or getting out to a new settlement. We are going to make it." Stated as reassuring as he could make it.

When they left the café, it was nearly time for lunch although neither of them was interested in eating, so they just moseyed on from one shop to another until they walked by a saloon.

James stopped for a moment and looked in. It was busy, with several men playing cards and some gathered around the bar. He had never had a drink of hard liquor in his life and he felt it time to grow up. At least having a drink and playing cards were in his book, part of growing up.

He had learned how to play cards on the sly with some of his school friends. He had purchased his own deck of cards at Johnson's mercantile when no one was around and practiced shuffling and playing by himself a lot in addition to his friends. He thought it necessary to see what it was like to play with real gamblers.

"Sis, why don't you go on and check out the stores. I'm going in here to see what it is like. It wouldn't be decent for you come in, but I just want to see what it is like. I'll be along and meet you back at the restaurant in a couple of hours for an early dinner. Ok?" said not even turning around to see the look of disapproval he knew she had on her face.

"OK, but don't come to me drunk or after you lost all of the money gambling, "as her tone and inflections sounded her dis-approval walking away.

He entered the saloon keeping his head high trying to look a little older and wealthy, so he might get invited into a card game. As he walked up to the bar the bartender asked, "What'll you have?"

"I'll have a shot of whiskey, whatever you have that's good." Not knowing what they served or if it was watered down. He thought whiskey was whiskey no matter what kind of bottle it came in.

The bartender was quick to wipe the area in front of James as he placed his shot of whiskey down. James took a sip of his drink and was prepared to walk over to attend a small group at the other end of the bar When he heard, "High there." From a voice behind him. A hand softly floated over his back, a beautiful young lady walked around him and sat down on the stool next to him. She continued to touch him leaving her hand on his knee as she asked him if he would buy her a drink.

"Sure" as he signaled the bartender. He was already pouring her drink anticipating that James wouldn't resist the request or company.

He had heard about the women in saloons and what was said about them. They were all prostitutes. The stories about the Gold Camps out West basically claimed that 90% of all the women around if there were any at all, were prostitutes.

It was a strange feeling to look at a beautiful girl not much older than him and think that this person in front of him was a prostitute. She looked gorgeous and innocent except for the low-cut dress which view he tried to avoid so not to embarrass her with his staring.

They had some small talk and he ended up buying her another drink. Then when the conversation came to the part where she asked him to go upstairs with her to her room, he would either call it courage or fear, as he told her that he was there to concentrate on poker and get into a game if everything felt good.

She said, "Don't you think I would feel good?"

He took that as his que to excuse himself and walk over to the game, seeing an empty chair he asked if he might set in.

11

Aces and Eights

"**A**nyone object to me joining your game?" James asked
The four men at the table looked weathered. No doubt
a couple of farmers or ranchers and one distinguished looking
character who seemed to have a rather large pile of chips in
front of him.

One of the older rancher types spoke up first, "Not at all son,
pull up a chair and let's see what you got. Headed North, South,
East or West?"

"South sir, and then West from New Orleans to California. "as
he sat down in the open chair.

"The boy is sick. Right son. Got a fever? Said the Old Rancher
causing those at the table to break into laughter.

"No sir, I feel good. Don't have a fever." James replied as the
rest continued to laugh even harder. He missed the joke.

"I mean "Gold Fever" son. Gold Fever. No one going to
California but for Gold these days. Gold, right?" said the old man
as the laughter toned down.

"Yes, that's the idea all right. Told the gold in Georgia is panning
out and I'm reading about one strike after another in California.
My fiancé' and I are leaving tomorrow morning on the Nominee."
Said James as he pulled out a few bills to get into the game.

"Me too. Looking forward to St. Louis." Said the wealthy Mr. Ward. "Looks like we will be on the same boat. As he called for everyone to ante up and started dealing.

It looked like most of those at the table had around a hundred dollars in front of them. James took out $100 and anted up. It was a lot different sitting at this table with real money in the center than on his bed dealing out four hands and playing them all, or with a couple of his friends for fun.

The bartender tapped his shoulder to see if he wanted another shot of whiskey. He had two already and a third might cloud his mind, so he declined.

One of the other men said, "Bring the kid a drink on me," and the bartender turned to get his drink.

James's first hand started out weak, yet he stayed in close to the final bet before dropping out leaving six dollars on the table. That seemed to have gone quickly, but not as quick as the next four hands. Which left him down under forty dollars.

He was starting to wonder after sipping the third drink if anyone was cheating at the table and if they were, how would he know. He also wondered about what he would do if he knew someone was. Would he call them out? Most of these guys carried guns that you could see and probably another one you couldn't with a knife.

James was starting to feel that he was getting in over his head when he was finally dealt a good hand. He tried to act disappointed reminding himself how good card sharks looked for signs through your actions that unconsciously told them what kind of hand you had. James didn't bet aggressively but matched the first round of betting. Mr. Ward kept betting the pot up so James assumed that he must have a really good hand. Either that or he was bluffing. That's always the big call in poker. High hand or bluffing.

After getting his final cards James had a full house, aces over a pair of eights. He pulled out more money and raised the pot. Then Mr. Ward raised James. With everyone still in but one person, the pot was sizeable. When they finally showed their cards, James had nearly $120 in the pot and that much and more again from everyone else.

Mr. Ward laid down three jacks which beat the other two still in the game. Then James laid down three aces over his pair of eights. Two of the men broke into laughter and congratulated the young man. The angered Mr. Ward put his hand inside his coat as he stated, "You got mighty lucky all of a sudden boy. I think I hear your mommy calling. Why don't you just get the hell out of here now before I get real upset."

James continued to reach for the pot with everyone staring at him. At that point it appeared the saloon girl had motioned the bartender who had come over and as he stood over the irate gentleman's shoulder said, "Son, you go ahead and take your pot and call it a day, ok?"

"Yes sir, thank you all, "as he swept up the money and chips, walked to the bar, cashed the chips and walked out, looking over his shoulder at the table, just in case. Wow, his first card game and he had won more than enough to pay for their passage, shopping for Sis, and hotel accommodations in New Orleans.

James got back to the restaurant before Sally, so he sat down in one of the chairs that were just sitting next to front window, so he would see her when she showed up. He had a good view of the saloon that he had just been in and hadn't seen Mr. Ward exit yet. He was going to keep his eyes open for him in the near future.

In a short while he saw Sis coming down the street. At the same time that she was walking by the saloon that he had just walked out of, Mr. Ward came out the door. The same man that he had the confrontation with. It appeared he was trying to talk to his sister. He couldn't tell what he was saying as she was about a block away, but he continued to walk alongside her. James could tell from a distance that she didn't act like she was having a friendly conversation.

He got up and started walking toward her. When she saw James approaching, she stopped and tried to tell the man to leave her alone and that she was already spoken for. She turned to walk toward James, while Mr. Ward continued to pursue her. When James was only about 30-40 feet from them, he could hear the man calling her names and telling her how she was acting all uppity.

He then looked at James like a child he was about to brush out of his way.

"That's my fiancé' your insulting. Leave her alone and take some of your own advice, get the hell out of here!" as James came up on him quickly.

"He reached again inside his coat and at that very moment, James moved quickly on him and hit him with his whole body in the air supporting his swing. James had lost his temper and could only think about this man abusing his sister. He guessed, he hit him pretty hard because he went right off the boardwalk, hit the horse trough, flew right over it and hit the ground. Before he had a chance to get up, James had his boot on his throat threatening to crush his throat if he moved. He just laid there in a daze looking at the young man as a small crowd gathered to see what was going to happen next. A gun had fallen from the man's hand.

"You there," James yelled at a young boy taking in the fight. "Come over here and hand me that gun!"

The boy picked up the pistol handed it to James who checked it making sure it was loaded as he aimed it at the man's face. As he slowly took his boot off of the man's throat the man remained frozen on the ground.

"Don't try anything stupid now, ok? Stand up and take off the gun belt and if... if you have another gun or a knife on your body, I suggest you add that to the pile, or I'll be forced to search you myself. If I find a gun, I'm going to beat you to death with it. If I find a knife, I'm going to stick it in your throat," James with a look that he could easily do what he said he would.

He got up slowly, dropped his gun belt, and a smaller caliber he had under his coat. Then he pulled a knife out of a hidden sheath in his topcoat dropping it on the ground. James nodded at the boy who picked up the smaller gun belt along with the knife and handed them over to James making sure that he was not in the line of fire. By now, the Mr. Ward just wanted to get up and away before the law showed up.

The small crowd was growing, and several people had seen him picking on Sis along with him attempting to pull a gun on James. He thought it an opportunity to get a nice set of guns in addition to a beautiful knife without any questions asked. Elsewise, James was going to wait for the town sheriff, file a complaint and have this guy put in jail.

James wanted the guns. Taking them from the boy, tipping him a dollar gold piece, he asked the man politely to go find some proper manners for the next time he spoke to a woman. James walked back to the restaurant with Sally. As they entered the restaurant, he remembered Mr. Ward saying that they were going to be on the same river boat to St. Louis. James thought about him boarding the same boat tomorrow headed for St. Louis. This was not going to be an uneventful voyage.

12

All Aboard

After all the excitement from the day before, Sally and James retired early after having a delicious dinner, along with a couple of drinks in the lounge for James in their little hotel. Then it was off to bed.

The next morning, they had all of their bags ready. They then went down to the restaurant to have breakfast hoping they wouldn't run into the man they had now called "Ward". Somehow it seemed like a new beginning having won his first time at poker. Then to add to that, he stood down a gambler in the street having confiscated the man's guns and a knife which he vowed to himself he would have to learn to use. He now realized the value of being able to move quickly to defend one's self.

They notified the front desk so the desk clerk could have their luggage taken to the boat. They paid their bill and relaxed walking down to the dock. As they approached the Nominee, docked and loading, they decided they might as well board early and get to their cabins. Their bags were likely in route to the rooms.

They boarded and were escorted to their cabins on the upper deck. They kept a lookout for Ward just in case he felt revengeful. The last thing he needed was to get into something that would expose them.

Asking one of the crew what the next big stop was they were informed that the Nominee would be loading more cargo at Cairo, in South Illinois.

According to people they socialized with in the lounge, Cairo was a boom town due to all the shipping moving from the Ohio River to the Mississippi River. It was built on a peninsula much like the port in Cairo, Egypt which is where it got its name from. Funny what you can learn from well educated people in the luxury lounge of a riverboat. They were not likely to learn the same information if they had been sleeping on the lower deck with the cabinless passengers.

The first evening on the boat found James and Sally walking into the casino. It was far more luxurious, and women were welcome. There was little chance of prostitutes unless they were so high class and stylish, they simply didn't look like one.

The games where plenty. Sally was excited to be able to accompany James to the casino and or lounge. She took a comfortable seat and struck up a conversation with an aristocratic woman who was a poker widow like several others.

There seemed to be a great number of wealthy businessmen traveling by water. From what James could see, a fair number of them had more money than gaming skills. When he finally watched a few hands at a table of weak players he approached them to see if he could join them. Again, James was invited in as if his youth made him a foolish target for these older men.

James found that he could purposely loose a couple of hands of poker to support their thoughts of how young and foolish he was. He was able to make up his losses with the way these guys played while he studied their ability to bluff. While he was waiting for the betting to get more aggressive one of the men suggested, as James was taking out some additional money to play with, that they up the ante and stakes all together. James pretended to think about it. He hesitated trying not to show his internal cheering.

The next couple of hands continued to show him how easy it was to look right thru these guys. He looked for signs in facial inflections or nervous movements that told him that they either had a great hand or were bluffing. This was getting fun in a whole new way from playing with his friends back home.

A couple of hands later when one of the good ol boys tried to bluff James. The man upped the bidding after taking cards to making everyone think he filled out a hot hand. James called and raised. The man looked at him with just enough surprise that James knew he had him. This poor guy recovering quickly still thought he had a winning hand over James. He reached for his stack of cash and said, "Looks like this is where we teach you a lesson young man, meaning no offense!"

"None taken" as James pulled out more cash to match the raise and raise him big time. In a fit of anger, the man was forced to drop out. He threw his cards at James, cussing, kicking his chair back and walking out of the lounge.

Everyone still there looked at James as he turned his cards up with a pair of jacks and an ace kicker. They found his weak hand and how he had bluffed the man extremely funny, not having especially liked the man that left. One of the men patted James one the back and called the bartender over to buy him and the table a round of drinks.

After a few more hands, the game broke up and the gentleman that had bought James the drink asked him if he was traveling alone.

"No sir, I have my fiancé' traveling with me to New Orleans where we plan to get married. She is over there in the blue dress with two women waiting for me to pay attention to her I speck" James replied.

"Sorry, I didn't introduce myself, Mr. Henry Wakefield, and you are?" holding his hand out.

"James, James Goodhue." Said James almost introducing himself by his real name.

"Would you join me and my wife for dinner this evening? I like your style son." having lost a sizeable amount of money to James with no hard feelings.

"It would be our pleasure. We would be honored to join you and your wife for dinner." James stated as he continued to ask questions.

"Traveling to Cairo myself, and you say you're going all the way to New Orleans? That's quite a trip, even on the river in luxury." The elderly man smiled seemingly aimed at making more than small talk.

James replied, "Do you have business, or do you live in Cairo? I've never been there. Are the two of you traveling on business?

"Both actually. I had to close some banking business upriver and yes, we do live in Cairo. I heard that you're getting married and then going to live in New Orleans?" spoken as a leading comment.

"We are getting married there and then heading out West to California. Hope to get lucky and get in the mining business." James said almost in an embarrassing fashion.

"Gold. It's a crazy thing isn't it? Effects everyone differently but mark my words son...it affects everyone. You're set on California, aren't you? I hear tell there is gold in the Arizona territory if you don't mind fighting Indians occasionally." As he laughed and studied my response.

"Sir, Indians don't bother me none. My...bride and I are expecting hardships and we are ready for them. Nothing going to stop us." Stated with all the determination James could muster as he stared him down.

"I believe you are son; I believe you are. Ever hear of the Arizona Territory, Tucson or Yuma? Let me tell you why I ask. My business is banking, but I took possession of some claims along with some information of gold discoveries in the Arizona Territory, Salt River Valley. I also have an interest in a couple of claims in California. They both need someone to work them and in the case of Arizona, follow the map and find the gold. Now, I'm not running out to California. If this were thirty years ago, you wouldn't be able to hold me back. But it isn't. Wife's gotten used to some of the finer things in life if you know what I mean. You'll see this evening at dinner. Please don't make a fuss over her jewelry." As he treated his comment as a funny joke.

James laughed or pretended to as the conversation had just taken an interesting turn. The man was still chuckling when James asked him about the claims he had.

"Sir, are you looking for someone to work these claims of yours?"

"Well, I'm meeting with a family in Cairo that might be interested in checking out the ones I have in California. One of them I know well because he's a trading merchant in Cairo. He has a whole slew of brothers, cousins coming in that have contracted that God forsaken gold fever. When I heard that one of the loans, I had out was going bad, I took a claim to these two mines in California as part of an extension I granted this merchant up in Galina." looking down at his drink.

He was slowing down on his drinking, as the conversation was taking on a serious tone. I was thinking about the California gold and saying something when he stated that there was a group of guys in Cairo, he already knew that he was going to have check out his claim or cut them in. He didn't need me, but his tone told me he wasn't done with me yet regarding the subject.

"Nice to know someone you trust to do that for you. What are you going to do with the information you have in the Arizona Territory if you don't mind me asking?" James was hoping he'd picked up on his leading comment.

"Maybe we should talk about this more over dinner? I have to catch up with my wife and make sure she is enjoying the trip." Laughing as we shook hands and parted.

As James started to walk over to Sally, he was followed by the elderly Mr. Wakefield to where the ladies were. Mr. Wakefield introduced James to his wife, Helen who had been talking and apparently having a great time visiting with Sally. Everyone now having been introduced, left excited to join up for dinner.

They were strolling back to the cabin when Sis suddenly held tight to my arm. As I looked at the far end of the deck headed our direction was "Ward". He was just coming out of his cabin which was on the very end of the row. They had hoped that he might have taken another boat since they hadn't seen him yet. They had guessed wrong.

Before he even noticed them, James had his hand inside his coat on the handle of his gun. The same one that he had taken away from Ward. It appeared that the man had a holster under his long topcoat, so James could tell he had repurchased guns and rearmed himself.

The second he noticed them, everyone stood still. James moved slowly in front of Sis just in case this hot head was going to try something stupid. The man's hand dropped resting on his holstered 45. He knew and I knew that if he was going to try something that he wasn't going to clear that 45 without getting shot at first. James's hand was already on his gun and halfway out of the holster under his left arm. James's coat concealed the gun, but the man knew why James had a hand inside his coat.

LOST AND FOUND AGAIN

As he passed by them, he had the image of pure hate in his eyes. He kept facing James as he passed him until he was walking backwards. That's when he said, "Look at your man carefully lady. You're looking at a dead man."

He then turned and kept on walking. James knew he would have to be very careful wherever he went knowing this guy was on board. They went back to their cabins where James practiced pulling one gun then the other. He even worked with the knife which he had in a sheath, high on his right side under his coat.

Before they left Galina, James had stopped by a shop that did leather work where he purchased a holster and sheath for under the left and right arms respectively for his newly acquired weapons.

He had learned to shoot a rifle, but he hadn't had much practice with a pistol. Everyone growing up had a knife and knew how to use it outside of fighting with one, he felt it would be easy to adapt if he had to. He couldn't imagine sticking it into another person, but it still felt reassuring to have it on himself.

13

Dinner and a Deal

James had worked with his newly acquired hardware, adjusting, and adjusting until he not only felt comfortable wearing everything, but also developed quick access. He was learning quickly that the game of chance had sore losers and if he were planning on winning, he would have to be prepared to face the consequences. He kept recalling a quote that he had heard from Mr. Johnson in one of their conversations. "Chance favors the prepared mind."

Knocking on Sis's cabin door, he was once again surprised by the beauty that stood before him when the door opened. The fact that she was his sister didn't deter him from admiring her beauty. He could only hope that someday he could meet a woman that would even come close to the beauty and stature in the way Sally carried herself. She was amazing. Being introduced as his fiancé' would keep most of the young men away from trying to court her.

"Over here you two!" yelled Mr. Wakefield from a corner table in a rather unorthodox manner for a gentleman banker, but non-the less he and his wife were felt they were quickly becoming friends.

The room was nearly full. There were a couple of serious looking games on the far end of the lounge. Most people were dressed up and enjoying the incredible surrounding. From the beautiful carpet below our feet to the crystal chandeliers, this was already a great evening. It could only get better.

"Sit down, sit down and enjoy a beverage before dinner." Said Mr. Wakefield as he held out the chair for Sis. James reached out and held his wife's hand, "Thank you so much again for inviting us. We really haven't had a chance to meet anyone long enough to enjoy their company."

"Our pleasure. Our pleasure." As Mr. Wakefield continuing to speak, "My dear, you should have seen this man play out a bluff today that won him the biggest hand of the game. He has a great style about him. One that displays confidence and success. Wouldn't you say?" as he waved the bartender over to order drinks.

"All he has talked about before dinner was how you bluffed this buffoon, as Henry described him. I guess everyone at the table was getting really tired of him moaning over one thing and then another. He even said he would have paid what he lost in that hand just to watch it all over again. Where did you learn to play so well? Asked Mrs. Wakefield.

Mr. Wakefield or Henry was laughing so hard by now he could hardly repeat what his wife just said, "Buffoon, that's right. I'd pay to see it again son."

"Mam, I'm no card shark, I just learned playing as a kid with my friends. It seems to come easy to me." James stated in a more quiet, humble way.

"Please just call us Henry and Betsy. We don't need formalities among friends." Said Mrs. Wakefield looking and enjoying how hard her husband was laughing and enjoying their company.

"See? The kid has real class. I think we need to order so we can get dinner out of the way. I Would like to talk a little business later and then see you perform your mastery over the cards if it isn't too late." With a serious look quickly turning jovial.

Sis was an eye full and James wasn't about to let her out of his sight especially with Ward on board. When Mr. Wakefield asked him to move to the bar for a brief business discussion, he was kind enough to ask his wife if she would keep Sally company. Sally was excited to hear what life was like for someone like Betsy, married to a successful banker and all. Maybe she would learn more about what kind of man she should look for. Since they thought they were engaged it would have to be by observation not discussion.

Henry and James took a couple of stools at the very end of the bar. James moved the spittoon to the side since neither of them were chewing. Instead, Henry offered him a cigar.

James didn't know it yet, but he and his wife had been discussing what was about to be offered to Sally and James, for a couple of hours. Betsy had told him how wonderful Sally was and that they were looking for a new beginning. She was impressed in the manner that they were heading out West with all the adventure and love of newlyweds. It reminded the Wakefield's of who and what they were 40 years earlier, ending up in Cairo when it was a frontier.

Henry was so open and honest with James that he started to feel guilty that he hadn't told him about their real relationship and that James wasn't who he was pretending to be. James waited for him to open the conversation since this meeting was by his invitation.

"I'll get right to the point. My wife and I have talked this over and we would like to know if you would be interested in partnering with us to explore whatever might come from the information, I have about possible gold findings in the Arizona Territory. It would mean sharing 50/50 on any claims that you file. I see you as an honest man and this might be an opportunity if you're up to it. If it doesn't pan out in a few months, then there will be no hard feelings and you and your wife by then can move on to California." Staring straight at James without so much as blinking now.

The next few moments seemed like forever. Even with all the people in the lounge and in the adjoining casino area, James felt like he was all alone, in solitude. Concentrating on Henry's proposal it actually seemed quiet as he was considering his comment. It was probably only a few seconds and James should have played it out longer or even negotiated, but the pride in having him Henry make him the offer was astounding. This man was offering him an opportunity of a lifetime with incredible trust. No one had ever done that for him. Again, James was feeling regret in that he knew who Henry was but everything about himself was a lie.

James's regrets didn't cloud him mind from having his voice ring out, "Yes, I mean, yes sir. I would love, I mean we would love to have the opportunity to partner with you. Are you sure that you want to do this? You don't even know us?" said James as he followed in thought with a ... why did he say that?

"I think I know you and through my wife, I think I know your fiancé' and the kind of people you are. It's not like you're not taking a great deal of risk heading into what I hear is pretty tough territory. I might add that the information I have is not detailed but shows some approximate areas that have historically shown to have gold. The maps I took in as collateral were from a miner turned businessman who was actually on the site, struck gold but left because of the Indians. His two partners weren't so lucky. He said he would never return. Have you really considered the risk?"

"Let me add this. If at any time you decide not to follow up this agreement due to the hostility of the region I understand. You will have a wife and it might be smarter to follow the trail to

California." James was thinking he should discuss this with Sally, but then decided not to let this opportunity pass another minute."

"I fully understand Mr. Wakefield. I will do my best to follow these maps and confirm their worth," sounding like a real businessman. James had just agreed to his first contract. No stronger contract than to give one's word.

"Let me ask you bluntly if there is anything, I might help you with to get ready for this journey?" Stated Henry.

"There is one thing I was wondering. If in the future I sent you funds, you know through your bank, would you be willing to forward it on to a person or persons for me without disclosing who it came from? I know that sounds strange, but I don't know a lot about how that works," a comment that might give his pretending aristocracy away not knowing anything about banking. "There is nothing crooked or illegal about it. Just saying, if there were a couple of people or a person that I wanted to send money to without knowing it was from me.?"

"Already planning to be a philanthropist. Sending money to people unanimously. I knew I liked your style. Of course, my bank could handle that for you. Son. What I read into your statement is integrity and honesty. I don't need to know; I'll just tell you that I would be proud to take care of your matters for you. Now what about the part where you might have needs in getting out there before you strike gold and become so rich your sending me money to give away to people." Said with an infectious laugh.

James was truly beginning to take a serious liking to this elderly man that he found was looking for adventure by vicariously living through him. James thought he might describe him like that to Sis, although down deep he knew that this man was a fair but very shrewd businessman. There was more to Henry than he knew. That would be just about everything, since he really knew nothing other than he had a bank and loved to play poker.

He knew even less about James, which left him wondering who was coming out on top in this arrangement. as they strolled over to their wives.

"Well ladies. Get to know each well because we are now business partners! Now Mr. Goodhue, James and I are going to enjoy a few hands of cards with some unsuspecting buffoons." As he had his arm around James's shoulders, he led him into the casino area, laughing loud enough to draw attention from everyone. James felt like he was out on the town with his dad. A person that acted in a manner a real dad would.

There were a couple of tables with two and three seats available. When approached, the first was a private game so they moved to the one that had three openings. It was a table big enough to hold seven chairs, so they were welcoming some additional players, or suckers, as they might have viewed a kid with an old man. They were sizing Henry and James up like an old man and his unexperienced son, pretending they knew how to play cards.

As James was looking over the players Henry spoke up and said, "Now listen up son, this is a man's game and it is time you really learn how to play. This is for money and I'm not going to bankroll your gambling. So, you're going to have to learn to take care of yourself." Waving over to the bartender who by now knew what to bring us.

The other men at the table tried to cover their glances as they must have thought they had a drunk and a newcomer kid with too much money that had never played cards. They were planning on lightning their load.

They didn't even get the first hand dealt when low and behold, who is standing next to the table but none other than Mr. Ward. James hadn't seen him come up behind him. James stood up as one of the others told Mr. Ward to sit down and join the table.

"Thank you" as he glared at James. Henry could read the tension in the air. He knew something was strange. James stood up and asked Henry to move over a chair before Ward even blinked an eye. This way he would be on his left side which is where he wanted him if anything were to happen. James was right-handed and with more freedom to move in that position.

Unsuspectingly, Mr. Ward just smiled and sat down in the last empty chair.

Mr. Ward pulled out a stack of bills that caused everyone, even the banker to take a deep breath. James don't know where he was getting his money from, but he seemed to have an endless supply which caused a couple of the players to snicker. They simply couldn't hold back on their actions thinking they now had three people to clean out.

As the game proceeded, James discovered that these players were far better than what he had previously experienced. Not so much as to ruin his confidence, but enough to put him on his sharpest behavior. He had won a couple hands out of a dozen which was keeping him even.

James had little knowledge of cheating or how it was done. He was a preacher's son and enough ethics had rubbed off on him to think that this was a game of chance and skill. Winning was left to how well you played the cards you were dealt. Henry had played enough on his business and pleasure trips to experience watching and learning how professional riverboat gamblers put the odds in their favor every so often with a big pot by what they called palming a card or with a number of tricky moves and devices.

Henry, even though he was sitting to James's right was able to watch Ward from an angle that was somewhat blind to the others at the table. Ward was more concerned with watching the majority of people in front of him when he would palm a card to fill a straight or full house.

As the game went on, James wondered if Ward was traveling alone. Looking around during the shuffle he noticed a man seated at the end of the bar closest to their table in the casino. James noticed a couple of times that he had walked around and was quite sure that he had nodded to Ward on one of his rounds. It was apparent that Ward was not alone which had James keeping an eye on both men. Every so often James would look out in the open lounge area to see that the women were ok. It appeared that they were having a great time chatting away with numerous hand motions as they spoke.

As the game went on it appeared that Ward was running a lucky streak. He wasn't winning all of the hands, but he was winning most of the large pots. That's when Henry leaned over and whispered in my ear. "Mr. Ward is cheating. I'll be right back." As he asked the men to deal him out for a hand, "I have to go see a man about a horse."

James noticed looking over at the bar that Henry had stopped to speak briefly to the bartender before walking out of the lounge. As the next hand was dealt, he spotted the bartender talking to a couple of the deck hands that he must have summoned. James figured out that Henry must have notified the bartender that Mr. Ward was cheating.

When Henry returned to the table the next hand was already under way. At a point that we had turned in our cards to draw new ones, Henry pushed his chair slightly back so to be facing Mr. Ward as he asked him, "So how long have you been cheating, palming cards? You have a card under your right hand that your palming right now.

"What in the hell are..." growled Mr. Ward as he started to stand up reaching with his left hand under the right side of his coat. His rig was just the exact opposite of James's. It wouldn't have made any difference because James had spent a lot of time learning to use his left as well as his right hand after breaking his right hand twice. He discovered that Ward was a south paw.

James didn't even know what all happened. The instinct wasn't natural, but with his right hand he reached under his coat for his knife pulling it and plunging it square into the man's right hand which was still supporting him as he rose from the table. At the same time, he screamed giving attention to his right hand. Not only did the knife have his right hand stuck to the table, but it went right thru the card he had been palming. An ace of diamonds.

Seeing motion from the bar as James rose, he pulled his 44, aimed it at the man at the end of the bar at the same time drawing his other revolver with his left hand, holding it to the Ward's head.

"Don't move! You at the bar... don't move." James couldn't believe that he had just pulled down on two men. He really didn't know what he was doing. He just reacted to Henry being threatened.

The crew members and the bartender moved quickly to subdue the man at the bar. When everyone at the table along with the crew members saw the card under his hand stuck to the table there was no doubt he had been cheating.

"You probably want this back sir," said one of the crew as he pulled the knife out of Mr. Ward's hand, freeing him from the table leaving a bloody ace of diamonds showing. He then flipped the knife handing it back to James with the handle first. "Well take care of these two from here. Thank you, sir."

The bartender immediately apologized and said, "I'll have a new table set up for you immediately."

Just then Sally and Betsy showed up fussing about all the mess and how cards might be too dangerous for both of us.

"Bartender, I think we are done for the evening, thank you." Said Henry.

"Gentleman, in this case it is customary to divide up the pot along with what the gentleman has on the table. He forfeited his right. "Said the bartender to everyone's delight as the pot along with Mr. Ward's cash were divided up among the participants.

Saying goodnight to Henry and Betsy, James and Sally agreed to meet up the next day with Betsy commenting with a smile, "I trust tomorrow might be a little less eventful."

James walked Sis quickly back to her cabin.

"Why are we almost running back to my cabin. Stop pushing me. I'm not a wheelbarrow. What is the matter with you? Said Sis in a very angry almost striking mode.

"I'll tell you later. I'll be back in a few minutes" as he literally shoved her in her cabin and closed the door.

James was already dressed in black suit and it was now dark. It must have been a new moon, leaving the only light outside coming from the lanterns along the walkways. The deck lights were always dim although lighting up enough, so one didn't trip or fall over anything. He had come up with a plan and had to move quickly.

When the man had pulled out his bank role his cabin key had fallen on the floor. Paying more attention to his money, James had reached down, picked it up and placed it on the table. As the man was being removed, James slipped the key in his pocket. It was cabin six, top deck. When the bartender and mates grabbed the two men, they were told to put them into the brig. Henry didn't know where that was, but the man wasn't likely to be returning to his cabin any time soon.

The locks on the doors of the cabins were made to keep honest people out, but it was really too easy to have the key. James went in quickly and closed the door behind him. James waited a couple of moments to listen and looked out the window to see if anyone might have seen him break in.

As it appeared, he had gotten into his room without anyone having seen him. He had to search for whatever valuables the man might have left there before a cabin attendant or another crew member might be sent up to secure and gather his things.

As James looked around it appeared that he had possibly put his money in the ships safe. Then he remembered having been told about putting a false bottom in their luggage by the merchant where they purchased their luggage.

James pulled the largest bag over to the bed. Throwing it on the bed he started to search the bottom area and found a separate stitching with a pocket opening. Sure enough, without having to check the other bags or drawers for false bottoms he had found the man's hideaway.

As he reached in, he could feel paper. The wonderful feel of pieces of paper. The size we all love. Even in the semi dark room he knew this was a lot of money and there was probably an unsavory story of how he got it or why he had it.

James must have looked like he gained 50 pounds after stuffing it all into his jacket and clothes. It was a good thing it was dark, or he would have been a dead giveaway for anyone seeing him in the daylight.

After finding the money it took only a couple of minutes to stash it on himself, put the bag back like it was and sneak out of the room. His guess is that they would probably be throwing Ward off the ship or turning him over to the sheriff at the next stop. He may not want to report the money gone guessing how he probably got it and questioning why he hadn't kept it in the captains safe.

Back in his cabin, James closed the door after looking around. He didn't notice anyone but a couple strolling farther down the walkway and they didn't pay him any mind. Turning up the light, he began to unload the nights take on the bed. It was incredible!

These were larger denominations and there were a lot. By the time he had counted it all, there was nearly $16,000. That was more money than he had ever seen in one place. Somehow, James felt no remorse in having taken it from the man. It seemed that there was almost a moral justification connected to having taken it.

James had a false bottom in his large bag where he put the money thinking that this may not be a very good idea given what he had just gone thru. Since this was the only place he could think of, he put it in the bag regardless. Besides, tomorrow we would be off the boat in Cairo before boarding the Nominee two days later for St. Louis.

14

Cairo

‚Å* (decorative flourish)

airo was a bit like they expected it. At least from the comments describing it as previously being a boom town, they still couldn't understand why all the empty buildings. All the necessities, bank, post office, hotel and merchants were all there, but it was obvious that it wasn't the city it had once been not too long ago.

James and Sally took their time walking over to the hotel. By the time they arrived, their bags were being brought in by the deck hand that was assigned to see they got to the hotel. James didn't want to show anxiety over the big bag causing any suspicion, but he was concerned knowing that the luggage with the false bottom and all that money had been out of his sight. But, alas, as he opened the bag in his room, there it was, looking a little stuffed, but beautiful none the less. Between poker winnings and Duke's stash, there was nearly $20,000 in there. James started to wonder if they should make a career out of playing cards, one river boat to another. Then the fever came back.

Once they were settled, they went to find the bank. Henry had told them to get their rooms then come over to the bank to finish up their business.

It wasn't hard to find since most of the buildings were on one side or the other of Commercial Avenue. The bank was just down from the post office.

As they walked into the bank a teller who was working behind one of two teller cages walked around and asked, "Hello, Enjoying our rainy weather today? Nothing I can do about it except smile and wait for it to go away. What can I do for you two?"

"We were supposed to meet with Mr. Wakefield. We were with he and his wife on the Nominee. Mr. Wakefield instructed us to get our hotels rooms and then come over to the bank for a meeting. I hope were at the right place?" James still couldn't believe that this partnership was really happening.

"Oh, you're in the right place alright. Mr. Wakefield stopped by on his way home, just to check on things and inform me that you might get here before he gets here from accompanying his wife to the house and back. I have both coffee and tea set up for you with some cakes fresh from the bakery in Mr. Wakefield's office. You can wait in there. Right this way." As he guided them into a massive office.

The office had all sorts of plaques and certificates on the wall. Some were school related, and some had company names on them. Other pictures and plaques were awards for community participation in various things. It certainly looked like Henry was a pillar in the community.

They had hardly started on their cakes and coffee when they heard his familiar laugh in the main area of the bank. They put their coffees down and prepared to greet him as he walked into the office.

"Oh my, sit down please. Let's be comfortable. Which leads me to ask, are your rooms comfortable?" Henry asked with concern.

"The rooms are great. It seems like a large two-story hotel with all of its luxury is unusual for such a small city or town." James said.

"City son, not town. Yes, thirteen years ago, in 1837 the State of Illinois let us Incorporate as a city. That's when things were booming. It looked like we were going to be the biggest city West of Philadelphia. A large finance operation out of London that was financing everyone went broke and overnight all the construction was halted, and people just started to move on."

"Now we're hoping for a revival. Looks like the Central Illinois Railroad is on its way here, rail by rail. Don't know exactly when it is going to arrive but there're saying in 5-6 years. That should change things quickly for those that are still around. Don't worry son, I'm not going anywhere."

"Now to our business. All very simple, as long as you don't lose this envelope. Nothing in it yet, but my attorney will have the papers showing our partnership and how to register any claims and an outline of our agreement. We can sign everything over dinner. My house tonight. Here is the address or just ask anyone where it is. Mrs. Wakefield is extremely excited to have you two over tonight...about 6pm?" said with a chuckle as expected.

"We don't how to thank you." James said

"Let's start with joining my wife and I for dinner. Our house, 6pm. By the way, the restaurant in the hotel was built first class and serves a meal to match in case you're hungry for lunch later. But save room for a big dinner...hahaha, "as he patted his belly.

Almost as an afterthought, Henry asked, "Say, would you have any interest in meeting the partners that are headed West to California. One of them has a merchant trading office here and I'm going to meet with them at 2pm. Maybe you would like to meet them and compare notes. We are all kind of in this together." Said Henry.

"Thank you I would like that." I replied

"Meet me back here and we'll walk over together. They're just up the street a little further. I'm right on the way. Be here a little before 2 then. Ok?" with a smile and a handshake.

"Yes sir" James replied as Sis and he left thanking the teller for all his hospitality.

"We need to find out when and if we can get on the Big Missouri to St. Louis and on to New Orleans. Let's head back to the hotel and see where we can get tickets." Just then they spotted a building by the docks that had a sign that read "Tickets for Passage" in big letters. There was another on the other end of the building that read "Shipping".

It was almost across the street from the bank. There was a large ticket sign on it. It was a long building that was used for shipping inventories more than passenger tickets and such. There was a door that had some steps to get up thru the doorway. The entire building was built on stilts. Probably had something to do with Spring flooding.

"We heard that we could get passage to St. Louis and on to New Orleans from here. Is that correct?" James asked

"Yes sir. We have riverboats coming down the Mississippi and Ohio headed down stream all the time." Claimed the attendant.

"I heard the newest and most extravagant is the Big Missouri and someone said it might be coming in over the next week or so?" More a statement than a question.

"Your absolutely right. The Big Missouri is due here tomorrow and heading back to St. Louis with a short layover in two to three days. Then it will start the trek all the way to New Orleans!" said with great pride.

"No better transportation on the river than the Big Missouri sir," said the agent who couldn't resist bragging about the river and everything on it.

The price of an average fare was $3-$5. A cabin was $20-$30 for the distance of the passage. The Missouri was the biggest riverboat on the entire river, although sadly they would read that it was destroyed a year later following their passage.

"Good. We would like two of the finest cabins. One for myself and one for my fiancé' here." As James pointed to Sally.

"Yes sir. I can take care of all that right here. Since you are going the full run to New Orleans, I will make sure you have the best cabins available for such a long run. We want the two of you to be comfortable and enjoy your trip." Now talking with a more relaxed tone. He knew that price was no object, so the agent gave them first class treatment.

They filled out the forms, their names and such and left instructions to have someone pick up their bags from the hotel and put them in our cabins on board the next day. Until then they would have to find something to do. James felt they were going to know this main street "city" quite well by the time they departed.

15

There's Gold In California!

The year was 1849 and George (Geo) Roberts and his cousin Abe Peeples had just moved up to Cairo, Illinois where Abe had a cousin that ran a trade station. The riverboats were slowly starting to crowd the Mississippi and Ohio Rivers and the two massive river systems met at the town of Cairo.

Geo was born in Virginia. The family had roots in Virginia dating back to his grandfather having fought with George Washington, at the Battle of Valley Forge. It seemed though that everything was moving West now. The excitement of the many stories, land, open prairies, and the ocean on the other side of the Territories all seemed to be calling to him. He felt a good start would be he and his brothers John, William, and Thomas to move to Jones County where his cousin Abraham Peeples lived. Abe and he were the closest of friends and worked together in Mississippi for a few years.

Now that they had both moved up to Cairo, they did whatever kind of work came up including helping at Abe's cousin's trade station in Cairo. They hadn't worked but a few weeks at the trade station watching the boats come in and out, moving goods from left to right when word of the California Gold Rush came out in one headline after another. The date of the first big strike was

January 24, 1848. Gold was found by James Marshall at Sutter's Mill in Coloma, California. That was in the Sacramento Valley. The papers make it sound like the nuggets were so big and plenty you could hardly ride your horse over them.

Now it was a little over a year later and they had read that the non-native population of San Francisco had grown to over 100,000 people from 1000 in just 18 months. Millions of dollars in gold was being discovered and gold fever was affecting people from every part of America in addition, they came from countries all over the world.

Abe had already known Mr. Wakefield. He guessed everyone knew Mr. Wakefield since he was the banker in town. Mr. Wakefield had his fingers into everything that mattered in the county. This was not to imply that he was in anyway anything but a gentleman. It was meant to emphasis that this man was one very astute businessman.

Thru Abe, the Robert's families were eventually introduced to Mr. Wakefield and he got to know who and what they were. He saw them as honest, and crazy hard working. The men and the woman that made up the Roberts clan were also tough and knew what the risk of the frontier offered, good and bad.

It was due to this growing relationship that Mr. Wakefield, hearing that they were going to set out for the frontier as soon as Abe sold his trading business, approached them with a proposal. Their display of hard work seemed to have paid off without them even knowing. The real payoff was Mr. Wakefield knowing and believing that he could trust them to become business partners.

After making a request that they all be present for a meeting, Mr. Wakefield showed up one morning while they all anxiously waited for him. They had no idea what he wanted to meet with them about unless it was something to do with one of his businesses that they were not performing well for in one way or another. The idea that the meeting would be of a positive nature never entered any one's mind.

"Good morning, Mr. Wakefield" Abe said as he extended a hearty handshake. If Mr. Wakefield took notice, he probably read the room with the hearty but sweaty handshake as an indication that all of us were expecting something unpleasant. He chuckled under his breath with his own anxiousness to see their reaction when he made his proposal.

"Gentleman, I have called you all together today, to make you a proposal. This being the result of getting to know your families and seeing the business risk and hard work that you are not only capable of and have already demonstrated here in Cairo. My compliments are to include the young ladies, your wives and family that I also asked to be present."

"In the event that you do not favor my proposal I want you to know that you will remain of high regard in my eyes and with my respect as the salt of the earth people that will settle the West if anyone can."

"Before I make this proposal, I also expect that you will want to discuss this among yourselves and members of your family. I have trust in all of you, but your collective commitment is very important to me. The future is not going to be an easy one, knowing now that you are all heading West into a land that humbles the strongest of men and can make the likes of a good soul disappear, never to be heard of again."

"To the point now" as he looked around. Everyone in the room was in complete silence. Not even a whisper. They were about to hear a proposal from one of the most important men they had ever known, and it didn't seem to have anything to do with bad news as suspected. What is going on? Everyone's thoughts were racing through their minds as mere moments of silent began to seem unbearable. The anxiety of not knowing what was going on was being applied like a slow torture.

"I have obtained ownership, how doesn't matter, to some mining interests in California. If I were thirty years younger, we wouldn't be having this conversation as I would be purchasing and setting up my outfit for the trip out West myself. But due to age, that seems to find all of us one by one, I am forced live the excitement of heading West by proxy. I thought I would have to wait sometime to find a partner I could trust if I ever did. However, as it were, not only do I think I have found one, but I think I found a number of people I can trust in the likes of your families."

"These claims are in a region known as Sacramento, out in California. I'm sure you have read about the gold strikes in that region. I only know that these two mines have produced ore at one time. I have not been updated as to whether claim jumpers have cleaned them out or if whatever law out there will actually honor the claims I own. The paper appears in good order, according to my attorneys. The previous owners claim to have covered up the find, and hidden the sights, best they could with watchful eyes overseeing their interest for the moment."

"I want you all to consider partnering with me over these claims and share 50/50 on whatever comes out of the ground. If your decision is yes..." And he was rudely but enthusiastically interrupted.

"Yes" yelled Abe. Everyone finally started breathing. Not only breathing but from one extreme to the other. Now everyone was hyperventilating. Yells and screams came up in volume from everyone without even hearing Mr. Wakefield's conclusion to what had appeared to that point to be a carefully prepared speech.

Abe and George were the patriarchs of their families. The second they both said yes, whatever the proposal or commitment was the families were in.

As the tone of excitement lowered, Abe apologized for cutting off Mr. Wakefield who by this time was belly laughing so hard he was about to collapse. Mr. Wakefield's wife had been just outside, but with all of the screaming and cheering, ran into the room, wanting to share in the celebration. And what a glorious feeling that room had. God had blessed everyone in a web of partnerships to describe business, friends, husbands, and wives.

"I guess I don't have to wait. Thank you for relieving my anxiety of having to wait for an answer. I will have the proper papers prepared for the sharing of the claims. May God bless this venture to all our benefits. Thank you." Then Henry and his wife left knowing that the group were likely to take the day and maybe into the night celebrating. It was a great feeling, and, in some way, Mr. Wakefield felt it was going to be an exceptional adventure even living vicariously through these men and women.

16

Robert and Peeples Clan

Sally decided to stay at the hotel concerned that Mr. Ward might still be around. Besides there wasn't anywhere to shop and if there was, it was doubtful there would be anything she was interested in.

James walked over to the bank and met Henry who proceeded to walk further down the block and across the street to a building that was near the docks. That only made sense, it being a trading company. Again, much like the building we got our tickets from, except much longer and larger. Inside and outside there were bales of cotton and numerous other mountains of goods. The cotton bales created a summer snowstorm with all the lose fluff breaking free in the wind and floating around.

There seemed to be quite a number of people working around the trading post or whatever it was that they called it. As they entered a large door where various types of inventory were being stored, a man approached them. He reached out to shake hands with Mr. Wakefield who in turn introduced James.

"James Goodhue, this is Mr. Abraham Peeples." Abe had been chosen to be the one to speak with Mr. Wakefield on behalf of the family. "His brother owns this operation and they do quite well with family and all. But not well enough to prevent Gold Fever once they caught it. Yah. Abe and his family plus the Roberts being cousins are all going to saddle up and head for California. Like I said, Gold fever does strange things to people." Said Mr. Wakefield.

"Heading for Sacramento and there abouts. Sounds like anyone that knows how to work hard and survive can make a fortune. I guess getting rich is what gold fever is all about." Said Peeples.

"Nice to meet you. I'd like to talk to you about how your fixing for the trip if you have some time tomorrow. Not leaving till the day after." James said to Abe, hoping for a positive response.

"Hey, there's nothing more we find more interesting than planning and talking our trip to California. We have had a lot of business lately which required everyone's help. It has caused delays in our plans to leave. But now my brother might have a buyer for the business and with Mr. Wakefield helping us get it sold we can all head out soon. We've agreed to partnership on some claims that he has in California. It might be a good start. We only hope that everyone out there hasn't discovered it and had a turn at it before we get there. We hope to be leaving in a couple of weeks." Said Abe.

"That's great. I'm looking to head out from New Orleans to head West. Guess I'll be looking for some gold in the Arizona Territory. If I don't find anything, I'll be moving on to California." Expressing a little doubt about the Arizona gold fields.

"Have a deal with Mr. Wakefield? "asked Peeples.

"Yes. He has an idea where there might be some places in the Arizona Territory to check out, so I thought I would see what's there. I don't really have any other plan as to where to start anyway." James responded.

"Listen, here come the other guys. I'll introduce you and then I must do some final business with Mr. Wakefield. We will definitely have some time tomorrow to talk about the trip. Always a lot to talk about." He said as he waved a small group of guys over.

"This here is James Goodhue. He and his fiancé are going down river to New Orleans and then heading West for the gold rush. He has an agreement with Mr. Wakefield to check out some places in the Arizona Territory, kind of like we do in California. Introduce yourselves. I'll be back in a few minutes." As he headed over to a table in a small office where Mr. Wakefield had some papers laid out.

"Well my name is George. George Roberts. Just call me Geo. These are my brothers Thomas, and William or Bill, and our other brother isn't here right now. His name is John. Then these three are my cousins Cyrus, Charles and Return. My other cousin is Abraham or Abe Peeples who you met. Abe is one of my closest friends in addition to being family. We are all going along with Abe's brother who you were just talking with. A couple more friends and family to boot. We nearly have enough families for a wagon train ourselves by the time we get to Castroville, Texas, just West of San Antonio."

"That's where my cousins from Beaumont, Texas are going to join us. Daniel, Mose and Gideon. All Roberts clan. Now that's a bunch of family thrown in with all of us here wouldn't you say. You have family?" asked George.

No, just my fiancé' and myself. We have the same excitement and we can't wait to start moving west. So far, we have only gone South. We're from Minnesota." Said without expanding at all.

"Any special reason that your all meeting up in Castroville, Texas, Fort Hondo did you say?" not knowing about the wagon trains yet.

"A number of wagon trains form up there. It's on the edge of the real frontier. They are forming up all the time with the Gold Rush to cross the South along the Old Spanish Trail. That trail goes all the way to California. Fact is it moves right through the Arizonian Territory."

"That's a pretty hard trip. Especially could be for your fiancé'. Are you sure you want to put her through it all? Our women have had over a year to think about it while we have been planning and running the trading station, so they have decided to go with rather than wait behind to hear what happens." Said Cyrus, Roberts cousin.

"I know. Don't worry, she's a lot tougher than she looks. We have had a lot of conversation and decided together on making the trip." James spoke with confidence, although stretching the truth a little.

"If you're seriously going, maybe you should think about hooking up with our outfit in Castroville. Your fiancé' would have plenty of women to visit with, you know... women socialize different than men. Might not feel so lonely for such a long trip. It might comfort her and help handle some of the hardships that some of our woman have already experienced. Just saying." Cyrus said looking and getting positive nods from his other relatives listening around us.

"I can tell you right now that I'll take you up on that. We'll meet you in Castroville. When we talk tomorrow if you don't mind, all I need to know is when you'll be there and my fiancé' and me, or should I say my wife by then, will be there. I want to thank you guys. Thank you so much. I feel like this was meant to happen." Said as the guys slapped James on the back with a couple saying, welcome to the family.

As both Mr. Wakefield and Peeples were returning, they noticed all of the guys slapping James on the back.

"Looks like you make friends fast son," said Mr. Wakefield

"He sure does," repeated Peeples.

"Looks like your boy and his fiancé' here are going to join up with our outfit when we reach Castroville, Texas." said Roberts.

"I like that. I like that a lot. All of you looking out for each other gives better assurance that my investments are protected. Again, I repeat, I wish I could go with you." Said with a melancholy tone in his voice. His eyes moist at the thought that age creates lack of capability. He was discovering once again that his youth had be taken and the sunset years of his life were upon him. He continued, "It truly sounds exciting. If I were only thirty years younger. Not that I couldn't whip half of you at this age." Laughing again with his signature laugh. This time everyone had joined in.

As Mr. Wakefield and I were leaving Roberts yelled, "Come on over late morning and we'll spend some real time talking over our plans for the trip. Maybe we can help you in planning your outfit."

The excitement generated by all these guys had grabbed James and for that matter, it had also had a real effect on Henry. James couldn't wait to get back to tell Sally. Then it would be near time to start getting ready for dinner.

"Once again, I find myself saying thank you Henry. You are a very special kind of person." knowing that somehow he probably suspected the outcome of his introduction and what it would lead to.

17

New Friends

⁓⊙

Sis was ecstatic when James told her about the guys and their woman inviting the two of them to join them all in Castroville. She admitted that to be heading out on this trip with no idea of what we are really up against was really hard for her and having some people that we have something in common with would be a blessing.

They relaxed for a while and then asked at the front desk where Mr. Wakefield lives.

"He said, "ask anyone. Everyone knows him and where they live. Just look for the biggest house on the bluff with red shutters."

They proceeded about three blocks. It wasn't far at all. There were a couple of blocks of Victorian style homes. One of the biggest with all sorts of fancy trim was Henry and Betsy's home of course. They knocked at the front door and Mrs. Wakefield answered wearing an apron. It felt more comfortable and normal to have Betsy answer the door than the maid they expected.

"Please, please come in. I am so glad that you could make it tonight, before you, as they say... shove off again." Said Betsy with a timid laugh.

"What a beautiful home you have. I'm so glad that you invited us over and that your husband took the time today to introduce

James to the Peeples and Roberts group. Did you hear that we are planning to join up with them in Texas?" Sis answered with some excitement and expectation in her voice for the first time since we left home.

"Yes, Henry has been doing nothing but talking about how he would love to go. That old man. I better tie him down when you all leave, or he'll find a way to saddle up. He forgets just how old we are. We played that role and had the same excitement when we headed West into the wilderness settling here in Cairo."

"You know what would be wonderful for us. If you had the time to write. Write often and tell us what it is like as if we were there. I think Henry would so much look forward to reading your letters as would I. We could probably publish them in the paper here in town given your all leaving from here, just for public interest. You can become everyone's adventure." Said Betsy, feeling like she just discovered a theme for a new book.

"I can do that. I enjoy writing. I will try to do that when there is mail available. Although, I don't know how often that will be." Said Sally.

"I know, but in a very personal way I will be praying for you two and worrying about you two on this kind of a trip. Your both so young. I hope you know what you're getting into. Oh… just listen to me! Or better yet, don't. I know you know what you're doing." As she filled the bowls with potatoes, gravy and carrots for the main table. Then she pulled this huge beef roast out of the oven.

"Son, I want you to know that I feel somewhat responsible for what happens out there so be careful. I know it sounds exciting when you read about it, but when someone is really shooting at you, or wants to take the top of your head off for a souvenir you must step up your game real fast. I know you can take care of yourself. I've seen it. Just be careful. Now, let's eat. "said Henry as he headed into the dining room.

As the evening went on, they bonded far more deeply in their friendship with this older couple. James felt that they were more than just business partners and it felt good that there was someone in the world that cared about what happened to them. He got a comfort, whenever he would recall Mrs. Wakefield saying that she would be praying for them.

Sally and James talked all the way back to the hotel about what a great couple they were and how they would have been great parents. Unfortunately, Henry and Betsy never had or could have children. James truly felt privileged to be his partner. It was hard to imagine all that had happened in the last couple of days. Tomorrow would come fast so they both turned into their rooms for the night.

That night Sally got on her knees next to her bed to give thanks for the events of the day. During the course of her prayers of thanks she ignored the ugly past. Although she understood and believed that God knew all, she found it difficult to bring it up. In due time. In due time.

"I knocked on your door over and over and never thought you would come down to breakfast without me." James said, looking at Sis as she sipped on her cup of black water as they called it on the trail. In addition, she had some bread and strawberry jam topping that looked fantastic. The smell of fresh baked bread, ham on the grill and assorted other foods played the senses of a hungry man. To a degree James felt her stronger showing such independence.

James waved to the waitress and pointed at Sis's coffee which had an addictive smell of its own. She got the message having a hot cup in front of me before I finished my sentence to Sis.

"Looks like I'll have your breakfast special!" which looked like everything possible to serve as breakfast on the menu rolled onto one plate. One very big plate. Eggs, Potatoes, Ham with bread, jam and an apple strudel for dessert.

"I'm having the pancakes please." Sis replied giggling like a little kid as she continued to eat the strawberry jam.

"I am going to meet up with some of the guys over at the trading post and talk about the trip. They are willing to help me with what supplies we might need to totally outfit us. The further away we get from Civilization the more difficult and expensive everything is going to be." Realizing just how much he didn't know about the trip they were about to embark on.

"If you can wait for a late lunch, I'll be back and join you. Tomorrow they will be loading and unloading the Big Missouri of its cargo. Come late afternoon they should be done, and tomorrow we would go on board and experience one if not the most luxurious riverboats on the Mississippi or Ohio river. I'll be back soon." And James walked off with a confident stride knowing now that it was all coming together.

All the men in the Peeples and Roberts families had gathered together to meet me for a shorter period than James expected. They had about an hour then two more ships were coming in to drop off and pick up cargo that they were responsible for. One of them mentioned that there were now hundreds of riverboats moving up and down the river carrying everything from cotton to cattle. There were several ships that were tied off to the shore waiting for a place to dock. The Big Missouri had taken up a lot of room on the docks and after a full day was loading now instead of unloading as when it had come in.

The time they had together was brief but informative. They had made a list made of the equipment needed from the wagon all the way down to the smallest of food supplies and horseshoes. John who James didn't meet the day before stayed with him a little longer after the others had to get to work on the doc and start unloading. He told him that he had spoken to a number of men that had been out West and come back to places like Kansas and St. Louis. He had met them from time to time when he had taken trips alone with the cargo run, to insure it was handled and counted correctly. What he learned spending the time they would give him was incredible. Unfortunately, James would have to learn a lot of what John knew when they had more time together when they found each other in Castroville or on the trail by experience.

James said good-bye to everyone in a rather haphazard way, with everyone walking off in different directions as he headed back for that late lunch with Sis.

First lunch then dinner. Following dinner, he didn't feel like looking for a game in Cairo, just in case something was to go wrong. He sure didn't want to get anyone here in trouble including Sis or himself. They both ended up going to their rooms early as they expected to get an early start. Attendants would be to the hotel for their bags first thing in the morning.

18

St. Louis and the Big Missouri

Sally and James stopped by the bank to pick up the envelope with the paperwork that Henry had talked about. After a heartfelt goodbye to Henry they went on to board the Big Missouri. What an incredible vision. The mire size and activity surrounding it made it look like it was a city to itself. The number of passengers and cargo that the Missouri could handle was enormous. They hurried about like they were just going to tour the boat and get off rather than spend the next couple of weeks aboard.

James wanted to look around with Sis, but he convinced her that he had to check on their baggage first. They went up to find their cabin rooms. Sally unlocked hers first and as James opened the door for her, they both gasped at the amount of room inside. They didn't know what the other rooms were like but when James asked for the best, he believed they got them. There was a sitting area and a large bed with curtains on the windows. That's right... windows, not window. Leaving Sally to enjoy her surroundings, James picked up his bags and headed to his cabin next door.

Once again, James was experiencing anxiety over the amount of money in the bottom of his large bag. The first thing he did once safely in his cabin, was to pull out the money and put the money on the bed. He had decided to move the money to the Captains safe. He was in the process of counting out $10,000 from all the money he had accumulated when there was a short knock on the door and in walked Sally. She was concerned about someone seeing her entering his room which is why she knocked, looked around and quickly entered. Now she was standing there after closing the door with her mouth open looking at all the money.

"What have you done? Did you rob a bank? Ok, I think it is time to explain where this came from. This didn't all come from the church offerings or Mr. Johnson's. He doesn't do that much business in a year. I think I deserve to know, and I've handled everything else ok so far. I deserve to know." As she stood there with this stern look with arms crossed.

"Ok. Pretty simple really." James said

"Simple, that's what you call it? Explain it!" she said.

"I had some of the money from the loan I got from Mr. Johnson. Then there was this man on the Minnesota that I helped one night and his money belt, money clip and watch ended up with me after he had passed out. I helped him into a chair so he wouldn't accidentally fall overboard. He was a very rich person. And... well... remember when I rushed you back to your room after the card game? Well... I went to Mr. Ward's cabin and found his stash of cash." Thinking that was an achievement, James smiled.

"James! you can lose that smile. What's happening here. Are you going to steal every time we need to buy something? Have you lost your mind? Did you forget it is a sin to steal?"

As he cut her off, James said, "Don't do this! You know why I have to do this. In addition, I haven't taken money from anyone that couldn't afford to lose it."

"What about Mr. Johnson? That man trusted you. Let me ask you... can I trust you? I'm wondering." With a questioned look on her face. "Are you going to steal from people like Henry and Betsy?"

That comment hurt him deep down because of all things, he had taken the responsibility of taking care of Sis and now she was asking him if she could trust him? How did this get so mixed up? He would rather be looking down the barrel of a gun than the expression she was looking at him with.

"Sis, I'm only going to say this one time. I am doing this for us whether you can figure it out or not isn't my biggest concern right now. Right now, I'm trying to get us to a new place. One that isn't moving all the time. A place that maybe both of us can have a normal life."

James continued, "I might be different than you in that I have a hard time believing in any God that would have let happen what happened to you. I'm the only thing or person you can trust. Because I can do things whether you think there right or wrong. You think God is looking over us. Let me clue you in. It's me that's looking over us. Now, I need to get this money deposited in the Captains safe. So, I'm putting it in the smaller bag and taking it to the Captain for safe keeping like a normal person would. We are done with this, ok?" with a tone of finality.

Sis was quiet. She was not going to challenge James. She knew when to pick her fights and this wasn't the time to fight him over the existence of God. It was hard enough for her to hold on to her sanity remembering the dark nights, the visits from dad, the touching as she tried to hold the tears back ashamed hoping she wouldn't wake the household. Yes, she agreed that "we" were done with this.

Money deposited, the next item was to have some dinner and look over the lounge and casino.

19

America!

~ⓔ

"Ah, Das ist einen guten tag!" as Jake greeted his closest friend Jacob. It was Spring, and year after year things were getting worse, but it did not stop him from yelling, "It is a good day!" at his friend. It was more of a joke given what the two of them, and their families were going thru. Jacob and Jake had spoken many times and dreamed about leaving Horb and heading up to Bremen, and then leaving Germany all together and taking a ship to America. It was more of a dream since the cost was nearly $100 in US money when labor was making around a $1 per week. Just a dream.

All dreams aside as they had to get to their jobs. Looking off in the distance at the Black Forest life seemed so simple. The animals had it better than we did. For a couple of years, famine had hit, and it was affecting everyone except the nobility.

"Listen to me Jacob. Do you really think we will ever earn the money to get to America by working in a factory? Every week that goes by we have to use nearly everything we make just to feed and clothe ourselves and we give what's left to our families." Jake's words were stinging, knowing that what he had just said he had said before. They were born poor and of uneducated peasantry. There would be no opportunity to get on a ship headed to America without finding a better plan.

"Jacob, I heard from my cousin that there are people in America, farmers I guess, that need help so bad, that they will pay your passage and let you pay back your debt by working for them. I even heard that the pay is much better than here, and wouldn't you rather work on a farm than in a factory here. Who knows what opportunities we might have after our debt is paid?"

"Another thing is that we are going to have to join the military here if we stay. Everyone has too and that is only $.65 a week. We are going to waste our lives in the military for a couple of years that we could be paying off our debt and living in America! Jake. This is what we must do. We need to find how to do this." yelling by this time to make sure Jacob felt the passion he had and the common sense of this plan, especially for a non-educated man.

Jacob at first, thought Jake was just dreaming big again, but the more he thought about the whole idea that day, the more he started to convince himself that this might be possible. They would have to try and find a contact that could get them to America and maybe this idea would work.

Jake wasted no time and went up to the port town of Bremen the following week. There were brokers of sorts in Bremen that advertised for good strong laborers for jobs in America and seeing Jake and his pledge that his friend was even stronger than him agreed to set them up for passage.

It was October 1, 1839 and the passenger registry had the names of Jacob "Jake" Weisner and Jacob Waltz on it. Jake and Jacob were only a year apart in age and had known each other their entire lives. At 29 and 28 respectively they felt they were quick to take on anything and everything that lay ahead.

The ship that was going to take them to this new land was the "Olbers". They were boarding in Brennen, a port town in Germany that was well known as a major connect to America. Immigrants by the hundreds lined up for the journey. They were from all parts of Europe and even Russia. The trip was not without hazards. Many ships were lost to the storms at sea along with sickness which spread with the close quarters and unsanitary conditions.

The Olbers captain H.W. Exter was heard frequently bragging about the sturdiness and speed of his ship. Then again, it seemed that all Captains seemed to have some kind of love affair with their ships. His bragging however was more fact than fiction. Jake had asked several agents in the port area and they confirmed that he was one of the best Captains and the ship usually make the voyage to New Orleans in around six weeks. This was an unbelievably short period of time to cross the Atlantic Ocean. Six weeks! It was hard to imagine that kind of speed over the water.

The anxiety of actually boarding this ship and thinking that in a few weeks they will be walking down the gang plank to take their first step on American soil was more than an answer to their dream. This would be a life changing miracle.

The parting with family members was difficult. They didn't know if they would ever see them again. The older members they had hugged knowing that this would be the last time they would ever see each other. Tears were aplenty, but they dried up quickly once on the road with the anticipation and adventure of the unknown. It took an unusual breed of person to risk everything, cross an ocean not knowing what was going to be waiting on the other side if you even made it across. The one and only thing they could count on for now was each other.

The word had spread as people in Horb heard about their passage. It was a small community and by the time of boarding a few weeks later their adventure grew to a couple of dozen additional people who had joined for the trip. Most of them had sold all their worldly goods and used the last of their money to pay for passage hoping that it had to be better on the other end than to suffer any more of the famine and disease they had put up with for so many years. A few others took advantage of what the two friends had found out about the servitude contract agreements for labor.

The days went by quickly and before they knew it the day of departure had arrived. It was early in the morning and the smell of saltwater thick in the air, was going to become normal in a few days. The birds were circling the ship as if to show their dismay at not being invited along. Everything the senses could grab in a stellar moment as this, one would remember for the rest of their lives. Prayers went out asking that the rest of their lives might be a considerable period of time and not a couple of weeks as they end up at the bottom of the ocean never to be heard or seen again. Many ships had disappeared on this journey.

As the ship left the harbor everyone hung on the side watching their homeland until it disappeared. Both men never having sailed nor very far from Horb, were having last minute remorse wondering if life would have been better to have stayed home. But now home was disappearing, the ship was not turning back for anyone, and the only hope was in looking forward. After a couple of days at sea they started to talk about their future in America forgetting for now the day they left.

20

New Orleans

Antoines's is the oldest operating restaurant in the USA, founded in 1840.

Jacob. Just think. We are only a couple of days from New Orleans. There will be someone to meet us that will take us to our new home. At least for now." Stated Jake seemingly losing some of the excitement in his statement as he said the part about the …" new home, for now". The uncertainty of it all had been slowly setting in over the last week. The closer they got to their destination the less conversation they seemed to have.

Jake had spent a lot of time speaking with other people on the ship and especially those from their village. The ship had a little over 200 passengers. After six weeks, unless you were an extreme introvert like Jacob, you had had an opportunity to share your anxieties with likeminded people.

Two days later they were looking at the harbor of New Orleans. The buildings looked like those at home, but then again why not. They weren't expecting teepees along the shore. As the crew were pulling down sail and preparing to enter the port area, everyone was talking and pointing with eagerness to get on shore. Everyone had their items packed and ready to go, as meager as the sum of their belonging were. Jake and Jacob simply had one bag each with all their worldly possessions in them.

The passage was roughly six weeks as was what we were told back in Brennen. We had left on October 1st and arrived on November 17th. The hustle of the people literally racing to get their feet on solid ground again was more than just stirring. The dock area was already full of people, horses and carriages waiting for those that were coming off the ship.

It was now time to find their contact. With their names displayed on a piece of paper they held in front of them, it wasn't long after the initial stampede of people that a tall thin man stepped forward and identified himself as Jim, the farm manager that had come with a wagon to pick them up.

"You two speak English?" was the first words out of his mouth. Jake replied, "A little", as Jacob just stared at Jim in his usual manner. Jacob never was one to take to anyone new. A true born and bred introvert.

"I guess we will find out how well you speak over the couple of days it will take to get back to the farm. "said Jim as he stared right back at Jacob. It was like they were having a stand-off.

Finally, Jim looking right at Jacob asked, "Hey, you ok? Can't talk, don't know enough English or what?"

Jake was hoping that Jacob would not take Jim's comments as an affront. He had seen Jacob before when he felt threated and the first response to rise was usually his temper. Jacob was the quiet type and everyone back in Horb knew to leave him alone unless you were one of a very few that for some reason he had befriended. Otherwise it was wise to stay out of his way. His temper usually led to someone getting badly hurt and it wasn't likely to be Jacob.

"I can speak little English, am ok, all this new." Jacob replied.

Jacob and Jake conversed in German but now they would have to try and learn all the English they could since this was going to be the language. It seemed at times that everyone knew some German until they got off the boat. Then they heard a little Italian, a lot of French, Spanish, but everyone seemed be trying to speak in English.

"We will have a good solid meal before we head out in the morning. There is a restaurant that the boss said I could take you two for a meal before we leave. It is as much of a bonus for me as for you two, so be careful how much you order. "Jim stated as they threw their bags into the back of the wagon. He signaled for them to take a seat on the back edge of the wagon.

The City of New Orleans was already a large city and it gave them a strange impression that the cities in America may not be that different from big cities we had heard about and seen in Europe. There was no doubt that the French had a left a great amount of influence around this place, looking at the buildings and their styles and hearing a lot of the language.

Very soon they pulled up near a stable where they left the wagon. Jim left instructions to feed and care for the horses for one night. We proceeded to look for a restaurant called, "Antoine's" which was on St. Louis Street.

Jim said, "This is just a small place that this young French kid had started, and the food is incredible. I'm glad that you two are dressed nice because we would otherwise be seated in the far rear of the restaurant. The owner, Antonine Alciatore and I became friends on one of my trips here with the boss when we were staying at the Grand St. Charles Hotel. The boss was born of a wealthy New York family and decided to build a farming business in the South raising cotton. On one of our trips here he went back to the hotel and I somehow ended up at a table drinking and telling stories with Antoine the chef."

"Antoine was the Chef at this incredible restaurant, and one late evening after the restaurant closed, he and I happened to end up sitting around sharing a bottle of wine. He told me how he planned to have his own restaurant someday soon and I talked about having a family and small farm. Guess he is ahead of me in reaching the goals we talked about. I try to stop by when I come into town."

"Ah, here we are. "proudly stating that they had arrived.

"Now, look smart and maybe you'll learn something." Said Jim as Jake held the door for him as we all entered.

The restaurant was small but, easily recognized as French with all of the decor that this Antonine had stuffed into it. Numerous pictures hung on the walls. So many that it made it hard to tell what color the walls were. As small as it was, there wasn't anything like it anywhere near their home village. The smell of the sauces simmering in the kitchen filled every inch of the room.

"How are you today, may I seat you?" stated a young lady displaying more class than all three of them put together motioned them to a table alongside the wall of pictures.

Ironically the first to speak after looking over the entire room was Jacob, who we finally found concentrating on the table stating, "I've never eaten in a restaurant." He was trying his best to speak in English. The surprise of his speaking and the way he referred to the restaurant caused Jim to break out in laughter! In a few seconds, it became contagious and all three of us were laughing.

"Ok, Ok, let's keep it down gentleman. Maybe you're having too much fun here", said the approaching Antoine, the appearance of a Paris chef.

Jim rose and as the French who liked to hug, gave Antoine a hug and a kiss on each cheek while he viciously shook his hand.

"I'm picking up some farm hands from the port and thought I would treat them to their first and last fine dinner before being worked to death." Said Jim laughing so hard he could hardly finish his sentence. Antoine joined him as we kind of smiled, the humor lost on Jacob and Jake with the suggestion we were going to be worked to death.

"Please sit. Now, I have to get back to the kitchen. Please don't go until we can visit a little. It might be some time before you are back again. Yes?" Stated Antoine as he quickly backed up, turned and almost ran to the kitchen.

"I love the Oysters here. Antoine prepares them with a sauce that he calls "Oysters Rockefeller". The "Rockefeller" is after a wealthy family in New York City that his family knew. His dad had once worked with William Rockefeller Sr. He had done some work for him some time ago. Antoine thought the prestigious name would add elegance to the dish. A couple of places in town have already tried to copy him, but he'll always be known to have created, Oysters Rockefeller. Try'em."

Jim added, "Don't get the idea that this kind of treatment is normal. Once we reach the farm you will be put to work alongside other men in debenture and our slaves. Everyone works. I just thought I would give you this meal as a bit of a welcome to America. My boss is fair, if you work hard and stay out of trouble. Understand?"

We both had heard the word slaves but thought it was a matter of speech and did not take it literally.

While we enjoyed the food and drink, Jake looked at the pictures on the wall and asked the waiter, "Who are these pictures of?"

The waiter replied, "Everyone that has a picture on this wall has eaten here. Like this one here of George Washington. That is thee, George Washington our first president."

As Jake and Jacob looked over the rest of the pictures, they didn't recognize most of them, but Jim continued to name more of them after the waiter left. They recognized some of the names as he pointed them out. They just hadn't ever seen their picture. By the end of our meal the two were feeling like they were part of the so-called nobility in this new country.

The meal was incredible and even more incredible given they were from a county that had been starving for the last few years. They seldom had occasion to eat seafood. The village of Horb was not on the ocean so any kind of seafood was a rare treat.

Jim took them to a hotel where the two shared a room for the night with an early rise. As they got their room and prepared for sleep their minds were buzzing with what they had seen and experienced in one day already. Their life was about to become more eventful as they took off in the morning headed for the farm.

21

Plantation Life

The St. Charles Hotel opened in 1837 as one of the greatest hotels in the United States.

Morning came quickly and sleeping in a bed that didn't move all night seemed strange. Jake and Jacob hadn't really adapted from their sea legs. It took them a few days to get their land legs. In the meantime, they would stagger every so often in their stride leaving the impression that they might have tipped a few too many.

Jacob, once his eyes were open, was up like a flash. Once they were ready, the two of them decided to go down to the lobby of the hotel and see what was happening out on the street of the big city. The entrance of the hotel led into a beautiful domed rotunda. It was very elegant room they referred to as, "The Exchange". Before going outside, they were drawn to all the activity going on as the room was being set up for some event by the hotel staff.

"Sir? What is happing. Important person today?" Jake stated the best he could in chicken English.

"Many important people will be here today, like every weekday from noon to 3pm", stated the hotel employee, acting like he should be getting back to his work.

"Every day?" said Jake with a strange look on his face.

"Yes. This room has the biggest auction block in the country, and it is held every day." He replied.

Jake was now curious and asked, "What is auction?"

"Sell, we sell Slaves. I have work to do," Said the attendant

The man looked at Jake now knowing he must have just got off the boat, "Slaves! Yes, some of the best available. Men, women, children, pretty much whatever you might be looking for. Lots of large plantation owners that grow cotton or sugarcane need labor and sorts, and our hotel has the best reputation for its slave auction."

He then turned and got back to work yelling at some guy in French, paying us no more attention.

Jacob spoke first after a couple of minutes of silence, "Did you hear what he said. People? Slaves? Buy and Sell? Auction? Men, Women and Children?"

Jacob replied, "Ya, I heard. I've heard about slaves in the old days of the Bible. I even heard that they have had slaves here, but

I guess I hadn't really thought about that until now. It's hard to think they were actually buying and selling people right on main street like bales of cotton. Owning people, forever?

Little did they know that they would be working off their debt working side by side in the fields with slaves in a couple of days.

They walked outside with a different view of everything. As they watched coach attendants, kids of color holding umbrellas to shelter the wealthy aristocrats from the morning sun, they realized that among the crowd that some of these people actually owned other people. What a strange, uncomfortable thought.

Reflecting on their situation and their future they could only believe they did right. There was no turning back now anyway.

"What a sight. Look at these people. We did the right thing Jacob. Remember how we wondered if we had done the right thing after leaving port in Bremen. Well, we did!" said Jake as his head spun from one direction to another trying to take in all of the movement of the city. St. Louis Street seemed to be a very popular street.

It seemed that a number of people must have been wealthy since they had carriages with attendants and clothes that looked like the people they imagined walking the streets of Paris as they had once been told about from a man back in Bremen that went to Paris every year for business. He used to enjoy watching Jake and Jacob as he told his stories about Paris. The women, coaches, buildings, art, flamboyant culture and yet, here it was. More interesting yet, here they were.

Jim found them standing out front of the hotel. He didn't seem too concerned about them running away since they didn't have anywhere to run. They had slept late, and Jim wanted to get something to eat so they all headed back into the restaurant in the hotel.

"Ah, the smell of cooking in the air. Grits, ham, let's eat up boys. We have some work to do today." Stated as a passing comment from a hungry man.

"Sir? What kind of work do we have today?" Jake asked, speaking for the two of them. Jake had worked hard speaking with anyone on the ship that could teach him some English. They would be thinking as they rode in the back of the wagon after hitching up a team to leave what represented real work.

"The boss, Mr. Dubuclet, wants me to purchase a couple really good farm hands. Young and strong. He has funds in the bank and arrangements with the auction firm here since we buy something about every month when I'm in town. The plantation, as we call large farms here, is growing which requires more workers. That's how you two got work so quickly." Said Jim, as calmly as stopping by the store on the way home to buy a sack of flour.

"The auction starts at noon, but we can go around back and look over the stock to see which ones I might want to bid for at the auction. Let's enjoy our breakfast gentleman, it's a beautiful day and only looking to get better."

Jake and Jacob looked at each other knowing it wasn't going to be a better day for everyone we were likely to see today.

Breakfast, although late, was another fantastic meal. One thing they knew for sure. They weren't going to starve in America like some unfortunate people back home did.

As they headed out the front door of the hotel following breakfast, Jim said, "This way. Let's go around back and see if we can pick out a couple of good strong ones." With a slap on Jakes back, as Jim seemed hesitant to get that friendly with Jacob, again we had to hear, "Ya, sure is a beautiful day!"

It was about an hour before the auction as they went around back of the St. Louis Hotel and saw the iron cages that were set up against the hotel that held dozens of Africans. They just followed Jim as he walked around looking at them like horses or cattle. Some were being taken out and cleaned up for the auction. Potential buyers were trying to talk to some to see if who might know some English or French. Especially the women since they usually worked inside the house and had to understand English to the degree they could respond and do their work. Jacob poked Jake as they walked by a cage with a family of three in it. The woman was a lighter skin color, more of a creole Indian cross. She was beautiful. The beauty faded as we realized the fear in her eyes.

"Sir? Can I ask how much they cost?" Jake speaking up to answer what both he and Jacob were thinking.

"Well sure. A good strong field hand usually runs around $1000 give or take. Around $500 for a woman and a couple of hundred for a child." Said Jim.

"That's' a lot of money. Do they work that off in some way like us?" said Jake.

"No. These are bought and paid for just like any other livestock. Find that unusual, do you?" looking curiously at Jake.

"Yes. We don't have this where we come from. Never seen this before sir." Jake spoke to Jim with more respect realizing that he must have a powerful position around this farm or plantation as they call it if the owner trusted him to handle money like that.

"Here's our two boys in the same lot! Look at the muscle on these two. Another important point is their look. If they look you in the eye, you know they are going to be trouble. If they look down, they know who is boss. That's important when you're out in the field. Ya. Those two are my choice out of this group. Let's go in and have a cold beverage and I'll show you how this works." Jim stated as he wiped his brow. Even in November it was hot and humid in New Orleans.

After they sat down and had some cool drinks, Jim explained that as long as we worked off their time, they were going to be free, and finding their fortunes in this new country in no time. "Maybe you two will get into farming and get some slaves yourselves. So, watch close and learn how this works. Then you can help load these boys up and watch over them as we head on home." Taking another sip, as the auction was about to start.

To try and describe the events of the auction would be more than either Jake or Jacob were capable of or cared to remember. People laughing and bidding on one side while women and children being sold were crying on the other side. One by one up to the block until Jim had purchased the two, he intended to get. Then it was time to go. No sense sitting around here when there was work to do back at the plantation.

They had the wagon hitched up and ready by the time Jim walked up with the two men he had purchased.

"Here, each of you two have one of these boys to watch," handing us the chains that respectively were connected to each one's neck. It seemed a bit much that they also had shackles on their feet, but Jim didn't want to take any chances of a runaway. Hang on to these fellows or you'll be the one wearing the chains. Understand?" Jim yelled.

They understood all right. They sat up front in the wagon holding the chains as they sat on the tail of the wagon. Soon they were on their way. It was going to be a couple of days up near some place called Natchez. Jim described the plantation as on the West side of the Mississippi river. It sounded like it was a big farm.

It was a quiet ride for a couple of hours until Jake spoke up.

"What is the plantation like, Sir? Is it anything like the farms at home where we come from?"

"I doubt it Jake. The plantation is made up of hundreds of acres of sugar cane with quarters for about 100 slaves give or take a few, along with horse barns, several buildings and a big ol mansion of a house where Mr. Dubuclet and his family live. Does that sound like your village home?" Jim laughed.

"No sir, no one has much more than what you call an acre of field and we don't have cotton plants or sugarcane. For that matter we don't have slaves and most people can't afford a horse." Jake noticed Jacob acting like he was disturbed and only hoped that he was going to stay quiet. Jacob was in deep thought as he continued to hold the chain connected to this man's neck. Jacob looked the chain up and down, from his hand to the man's neck, over and over. Neither of the two slaves had made a sound in a couple of hours.

Nothing eventful happened throughout their first full day on the road. They found out that their passengers didn't speak any English or French so there would be some instructions to learn when they arrived. They were expected to arrive at the farm later the following day.

Sitting around the fire that evening, having had some stew for dinner, Jake asked Jim if he would tell them something about this Mr. Dubuclet. What was he like? Jacob had been nodding off, but he sat up straight with wide eyes to hear what Jim had to say. Jake took in what he could understand and restated it to Jacob in German so he would at least get what he could make out.

"Well let's see. Mr. Dubuclet is one of the wealthiest plantation owners in entire USA. He was wealthy to begin with and then he married his wife Claire, who was also already very wealthy. They have nine children with two of boys going to school in France. Big money."

"He got the Cedar Grove plantation from his dad. The plantation is in two locations. One part is West of the Mississippi the rest is on the East." Shared Jim.

"How big is the Plantation?" asked Jacob.

"Well, he has around one-hundred slaves not counting guys like you who provide low cost labor for a few months at a time. We grow mostly sugar and some cotton. Don't know how big the plantation is land wise. Let's just say big and growing." as Jim seemed to have a look of pride for the part he played.

"Did you hear all that Jacob?" as Jake spread out his bedroll.

Jacob replied, "I heard all right. I just wonder what kind of man owns one-hundred people. He actually owns people. Just wondering."

22

Dubuclet Plantation

The morning sun was up before they were. They were going to reach the plantation later today and Jacob and Jake were both wondering what to expect. The first thing that that the two did was to look over to the tree that they had chained the two slaves to, just to make sure they weren't going to get their own iron necklaces. Both were sitting against the tree. Neither had said a word yet. They didn't speak any English or French, which had them wondering how anyone was going to communicate with them. They guessed Jim wasn't too concerned at this point. He would turn them over to the overseer who was responsible for the slaves once they reached the plantation.

They fixed some coffee, had some jerky and left on the last leg of their journey to their new home. Arriving just before sundown, it still took a long time to reach the main house after Jim pointed out that they were on the Cedar Grove Plantation.

As the wagon approached an area on the side off the main house several people were grouping to greet them. The house was a mansion. It sat on the top of a hill overlooking acres of plantation. The air was thick but sweet with the smell of flowers. The main road up to the house had huge trees on either side leading up to flower beds that were all around the house. It was a sight. They were anxious to meet Mr. Dubuclet.

The wagon stopped and after the two slaves moved off the end and out of our way, Jacob and Jake jumped off still holding their chains and stood still for instructions. Jim handed the reins over to a farm hand as someone was already taking the wagon over to the stables.

A small framed man of color approached Jim and stated, "So it looks like you made two excellent choices. You never disappoint me when it comes to the auctions. And I see you found our two foreigners. Bet you all can't wait to get to work. (laughing)"

"How was your trip? Hey Jim? Do they talk? Do they know any French or English? My German is very rough. (laughing even louder)."

Jim stepped forward, "This is Jacob Weisner, likes to be called Jake and this is Jacob Waltz, Mr. Dubuclet. They speak a little English, don't you boys...?"

"Yes sir, Mr. Dubuclet," said Jake with Jacob following in suit, "Yes sir, yes sir, we speak some English. I speak more than Jacob here, but I can translate to him in German. No problem."

"Hey Cody, over here, take these new boys down and introduce them to their overseer and I'll leave Jim here to show you two to your quarters as you will report directly to Jim even though you all will be working the fields with everyone else." Said Mr. Dubuclet with a smile not realizing why we seemed to be speechless and in mild shock.

Both of them took glances at each other but said nothing as Jim took them over to a small cabin on the end of a row of slave quarters. The first couple of cabins were nicer than the others so they were usually reserved for the debentured workers.

"Here is your new home. Get settled in and I will have one of our guys show you the layout and what you will be doing tomorrow for your first day." As Jim walked off.

Jacob wasn't lost for words this time when Jim had closed the door to the shanty behind him as he walked out. Able to speak his mind in German to Jake there was no holding back.

"The owner of this plantation is Black? Did you see what I saw or am I color blind? Am I right? Is that what I saw?" Jacob's voice was edgy bordering rage.

"yah, you saw what I saw. I don't know if the two of us believe what we just saw. How can a black man own a plantation and buy and sell slaves? Black slaves! Where are we? "

The two of them didn't have much time to think about their statements. A knock at the door, door opened, and a European guy said, Hi you blokes! Let's get to it. Going to show you around. You already know where you sleep and eat when you're not in the field. Next, I'll show you what you will be doing for work starting tomorrow.

Jumping up they were pleased to meet someone that seemed more on their level. Their questions were rapidly building up and here was someone they felt we could ask them of.

"My name is Richard or Rich. You'd be Jake and Jacob? Right! Great! Let's get going."

"Now, over there are the food supplies. You have a stove of sorts to fire up in your shanty so you can cook. Rations are distributed once a week." Rich stated.

Heading down the road toward what were the gardens that all the produce for the master's house were grown, Jake asked Rich his first question.

"How is it that Mr. Dubuclet, a black man owns this here plantation?"

"Mr. Dubuclet inherited this plantation as an original part of his father's plantation and grew it larger and larger. His father was wealthy with his grandfather having started the farm. He is now one if not the richest Blackman in the entire USA. He was born free of free parents. There are a number of Blacks that got their freedom and managed to work themselves into owning some large tracks of land. Many live right South of us around New Orleans and own their own slaves."

"He has business partners in New York where he sells his cotton and big political friends in Washington DC. You are very lucky as a debentured slave to be working for Mr. Dubuclet. I only have a few months left and I will be moving on. Might go east to Georgia. Heard some guys found Gold and everyone is running over to stake a claim. Figure I'll join them." Rich continued talking like he hadn't had anyone to talk to for a long time.

Over the next few days our introduction was eye opening. Not only did we end up working harder than we ever expected with twelve-hour days, but the food was everything from salt Pork to corn meal with a catfish or Possum thrown in on a good day.

The two chose not to plant what they called a truck patch on the provision grounds where the slaves could plant vegetables as such because they weren't planning on being there that long and for the time they were, they weren't interested in gardening after a hard days work. Months of hard work along with the activities of watching severe punishments to slaves, at times... less food and more work, they couldn't wait for it to be their time to leave. Leave before it all repeated over and over with more inhuman treatment. It was one sick cycle of pain and frustration after another. They were under a contract and had to work off their debt. In the meantime, they were forced to watch beatings, slave breeding, you name it, they saw it.

The best times were during their breaks. This allowed time to visit with other indentured workers and plantation hands. Most of the indentured workers worked right alongside the slaves, day after day, month after month. Almost all the indentured workers were from Europe and England. During the conversations they enjoyed, there was more and more talk about the gold. Rich would talk for hours about gold being found in Georgia. The stories that were told, made it sound easy to find. Gold fever was starting to affect them, and they didn't know the first thing about looking for gold or anything else.

23

Moving On

The two Germans worked hard and kept mostly to their own business. Jacob did give a threatening look a couple of times that likely caused the overseer to go easy on a field hand that might have made a simple mistake or showed up late for work. Jacob was like that silent nightmare that you just didn't want to get into. He had a penetrating look that said all he had to say, which is why he was probably unlikely to talk at times. Especially when his anger was rising.

Jake had told the story to the field hands and such, of the time Jacob got into a brawl in Horb, their village back in Germany. He described how this big guy and a friend of his picked a fight with Jacob. After hitting Jacob three times with what should have been knock out punches, Jacob refused to fall. Instead he took a deep breath, got that look in his eyes of pure evil and exploded in a fury of swings and kicks which rained down on the two attackers. When Jacob did get hit, it was as if he didn't feel it. Instead being hit seemed to make him stronger. It fueled his hate, creating an even stronger response. Once angered there was no putting down Jacob or trying to reason with him. He didn't stop until it was over. The meaning of "being over" in the story Jake told, was when a half dozen of the men in the bar held him down. If they had let him free, he would have clearly killed the two men.

Those that would become a chosen few to have friendly conversations with Jacob felt a close connection. Those that were not among the chosen, stayed away from him. All and all, by the time it was time to leave the plantation, the two of them had made a lot of friends. One was Rich who had educated them about finding gold. Having decided to head off to the gold fields of Georgia, they had agreed to partner up with Rich.

Jacob and Jake were going to be paid up and ready to go before Rich so they struck an agreement that they would stake claims as a partner with Rich until he joined them. He gave introductions and directions to relatives that knew how and where the potential was for finding gold.

When the day came for them to say goodbye, even with all the work and hardships they felt grateful and expressed that to Mr. Dubuclet. Mr. Dubuclet said that he would always be available to assist them if they needed a reference or work. It was hard to look at those that they had worked with in the fields knowing that they were on their way, yet others had very little hope of ever living a free life. The hope they had risking everything to have a new life, was not available to them and they showed it in their eyes. The two had to realize once again that life wasn't fare and never would be.

Over the next several years the two men worked the mines in Georgia. Rich soon caught up with them. Then it was off to the Carolinas where the three of them learned more on how to search out good ore, pan gold and locate likely places to hunt down the yellow dust.

Eventually, the gold became harder and harder to find. It was time to move on. Jacob and Jake decided to leave Rich with the best of wishes and head back to Louisiana. They worked around

Natchez, traveling down to New Orleans every so often until the stories of the California gold rush started to headline the papers day after day. The 1849 California Gold rush was at full strength.

With what they had learned from their time in Georgia and the Carolinas and never having fully recovered from "Gold Fever", the two of them decided to head West. They decided to head for Castroville, Texas where they knew people were forming up wagon trains to California. The pathway was known as the Old Spanish Trail or Immigrant Trail. In a few days, they would be on their way following that trail from New Orleans to Castroville just west of San Antonio.

24

The Big Missouri

✌☙

The dining room of the "Big Missouri" was indescribable. Huge chandeliers hung from the ceiling giving the room an elegance they had never seen in their lifetime. It was a good thing that they dressed in their best as the people being seated and those already enjoying their dinner drinks were the upper crust of the upper class. The women wore incredible jewelry and the finest in dresses from back East, New York if not Paris itself. The men all looked alike in their formal attire smoking their cigars seemingly without a concern in the world unless it were not finding an ash tray when needed.

Once again, they were in an environment they intended to enjoy, but realized how soon this was about to end. They would be trading in their fancy duds for britches, oilcloth dusters, chaps and boots. James could tell once again that Sis was thinking the very same thing he was.

"Hey, let's enjoy the hell out of this until we have to pull our boots on. What do you say Sis?"

"I think I would like to stay right here for the rest of my life, but I know...I know that we really aren't the people that everyone here might think we are. Sometimes I think this is what life is all about and then I just want to run from this and put those boots on and get real. I think you know what I mean, don't you?" Sis stated with ever changing emotions coming and going every time she moved her head.

"I know what you mean. Let's just live one day at a time and enjoy this evening." Hoping to cheer her up.

The smoke got thick and the voices rose as more drinks were consumed. The dinner selections were so extravagant that they had problems figuring out how to order and not give away the fact that they were two young people from a small town that almost nobody ever heard of. Dinner was finishing up with a southern desert of some type and it seemed that the card tables were being prepared for the evening on the other side of the room.

There wasn't much that went on outside of this area. Rather than head back to their rooms, most passengers chose to just linger around and carry on conversations trying to show each other up. Either the women where showing off their jewelry or their husbands. The men were showing off their wives and trimming the conversation with their financial holdings whenever they could in hopes that their wealth would raise eyebrows over their companions at large.

Then there were the misfits. James guessed in a way they were in that category because of their ages. They were very careful about what they said so as not to give away their lower-class distinction. You could tell that there were others in the room that were more middle of the road and not the cigar smoking, jewelry laden folks.

One such person caught James' eye because he kept staring at Sally. It seemed that he couldn't take his eyes off her at times. A couple of times that James caught him looking at her, he quickly looked away, uncomfortably as if he were embarrassed.

James had to admit that Sally was starting to fit into this glamorous setting. She was a very beautiful woman. Stunning would be an even better description. He couldn't look at her and see the little girl in jeans anymore. "Mr. Stare at her" was not looking at her like a little girl in jeans either. It was easy to notice how men of all ages would look at her with different degrees of approval to downright lust in their eyes. "Mr. Stare at her" didn't seem to lust, but more looked at her like someone looking at beautiful piece of art. A masterpiece. None the less, James didn't like it.

It was disturbing to think that after all she had gone thru that she was here, pretending to be her brother's fiancé, and thus, it was not proper for her to speak with other men without introduction. Some women her age were already married with children. James started to wonder if he was taking that opportunity away from her? Disguising their names was meant to throw off the unlikely chance that authorities might come looking for them.

At the speed that they were moving down the river, it was unlikely that anyone would have heard of his shenanigans back in Stillwater. Even the telegraph hadn't made it to most cities on the Mississippi yet. He knew they would be living a new life and lost from the past the minute they turned to head out West.

It was about that time every evening, that the men started to move toward the tables for the evening's games. James had spent a lot of time practicing being a good poker player, one bent on winning, but not a cheat. Even during their brief riverboat experience thus far, he had learned and experienced the personality and ethics of many of the "Riverboat Gamblers" who made it their living to cheat people less aware, out of their valuables.

Sally had made friends with two other young ladies and was enjoying conversation when James decided to join a game just being put together. With one chair left, non-other than "Mr. Stare at her", now properly introduced as Mr. Patrick Comings decided to join them, pulling out the chair and placing his money on the table.

He was a nice enough looking man and seemed to have good manners, which was also a trait of the riverboat gamblers that would have one hand on your wallet while they shook your other, smiling all the time. James couldn't help but notice how he was seated so that he could look over James's shoulder to where Sally was socializing on the other side of the room. Maybe it was circumstance, but he could see his eyes wandering to watch Sally more than the game at times.

The game got started with six players. It seemed like the same mixture of people night after night. Tonight, was going to be a little different as James noticed that one of the elder players was indeed cheating. He was doing a very poor job of palming a card here and there. He had a young, beautiful lady standing behind him that would make a fuss at the same time he would palm a card, distracting everyone's attention for a second. That's more time than he needed to end up with four of a kind.

As the evening went on he managed to bluff his way through some good hands and was comfortably ahead. Content on winning, even though they had a cheater at the table, James was still annoyed every time he saw Mr. Comings look over his shoulder. It was becoming too obvious that it didn't seem to concern him that Sally was his fiancé. Mr. Comings was enjoying the view but not the game. It seems on a couple of hands that James had dropped out of early, he had stayed in and was eventually taken to task by their resident cheater and his traditional full house or four of a kind.

When Mr. Comings attention finally started to return to the table, he started to look worried. James feared that Mr. Comings was losing far more than he had planned for. This wouldn't have bothered him, especially with the interest he was showing his Sister, but James just couldn't stand to see anyone lose their money to a cheater. It was time for a break.

James called for a half hour break on the pretense of enjoying a drink without the tension of the game. He got up and immediately moved toward Mr. Comings asking him if he could buy him a drink which he seemed happy to accept.

As they stepped up to the bar James asked, "What kind of business are you in Mr. Comings? Don't believe you mentioned anything at the table."

With a scotch in hand he replied, "Just call me Pat please. I represent a gun manufacturer back East on my way to San Antonio, Texas. I have traveled the entire length of the Ohio river and now it appears I'm close to completing a large portion of the Mississippi. Might I ask where you are headed Mr. Goodhue.?"

"Just James will do thank you. My fiancé, who I noticed you are aware of, and I are on our way to New Orleans to get married. We are thinking of heading out West."

"I'm sorry if I appeared to take an interest in your fiancé sir. I didn't realize that she was your fiancé. Beauty like that is hard to turn away from. Seldom seen to that degree. Again, my apologies for my comments. I seem to be stumbling this evening which would include my lack of skill at poker. I'm sorry." Showing embarrassment again as he started to turn away.

"Hi dear," Sally said as she approached. "Who is your friend and how are you gentleman doing at cards tonight."

Not realizing she should have been properly introduced among distinguished company, she moved right up and in between the two of them.

Mr. Comings was almost speechless. James was trying to be polite and not laugh. After Pat's comments to him, Embarrassingly, he was trying to be non-attentive with Sally almost on his arm. Her blue eyes exploded with the deep blue of her gown.

As the men remained silent, she stated, "That bad? I do hope we have enough money left to get to New Orleans dear." She then took a double take of Mr. Comings who was embarrassingly spellbound. "Are you ok?"

"Forgive me, I was distracted in my thoughts for a second. A pleasure to meet you."

"Allow me to properly introduce you to my fiancé Mr. Comings or should I say Pat, this is Sally Burbank. Pat is traveling to San Antonio, Texas. Weapons seem to be his business."

Sally replied without further formalities, "How interesting. Where are you traveling from?"

"Hartford, Connecticut Ms. Burbank. I am representing Colt's Patented Fire-Arms Manufacturing Company."

"My, my, that's a mouthful." Replied Sally as both James and Mr. Cummings broke out in laughter.

"I guess that is a lot. Looking to meet up with Mr. John Hays, Captain of the US Mounted Rifles." Looking down as to not seem to be bragging. Many people had heard the stories of John Hays and the US Mounties.

"I guess we had better get back to the game." But before James made his next comment, he pulled Mr. Comings aside and quietly stated, "Be aware that Mr. Steele is cheating. Don't play into his hand when the young lady behind him is creating distractions."

Pat's eyes were wide as he asked, "Why haven't you called him out? Are you sure? Shouldn't we say something?"

"Let's just go quietly and play a little poker. Don't worry. I'll get your money back. We'll talk after the game." James's arm on his shoulder as they walked toward the table.

In a strange way, even though he took too much interest in James's Sister, he liked the guy and didn't like the idea that he was getting taken. It hadn't escaped James as to how Sally looked at him either. If emotional sparks could start a fire, this boat would be smoldering at the bottom of the river by now.

As the game went on that evening, Sally made it a point to come over every so often until she finally announced that she was going back to her cabin and that the first mate would accompany her to her door while all the while Pat was once again, doing what he did best, staring at Sally. This time James noticed that although she was talking to him, she was looking only at Pat.

With Sis having left it seemed that the game finally got Pat's attention as his loses continued to build with the cheating going on until he declared that he was cashing in and heading for the bar for a drink. James could tell he had some hidden rage over Mr. Steele's cheating. He had seen him palm a card which won Mr. Steele a hand that ended up nearly breaking Pat.

As Pat stood up, James took the liberty to say, "If you stay around a bit, I'll join you in a drink. I think I'm getting a bit tired of this game too. Everyone at the table was getting tired of losing. Mr. Steele wasn't even a good hustler. He won too much too fast. Not a sign of a skilled gambler. A few rounds later, James retired from the game to join Pat at the bar.

"Pat, let me buy the next round, as I'm assuming you have lost more than you could afford. Hard to stand up against a crook unless you act like a crook."

"I am embarrassed to say that your mostly right. I could wire for more funds from the company, but they're going to want to know why this trip is costing so much. I have to ask how you can sit there so calmly and let this man win the way he did," said Pat with an expression that confirmed James's guess about his finances.

"Don't be concerned. I am simply going to ask him for our money back along with a small fee for supporting him in the game so he can continue to fleece the other gentleman at the table without any conflict for the duration of the voyage. He made a good haul off them and it appeared that they all can afford it." As James turned and observed the table. What was left of the game was about to break up for the night and he didn't want to lose the opportunity to confront Mr. Steele.

"You don't seriously think it's going to be that easy? Do you?" said Pat staring in disbelief at James. He looked really depressed now that he had heard the plan. Pat had just written off his losses in his mind, thinking James had lost his mind.

"Enjoy your drink, please. It is a beautiful evening, isn't Pat," Laughing inside as this poor man was looking so conflicted. Seemed like little payback for staring at James's Sister the way he did all night. Especially since he was now aware that she was my fiancé.

25

Poetic Justice

The card game was breaking up. Reluctantly each player picked up what was left of his chips and shook hands, not knowing that, Mr. Steele was not as lucky as they thought. If he had any luck it ran out when James spotted him palming cards. As the group broke up, Mr. Steele had an attendant come over to cash in his chips as there were too many to simply carry to the cashier. A few minutes later he was handed a bundle of cash and he headed for the bar with a smile for a nightcap.

As James looked around the large room, he noticed a number of small groups of gentlemen drinking that looked like a tougher breed than the sophisticated gentlemen from our table. He then picked out a couple of tables and told the bartender to send over a round of drinks on him to each of them. Then he asked Pat to accompany him over to speak with Mr. Steele.

Pat reluctantly followed James. Again, it was comical how uncomfortable James was making Pat feel in confronting Mr. Steele.

"Ah, Mr. Steele, may I buy you a nightcap. You are an exceptional card player."

With a big grin he extended his hand, smiled and said, "That's mighty friendly given what you two lost tonight. Real friendly indeed. Maybe you'll win it back tomorrow night?"

Appearing nonchalant, James looked Mr. Steele straight in the eyes and said, "You won't be here tomorrow night or anywhere else unless you listen very carefully. What's about to happen here is a form of extortion. I think that's what they call it. You're going to keep smiling, smile Mr. Steele", as James pulled his coat back to show that he had a gun in an under the arm holster. Then James asked him to look around the room. The men that had received their free drinks were looking for a chance to catch James's attention, so when he turned two different groups of men waved to him in gratitude for the drinks. Mr. Steele immediately took that to mean he had his crew, a sizable one at that, in the room.

Taking James's advice, he was still smiling. It wasn't with a lot of conviction, but from a distance it looked like we were friends.

"You are very good at palming cards. Amazingly good. Let's get one thing straight, I don't care that you cheated. I only take offence that you cheated my friend here, Mr. Comings and myself. So here is what you're going to do. You're going to give us your winnings for the night and continue to enjoy this wonderful trip all the way to wherever you are going without our interference. Or, I will make sure, that by the time that big ol' clock over there on the wall strikes midnight, you won't have any hands to play with. The catfish will be feeding on them. I haven't decided yet what to do with the rest of you. What would you like to do Mr. Steele? The next play is entirely up to you." As James's expression became sinfully stern.

Pat didn't know if he should run from this scene or try and play it out. Since he felt his legs wouldn't move if he tried to run, he had little choice but to stand there providing a look of supporting James.

"Mr. Steele, I'm waiting. Smile Mr. Steele, smile." As James laughed, as if they had just told a good joke.

Mr. Steele had a strained smile on his face. He looked like a man trying to smile or laughing at a joke while he was having a heart attack. Without saying a word, he reached into his inside pocket of his coat, drawing some alarm from myself, then slowly drawing out his wallet. He took the huge bundle of cash from the evening and with a smile on his face, discretely put it in James's hand.

"Looks like our business is done. Please forgive us if we don't choose to sit in on any of your games during this trip from here on out. Like I said, we won't interfere with your game. Enjoy your trip and your winnings Mr. Steele." As James turned and walked over to the bar, he almost forgot that Pat was walking in his shadow.

James sent the two tables of men another round of drinks. Some came and thanked them and as they walked away, he looked over and noticed that Mr. Steele had left. In fact, they never saw him again. James guessed he decided to leave when they docked the next morning.

It took a few minutes before Pat could even talk. "Are you all right?" James asked.

"How could you do that? What if he would have yelled for help? What if he's telling the authorities about this right now?"

"He's not. That's not how a man like that thinks. He runs from conflict if he can. He was not a fighter. Just a cheap card shark. He played into my bluff, thinking I had a better hand, to include the men in the room, than he did. Thinking that the men in the room where associated with me, makes me think he may not wait till we dock in the morning. He might be swimming to shore right now." Keeping his back to the bar, just in case he had figured this Mr. Steele wrong. James kept both doors in his line of vision.

That didn't stop them from laughing and making more fun of Mr. Steele as the night went on.

James hadn't really lost that much, so he gave Pat a big thick slice of the bundle before they parted and stated, "Here, this should cover your losses!"

"James, this is three or four times what I lost. I can't accept this. Please I can't." as he was starting to get his words out. His mind was clearing up about what just happened.

"There is something about you I like, even though staring at my fiancé is not one of them. I can handle the idea that she is not difficult to look at when she is in the room, but she is my fiancé. Look, you keep the money, as I'm guessing you need it right now more than I do," Said James taking note of what he liked about this guy.

James walked back to his cabin with caution. After entering his cabin, he pushed a table up against the door and put a gun under his pillow just in case. He was tired and when he laid down, immediately went to sleep. This was one of those nights like a couple of others that he had the same nightmare where he found himself drowning. Then a hand reached into the water and started to pull him out. He had never seen a face. There was simply a lot of light above as he looked up and couldn't breathe.

James woke in a sweat wondering who was saving him. Why was he drowning? Why the reoccurring dream. It had been Sis that almost drowned, not him. He started to think about the dream more and more and decided at some point that he was going to talk to Sis about it.

26

Romance

Although the luxury of the Missouri was exceptional and unique, they seemed to have gotten comfortable with the surroundings all too quickly. A couple of days walking the decks, fancy dinners, and spending time with friends like Pat and some of the guys that James had bought drinks for the night that Mr. Steele left, and they were right at home. He guessed the Missouri was as good as many and better than most places to refer to as home.

James seemed to keep running into Pat, at least that's what he was thinking until he realized that Sis was with him most of the time. They had dispensed of formalities and were close enough after sharing a crime to call each other by first names, displaying the beginnings of a friendship. Thus Patrick, now Pat became a third wheel. Sis would dominate the conversation and at some point, it seemed that James would become the odd man out. He could hardly scold her other than to call her a tramp in a comical manner when they were alone, for taking such an interest in Pat. He reminded her that he didn't want to appear to be the doting fiancé, but we were still engaged. This idea of being engaged was putting a strain on her. He hadn't taken notice of the young single woman aboard. Once they knew James was engaged, they gave him a wide birth.

It was early one evening as James was enjoying a cigar on deck when Pat approached, asking if they might join him.

"Of course. Pat, very nice to see you again. I was just reflecting on our successful evening at cards. I can't remember that last time I had so much fun. Have you recovered from counting your winnings from the night?"

Pat was caught off guard by James's comments and didn't know what to say. He was stuck by James's humorous sarcasm. He finally found the clearness of mind to comment. "Yes, it was a rather grand evening, wasn't it? Not only was it enjoyable, but the entertainment provided some very intriguing moments."

While the men were out on the open deck some of the women chose to meet in the lounge for some social time. The first subject they all seemed to have in common was the extremely good-looking young man, Patrick Coming from Hartford. The comments were all light and since most of women were married, but it didn't stop them from commenting in a jesting manner about the gentleman. And a gentleman he was.

Some of women had their complaints about some of men that traveled these river boats. The boats, big and glamorous as they were, still made it was easy to spot someone that shouldn't be on the upper deck. Some of these men had money but not manners befitting a true gentleman.

One of the women then commented, "Like your fiancé, Miss Sally. He is a real gentleman thru and thru. You can tell he has had a cultured upbringing. You better keep a close noose on him or one of those Southern girls might make a play for him."

Sally felt beside herself. One, she knew they were living a lie and second, she had to speak of her brother about being the best fiancé' to hit the planet. She loved her brother, but, but having to talk about him as her fiancé' to all these women seemed short of immoral, even if it was only conversation.

Sally took a deep breath to move forward with their charades stating, "I feel like I have loved him all of my life. You know, Jim and I were just waiting for the right time and place. He is a gentleman. He treats me like someone that needs taking care of, although I certainly know how take care of myself if I had to." Deciding to project a little of her own self-worth into the conversation.

"Ah, but dear, to have a real gentleman that is obviously wealthy, handsome and can take care of you in the style you are accustomed has to seem heavenly sent." Comment one of the older ladies.

Sally doubted that anything since they left home, would be considered heavenly sent in James's mind. And the fact that her good-looking brother wouldn't have to do too much to keep her in the style she was accustomed to. A room and a couple of dresses for Church and that was what she was used too.

However, Sally said, "You are so right. No need for me to be concerned about anything once we are married."

She was thinking, if only that were true with someone like Pat. Her mind was really get mixed up. Once again, she felt strange not knowing what was in store for James and her. She wanted to get back to the exciting feeling of adventure she would feel when James would get excited and describe the trip they were about to take.

27

The St. Louis Fire

The announcement went out that they were going to be arriving in St. Louis in a couple of hours. They had heard about the cholera epidemic that had taken a toll on the population the year before. There was a lot of conversation on the boat during tea and drinks about how the city had bounced back from such misfortune. It was a beautiful city, by the description Joe provided and they were looking forward to seeing what the city was like. They would be docking at night. They were planning an early rise to tour the town. According to Joe, it was the largest city West of Pittsburg, with the second largest port in the country. Joe was really proud of St. Louis. He had offered to show them around for their short time ashore.

The sun was just setting over the horizon as we looked South and saw unusual clouds. Everyone was hoping that they would not arrive in a rainy downpour. They were looking forward to seeing what some of the nightlife was in St. Louis if they arrived early.

Sally caught up with James on deck as he excused himself from a small group of gentlemen that he had been sharing conversation with. They walked a bit then stopped, standing on the bow looking South. The clouds were getting bigger. Over a short period as they observed, it became evident that what they were looking at was not a natural cloud formation, but smoke. Yes, smoke from a fire.

The cloud of smoke appeared to be rising from one concentrated area then drifting for miles and miles to the East. By the minute we were drawing closer and closer. By now we could tell it was clearly not clouding, but clouds of smoke from a huge fire of some sorts.

The deck was getting crowded as more and more people were coming out of their cabins and from the lounge inside to see the smoky clouds that seemed to come from exactly where we were headed.

James felt a hand on his shoulder and to no surprise there was Pat. He didn't say a word. Pat was simply staring at the horizon as everyone else was. It would only be another hour or so and they would be approaching whatever they were looking at. They would then arrive just after nightfall. Whatever it was, it looked threatening, thus the silence on the deck confirmed.

As James turned to speak with Pat, he noticed that Joe Murphy was right behind him.

Joe spoke first, "I have a feeling this is going to be an evening to remember."

"Let's stay close until we know what is going on, just in case." Pat stated as if to take the responsibility to watch over them, "Just in case."

As the next hour or so passed they observed what seemed to be a bad dream. A fantasy of hell. They were now only a few miles away. The sun had gone down in the West which seemed to make the inferno ahead of us grow and reflect even bigger as the night sky moved in from the East. We were headed directly at it. Crew members were telling passengers to remain calm and return to their cabins to no avail.

The four of them along with Joe, stayed together on deck watching and listening to the passengers who were beginning to panic even though they were on the river with a very capable captain at the helm.

They saw men on the riverbank flagging the Captain's deck and yelling to pull over up ahead. They had passed a couple of these men signaling before the captain got the message and started looking for an area along the bank or shore area to pull over and tie up. Men appeared up ahead on the bank of the river signaling a place it appeared they wanted the Missouri to pull into.

They were moving very slowly now and as we came around a corner there were men all over with lanterns and big fires on the beach, flagging every riverboat coming down river into St. Louis to tie up to the sandbar. There were a couple already tied up as we approached a large area, they indicated for the Missouri to shore up as well.

As the Missouri docked, it was at an angle to where the fire could be seen on the starboard side facing South. The entire horizon was in flames. Was all of St. Louis burning to the ground. The lower the sun got the higher the flames seemed to go. The sun had set and from their view point it truly looked like what they all envisioned hell to be.

Once the Missouri was tied up the Captain wasted no time getting to one of the men on shore to assess what was happening. They could see him shaking his head as if he was in disbelief to whatever he was being told.

Moments later he came to the shore in view of the passengers of the Missouri, still all on board. Everyone had moved to one side to hear what the Captain was about to say.

"Listen! Listen! Quiet everyone! Please be quiet!" as loud as the Captain could yell with the first mate and other members of crew repeating to everyone to listen to the Captain.

The Captain was thinking of his words so not to panic the passengers any more than they already were. Afterall there wasn't any threat given where we were.

"Listen! Fire has broken out in the harbor area of St. Louis." The Captain continued as some of the passengers started to act like the fire was licking at their feet.

"None of you are in any danger here. The fire has spread to several of the large riverboats docked there and to a portion of the city's building that border the docking area. Again, there is no threat to any of you."

"We are only a few miles as you can see from the city and the fire seems to be contained to the waterfront. Here is what will be happening. If your destination is St. Louis, you can disembark at this location and men and wagons are here to take you to where you have to go whether homes or hotels. They will see that you are safe."

"All merchandise that can be unloaded will be unloaded on the shore area with some of our crew to guard over it. They will stay with the cargo and catch up with the Missouri down river. The rest of us will proceed down river remaining far from the shore to avoid any threat of fire. Crew will be on deck prepared to address any sparks or emergencies that may arise. We do not feel there is any risk if you remain calm."

The crowd now broke out yelling and screaming, "Why can't we just stay here until it is over? Why do we have to going anywhere until the fire is out?"

The Captain again yelled out, "Listen! Let me speak. Listen! There will be other riverboats coming down river during the night to dock. There isn't enough room on the sandbar. Cargo must be unloaded and moved on shore. We need to make room for other riverboats that will be following us up. It is unlikely the fires are going to be going out anytime soon. Besides, there is no real threat in moving down the river if we keep our distance. If you chose to get off here, you are welcome, and the shipping line will make sure you get reimbursed for your inconvenience. Otherwise, we are moving on as soon as we get the cargo to shore."

He walked away from the people yelling already having made the decision for the Missouri. The display was no more than the Captain, a very competent man, doing his job and performing it well under pressure. Now it was up to the passengers to make their decision.

"Shall we retire for a moment to the lounge where we can talk?" said Joe as he turned and we in turn all followed him.

That fast, there were only a couple of tables left. The passengers were flooding the lounge. Joe quickly walked over and secured one of the last tables. The noise level in the room kept rising as more and more people moved into the room. Standing room only whether at the bar or just around the room. Nobody wanted to be alone in their cabins. Extra chairs were brought in by the crew members. Bartenders were busy pouring. If nothing else this night was going to be a grand night for the bar receipts.

Sally seemed to end up seated between Pat and James which lead to Pat and Sally talking to each other while Joe and James discussed Joe's departure. This was where his passage ended. He was a little concerned since his factory wasn't too far from the waterfront. At the same time, he knew that his wife and family lived far and away in an influential area on the out shirts of St. Louis. Even though he had joined them this evening for a quick farewell drink trying to act as normal as he could, inside, he was concerned and worried over his family.

In a rather unusual gesture Pat spoke first, "I don't have to be anywhere fast if my services might be of use, I'll go with you Joe."

James couldn't stop himself either from saying, "So will Sally and I. We would like to help."

"Woooaaa there folks. Your about to bring a man to tears having such a desire to help, but I have many employees, that are there to take care of what needs to be done. And my house staff will more than take care of my family. Another thing you should be aware of is our just having gotten over a serious breakout of cholera that spread to all areas of the city a few months ago. We think it might have been caused because of the immigrates that have moved upriver. I don't know how many lives this fire is going to take, but last year we lost over 5000 people from the cholera. Maybe better you just stay on board, stay safe and move on."

"I don't know how to thank you except to say we have exchanged information and friends stay in touch. Send me a telegraph if there's anything you need. And young man, don't forget about my pistol when its available. Now, I must get going. I must find my family. Take care my friends," and with no further conversation, Joseph Murphy, of the Murphy Prairie Schooner got up and with a quick step, left the room.

Pat and James had another round while Sally sipped her sarsaparilla.

James addressed Pat, knowing that Sally would move along with whatever they decided. "Pat, what do you think about moving ahead on the Missouri? I don't think the Captain would make a move with this boat unless he knew it would be reasonably safe."

Pat seemed to have already made up his mind, "I feel sure of that James. Are you ok with moving downriver tonight Ms. Burbank?

It seemed like Pat was looking out for Sally as a gentleman. James liked that and thought for the first time, how interesting it would be if these two could face each other with no fake identities.

"Yes, of course if you two think it is ok, then it is ok with me." Responded Sally, looking at him instead of James. You could tell her look made Pat uncomfortable, but then she knew she was single, and her flirting wasn't really going to hurt anyone. Unfortunately, Pat couldn't see it that way and didn't know.

"We had better pack our bags just in case something happens. We should be prepared. Then we can all meet back here no later than when we shove off. OK?" as they stood and left the lounge.

28

Dante's Hell Up Close

It was less than an hour and the Missouri was preparing to leave with a handful of passengers being loaded into wagons and crew guarding a couple large stacks of cargo destined for St. Louis. The shore was busy with men running around like ants. Two of the riverboats that had arrived before them had already left and would be far ahead of them by now. It looked like their next stop was going to be Natchez, Mississippi and then New Orleans. They had in no way expected to meet the people they met or had the experiences they had had. To further that, James knew they were still far from their goal. At least far from his goal. James felt that Sally and he would have to talk about the outcome of their engagement which seemed to be getting problematic. He often thought about what would happen if he met someone that he felt about like he thought Pat felt about Sally. He would probably pretend to drop Sally as his fiancé and be the bad guy and moving on to a new life. Well, that wasn't happening right now so other matters had to addressed, like finding Sally and Pat.

James knocked on Sally's door. When she opened the door, he could see that she had her bags packed, just in case, sitting in the middle of the room.

"We should go and find Pat?" James looked at her face. She had this little smirk of a smile just hearing his name. What was he doing and how was he going to handle this issue?

A few minutes later they had found Pat and the Missouri was moving backward out into the channel of the great Mississippi. Looking ahead and thinking about going forward was going to be like going thru hell.

Suddenly there was a shift and everyone on board could feel the forward motion of the boat. Most of the passengers were on deck even though at one point the Captain and crew told people they would be safest if they stayed in their cabins. That request went as if unheard. It appeared that every single passenger on the Missouri was now on the starboard side so they could see the port of St. Louis as they passed.

If the Missouri wasn't as large and mostly a flat bottom boat, there was no doubt in everyone's mind that it would have rolled over. One could feel it lean towards the starboard side from the weight of all the passengers waiting to get a glimpse of St. Louis and the fire in the port.

Closer and closer we moved. The flames went up for a hundred feet lighting up the surrounding area in a mysterious manner but with light enough to render it nearly daylight.

As they finally saw the harbor, Sally grabbed James's arm and Pat's in fear. She prayed softly for everyone's safety. A few hundred yards upriver they had the view. It took their breath away. They were expecting to see a couple of boats burning in the harbor, but the fire had spread into the city and throughout the entire harbor. The harbor was like a blanket of fire that covered the area whether boats or buildings. It looked like it was all one inferno.

At any one-time St. Louis would have dozens of ships of all sorts docked three abreast in the harbor. They were all lashed together which made it nearly impossible for a lot of them to escape the flames. Those that could had already cut their ties and with whatever crew was around had moved out into the channel and downstream.

At least 20 to 25 of the large riverboats were in blaze. They were built of wood and had huge wood reserves which more than fueled the fires that were going to be burning a long time. The attempt to fight the fire on board the riverboats was looking futile. It looked like the fire departments and men that were trying to save the city weren't having any more success than those that were trying to save the harbor.

Captains and crews were fighting to save their boats, cutting them free from the pack. Some thought drifting down the river until they had themselves under their own power was better than being tied to certain destruction. This made the passage past the harbor a challenge that the Captain had not planned for. Regardless, there was no turning back now.

They had moved close enough that the smoke burned in their nostrils and their eyes. The smell of everything imaginable burning woke the senses to a new level. One that created a memory that years later one could recall as if being in the midst of it all over again.

"Let's hope we never have to see anything like this again." As James wondered how Joseph Murphy and his family were.

It was almost hypnotic watching the fire whipping and dancing into the sky. From their viewpoint it seemed to have consumed everything in sight. Sally continued to squeeze James's arm and eventually was holding tight to Pat's arm too, tighter as we moved closer.

James looked over at Pat with Sally squeezing his arm and her head close to his shoulder. James could see Pat becoming very uncomfortable. Not wanting to leave her grasp but not knowing how to react, he just stood stiff as a board looking forward James knew that he and Sally were going to have a talk sooner than later.

The view as they passed St. Louis burned into their memories. The heat was like that of a blast furnace. The river wasn't wide enough at any width to move outside the heat and smoke. They could hear people yelling and women crying. Part of the pain in watching this tragedy was their inability to do anything. People seemed within reach that needed help and yet they were simply watching as if they had purchased a ticket for this horrible show. Then it dawned on James, as felt his ticket for the trip in his pocket, that it was exactly as he described it. He had a first-class ticket in his hand for the biggest tragedy he would remember. He would have an interesting question for Sally the next time she brought up God. Where was He tonight?

In a few minutes they were looking back on the fire and slowly as they moved downriver around one bend and another it disappeared from the night sky. The captain avoided the drifting boats. A couple of the boats that had their ties burned and broken floated out in to the river creating extremely dangerous obstacles. Eventually they seemed to run aground and burning to ashes.

On a personal issue, there was that moment when Sally realized she had her head on Pat's shoulder while holding James's arm and she jolted up and suggested they all get some rest for it was getting late and the excitement was over. Many of the passengers had cleared the deck, going to their cabins to try and forget the night they would remember forever.

A couple more days went by and we proceeded to dock in Memphis, Tennessee and then Natchez, Mississippi. Their trip to New Orleans was nearly over. One grand run to Houston, then San Antonio for supplies and they would join up with the wagon train West. Each moment that went by seemed to have Sally and Pat bumping into each other. James had planned to discuss the nature of their engagement on the trip from New Orleans to Houston.

As they went down the last stretch from Memphis, they viewed the riverbanks of the huge plantations growing cotton and sugar. It was moving into summer and the planting season was done with the harvest far off yet, but you would still see people working. It was also the first time that Sally and James had seen slaves. Once they had realized that the field hands were slaves, they seemed to recognize them all over. Multiples of slaves started showing up at the two dockings now that they were in the deep South to unload cargo. This was very strange to them. They were certainly aware of and had heard about slavery, but to see it in real life was totally different. The feeling that you could be near one and walk away was more than they could ever do. That didn't settle with either of them.

The trip seemed to get slower as the river seemed to be in a constant turn one way or the other. As they would sit on deck the sun would be on one side and in a minute or two on the other as they wove their way back and forth to New Orleans.

When they arrived in New Orleans, Sally and James had asked Pat to join them for dinner that night. James was told about a place called Antoine's that had fantastic food. It was also said to be the oldest restaurant in New Orleans. Pat accepted the invite. They all walked over to check into the St. Charles hotel which was recommended to them by the First Mate of the Missouri.

As Pat checked into the hotel, he mentioned to James that he was also heading to Houston and had decided to book the same passage that they had. From there he was heading out to San Antonio to meet up with Captain John. James realized that Sally would be seeing a lot more of Pat on that leg of the trip too. Castroville was just a little West of San Antonio.

29

New Orleans

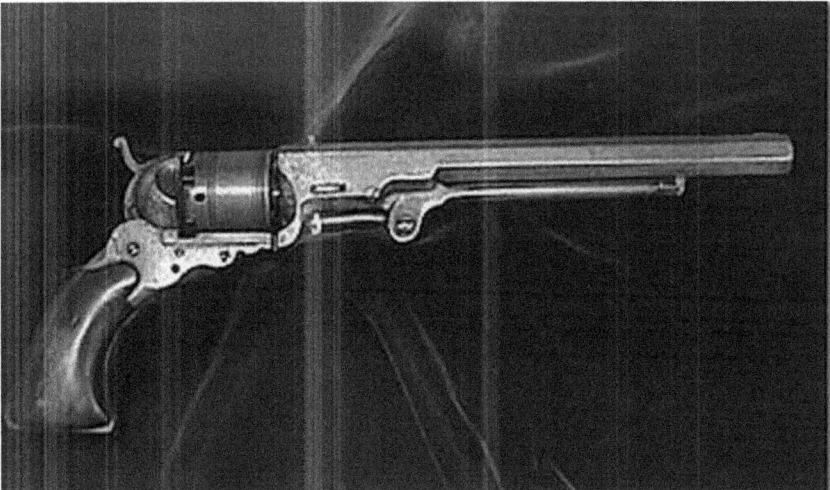

The 1851 Navy Colt was first called the Colt Revolving Belt Pistol, designed by Samuel Colt.

As James met up with Sally for breakfast their first morning in New Orleans, the matter on his mind was their so-called engagement. This seemed an important issue and he decided that he couldn't wait until they were on the boat to Houston to talk with her. He decided that today would be the day. He didn't know exactly what he was going to suggest, but to open this discussion. He was feeling more uncomfortable by the day, and he felt he was robbing her of a chance to have a relationship.

"Hey Sis, how is my beautiful fiancé this morning! Your gorgeous as usual." Thinking a humorous approach might be a good approach.

"Morgan! I mean James! Oh, can we just stop with these charades. I don't know how to tell you this, but I don't want to be your fiancé' anymore. The whole idea around this with you as my brother isn't allowing me to show my feelings toward anyone else." Sally blurted out.

There were two elder ladies sitting down at the table next to them, until they heard what Sally had just said. They stared for a second, got up and went to the other side of the room, obviously appalled at the idea of a brother being engaged to his sister. James tried not laugh since Sis was looking as serious as he had ever seen her.

"Stop! This is exactly what I wanted to talk to you about for some time now. I think our engagement has gone as far as it needs to. It is time to stop the engagement, but we still should maintain our fake identities. There might be someone looking for us." James was struggling to be serious until he saw the two ladies across the room pointing them out to two more ladies that were sighing now and looking our way with the most disgusting looks on their faces.

The waitress approached and they both became silent. She picked up their menus as they ordered their breakfast. When she left, they looked at each other as if wondering who was going to break the silence first. They were both digesting the idea that both of them were about to be unengaged.

"James, since I can't call you Morgan anymore, have you met someone? I haven't seen you with anyone nor have I seen you take an interest in anyone." Sis looked down at her coffee.

Sis continued, "I've taken an interest in someone that I think is a really fine person. Someone that I think, or should I say has a tremendous interest in me but is far too much of a gentleman to disrupt our engagement."

James stepped in, "He is someone that I can easily see has become your friend and would like to be more if I were not in the way. I like him Sally. And I can see how infatuated you are with him. You have the people around us wondering if you're going to have an affair with him." Morgan laughed and Sis hit him in the shoulder. He could hear the women across the room sigh in the loudest manner, causing him to laugh out loud this time.

"Hey, all I'm saying is that whether him or not, you deserve to be free to meet men and enjoy your freedom. I feel it is my duty to explain to him that we ran away from a bad situation and don't want to be followed. I need not explain anymore. I won't explain anymore. I don't feel he will be thinking of you as a criminal, having committed some dastardly deed. Someday we will take our names back and move on with life, but right now we need to stay hidden to some degree. At least by name." as Sally started to smile like a bird just told to it was free to fly.

"Oh, James. I hope you can explain everything, so he understands. I trust you. Tell him all or part if that's what you feel. I don't care. It is important to be as honest as we can right now." Showing a couple tears of joy.

"I will pull Pat aside and talk with him as soon as I see him and then ask him to come with me to meet up with you. I'll excuse myself so you two can work things out. OK? Hey, ok?" breaking her thoughts about meeting with Pat over all this.

"Ok." Sis said in a weak voice.

Sis decided to go up to her room and wait while James went to the front desk to try and locate Pat. Their tickets for passage had already been purchased and tomorrow they were leaving for Houston, so James had to try and talk to him today.

"Have you seen Patrick Comings," as James approached the clerk at the front desk.

"He just left sir, asked where there was a gun shop nearby and I sent him two blocks down. Can't miss it." Replied the clerk.

"Thank you," as James turned and walked out of the hotel noticing that they were getting the ballroom prepared next to the lobby area for some big event of the day. He didn't stop to find out as it was important to find Pat, while he still had the courage and heart to enlighten him on who Sally, and him were. James decided to leave a lot of the more sensitive reasons for another time.

James walked into the gun store to a display of firearms, leather holsters, and several accessories for the gentleman carrying firearms, outright or hidden. Pat was at the counter showing the store owner the Colt line and introducing the new 1851 Navy Colt, to be available soon.

"Pat, glad I could find you. I don't mean to disturb you, but I really need to talk with you when you have the time. It's important." He could tell that James was serious and uncomfortable.

"Sure James, we can go talk now. Let's go to the saloon next door." Saying good-bye to the shop owner, they walked in next door and found a table off to the side that would make their conversation private.

Once they had their drinks, Pat could tell James was stalling a bit, so he finally asked if he had something to talk about or not. James moved his head up and down to indicate yes. At the same time, he realized that he needed to tell someone his story, to get it off his chest as well as clear up Sally's availability. Let the chips fall where they may. For some reason James trusted Pat and felt, whether he continues with an interest in Sis or not, he had made a friend that will keep the secrets that friends keep.

"Pat, I have a story to tell you and I need you to let me tell it before you start asking a bunch of questions or walk out. Ok?

"What makes you think I'll want to ask a bunch of questions?"

"See, there's the first question and I haven't even started. Just trust me. You will." As James prepared to tell the story of a couple of runaways.

He had hardly gotten to the part where Sis walked into the river and he could tell Pat was already choking on all the questions he had to ask. James had no idea what Pat was going to think of Sally and especially himself when he was done.

An hour later, Pat had consumed three beers and was looking at James, sharp as a tack, as if he were memorizing every word he was saying. As James finished up the story with them finally arriving in New Orleans, the bar tender placed a shot and large pint of beer in front of James. He didn't stop Pat from ordering for him since James had been sipping on one beer from the start of his story. It was time to sit back, have a drink and see how Pat plays the hand in front of him.

Pat was wide eyed, confused and probably couldn't decide if he should ask questions or just run away as fast as he could. Finally, after a couple of minutes of silence as they stared at our drinks, Pat asked, "Why did you decide to tell me all this. Why me?"

Still looking down at my drink, playing with his glass, James responded, "Because I can see that you have a serious likeness for Sally, and you need to know that she seriously likes you. Hell, I even like you and I tried pretty hard not to."

"Sally likes me?" Said Pat.

"Are you blind Pat? Of course, she does. I should make it clear, in a much different way than I do. Now, that said, let me tell you that if you hurt my Sister, you won't live to regret it." With his best poker face on display.

"I have so many questions and yet I don't really have any that seem more important than asking where Sally is right now." With a shy grin.

"She is waiting in her room to see how this meeting between you and I go. I suggest that you go back to the hotel restaurant and get a quiet table. I'll go upstairs and bring her down so you two can visit. I'll be waiting here if you need me. Maybe you can ask her questions about our story. Remember! She does not know what I did to our father. Please leave that card for me to turn when I feel it is best. Our secret as friends. Obviously if someone is hunting for us, I'm trusting you will not talk about any of this except with Sally. Let's head for the hotel." As James walked out with Pat in tow.

30

Turning West

When James knocked on Sally's door, it opened so quickly it was like she had been standing on the other side with her hand on the doorknob.

Then, almost as slow as he had ever heard her speak, she asked. "Did you find him?"

"Yes, I did. He has been listening to me for nearly two hours." Holding his poker face.

"What did you talk about all that time?" she asked

"Everything" James said

"Everything?"

"Yes, everything. I couldn't help it. Once I got started telling him the story it just came out." looking at Sis with her head in her hands.

"Oh no, he will never talk to me again. He doesn't want anything to do with me now." She started to cry, then sobbing.

"Stop that! Now!" as James pushed her back into her cabin and closed the door so they wouldn't be heard. "He is downstairs in the restaurant waiting for you. He wants to talk to you. He will have questions, so this is your turn to be as honest as you want to be. I feel he can be trusted. Besides, it's not like we have a bounty on our heads." The last few words drawing a dirty look from Sis.

"What do I do!"

"Simple, fix your face, comb your hair and go downstairs. I think you'll be surprised at the outcome." Stated with a reassuring smile and a hug.

After a couple of minutes of fix up, James opened the door for her and escorted her downstairs. At the restaurants entrance He excused himself and went straight ahead and out the front door.

Pat had stood at his table, watching Sally's eyes follow James out the front door. He started to wonder if she was going to turn and join him? When Pat saw her turn and their eyes met, he seemed to instantly be consumed with his feelings for Sally like never before.

Sally made her way over to the table. Pat held a chair out for her and the next couple of hours had two friends sharing their inner most secrets. Pat asked his questions in a far more delicate manner than if he had been asking James. He still couldn't think of him as Morgan. Eventually they stopped talking and started staring at each other. Pat put his hand over Sally's hand which sent an electric charge through both of them. They said goodnight to each other after Pat had walked her to her room. He then returned to his room, feeling the need to just sit down. He had wanted to embrace Sally, knowing that she cared for him, but there was just so much to digest that Pat hadn't even given her so much as a hug before walking away.

James had walked out, played cards half of the night and returned with some meager winnings. He had become a good card player, at least better than most of his adversaries. The next day, he was going to hear all about Pat and their dinner and then they were going to board the riverboat that would take them to Houston, given the weather was good to fair.

There was a lot of activity on the dock as the final loading of cargo and passengers took place. The three of us had met up and had breakfast together. Pat insisted that James join them even though he thought they might have more to talk about. Especially, questions that Pat might now have that he didn't think of last night. It was what he thought it would be. Quiet. A very quiet and slightly awkward breakfast with those two sneaking looks at each other.

James asked Pat to escort Sally on board while he went to the telegraph office to send a couple of telegrams before joining them. The first telegram was to Mr. Wakefield and his wife to let them know that they had arrived in New Orleans and were headed for Houston. The second one was to Joe Murphy stating they had made it to New Orleans. James had arranged with the bank in Memphis to wire adequate funds to purchase two schooners from Mr. Murphy and have them delivered to San Antonio. They would be in San Antonio moving on to Castroville where the families would be forming up the wagon train. The wagon train wouldn't' leave until late fall so they would be moving across the hot desert territory in the winter months. James had asked Joe to respond by sending him a telegram in New Orleans confirming he had received the money and could make delivery. For the extra amount that Joe had received which was well over the purchase price, he was making sure we had plenty of extras to try and make their trip a little more comfortable. In his reply he let James know that he, his family and business were all untouched by the fire. Truly blessed, was how he described it.

The whistle was blowing as James was walking on board. In a little while we would be leaving for Houston. When he got up on top deck, he saw Pat walking with Sally. Pat had his arm around her. He guessed he wasn't going to introduce her as his fiancé' anymore.

The trip to Houston was rather uneventful for. He tried to stay out of the way of Pat and Sally. If he were on deck, he could hear them laughing before he saw them. The same was true in the lounge or restaurant area. James often wondered if he would ever see her laughing like this. In fact, he didn't think he had ever seen her laugh like this. It gave him a warm feeling to see that someone else was looking after her with what appeared to be the same protectionist love that James had for her.

31

Houston

James expected Houston to be a city like New Orleans. What a surprise. With all the stories about Texas, Sam Houston and the number of events he had read and heard about, the Mexican War, The Alamo and such, he thought he would see the city of Houston as far more advanced than a bunch of squared off streets and a population of under 3000 people. It didn't seem much larger than Stillwater, where they came from. What made it different was how it was stretched out. The harbor was nothing next to St. Louis or any number of other harbors we had been through on our travels down the Mississippi. He guessed they were a whole lot closer to the real frontier than he thought.

He went to help Sally with some of her things and make sure that their luggage would be moved to the hotel. They would be there a couple of days before they took a coach to San Antonio which they assumed now would be even less populated and wilder than Houston.

Pat was already ahead of him walking down the corridor approaching.

"We have arranged for all of our baggage to be moved to the hotel. We were looking for you to let you know. I hope that's ok." Said Pat as he seemed to now be taking care of both of Sally and James.

"Of course. Thank you, Pat. I only have this one bag that I'll carry. The rest are in my cabin to be moved. Again, thank you. Shall we head over to the hotel and check out our accommodations?" as James followed the two of them off the boat.

They were staying at the Burnet House. It was right on the main street which in total didn't have much to offer. Following Pat and Sis down the walkway to the hotel it started to hit James that he was in a funny way a free man now. He was thinking he might gain a new appreciation for the lady's he tipped his hat to. He started to laugh to himself expecting that this new-found freedom had all sorts of possibilities. But, how was he going to explain Sis and him breaking up when they met up with the Peeples clan in Castroville? This group took them in as friends and offered their help getting them equipped and looking after them on the trail, so James felt compelled to be honest and simply explain their running away and pretending to be engaged. Yes, that's what he was going to do. That meant that he had to also fess up with Mr. & Mrs. Wakefield as a business partner. Somehow it didn't seem right to go any further with deception about who they were.

Suddenly, James felt like a burden had been lifted and his conscience was a little cleaner. It had started to feel better ever since he had confessed what he had done to Pat. He wasn't going to treat Pat like a confessional, but just telling someone and explaining the circumstances made a difference. It didn't correct anything. It just made a difference. Not so much as to jump into a religious conversation with Sis, but enough to know that being honest with your friends felt good. After having checked his cabin, still carrying his smaller bag with the money in it, he headed over to the telegraph office again. He had decided to take the funds and put them into a simple smaller carry bag that no one would notice and keep it close to him at all times.

James had two telegrams to send, one was a very lengthy and expensive telegram of explanation he had to send to Mr. & Mrs. Wakefield. He decided that they deserved to know the truth about Sis and him. Allowing a proper time for response. He would give them an opportunity to back out of our agreement knowing he had lied to them. The other telegram was to Mr. Murphy, checking to see if the schooner wagons were on the road yet and how long it might be to get them here. James decided it would be best to wait for his response, even though he told him where they would be staying in San Antonio.

He headed out from the hotel to the telegraph office to take care of first things first. He had everything written out for the telegraph operator to send before he walked in. It was a good thing that there wasn't anyone else in the office as his correspondence was lengthy and he didn't want everyone to know the story of his past as he might be telling his story to the town sheriff.

As James greeted the telegraph operator, the man kept staring at all the paper he was holding in his hand, as if to say to himself... this is not my day...

He started to figure up what it would cost when James simply told him to send it, it didn't matter. He immediately proceeded to sit down and start clicking away. James was always amazed how some of these guys could send and read Morris Code so quickly. It was truly a new age. The telegraph seemed to be following us and moving West. It was connecting city to city now up and down the Mississippi in only the last few months. It wouldn't be too long before it would be all the way to California.

This would be one of his last chances to telegraph Mr. Murphy or Mr. & Mrs. Wakefield. The telegraph was moving West, but he was about to say good-bye as the wagon train would move beyond that part of civilization on this journey. Mail would be slow as it was sent back and forth with supply wagons as they moved in and out of the frontier.

As the operator sent his story about Sally and him running away, he kept looking back at James. He hadn't included any of the gory details except that he tied my father up to the bed and left. James thought the man was uncomfortable about having to turn his back on him. In a couple of minutes, the operator seemed to settle into what he was doing. He started to act like he was reading or sending someone a good novel to read.

Messages sent, James paid the man and gave him a little extra to find him the minute that any reply came in. He smiled at that point and knew there would be a big tip for delivering any reply. As James left the telegraph office, again he felt a relief having told some of the story and having been honest with Mr. & Mrs. Wakefield. He held his breath waiting to see how they took the bad news. They might decide that they didn't want to deal with him. Henry still having an arrangement with the Roberts and Peeples families, their mentors for the journey, meant he would likely notify them, and the two of them would be on our own.

The next thing he had to do was figure out how they were going to get to San Antonio. Not too surprising as all things were going, Pat approached James as he was returning to the hotel to see what the plans were for the next leg of their journey which was to get to San Antonio.

"San Antonio is my ultimate destination for this trip." Said Pat. "I need to meet up with Captain Jack Hays. He is expecting me with the new pistols I personally wanted to deliver to them."

"What is so special about these new pistols again? Say let's see what some of these saloons have to offer while we talk. Sis back in her room?" James asked.

"Yes. She was going to take a nap. Let's check this one out," as they walked in to see what it looked like, "... and if there might be a good game to join this evening.

The place was a serious step down from the saloons and card rooms on the riverboats and the riverfronts of the towns and cities that we had just been through. Yet the bartender was polite and said there were many a high stakes game late in the evenings.

As we walked around town going in and out of several saloons, Pat started telling James about the pistols that he was delivering to the US Mounted Rifles (Texas Rangers), more specifically, his hopes to open up the West to distribution and sales of the new guns being designed and built by Colt. Pat kept saying, "If there is one thing the West needs more than anything is a Colt. Not one to ride, but one that shoots."

"When we're done with our checking out a good place to join a game come night, I'll show you what I'm talking about. That crate that keeps following me from boat to boat, has a two dozen of the new Navy Colt pistols in it. I'll be showing them to Mr. Walker for the first time in a finished version when I reach San Antonio."

It was very uneventful walking around the waterfront going in and out of the saloons. There wasn't that many, and with time they all starting to look the same. They had stopped long enough to have a beer or two at a couple of them. Feeling strongly that it was time to put some food in their stomachs and thinking Sally was done with her nap, we headed back to the hotel.

"There you two are!" hearing Sally's voice as we were walking toward the hotel. "I have been up for a long time looking for the two of you. Where were you?"

Pat replied, "In places a proper woman as yourself wouldn't be seen. You wouldn't have found us unless you had been checking all the saloons. I think that would have been a bit unlikely thank God."

They all had a laugh as James suggested they head over to a restaurant that they had been told had great food, especially known for their pies and bread pudding. When the bread pudding was mentioned James couldn't help but think back to Mr. Johnson. He was so kind and supportive. He remembered how he took him over to celebrate a hard day's work for dinner and bread pudding. Then his heart sunk as he remembered steeling from him before he left town. Mr. Johnson must think he's the worst of the worst to do what he did.

"Heard you had great food." James said as the waitress approached.

"T-Bones, potatoes as you like them all covered in our special dark gravy. That's our special. "said the waitress with a broad smile.

Suddenly, he found himself looking at the waitress with a different feeling now that he wasn't engaged. Then again, he needed to wake up because he wasn't really engaged. She got his attention with a friendly smile that immediately made him feel like he was cheating on his fiancé. How mixed up can one man get. He seemed to have fallen into the role easily having always loved and protected Sally the best he could. Now he had to let go of it and enjoy life.

James could see her blush a little as he smiled back and stared her straight in the eyes. It seemed to draw the attention of Pat and Sally since his look wasn't very subtle. The waitress seemed quick to acknowledge him by flirting whenever she approached our table. Then James became aware that Pat and Sally were observing him with great interest, and he came to his senses, feeling incredibly embarrassed.

"I'll for sure have the special, rare, with a cup of coffee. Potato mashed. Thank you!" as he attempted to hide his embarrassment by ordering Sally, putting into question his being a gentleman.

Pat and Sally enjoyed the display. They laughed under their breath and ordered. The conversation then started with what they were going to do next for the trip West.

32

Game Night In Houston

～◎

The discussion was light as they were all hungry. Their T-Bones hung over the sides of the plate signifying no shortage of beef in Texas. They had heard about the continuous stream of cattle moving north to Kansas to be shipped East. The trails north were so crowded at times you could see one herd starting to mix with another. When the herd ahead bedded down for the night, so did the one behind it and so on down the line. The pathway to the markets in Kansas and Missouri moved only as fast as the slowest herd causing tensions to rise at times among the cowboys getting paid to drive these herds to market.

Near the end of our dinner Pat and Sally took the liberty to make fun of James and the waitress, reminding him that he was now a single man. They enjoyed desert and then it was time to start thinking about getting into a game for the evening.

Pat and James walked Sally back to the hotel and she went to her room to turn in early and read. That's when Pat asked James to come over to his room and see the pistols they had talked about.

In the corner of his room was a sizable wooden crate. James was aware of it, as Pat had to have another person to help move it any distance. James had seen it get loaded and unloaded from the riverboat, assuming that it contained something pertaining to Pat's business. It wasn't standard luggage. Pat unlocked the huge padlock on it and lifted the cover. There packed in oil cloth were nearly two dozen of the new Navy Colt pistols.

He pulled one out, unwrapped it and proceeded to wipe it down so it wouldn't be all oily and handed it to James.

"What a beautiful gun." It almost looked like a piece of art to James. "The feel to the hand and the weight and balance are significantly different than the dragoon he carries around."

Pat looked down and then up stating, "I have thought all along I wanted to give you one of these and now is as good a time as any. I only need a dozen of these for the Mounties. Plus, there is another shipment not far behind me that will outfit all of the Mounties. Would you do me the honor for having befriended me and in return for having helped me get my money back on the riverboat."

I couldn't possibly refuse such a gift. It was an incredible piece of engineering and having made the statement he made in offering it, James would have broken Pat's heart to have refused.

"It would be my honor Pat! As I replaced the gun in my holster with the new colt.

"Why don't you carry one of these?" James asked.

"I do have one, but I have chosen not to wear it. As to the rest, I guess I just wanted to make sure they all made it to San Antonio without drawing to much attention to the guns." Pat replied.

"Nonsense! Holster up yours and if you can spare one more, I will love to be your first customer. That is, if you have enough for the Mounties and your meeting. Can you sell these?" displaying a look of desire.

"I signed out a dozen for the Mounties. The rest I purchased to resell, but I wanted to make sure in case anything happened that I had some extras. Sure, I'll sell you one as my first step to my new future as a gun distributor and salesman." Stated with a broad smile.

"Then let me get these cleaned up, holstered and so we can head out for a night of wrangling up some money from some lucky cards!" as they shook hands knowing there were now three things they had in common. Sally, guns and cards. James thinking the order of priority might be optional depending on place and time.

A couple hours later they met up and were walking out of the hotel toward the saloon that they determined would have the best game and most potential. Potential meant the most unskilled players with the most money.

"Well, well," stated Pat, "you sure took up the role of gunslinger in a hurry. Double holster, low-cut with two new Navy Colts. Ya, let's not draw any attention to the guns. How come you don't have one under each arm too with cross holsters. You better watch out partner, that someone doesn't draw down on you thinking there's going to be a reward on your head or that they might become famous for killing some gun fighter."

"I couldn't resist the holster from the shop next door. It might not be perfect yet, but I couldn't wait to wear them and start working with them a little. They give me a feeling of being well protected." Said James as he kept adjusting the holster to feel right.

They both laughed, walking on with a feeling between them like that of two brothers.

As they walked in, they looked around and saw a couple of games going on. They decided to take their time and head over to the end of the bar where they could watch over the room as they ordered drinks and asked the bartender for a little advice, for which they were always happy to provide for a good tip.

They ordered two beers and James asked, "Any good games going on with your recommendation?" knowing that the bartenders always knew the regulars and kept an eye on the stakes going on at the various tables.

"Ya, there's an interesting game over at that table. The stakes seem to be getting higher and the strain of four hours of playing is taking a toll. Plus, I might have to throw a couple of those gents out of here in a little while. Been drinking steady which isn't helping their game." He stated as he reached around and served their beers.

"Thank you, sir," hitting him with a hefty tip, then nodding his hat to him, James had a feeling they were already getting lucky.

They moved to a place where no one would pay any attention to them watching the game next to the stairs that went up to the lady's rooms, using the term lady loosely. The steps turned out to be quiet a distraction as business was booming tonight.

One older gentleman at the table seemed to be slowly losing with every hand dealt. James assumed that he had started with a fair amount of money seeing how the betting was going and had lost most of it. He was not the gambler type in my eyes. Pat commented a couple of times, questioning why the old man didn't lick has wounds and go home.

If I was going to join the game, James wanted to try and read their motions that gave away whether they had a high hand, or they were bluffing. It only took one beer to get most of that figured out and the easiest in the group was sadly enough, the old man.

He would rub his nose when he had a good hand, in a rather unassuming manner, but it was none the less accurate. When he had a bad hand, he would stroke his beard like he was in deep thought. It was just too easy for anyone skilled to miss.

They had watched the game for some time and thought a chair would open soon when the old man was finally cleaned out. Sad, but that's life. Then something happened.

As plain as can be the man was dealt a hand that had him rubbing and scratching his nose making it turn red. He was so lit up with what he had before the draw that I knew it was not only a good hand, but a great hand, maybe the best he had had since they had been watching. James shared his evaluation with Pat and as he was quickly learning the new science, fully agreed.

Now, most everyone else at the table must have known too, but the card shark at the table who had been slowly, skillfully cleaning everyone out without being too obvious didn't seem to care as he kept raising his bet. These two gentlemen both had a hand they thought was a winner. No one was backing down.

The raises got to the point that the card shark laid down one huge raise that was about to put the man out of the game. The tension and theater in this game was better than any entertainment James could have bought a ticket to see. He felt it was about time to pay up for the entertainment.

James turned around and discreetly counted out one thousand dollars in bills and carefully rolled it up. Having heard them call him by his name "Bill" and "Mr. Overly" he moved toward the table leaving Pat wondering what he was about to do.

"Excuse me gentlemen. Mr. Avery, I'm so glad to have found you. I've been looking all over town for you. I was able to put the money together that I owed you. I hope you'll forgive me for the delays." As he put the rolled-up cash in the confused man's palm, he quickly walked away leaving him looking bewildered, then having figured out enough to play on he covered the bet and turned in one card.

Pat was laughing as James walked back to him and turned to watch the game. Taking one card meant he was looking for a straight, flush or full house.

His opponent asked for one card also looking like he had already won. He also hadn't shown this kind of emotion. It is a bad sign for card players to do, but he was so convinced by what he was holding that he didn't care.

The raises continued and the old man finally called, and the betting stopped with most of the thousand he had given him on the table. By this time near everyone in the saloon had an eye on the game. The old man turned over his cards.

"Full house, Aces over Queens" the old man said with a hopeful smile.

"You son of a bitch!" as the shark threw down a full house of Kings over tens.

It seemed the man was about to become belligerent, so Pat and James moved quickly toward the table until James was on one side of the man and Pat with his coat pulled back, pistol showing was on the other side.

The card shark looked us over quickly but intently. He also saw the bartender coming forward. He decided to leave the game with what he had left before being thrown out.

He collected his money and as he walked past James, he leaned in so others couldn't hear what he was about to say, "This isn't done. Don't lose your money because you own me and I'm collecting." Hardly breaking stride, he continued out the door.

At that point, everyone called a break in the game to provide a little time for everyone to calm down. James yelled at the bartender who was almost to the table, "Round of drinks for everyone at this table please, on me."

The old man raised his head, shaking it back and forth as he got up to his feet.

"Young man, I don't know you, do I?"

"No sir, we have never met. I just saw an opportunity to even the odds and keep you in the game to play that hand of yours. Although I might suggest that you find another form of pleasure. You never do to well at cards do you.' James said with a smile.

"Not really, but I expect I'll improve." Stated firmly by Mr. Overly

"Mr. Overly, what do you do to make the money to fund your card games, if I can ask?" James wanted to know how men like this made their money.

"Son, after tonight you can ask anything you want. I buy and sell real estate. I'm quite known in these parts to include San Antonio and Austin." Stated with pride and distinction. A different man seemed to be speaking now.

"Then sir, with all respect, if you make enough money to continue to support your card playing the way you play, I would like to hear about what you do and explore opportunities. And, until you learn how to look in the mirror without expression, stop scratching your nose with a good hand, and playing with your beard when you're holding a bad hand, I suggest you slow up on your card playing and make a bigger game out of your real estate," James's words hardly finished as Mr. Overly started laughing until he was in tears.

"What does someone call you instead of son? And Please call me Bill. Bill Overly which I take you already knew when you handed me a small fortune. Oh, by the way, thank you and I'll count out your money before we leave with let's say half of the winnings? Again, thank you. I don't know if that sounds fair." Tenderly stated by Mr. Overly.

"My name is James Goodhue, and this is an associate of mine who happens to be in the gun business, Patrick Comings. Please just refer to us as James and Pat." As they all sat down at the card table to relax before the next round started.

They spoke for a while and then when the other players decided to play again, bringing with them a couple of new candidates, Mr. Overly decided to leave the game and asked if we would join him continuing our conversation.

As he explained his ideas in real estate and how he figured this area around Houston was bound to grow, James became more and more interested. Bill was considerably older than James, in his forties, and knew more than James ever wanted to know about the buying and selling of land for profit.

He and his wife had done well back East in Pennsylvania before coming out to Houston and Galveston. He was convinced that the port side of these cities would grow like New Orleans. James felt that this was an honest man that he knew far more about than Bill did him.

Hearing that Pat was meeting up and dealing with the US Mounted Rifles didn't hurt our credibility either. Pat decided to leave and walk back to the hotel to turn in for the night. Bill and James continued their discussions with real intensity for another half hour. They seemed to have hit it off. They had more to talk about than the will to talk at this hour, so they decided to continue their business conversation the next day when their heads were clear and rested up.

They walked out together. Bill lived in town only a couple of blocks over, so he headed one direction as James headed back the other direction, toward the hotel. James was about a block down from the saloon when suddenly, a bunch of men came out of nowhere. They were on him before he could draw his gun. They held him while they shoved a gag into his mouth and dragged him to the back ally where they had their horses. The man was still mounted holding on to the reins of the other horses was the card shark.

As four men held James, the man on horseback looked down at him and said, "Told you this wasn't over. You're going to hurt. You're going to hurt for a long time. Might not be able to walk right again or never so you'll always remember me. And you'll remember not to ever interfere in a game that I'm in, if you ever see me again. OK, boys, have some fun!" as he grinned.

Just then a shadowy figure came out from behind the men with two guns drawn. They didn't have time to turn before the first two got hit with the barrels. One slammed the guy in the side of his face, surely giving him a lifetime memory. The other never knew what hit him. He simply fell after being struck. James pulled around on the two that had a hold of him. They had let go to turn on the man behind him leaving him to grab the man in the saddle, pulling him to the ground. He hit the ground headfirst. He lay there semi-conscious, most of the work for me by his fall. James was angry, and as the started to raise up he kicked him the head rendering him unconscious.

James felt another man fall almost over him with several of his teeth flying around like hail in a hailstorm. The last one as James stood up was standing with the barrel of a brand-new Navy Colt in his mouth with eyes the size of dinner plates. It was Pat holding that gun. James could only stare in amazement. Pat had a look in his eye that looked like Satan himself, yet he was as calm as if he were listening to a Sunday Church Choir.

Pat said, "Now you listening? Have any money? Maybe from having stolen from other defenseless people. I'm only asking you this once."

The man nodded yes and slowly pointed to the saddle bags on two of the horses.

James quickly grabbed the bags and looked inside and sure enough, it contained a small fortune. These guys must have been working the saloons and the card games, either winning at the table or robbing them as they left.

Pat continued, "Thank you. Now, for being so helpful, I'm not going to kill you, if you do your part right. If not, I'm going to beat you to death and show how the five of you robbed me. We clear?"

"Yes sir" now crying in humiliation with one man holding his mouth which was missing several front teeth.

"Good, now load up your friends here on their horses, leave the guns and get out of town. They say there is a good doctor in Galveston. If I so much as see you on the street, I'll shoot you down cold and explain to the sheriff along with my friends among the US Mounted Rifles how I was robbed along with my witness here, understand? Now, please don't take advantage of my generosity and try anything as you leave. Ok?" Pat said as I walked over to his side picking up my new colts that they had tossed on the ground. I also picked up the guns from the other men thinking I could give them to friends that might need them more than these guys and use them more wisely. The pile also included a newer looking Winchester rifle that the card shark had in a scabbard on his saddle.

"Yes sir, yes sir, thank you, thank you." As he started to load up his friends.

James and Pat made their way to the main street, quickly walking to the hotel, just in case the men decided to challenge them again. James couldn't help but ask Pat, "who are you? I didn't know you could handle a gun. Why didn't you just shoot them." With a shocked expression on his face.

"There wasn't any reason to kill anyone. Besides, we wouldn't have been able to rob them if people were running in from the shots. They might show up again, but I doubt it. Regarding the guns. I have been handling guns and practicing since I could hold one. Why do you think I'm selling guns? It's because I love them.

I also know how to use them. I'll teach you a few things when we get out on the trail with some free time."

With amazement they walked back to the hotel like a couple of modern robin hoods. Not only had they made a great friend in Bill, but they ended up with more money than if they had won every card game played that night at the saloon. And yet, they had never even touched a deck of cards.

33

Business Startups

The Prairie Schooner designed, built, and sold by the thousands by Joseph Murphy, an Irish immigrant.

Everything seemed normal to Sally the next morning as Pat and James took her for breakfast until she noticed that Pat was wearing not just a holster, but a double holster. Usually only outlaws or lawmen carried two pistols just in case something happened to one of them, they had a back-up. Sally was the first to comment. "Why are you wearing a gun, or should I say guns. Both of you, with your double holsters look like you're looking for trouble and from what I know, if it is going to involve guns, neither of you know what you're doing."

"Well, good morning to you too. You look so refreshing in the morning light." Said Pat.

James couldn't help but to start laughing which seemed to get Pat into the mood when he looked over him. They were both recalling the mischievous evening they had had without killing anyone. Sally looked stern, waiting for an answer to her question.

"Sally, I'm a gun salesman. I'm simply displaying my wares." Pat said.

"You look like a gunfighter! Someone that makes a living with a gun" she blurted out.

"Actually, I do make a living with a gun. I just do it in volume. These are the new 1851 Navy Colts. Soon to be the envy of every man who owns a gun" As he lifted the pistol out of his holster.

"Is that supposed to impress me?" she struck back.

"Sally, you might want to think about what lies out ahead of us and start getting ready. In a couple of weeks, you won't be wearing dresses like that or eating in restaurants like this. There will be varmints, rattlesnakes, coyotes and wolfs out to feed on you and the livestock we depend on if you cannot defend your-self. Then there are Comancheros, Indians, bandits, and plain old undescriptive bad people to deal with. They will all be strong. Nothing weak will sustain through this trip and the settlement of new territory. Only the strong survive on the frontier. The only real equalizer is the gun. If one helps a little, two will help a lot. Now, that's the end of my speech. Can we eat?" ended Pat.

Sally decided after that to remain silent. In fact, she had been enjoying most of the trip so much and seeing all the sights and meeting new people that she hadn't thought much lately about the trials of this venture they were about to embark on. How different things were going to be starting day one. They would remain that way maybe forever. It would be a long time for telegraphs, trains, and streetlamps to catch up to the far West where they were going. Yes, things were about to be life changing. That said, a gun now seemed like a good idea. She figured she had better learn how to use a gun.

"There is only one thing I have to say about all of that." Said Sally knowing she never knew when to quit. Looking straight at Pat with a melting look she said, "Will you teach me how to shoot? I want to be able to shoot a rifle as well as be a great shot with a pistol."

It was a good thing James didn't have a chunk of steak in his mouth or he would have choked to death hearing those words. Instead, he just blessed the table as he sprayed a little coffee around, choking on the last swallow. She was a much faster thinker than James had ever taken her for. Not only was she using common sense, but she was going to please her man at the same time.

They were just finishing up when the telegraph operator came running in with the first telegram. James tipped him big and he ran out the door like he couldn't wait to get another for him. He probably already had the second one back at the office but wanted to deliver them separately so he could get two tips.

This one was from Mr.& Mrs. Henry Wakefield. It said.

Mr. Sommer (stop) Admire honesty (stop) Will continue partnership (stop) Advise anyway to help (stop) Will investigate father (stop) Await adventures (stop) God bless you Henry & Betsy (End)

Brief and to the point. James handed it over to Sally to read and as tears came to her eyes, she handed it to Pat, since he was the only other person that knew what the telegram meant.

James spoke first, "This is a miracle. That Henry and Betsy want to continue our partnership. What a blessing that we have that disclosed and off our back. The part about checking on our father bothers me, but he can't reach us or do anything about us now. It would be good to see that mom is all right and that father didn't somehow die because of that event."

Pat looked confused, "How would he have died from you two having run away?"

"Sally, best you tell Pat the rest after I'm gone. Maybe you don't know me like you think you do. I didn't really know a part of you before last night. I'm leaving to go meet with Bill about real estate."

Sally confused now asked, "Who's Bill, what happened last night? I think you have some things to explain to me too."

James was going to be as far away from that restaurant as possible before those conversations started. Besides, he was really interested in speaking with Bill about his real estate dealings.

It was only a short walk to Bill's office. James could see Bill sitting at his desk thru the window as he walked on the boardwalk to his front door. As quickly as James opened the door, Bill was out of his chair, coming around to shake his hand.

"Son, I mean James, I have to tell you that last night provided me a story that I will be telling for the rest of my life, however long that might be depending if that varmint returns looking for me. What an adventure. One of the most exciting nights of my life. Nothing like my wedding night but exciting none the less." As he laughed and tried to pour coffee at the same time, he spilled some, but paid no attention to it.

"Bill, you should know that Pat and I had a run in with that varmint and four of his friends after we walked out, and you left the opposite direction. The way things were settled, I believe it is safe to say they will never return to this county again. I also think

I should tell you that my name is Morgan, not James. Morgan Sommer to be exact. "as he shamefully looked down.

"James, or Morgan or whoever you are going to be next, why don't you explain a little before we talk business. I'm really confused and want to know who it is I got to know last night. Hell, so far I like all of you." Said Bill.

"I ran away from home with my Sister because we had an abusive father. We traveled from Minnesota and are headed to California to join the gold rush. We changed our names thinking people would be looking for us. Now that we have moved on from that we are changing our names back to our real names. I have also been protecting my Sister, by pretending to be engaged to her. That worked until she met a guy that seemed to capture her attention. In addition, I really like him." Stated James looking for an excepting gesture from Bill.

"Wow, you continue to be full of surprises aren't you. Might that other man be Pat?" shaking his head as he started to laugh. "I think we can cover more of this after we talk a little about business."

Morgan noticed he had several pictures of his wife on his desk and wall. At least he thought it had to be his wife.

"Is this your wife?" picking up a younger looking picture of the two.

"Yes, she has been my partner since grade school back East. We have had one adventure after another. Moving to Houston turned out to be our biggest move. We miss our two sons. They're in college getting a real education. With times changing like they are a man with a good education in business will be able to perform miracles out here and further West. They are two years apart and looking forward to moving out here as soon as they finish up school." said Bill.

"Take it your still single under whatever name. You might be big for your age, but I think your young. Am I guessing close?" said Bill.

"Yes, you are. Too bad you don't size up card players like you do everyone else. My Sister and I are about to head West. We have some interests to check on in the Arizona territory and may not find our way back here for a long time. That's if we survive the extreme weather, Indians, and wild animals and such. I'm just being realistic. I notice by those papers on the wall that you are also an attorney. Is that so?" as Morgan had another thought building.

"Matter of fact I am. I handle a little bit of everything, but my love is in real estate and watching something grow. Kind of like a farmer that grows buildings." Laughing as he pointed to his diploma from law school in Philadelphia.

"I would like to talk to you about having some kind of will, which in case something happens to me certain people get certain things. Then I would like to leave you with a modest amount of money to invest in real estate with the two of us as partners. I'll put up the money and you find the real estate. How much of the company would you think is fair?

"Well, this is a surprise. Let me think a second. Of course, I can help you make out a will and help maintain that if we are in contact. I guess we would have to be in contact if we started a real estate company too. If you put up the money, I would need 10% to run the business." Bill was looking at Morgan like he would have no hesitation.

"Bill, that doesn't sound right." Morgan replied with Bill looking confused.

"I would rather you own 25% so you would put your best work into what we are doing. I think that sounds better, don't you?" Smiling at Bill who was scratching his head.

"Son, I mean to tell you, I'm going to have to teach you something about business, while you can teach me more about cards. In any case I will throw in my services at any time for the will or any other help you need." Shaking hands and laughing they spent the better part of the day getting things done. It was midafternoon and I was just about to leave when the telegraph operator came in the door.

"Your Sister and associate said you were with Bill. Sorry to interrupt you two, but I figured you wanted this one as soon as it got here." Waiting for his next big tip which Morgan gladly provided. At the same time, Morgan told him that he would have a couple more to send before he left which brought a gleam to his eye.

"Yes sir, Mr. Sommer. Be waiting on you when you're ready." He stated as he left.

"May I Bill? Been waiting for this" Bill nodding politely to the interruption.

The telegram said as follows:

2 Schooners by riverboat arrive Houston 2 days with some supplies needed (stop) Funds more than adequate (stop) what do with extra funds (stop) Hello Pat Sally (Stop) Stay contact Joe (Stop)

Morgan couldn't have been more excited that the wagons were arriving in Houston. They wouldn't need to find a coach to get to San Antonio. They were going to start their adventure from here.

Morgan suddenly realized that they would need horses for the wagons and the cost to ready them as they came off the boat. There would also be the need for a place at the stable to store them as they gathered the supplies that they needed. There was a lot of work coming their way.

"Ah Morgan, right? good news I take it. I'm trying to learn how to read your emotions." Said Bill.

"Yes, it is. Turns out our new Prairie Schooners, built by Mr. Joseph Murphy will be arriving here by riverboat in two days. Morgan guessed he was going to have to purchase some horses and supplies here before they headed off to San Antonio and then Castroville.

Bill was familiar with Castroville and Fort Hood known as the edge of the real frontier. When it was time to leave, their business quickly taken care of, there was a large sum of money left behind for their real estate investments and a copy of a will leaving Sally and Pat whatever he had accumulated. Bill held Morgan's hand with both of his hands wishing him Gods speed and offering to help them with their outfitting over the next two days.

As Morgan walked the boardwalk toward the hotel, he noticed across the street was Pat and Sally walking slowly and talking. He sat down on a bench partially hid by a post and a tied-up horse as he watched them hold hands and talk. Morgan was concerned since this was the first man she had ever really spent any time with and yet, he had to admit that if looks told the story, they'd be a couple for life.

That night they were invited to join Bill and his wife for dinner at the café. Morgan, Sally and Pat had all insisted that they didn't want Bill's wife to labor over dinner for them, but to have more time to enjoy the conversation and give Sally and her a chance to know each other, thus the restaurant instead of their home.

It was a great time with Bill introducing them, by their real names, to several other people that stopped in. There was no doubt that Bill knew everyone in Houston. Some had already heard the story about the card game and gave a heartful thanks to Morgan for being there for Bill. His wife gave both Pat and Morgan a kiss on the cheek for having taken care of him that night.

The evening was over far too quickly as they all walked out, saying their good nights. Soon it would be good-byes.

34

Load'em Up

The next morning found them making a list of supplies they needed comparing it to the lists that we had gotten from the Peeples and the Roberts families back in Cairo, Illinois. They still planned to get most of the food supplies in San Antonio before they headed West. They were informed that they still had a good three to four weeks before the next wagon train would be leaving. There wasn't any real schedule. It just mattered as to how many were there that were ready to go and if they had someone to lead them.

They kind of guessed as to what might be coming in with the wagons, but at the time had no idea that Joe had thrown in extra wheels and wagon parts, harnesses etc., not knowing at the time what they would be purchasing for the trip before the wagons showed up.

A big issue would be clothing. They only experienced summer during their runaway and frills on the riverboats. Now they had to get real trail clothes. Pants, dusters, boots. Canvas, rope and the list went on. At one point they had to think about the room they had to carry everything. They were far more fortunate than most others with the two large prairie schooners. Most people were using two wheeled carts pulled by oxen. It was a rough ride. Most people had not even seen a schooner since Joe had just created them. They were just becoming available. They were so grateful that they ran into Joe. At the time they first met they had no idea the role that Joe would play in facilitating their adventure.

Throughout the day they assembled supplies that the local merchant held in storage awaiting the arrival of the wagons. In addition to the smaller supplies they purchased twelve horses and four saddles so they would have saddles to ride in case something happened to the wagons or there wasn't a place along the way to purchase saddles that actually fit them and were to their liking. By evening they were all shopped out, with some serious anxiety starting to set in. They were all wondering how life was about to change.

The next morning had them up early. They all figured to have a good breakfast knowing that this was going to be a busy day. They decided that if the wagons came in today, they would get them set up and stored at the livery stable overnight, ready to hitch up and leave the following morning.

They were just about done with breakfast when a young boy ran in to say that a riverboat was docking with a lot of people on board.

They didn't know what boat the wagons were going to be on, but Morgan had been given some numbers to identify their goods to the officials on the dock. They took their time finishing, knowing that it would be a while before the boat would complete docking and start unloading. Passengers usually get off first and then they would start to hoist the cargo over to the docks.

Morgan had already arranged for some men from the livery stable and blacksmith if necessary, to help assemble the wagons. They didn't have any idea what had to be done but felt it would be good for them to be there also to watch. Then they would know how things worked in case something broke down on the trail, which was bound to happen, so they were told.

It was another hour before they walked to the dock against the groups of people coming off the boat. It was surprising the number of people. Families that for sure were headed West. Most were in trail clothes and ready to be outfitted. They all commented on how it was a good thing they purchased what they needed yesterday before these people showed up.

The first mate was holding a clip board directing the offloading of the cargo. When Morgan asked if he had two prairie schooners to off load, he stopped and commented how he did and that he had never seen anything like them. He called it, "Heading West high on the hog". He chuckled and pointed to one of them being lifted off with a small crane.

Morgan recognized a man from the stables among a group waiting in the shade not far from the dock moving toward the schooners. He waved to Morgan as he moved toward him.

"We'll have these together and ready to hitch up in no time Mr. Goodhue" he stated.

"We can just bring them up back of the hotel when they are ready if that's ok?" said the stable attendant.

"Yes, that would be perfect. Thank you." Giving him a tip up front to pay for a round of beers for the men when they're done.

Walking back to Pat and Sally, Morgan told them that he was going to send a couple more telegrams, stop by and see Bill and catch up with the two of them when the wagons were delivered behind the hotel. Morgan asked if they would mind them watching the men put the wagons together just in case there might be some trick to do something they might want to know if they break down out in desolate countryside.

Bill and Morgan went over to the bank to open an account for their new business. Morgan was introduced to everyone in the bank. It would have been nice to have spent a few more days, as by that time he would have known everyone in this growing hub.

It was midafternoon when Morgan got over to the hotel and caught up with the wagons. Both were hitched up to a couple of horses each that he had purchased as part of an even dozen in total. They were ready for loading. They were drawing attention from people having heard about them and having seen them being assembled. Those that were preparing for the long road ahead admired them.

The three of them with help from the merchant store, livery, and a couple additional places managed to get the wagons loaded and back over to the livery, locked up for the night ready for the next day's adventure.

The day's work was done, and Sally and Morgan were setting out front of the hotel enjoying a moment together without Pat. They felt the evening breeze anticipating the next day's adventure. You could tell that both of them were trying not to show their anxiety. They had both made the decision to go West. In addition to the anxiety they were a little scared and excited.

Out of nowhere Sally said, "Do you ever think about how we got here so far, the friends we have met like Pat, Joe, Henry and his wife and Bill. Do you believe that it was meant to happen in some way?"

Morgan responded, "In what way?"

Looking Morgan straight on so not to miss his reaction, "Do you think God is looking after us and has a mission for us? That's why he had put these people into our lives."

"Wow, now where did that come from. It's enough you constantly say, thank God, or in some way try to get me to think about being God fearing. We got here because you tried to drown yourself because of what a God-fearing father did to you. Am I wrong? I suppose God wanted to make sure we had money, so he laid a drunk out in front of me to rob. Or he had me sit with some bad pokers players I could extort money from. Did God bring us friends, or did we just happen to get lucky with the people we met. I suppose God is responsible for all of that. Sis, you need to take a deep look at the way you're thinking."

She wasn't looking at Morgan, eye to eye from the moment he mentioned their dad. Suddenly, she was silent. Too silent. He had really hurt her. He had cut her deep reminding her of their father and criticizing her faith, all in a couple of comments. It was too late like it always is to take back words that just deeply hurt someone. Someone you didn't want to hurt. She got up and slowly walked inside without saying a word. Morgan was left wondering why, why did she have to bring the God thing up.

As Morgan continued to sit and watch the people walk by and the sun disappear over the horizon, he continued to think about what Sis had said and how cruel his comments were. He still couldn't figure out how she could continue to have faith in God and spew out Jesus talk every other day after what she had gone through. Church and God was represented by their father who for all the years he had studied and claimed to congregation after congregation that having a relationship with Jesus, God's son, was the answer. Did he have a relationship with Jesus? What a hypocrisy. Morgan chuckled at the thought of what a conversation with Jesus might be like.

It was going to be a long day and a very different one tomorrow, so he decided he had better get some sleep. Later as he laid in bed, he kept hearing Sis's comment. Translated, "Was any of the good fortune we had experienced a gift from God for some kind of mission he was preparing them for."

35

Wagons Hoooo!!

They were up with the sun so they could all get an early start, not knowing what the day was going to bring. They had all met up in the main floor of the hotel. It was site to behold to see Sally in jeans looking like one of them referring to Pat and Morgan. Then again Pat and Morgan had not been dressing so casual until now either. Now they all stood there in their riding clothes and side arms, looking like two brand new shinny cowboys and one cowgirl. All of them started laughing at the same time, each observing how the other was dressed. Morgan reminded Sis and Pat why they were dressed this way and carrying guns. It put a slightly more serious tone to what they were about to embark on.

They decided to head over to the restaurant and get a good breakfast before they headed out. It seemed strange to be walking around town, even just over to the restaurant dressed like a wrangler. Not a single head turned so it was only them that seemed to think they would draw attention dressed like this. Not many people knew them, and their dress was not abnormal.

After breakfast, Pat and Morgan went to the stables to hitch up the horses. They paid the livery owner and drove the two teams around and down to the front of the hotel.

Sis was waiting, standing alongside the bags they had kept in the rooms. Not wasting any time, Pat packed the luggage in the back of the wagons as Sally and Morgan got ready to climb up into their seats, Morgan driving one team and Pat the other.

Morgan could tell that Sis was still upset with him since she hadn't said much to him all through breakfast. She was heading his way as he climbed up and offered her a hand to climb on board.

"I'll be riding with Pat." Was all she said as she turned and headed back to Pat's wagon.

Morgan snapped the reins and whistled loudly. The horses knew their que and started pulling everything in the world that Sis and he had.

They had an eight to ten-day trip ahead of them depending on how far they drove the horses each day and the weather. They figured that they should be able to make 20 or maybe 25 miles a day on average. That would put them in San Antonio which was within a day of Castroville. They would be in Castroville in time to join the wagon train that the Peeples and Roberts said they were going to be with.

The excitement wore off in the first couple of hours. Driving a team with a wagon and following the trail had already become work and Morgan's rear was already tired of bouncing up and down on the wagon seat. He kept telling himself that this was a luxury wagon. He was reminded that it had springs and was the most comfortable ride built.

Morgan pulled up on the reins bringing his team to a halt. When he had heard Pat yelling and stopping his team, Morgan yelled back, "This looks like a good enough spot to take a break and give the horses a rest."

There was only an "ok" in response.

They settled down for a little rest along with the horses. It seemed that Sis was keeping her distance from her brother.

Eventually, Morgan had a chance to catch Pat while he was arranging the baggage that had been banging around in the back of his wagon.

Pat spoke first as Morgan looked into the back of the wagon.

"Whatever you said to Sally has left her almost speechless. She won't discuss it with me even. What did you say? Since I'm the one that is having to deal with the awkward silence as we sit next to each other, I feel it might be my business to know."

Morgan responded, "She told me last night that she thinks that all of the good things happening to us and maybe some of the bad are because God is looking out for us. That God is taking care of us because he has something important in store for us."

"Do you so strongly disagree? What did you say that made her silent?" said Pat.

"I just get tired of her always trying to talk about God or Jesus because it reminds me of our father. I don't know how much of that story you know, but I don't think anything that my father did, made him a blessed man. What he did and how he treated the family makes me wonder if there is a God. If I can't get to there being a God, I'm surely not ready to think about His son."

Pat had tied the baggage up inside the wagon and was now on his way out. Morgan stepped back as he climbed out. As he walked over toward Sally, Pat turned and said, "Maybe this trip will give you some time to think about what Sally believes."

They continued on their way, meeting up with an occasional drifter and in one case a couple with two children that decided to turn back before they had really even started, after hearing from some of people going West and some of the soldiers from the Fort Hood what the trail was really like.

Outside of that it was uneventful, as they repeated one day after another until we found ourselves just outside San Antonio. They stopped short the risk of arriving at dark. Sally had only said a handful of words to Morgan. He had thought more about her faith and what it meant to her than anything else since they left Houston. At times, he was so deep in thought that after a while Pat took the lead in his wagon as Morgan's team would slow down and be without anyone really driving them.

The thought of joining the wagon train and meeting up with their new friends from Cairo, Illinois finally helped move his thoughts onto another subject. Morgan couldn't wait for tomorrow to arrive.

36

Waltz and Weisner

Jacob Waltz and his sidekick Jake had a severe case of gold fever. They were ten days out from having left New Orleans. They were on horseback with a couple of burros packing some of the things they would be needing. They had good gear for panning gold from working the creek beds in Georgia and the Carolina's. They were planning on getting the rest of their outfit put together in San Antonio.

With time a wasting, they decided that they would move faster by horseback to San Antonio and Castroville than with a wagon. They had moved along the "Old Immigrant Trail" from New Orleans West.

They rode mostly in silence, but at night they would sit around the fire and talk about how different things were from back in their home country of Germany. The memories were not that good. Since coming to America, they had food every day and even managed to work enough after their time at the plantation to save the money they needed to grubstake themselves for the trip West and do some prospecting.

Sometimes they would talk about their chances of finding gold. Didn't seem like there was enough for all the people answering that devilish call. The mind of a man as he heads out to the gold fields changes. It's almost a sickness the way it creeps into their thoughts and eventually corrupts their common sense.

The two of them swore to each other that they would not let their gold fever overcome them. They mostly wanted a fresh start where they didn't have all the concerns and struggles that they had back home. They weren't afraid of hard work and had already proven that over and over. They just needed the right place to apply it.

Soon they would be riding into San Antonio. They really didn't expect much of a town given what they had already experienced on the trip so far. Yet when they finally arrived the history of seeing the Alamo Mission in the center area of town gave them a real lesson about the type of people that were building America.

They had tied up their horses and burros, not far from the Alamo outside a small salon to take a rest. After they each had a beer in hand, they went out front of the saloon and sat down in a couple of chairs and watched the town. They knew enough English to have a conversation with a couple of men that were already outside enjoying their beverage in the shade.

Jake looked over to one of the men and asked them what had happened at the Alamo that made it so famous.

The man took a drink from his mug, cleared his throat and said. "Well, to start with 189 men died there fighting a Mexican army of 1700. They killed hundreds of the Mexican soldiers before they fell. At one point, they were all given a chance to walk away and they all chose to stay pretty well knowing it was going to be a fight to the death."

"You have to try and imagine what it would have looked like to them to look over that crumbled wall at the campfires of 1700 professional soldiers. I'd guess the fires would make it nearly daylight. It had to be hundreds of fires burning. Then during the day, they would continue to see more soldiers arriving with cannon being set up in a number that would be more than enough to eventually level everything."

"Those were special men alright. That story will be told forever I recon," said Jake

Both Weisner and Waltz sat quietly looking down the street toward the old Alamo, wondering what that battle would have been like. They had heard of numerous battles in Europe and surrounding regions, but except for Napoleons Royal Guard who rode to certain death, they had not heard of another group that was ready to fight to the death and in fact did. This had happened only a few years ago, a few hundred feet from where they sat. It turned out to be a quiet moment of reflection for both men.

They would be looking for a place to bed down for the night and in the morning, they would be getting the rest of their supplies and start the ride out to Castroville near Fort Hood to catch the next wagon train West. Their thoughts about the Alamo slowly turned over in a crazy way to thinking about gold. It was a constant thought that little would distract them from it.

As the sun rose Jacob Waltz was already up and getting ready to ride over to the merchant store. He had told Jake the night before that he wanted to get an early start so they might bed down in Castroville by nightfall. It was roughly 25 miles. That was a long day's ride and he was anxious to get on with it.

Weisner was awoken by Jacob and quickly got ready and mounted up to join him to fulfill purchasing the last of the supplies they needed before heading over to Castroville. On the way over there was one house being built that stood out so much that the two men stopped for a moment to admire it. The house was being built right along the river that ran through San Antonio.

"You two looking to have a house built?" said a man walking up from behind them.

The man startled Weisner and Waltz. At the same time the burros started to act up. Weisner answered above the noise of the burros, "No, headed West. Nice house."

"Gold Rush I bet. Maybe you'll be back and spend all that gold on having a house built here in San Antonio," as he laughed and waited for a response.

Waltz was getting angry when he realized that the man was laughing at the idea of finding gold. Weisner wasn't taking a liking to him either.

"Name's Kampmann, J.H Kampmann. Contractor and Stonemason. Building this house for Major Jeremiah Dashiell. Didn't mean to sound like I was making fun of Prospecting. Just that so many are starting to return. They ride through here never having made it to California. They turned around due to all sorts of misfortune on the trail."

Weisner spoke ignoring his comment about the people returning from out West, "Major must be an important person to be building a house like this."

Kampmann was surprised that the two men didn't know who Major Dashiell was. But these guys were simply passing through.

"Good luck gentleman." As he continued to walk toward the house to see how the construction was doing.

Weisner glanced at Waltz, shrugged his shoulders and the two continued on. In a couple of hours, they were on the trail heading for Castroville. After riding most of the day they found themselves with the sun in their faces as they approached Castroville. They set up their own camp just outside of town on the opposite side they rode in. The town wasn't much as they rode thru.

They crossed the Medina River looking over the general store which stood out again because of the limestone rather than lumber. A couple of buildings were part building and part tent as the town was growing like a mining town. There were a couple of saloons, brothels, and merchants, but nothing fancy.

Seemed like a lot more men than women, likely due to most men thinking they would go out West, strike gold and then send for their wives and children.

37

The Clan Comes Together

~⁖☙

George Roberts and his cousin Abe Peeples had been preparing a long time to head West. Every day they talked about the gold rush. They wondered how James and his fiancé were doing and if they had reached New Orleans. They had found a buyer for their business with the help of Mr. Wakefield, the banker that had gone into business with them.

The two families were planning on meeting three more family members when they reached Castroville. They had all agreed to wait for each other, even if there was another opportunity to hitch up to a wagon train, until they were all there and accounted for. In addition, they were now looking forward to meeting up with James and Sally. It wasn't going to be lonely on the trail.

They were all invited to the banker's house for a barbeque as a going away kind of party. Several other people from town were invited and the group knew that leaving the friends they had made for a wilderness that they really didn't know was going to be difficult. The women would be trying to hold back tears while the men tried to act manly, saying very little for fear their voices would show emotion and that they might even show a tear or two in their eyes.

The group worked right up to the day of the party getting ready to leave. They would head cross country down to Castroville. They had purchased all their supplies. If planned correctly they would be arriving within a week or two of James and Sally and their other family members.

As the day moved toward late afternoon Abe took the opportunity to pull his wife aside just before the party. "life is going to be different starting tomorrow. If there is any doubt about what we are doing, or that we should stay here and raise our family this will be the last time to talk about it."

"Abe, how dare you say this to me at this time. The very day before we leave. If you're having any thoughts about not leaving you better get rid of them. Especially if you think you would be doing me a favor by staying. This is something that was decided on a long time ago. Even the children have grown to be excited about heading West. I have spent a lot of time praying that God will protect our family for this journey and give us a sign we recognize if we are to stay here. The business with Mr. Wakefield, meeting up with James and Sally and then your cousins from Texas joining us are all signs God has given us that are showing the road ahead. Not that we should be afraid and be held here by our comfort. Let's worry about our comfort when we get old. I love you and want you to know that this family is headed West. Are you coming along?"

The last parting comment made Abe break out laughing as they hugged, and he replied how much he loved her. They imagined the same last-minute thoughts were being shared between his cousins and their wives.

"It's time to party" yelled Abe as they all headed on up to Mr. Wakefield's house to join the party already underway.

The neighbors and friends that had already arrived for the barbeque surrounded the prospective travelers, back slapping, hugging, and expressing how much they will all be missed. They knew it was going to be difficult to say goodbye to time-tested friends and neighbors. Abe was thinking it was too bad they couldn't just move the whole town of Cairo west.

The crowd seemed to close in around Mr. Wakefield and his wife Betsy as they approached the group.

Mr. Wakefield spoke first by saying, "Let this be a celebration of the new life our friends have chosen. Friends stay friends forever and we need to let you know that if you change your mind and think about coming back, remember, you'll simply be coming home."

Just as Mr. Wakefield finished, his wife, Betsy said, "Know that we will be thinking and praying for your safety and success. Take comfort that you have a great group of friends that will pray for you every day. You don't forget someone you pray for every day."

"Anybody want some ribs? Let start this celebration!" yelled Mr. Wakefield as everyone followed him and his wife to the rear of their house. The back yard was busy with smells of ribs on the grill along with a vast number of other food dishes. There was chicken prepared in every manner.

The group was reminded as they looked over the tables of food that they may never see a spread or variety of food like this again. The trail was going to be very different when it came to meal selections.

As dusk turned into night, the party started breaking up. Mr. Wakefield took the opportunity to invite the Roberts and Peeples into the house as the last of their friends left with more hugs and kisses.

"I just wanted to talk to you all about our friends, James and Sally." Said Mr. Wakefield as everyone became silent as if expecting horrible news.

"A telegram arrived the other day from Jim explaining a situation that none of us were aware of. He wanted me to inform you all before you meet up with them in Castroville, so you would have some time to think about their predicament before you all arrive. They hope and pray that you will understand and not think that they were in any way deceiving you. After making an admission to me with this telegram he asked me to forgive him and would understand if I didn't want to be in business with him. That he would respect me for the offer and never forget the opportunity I gave him. If I so chose to go forward with our business arrangement, he would never deceive or lie to me again."

"I wanted to think about this a couple of days before telling you about it, so I could clearly make up my decision. I think it important to know that I feel proud to know and be a business partner with Jim or should I say Morgan and Sally, his Sister. I hope you will feel the same after I explain his dilemma."

Abe jumped up taking the floor, "Do you mind backing up a bit? Did I hear you say Sister? Who are we talking about? Who is Morgan?"

Mr. Wakefield cut him off waving his hands in the air as he proceeded to speak, "That's a part of the dilemma. Please just sit down and listen. This won't take long."

"Sally is James's Sister and his real name is Morgan. Sally and Morgan Sommer. He claimed that she was his fiancé- to protect her and help hide him. Remember that he wants you all to know this. He and Sally ran away from home. They had an abusive father that was a pastor, so they jumped on a riverboat, took different names and suites, leaving everyone they ever knew and anyone that would be looking for them, they appeared to be just a couple of rich kids going to New Orleans to get married."

"Is he or they rich? They bought all sorts of things and dressed like they had a lot of money. Where did they get that? What are we to believe if they can come up with a lie like that?" stated Geo firmly.

Mr. Wakefield now stood up to emphasize his statements. "I believe that we met a couple that needed help. They needed friends and people that acted like family to them. We all seemed to fill that need putting some love into their lives, which is why Morgan felt he had to tell us the truth. As far as the money, he admitted that he stole most of it with the sincere intension of paying it all back with interest. He realizes that what he did in obtaining the money was wrong and playing poker with old men while they got drunk and lost all judgement wasn't right either, but he had to protect his Sister and survive somehow. I think they both need us very much. I only hope that when you meet up with them that you have thought about what short falling you have experienced and what you would have done in the same position."

"I guess I've said my piece, so I bid you safe travel, may God be with you."

As the two clans filed out, Abe was last and before he went out the back door, he turned to Mr. and Mrs. Wakefield and said, "Don't worry about them. We'll look out for them when we catch up with them. I think we can adopt them into our family."

Laughing he went out the door to the soft sound of Mr. Wakefield saying, "Thank God."

With the wagons, all pulled together and the families ready to head out, Abe spoke up, so all the family could hear him. "I told Mr. Wakefield last night as I was walking out that we would be looking out for Morgan and Sally when we meet up with them. I believe their reason for telling us what they did, was mostly to protect his Sister. I believe that to be admirable. Does everyone else here think about the same or do you want time to think about it?"

Peeples spoke up for his family, "I heard you as you spoke last night and agree to the part where you said, "We will adopt him into our family". I think that's a right good idea. Any objections?"

Everyone, including kids cheered and yelled in agreement.

"Good, now let's get on the trail so we can meet up with the rest of our family!" said Abe.

38

Confessions and Confusion

The days went by and they were now approaching San Antonio. The three of them had been on the trail for a week. They learned a lot and found out that making camp was a lot more work than walking over to the hotel and eating in a restaurant. They were getting into a rhythm, unhitching the horses, feeding them, starting a fire, cooking, and a few other tasks everyday one after the other.

Pat seemed to be getting very close to Sally. She still hadn't spent much time talking with Morgan. Her time was being spent with Pat except for two nights ago. Pat was tending to the horses and must have been told by Sally to take this time so she could speak with Morgan.

Morgan knew by her look that something was up, as she approached, but he didn't expect a sermon.

"I need to speak with you, Morgan." Said Sally as she sat next to him with the fire starting to finally blaze up a little.

"Is there something still bothering you?" Morgan said.

"Yes. I want to know if you remember the lessons that we learned in church. Do you think the Bible has meaning or have you decided that you know what is best? Have you really deserted your faith?"

Sally continued, "Regardless of what happened regarding our dad, it was not God's doing. If it was, it was to fulfill a part of a larger picture. Look at where we are and what we are doing. This is incredible and it would have only happened with God's blessing."

"Are you telling me that God approved and wanted me to steal the money I stole? Did he want me to lie about who we are and deceive our friends?" Morgan responded.

He continued, "I remember our lessons and I have read the Bible more than once. Not lately, but I have read it. I believe in God but asking for forgiveness every time I steal or play cards gets tiring. He might just be done with me. Why don't you work on Pat?"

"Pat doesn't need working on. I don't think you know him as well as you think you do. Pat accepted Christ years ago and tries to live his faith and accepts that God acts in mysterious ways You my brother on the other hand used to be a strong Christian. Do you remember how we spoke over and over about God and what heaven would be like? What it would be like to speak with Jesus? Remember us praying together about mom and dad, asking for His help?" said Sally trying to find a nerve to help Morgan remember his early convictions.

"Lots of good that did. A faithless pastor as a father. The only thing that served him right was me nailing him to the headboard of the bed!" realizing what he just said in my haste.

"Oh my gosh! You didn't just say that you nailed him to the headboard? What does that mean? Don't look away and don't you dare walk away or I swear I will never talk to you again. This trip is about to get very lonely for you." Screaming as she said it, "Talk to me, now! What happened back home with Dad?"

"When I saw your room and figured out what he had done to you, I lost it. He was sleeping when I hit him in the head with a chunk of wood to knock him out. Then I pulled him up further to the headboard and nailed his hands to it. After that I broke his legs for good measure. Then I left! He had driven you to kill yourself. He is lucky I didn't kill him, and take my time doing it."

Then Morgan looked at his Sister in pain given the horror in her face. She had her mouth open a bit and her eyes looked wide and crazy. She couldn't speak. In even more pain she looked past me, over my shoulder. As he turned around, there was Pat with the same type of expression. He had come over while she was yelling before Morgan's explanation and heard everything he said.

Morgan stared at the ground and realized that the rage and hate for his dad was just as strong now as his love for his Sister. Love and hate are separated by a thin line. This was not his best moment, but it was one that was predictable and now had to be dealt with.

'I have spoken out this time but never again. That's the entire story. It will never be told by me again. You are free to tell anyone you want in the future to let people know what kind of person I really am." Stated as Morgan looked around with nowhere to go.

There was complete silence the rest of the night. He remembered staying awake most of the night thinking about what he had done and whether he had lost any and all connections with God. He had been a Godly child and Sis and he had prayed together as they mostly asked for things as kids do, but they prayed. It had developed an extreme closeness. He hadn't prayed for a few years now. When his prayers about his dad were not answered Morgan guessed he felt more compelled to handle his dad the way he thought best.

Sally and Morgan had not said anything to each other since they had gotten up. They were now approaching San Antonio. The day was clear and dry as the dust floated up from the activity in the streets. They pulled up to the livery stable to see if could bed down the horses and store the wagons for the time they would be there. Morgan didn't know how long or what type of business Pat had with the US Mounted Rifles, but he knew it would be at least a couple of days and then they would head out to Castroville.

Pat and Sally headed off toward the hotel leaving Morgan behind without concern. He knew he had to sleep in the bed he made. He decided to walk the town a little while he continued to think. Think about what he needed to do to correct this situation. His stomach reminded him that he did some of his best thinking with a full stomach. The thought of eating in a restaurant seemed attractive, even before checking into the hotel.

Pat and Sally had hardly spoke since the outburst two nights before.

"Sally, can we sit down and talk after we get our rooms? I have some work to do. I must find Captain Jack and discuss the reasons I'm on this trip. But before that, I really need to talk to you. Is that alright? Let's get our rooms." Pat said.

If the look on Sally's face could tell a story it would be of a man about to leave a woman. The woman had fallen in love with the man who she knew had to tell her that he chose to move on. Her history and that of Morgan's was more of a burden than he had first imagined dealing with.

It only took a quarter of an hour to get rooms, Sally freshened up and as Pat knocked on her door, she had a chill shake her whole body. She opened the door. To look at Pat standing tall and handsome filling the frame of the doorway, she wished she had the words to make him hers.

In an attempt to avoid crying in public over his rejection, she asked if they might simply have their conversation in her room, inviting him to come in to sit in the only chair while she sat on the edge of the bed.

Pat was a little uncomfortable about being in the room alone with Sally. What would this look like to Morgan if he came looking for Sally, but to look into her eyes made any concern fade.

Pat started speaking as he sat down. "Sally, this is not going to be an easy conversation. Best to say, I learned a lot about myself the other night when Morgan said his piece."

Sally looked down realizing she was about to hear how different his family is than hers and that he would not be able to handle it. He was going to tell her that it would be best for the two of them to be friends and not get romantically involved any further. Sally decided to take a quiet offensive action and pray without speaking.

(silently) "Lord, I need your help and want to serve your will. Morgan has gone astray and now Pat is about to tell me he is leaving. If this is your wish, I will try and understand, but know that I'm in love with Pat. Give me strength"

"Sally are you listening to me?" said Pat

"Yes, Yes, I am, I'm sorry, I just had some distracting thoughts." As she gathered herself.

Pat started again, "Sally, I want you to think about what Morgan did. His anger and his actions were because of you. As a brother, he must love you a great deal to risk doing what he did. The degree of his actions was excessive, but he didn't kill him. He could have easily shot him. If he was caught, the punishment won't be much different."

"There are two things I want you to consider. The first is how much your brother loves you. The second (as he stopped speaking for what seemed minutes) is how much I love you."

Sally looked up completely speechless. What was happening. She got the part about her brother and was ready to forgive him and talk our what he had done, but the second thing. The second thing to think about was Pat's love for her.

This was becoming very confusing, trying to figure out why he would tell her he loved her just before he was going to leave, or was he?

Sally spoke next, "If you love me, why are you leaving? I know that my family is not what you want in your life, or a woman who has deceived you by not even using her real name. I'm so sorry about all this, but I really wish you would reconsider. Please don't leave. Not like this."

Pat's face had one big question mark on it. "Where am I going? Do you know something that I don't? Are you leaving me? I'm a little confused. No, actually I am completely confused."

"OK, let's slow down and talk this out." Said Sally as she tried to calm her emotions.

"You said you love me", she said first.

"Yes, I do." Said Pat still looking confused.

Sally continued, "You're not leaving, maybe?'

"What! Maybe leaving? Not without you. I want it to be wherever you're going. What's the problem here. Do you love me?" Pat said.

It was as if her prayers were answered. That fast, she was just told that the man she loved, loved her and was only going where she was. Under her breath there was a quiet, "Thank you Lord, thank you" and then she burst out, "Oh Yes! Yes! Yes! I love you so much Pat, I don't ever want to be without you."

Pat rose as did Sally to embrace. As they leaned backed and quietly looked at each other, Sally moved first to capture the moment with a kiss. As they kissed, they lost their balance and fell back on the bed. It was a long and passionate kiss. When they broke it off, they both jumped up knowing that if they remained on the bed, their passions rising, things would happen that they might regret later as too much too soon.

Before they headed out the door, Pat reached out and pulled Sally to him. Holding her tight up against him as they kissed, he felt the heat from her body and his hand felt the delicate curve of her back. Once again, they stepped back, straightened up and headed out to get something to eat.

As they entered the restaurant, they had a glow about them. One that Morgan even noticed was different as he sat back in a corner trying to enjoy his meal.

The moment that Sally saw Morgan she ran to him, leaned over and hugged him before he could even stand up. Right behind her was Pat tipping his hat and extending his hand for a handshake.

"OK, what's going on? Did you two find the mother lode or something?" said Morgan.

"In a way, "stated Pat giving Sally a very loving look.

"You didn't go out and get married without me, did you? I didn't think you two were speaking to me." Said Morgan with a reserved kind of smile.

"Brother let's just forget about the other night and write it off to brotherly love. After speaking with Pat, I have a completely different take on it. We didn't find gold, but we found love. And no, we didn't and wouldn't run off and get married without your blessing. Besides Pat hasn't asked me yet." Sally running off at the mouth.

"Yet? Seems there's a lot of love in the room all of a sudden," said Morgan as they laughed and sat down to join him.

39

US Mounted Rifles
(Texas Rangers)

The legendary Captain John (Jack) Coffee Hays.

With breakfast over, Pat informed Morgan that it was time to get to work and find Captain John (Jack) Coffee Hays and see what the Captain will think of the new Colt 1851 Navy Revolver he was sent to show him.

Captain Hays was familiar with the new Navy Colt. He had supported the development having used the legendary Dragoon revolvers from Sam Colt. He had even assigned one of the men in his command, Samuel Walker to work with Colt on the design which led to the Navy Revolver. Hays carried two Dragoons which were so heavy that they were usually in a holster slung over the saddle. The stories of Captain Hays riding into battle with his Dragoon pistols was legendary. They were the most powerful handguns made. His escapades made them famous. Pat couldn't convey to Morgan how excited he felt Captain Hays would be to receive them. Specifically, his new revolvers.

Morgan offered to help Pat carry the crate of hardware over to the ranger's office once they knew he was there. Pat treated his crate of firearms in the same manner as Morgan treated his satchel of money. Neither left eithers sight for very long. Both seemed to know that their individual treasures were going to change their lives.

A young boy was walking by the hotel as the two walked out of the hotel restaurant to take in the morning air. Instead of walking over to Hay's office Pat yelled out to the boy walking by who was about 10 to 12 years old and told him that he would pay him a nickel if he would run down to Captain Jack's office and see if he was there. The boy was running off almost before he finished his sentence.

"I might have gotten lazy on the river trip", as he moved a few feet over to a rocking chair on the porch, watching the boy run off disappearing around the next corner.

Morgan laughed, "I guess I can handle that other rocker as I let my breakfast settle a bit."

"What are you going to do after this meeting with the Mounted Rifles if it goes well. Heading back to Connecticut?" asked Morgan. The question was a loaded question and Pat knew it well.

Morgan, not hearing an immediate answer looked over at Pat who was staring into the distance, totally lost in the many options one has at certain pinnacles of one's life. The answer to this question would disclose a selection of options far different than if he would have been asked the same question a month ago. For now, the options from the mind continued to push hard against those of the heart.

"You don't have to answer that question for me right now, but you know you're going to have to come up with an answer fairly soon." Said Morgan signaling Pat that he knew all too well what and how his thoughts were in conflict.

Pat now drawn into thinking about Morgan's question was concentrating on one of the options and that was where his relationship with Sally was headed. If he listened to his heart, he would be making that all important proposal. Yet he knew they were young and seemed to be headed in different directions of the country soon. He was breathing the morning air in a quiet shallow manner now as Morgan studied the trance that Pat seemed to be drawn into with deep thought.

Pat broke out of his trance with the sudden crack of the boy's voice coming near him yelling, "He's over there, mister. He's there right now and said to come on over."

The boy looked like a dog panting for a treat as the nickel he was promised was flipped into the air. With a quick catch, the boy was running off, likely to the candy case in the merchant store.

"If you'll give me a hand with the crate in my room, I'd like to go right over to the Captain Jack's Headquarters now." Pat stated asking Morgan for a helping hand at the same time.

"Let's do it" replied Morgan.

A few minutes later they were walking toward the Mounties office carrying Pat's treasured cargo. The crate seemed well balanced with the handles and two carrying it. The weight of the couple dozen Navy Colts inside was well distributed. The journey to deliver these had been a long one for Pat.

Before they even got to the office, a small collection of Jack's men, anxious to see the new weapons, came walking out of the office. A couple of them generously offered to carry the crate and proceeded to take it inside.

Introductions were being made quickly as Pat and Morgan entered the US Mounted Rifles' headquarters. Time suddenly seemed to slow down as Captain Jack walked into the room from the rear of the building somewhere. His stride seemed as long as he was tall. He had holsters carrying two very heavy five shot, .44 caliber Dragoons, a reminder again of what he and his men made famous throughout Texas.

"So glad to see you made the trip. I was told you would probably show up soon. I'm leading a wagon train to the West Coast but intended to wait as long as I could so I wouldn't have to leave that crate there behind. This is a glorious day!"

"As you well know, for those here that don't know, our own Sam Walker made some suggestions which our friend Samuel Colt added to make these creations as he pulled one of his 5 pounder Walker Colts out of its holster. Especially proud to have it called the Walker Colt. I hear these are lighter, so I won't have to have shoulder straps connected to my holster just to hold the weight of these things."

From the stories Morgan had heard, he could imagine the Captain and his men riding into battle firing both revolvers. At his side Morgan could imagine his close friend Chief Flacco and the Apache warriors. They rode together in many campaigns against the Comanches. He and his men known to carry the fight, being labeled "Los diablos Tejanos", the Texas Devils.

Jack didn't speak much, but when he did, you would have thought he should be a Politician. Now that he was done speaking, everyone remained silent for a moment until Jack made one more statement, "Let's get on with this unveiling!"

The men raised the crate up onto a sturdy table and pried off the top to revel twenty-two pistols covered in grease all sticky with straw bedding around them. What a beautiful sight. These were 36 caliber, lighter than the 5-pound Walker Colt. Still the crate was well over 120 pounds. The other huge improvement was that it held six rounds. First named the Colt Revolving Belt Pistol it became identified quickly as the Colt 1851 Navy pistol.

The men immediately started to pull out and clean the revolvers. As they handed them out and around, the men kept making statements like, "I could ride in and out of hell with two of these."

It didn't go unnoticed to Captain Jack that two of the two dozen were missing and that the young stranger who walked in with Pat was carrying two of them in holsters similar to Captain Jacks.

As Pat introduced himself formerly to the Captain. The Captain seemed to have more of an interest in Morgan, who was quiet and standing out of the way.

"My friend Pat, maybe you would introduce me to your one-man army or security man in the corner. Quiet... yet seemingly formable in conflict I would guess, as an indication of his silence and hard stare. Likely has good instincts. I also see that he is wearing two of the twenty-four revolvers that we were expecting to receive." The Captain speaking slowly, almost calling out Morgan.

Pat spoke up quickly realizing there was a tension rising in the room. "Captain Hayes, I would like you to meet my very dear friend Morgan Sommer. Morgan's actions are responsible for the successful delivery of the twenty-two revolvers in the crate. "

At this point the room seemed crowded. Then the Captain reached out to shake Morgan's hand. I guess a friend of Pat's is a friend of mine. Think I'll clean up a couple of these pistols myself, so we can go out back and see how they perform. What do say Morgan, shall we?"

Morgan replied, "I would enjoy that. They're a bit heavy, but very accurate. Haven't had a situation that I had to use them yet other than target practice."

Sharing a pot of coffee while everyone cleaned their guns, it seemed that the Captain and Morgan struck a silent bond in a professional/business sense.

Captain Jack went on to talk about his planned expedition leading a wagon train West of New Yorkers that had traveled to Texas. They were going to take a cutoff called Cooke's Wagon Road (later to be called the Tucson Cutoff). Captain Hayes was destined to become the Sheriff of San Francisco County (and one of the founders of Oakland County, appointed surveyor general of California by the President of the United States in years to come).

Before we had a chance to go out back and fire a few rounds, a rider came into town. Dismounting and landing at a run into the headquarters, he was yelling about his people being attacked by Comanchero's about ten miles West. Everyone in the room faced the Captain as if by order.

"Five-day provisions. We ride within the hour. Straight through to Castroville and Ft. Hood if we don't find them. Men moving in every direction. Everyone grabbing a new Colt with ammo for the trail. Within half an hour, horses were mounted, saddles packed, and guns loaded. It was as if Pat and Morgan weren't there. They had moved out to the porch right away to observe the activity and get out of the way.

Before riding off, Captain Jack yelled over from his mount, "See you in Castroville or Ft. Hood if your headed that way direct."

The heat and dust kicked up by a dozen men riding out lingered in the air until everyone in the street was probably thinking about getting a drink to wash it down. Morgan and Pat decided to act and let their adrenalin go down over a cool beer.

The conversation over Sally picked up quickly as soon as Pat and Morgan sat down in the saloon to have that cool beer. The mere mention of Sally by Morgan caused Pat's anxiety to start to peak.

"just stop a minute, just give me a minute. Did you, or haven't you thought that it could have been us out there that the Comanches might be killing off right now or worse. By the time those men get out there, it will likely be all over and not a pretty picture. Even in a wagon train, it is still just numbers. More settlers, more Comanches, Apache's or Comancheros. I don't want to risk Sally to that!" said Pat, picking up tension and volume in his voice.

Morgan could understand what Pat was saying. He was so taken by watching Jack's men saddle up, that he wasn't thinking about the people out on the trail that were likely all dead by now. Knowing what the Comancheros did to captives, one prayed that they had either fought them off or that they saved their last bullet for themselves.

"I think you had better stop and think about who you are talking about. The biggest mistake you could make right now is to act by telling Sally you won't have her head West because you won't allow it. You better calm down and weigh what it is your thinking of. As much as she might love you, be very careful about demanding what she will or won't' do. She is not your ordinary farm girl looking for a man to take care of her." Morgan replied.

They were both now quiet thinking about the people out on the trail and what might be happening.

Over the next two days everyone waited for word about the settlers and whether some or any had survived. Then in the afternoon of the third day a rider came into town who was one of the Jack's men.

Once people heard that one of them had returned, it seemed most of the town came to gather outside of their headquarters to hear about what had happened.

Pat, Sally and Morgan joined the rest and headed over to hear for themselves what had happened. The man came out of the front door to address the crowd. You could tell as he looked down, avoiding any eye contact that he was uncomfortable facing or speaking to a crowd. More than that, it implied that we were about to get bad news.

"Sorry folks. Wish someone else was talking to you right now. I'll keep this short. By the time we got to them people out there on the trail they were all dead. Don't want to say any more about how they died. If you're a relative or something we can talk about it in the office. Otherwise it wouldn't be proper to carry this on any further amongst the women and children" as he turned and went back inside.

As Morgan looked around, you could read the fear in people's eyes. They were probably wondering if these Comancheros might be so bold as to attack a town like San Antonio. With a population of three thousand, many of them were women, children, and shop owners, we wondered how many Comancheros were there and are we under any threat here. It was a thought in many minds, but no one asked the question.

That evening as the three of them had dinner, they couldn't help but think about those poor people. One question Morgan continued to ask himself was why. Why would God, which he was always told was a loving God let those poor settlers get killed and in such a horrific way. That's when by chance, Sally said, "May God have mercy on their souls".

That was all that had to be said to set Morgan off. Once again, he had to hear these references to a loving God when so much was in question and so obviously wrong.

"Why would God need to have mercy on their souls unless you're talking on behalf of the Comancheros. They are the ones that need Gods mercy. Sally! I know you mean well, but can we stop this talk about a loving God that allows these things to happen."

Sally replied as Pat remained quiet, "Don't you remember what we were taught? Have you forgotten that this world is Satan's world, not God's? When God threw Satan out, this world became his, filled with sin. Satan rules over this earth. He is constantly spreading his evil in every form and fashion he can. He is everywhere, even here in Texas."

Pat knew better than to jump into a charged conversation between brother and Sister. Especially about God and religion. Morgan on the other hand felt truly conflicted. He remembered what he had been taught and what he had read in the Bible. He just couldn't understand how it all fit together. It seemed better to take Pat's lead and remain silent.

40

The Gathering

~◎

A few more settlers each day would come into San Antonio, passing thru to Castroville to hook up with a wagon train. Their numbers were increasing because a couple of wagon trains were numbering up to leave soon. One was headed up by the famous Kit Carson. He charged as much as $8000 to lead a train to the California gold rush. A sum large enough for the average man to retire on. Trail bosses, merchants, gamblers, and thieves were all making a lot of money off the number of people seeking their dream in the wild west.

The reality would sink in after a few days on the trail. A good day on the trail would be fifteen to twenty-five miles. It was one thousand miles to Salt River (Phoenix) and over six hundred miles further to Sacramento where most of the miners in the wagon train were headed.

Pat and Sally were spending nearly all their time together. Breakfast, lunch and dinner. Add in the walks and short rides around the countryside and one could see their love for each other exploding.

They had decided that it was getting near time that they move on down the trail to Castroville themselves. They had agreed to meet up with the Roberts and Peeples families in San

Antonio, but time was running short. They had received word that they were on their way and would arrive soon. Morgan was also informed that more of their relatives would be coming up from Southern Texas to join the wagon train. They could leave word that they had moved on to Castroville to wait for everyone, but they didn't feel comfortable after saying they would be here when everyone arrived.

The day before they had decided again among themselves to leave. Morgan kept delaying every decision every time they set a date until the decision was made for them. The day of coming together arrived. Slow moving with their own little train of Prairie Schooners, came the Roberts and Peeples. Nobody gave much attention except for a glance or two when more of those prairie wagons came into town, but that changed when Sally spotted them coming down the street. After Sally screamed, all the wagons pulled up as the women jumped down to rush Sally. It was an incredibly warm reception.

With all the screaming and commotion going on, it wasn't but a few minutes that Morgan and Pat joined the celebration. The men at this point simply moved the wagons over and climbed down for hugs and handshakes. It was as if they were surprised, wondering if Morgan and Sally were going to wait for them, and then out of nowhere, here they all were.

Morgan introduced Pat to everyone starting with Abe. Everyone decided to meet at the restaurant as soon as they had left their rigs at the stable. They were going to camp on the edge of town, but right now it was time to catch up.

As strange as it might seem, the whole group wasn't in the restaurant more than a couple of hours getting the stories from Morgan and Sally's trip on the trail, when the rest of their family members from South Texas walked in. There seemed to be Roberts clan everywhere. The members from South Texas looked a lot like their cousins from Cairo. So much so that you could easily tell who was and wasn't related.

The atmosphere was one of excitement with everyone enjoying the massive reunion. The by standers had smiles on their faces to see so many people, so happy in the moment. After a while as everyone relaxed and got their emotions under control, the men decided to drift off to the saloon across the street. The women were already off in conversation describing their experiences on the trail to San Antonio and what was to be expected moving on to California.

As the group of men moved outside, Geo Roberts lead the way. He seemed to take the position of patriarch of the family with nine more of the Roberts clan following him. Pat and Morgan were trying to remember names, but there were too many too fast. It was even more confusing to say Mr. Roberts, because you would have several men turn to respond. When that happened in the saloon it filled the room with laughter. Then there was a round of Mr. Roberts calling over to Mr. Roberts to the next Mr. Roberts until everyone, including bystanders were laughing and calling everyone Mr. Roberts. The drinks flowed freely, and the men had story after story of their journey to San Antonio. The cousin from Texas with fewer stories due to the short rather uneventful trip as compared to their counterparts from Cairo.

Later that evening as conversation moved to the serious side, questions came up to Pat and Morgan, and if we had heard about the trail ahead. It was difficult having to tell them about the Comancheros and what happened to the settlers only a couple of days earlier. The faces of the men had a sobering look as they heard the details of the attack and thought about their families.

Adventure was one expectation, survival another. The men decided not to tell their wives about the attack until they were ready to leave Castroville. They would try to comfort them in the fact that there was strength in numbers and the wagon train would likely have forty to fifty wagons and plenty of men and woman that knew how to shoot to defend themselves.

As the evening came to an end, everyone said their good-nights and went on their way to tend to their livestock and settle into their bed rolls. Pat, Sally, and I retired to our hotel rooms. The three spoke about how they were appreciating their hotel more and more as it got closer and closer to living on the trail.

The following morning the decision had been made from the night before to get the families together to plan their move to Castroville. The group was large enough, with enough well-armed men to fend off any attack between San Antonio and Castroville. It was only a one-day trip.

With everyone assembled, Geo and Abe took the liberty of starting the meeting by notifying the women that a pervious group had been attacked going from San Antonio to Castroville. The response was expected. Concern but determined. These women already knew the trip was not going to be easy. The other surprise that an attacker might not expect was that every single one of the women not only had a gun but knew how to shoot. With families at risk, they could easily shoot to kill.

The decision was made to leave early the next morning so they would have plenty of time to make the trip and get to Castroville while it was still daylight. There would be no rush to find and make camp. Just as fast as the meeting broke up, everyone was headed in a different direction.

I heard Geo speak out, "Morgan, we haven't had much time to talk one on one," as he turned towards me.

Geo was usually quiet in voice but strong in character. He took on the look of a man that knew the trail and the hardships like the back of his hand.

Morgan decided to speak first, "It seems like a long way from Cairo. I did want to ask you how Mr. and Mrs. Wakefield were doing the last you knew."

"They were just fine. Mr. Wakefield continues to speak highly of you. I would guess that he feels he knows you better than yourself at times. Anyway, they continue to talk about how they wish they were young enough to make this their adventure. Guess they will have to be satisfied hearing through us. Right Morgan?" Stated Geo as he glanced away from Morgan, but strongly awaiting his response.

"Mr. Wakefield has put a lot of faith in both of us. I felt more like a son to him rather than a business partner when we were together." Said Morgan.

"So, did he. So, did he. I just wanted to say that Mr. Wakefield informed all of us about you, Morgan, and your Sister Sally. You might have been thinking that no one knew yet because no one mentioned anything tonight. I even heard you called James a couple of times at the saloon. We know and were ok with it. Just felt you needed to know up front. Got to get ready for tomorrow." As Geo turned and headed back to his wagon.

Returning to the hotel, Morgan found Sally and asked her to meet him for coffee or tea in the restaurant.

"Sally. I want you to know that I think you and Pat seem like a great couple. Your falling in love with him, aren't you?" Morgan stated.

"Brother, I've already fallen. I love everything about him. He is gentle, yet strong. He already looks out for me and feels he needs to protect me. I've only had that feeling of protection from you. Are you concerned?" in response.

"I just want you to be happy. This trail is going to be rough on all of us. Nobody really knows what to expect. It is important that I know that you are doing this for yourself and your own desires.

I feel like I have forced you this direction since we ran away." Said Morgan with a sad look."

"Morgan. If you wouldn't have taken me away, I would never have met Pat. I really believe that Pat is the one I want to be with. I love you for being the brother that no one should have to rely on the way I have with you. Now I think you can feel that Pat is the right person to take on some of that responsibility."

"To bring up another subject you don't care for, I feel that you need to think more about who you are. I'm so scared that you might become someone that is Godless. And in addition, runs from relationships. This new land we are headed for has less God and good woman than anywhere I can imagine. I'm afraid of what you might become. I can't help but think about some of the things you have done that already shock me. I took the liberty of purchasing this at the merchant exchange as a gift to you. I want to give it to you as we set off on the trail ahead."

Sally reached in her bag an pulled out a small but complete Bible. She quietly handed it to Morgan.

Proceeding to speak, "Please understand that I love you and want you to have God as a comfort more than a gun. I have seen you practice with your guns. Your quite good. But it is more important to have God in your life to give you the kind of comfort and support that a gun can't. Please don't forget that or get angry at me when I bring it up," Said Sally with tears in her eyes.

"I'm trying to work out where I am with God, Sis. I really am. In a strange way I feel that we have experienced several miracles just getting to where we are. I know there is a God and I believe that. I just don't know how to connect right now. It may come as a surprise but I'm trying Sis. Now go find Pat and enjoy the day. Tomorrow things are going to be a lot different," as Morgan remained thinking about what she had said. Out in the frontier it seemed that someone could be whoever they wanted to be and do about anything they wanted to do. With easy temptations, she knew more about the challenge of being a good person than he did.

Deciding to go for a ride on his own, Morgan saddled up and rode along the San Antonio river a way until he found a comfortable place with grass for his horse to graze and a nice place to sit next to the water and take some more time to reflect on Sally's comments. Morgan decided to take a couple of hours for the first time since the journey started to sort his thoughts. Sally had him doing a lot of thinking. He knew what she had said was real. Even though he had fought with her over the subject, today he was remembering what it was to pray. Even with the failure to understand God, Morgan felt the need to ask Him for help. He had his Bible in hand.

First, he pulled the saddle from his horse and laid it in the tall green grass to make a pillow of sorts. It was such a beautiful day, clear sky, except for a few big white on white clouds. The air carried the smell of the surroundings, the grass, the river and of course the early fall season. The leaves were just starting to fall. Not enough to show any real change yet, which you could anticipate would be beautiful when the forests along the river exploded in their fall colors.

"God. God. God" Morgan repeated out loud as he thought about his earlier conversation with his Sister. How could she have such belief and faith in God after what she had experienced. A father, a pastor had abused her, and he considered the possibility that their mother knew what was happening also. If a pastor couldn't keep his life straight, there seemed no hope for the rest. Sally would continue to refer to God's bigger picture.

Still, why would a loving God allow such a thing? Especially to someone like Sally who had such strong faith. If He was as is described in the Bible, all seeing, how could He not see what was happening? Why wouldn't He have stopped it or revenged what happened? Why was it up to Morgan to seek revenge?

His thoughts were only beginning to pour out. He remembered thinking about stories in the Bible where Jesus lost his temper, turned the tables of the money changers in the temple or worst yet when God rid the earth of the human race except for Noah and his family.

The loving God didn't seem so loving at times in some of the Old Testament stories. So why would He stand by and allow this abuse. Morgan kept trying to think of the stories where God struck out because of his disappointment. Where He destroyed the enemies of his people. Wasn't Sally clearly one of His people? Whether it was plagues, drowning with floods, empowering forces over his enemies, it seemed a simple task to have given his father a heart attack, anything to get rid of him before the abuse to his Sister would have even started.

The time went by quickly. It would be getting dark in a couple of hours and friends were not used to him riding off on his own so they might think something happened if he didn't start back. With his thoughts still mixed, between God, his Sister, the long road ahead and the recent past couple of months, he looked up to see someone walking along his side of the riverbank. Walking, sprinting at times and crouching low as if hiding as they moved towards him.

Whoever it was, they hadn't noticed him. As Morgan watched, the person seemed to be more concerned about looking back and at the woods adjacent to the riverbank as if someone might be following them. Morgan lost view of the person at times because of the underbrush and trees along the riverbank, but as the person drew closer, he could make out that it was a woman. It was an Indian woman.

41

Strangers In Love

It didn't take long for the Indian woman to get within a few yards of Morgan. Morgan kept out of sight, but now he didn't want to scare her by surprising her as he was within talking distance.

She heard his horse before she noticed him. She bolted and jumped back, holding a gun out that looked too big for her small hands to even hold.

"Who are you? What do you want?" said the woman with fear in her voice and her hands, that held the gun badly shaking.

"Hold on miss, please don't point that gun at me with your hands shaking like they are. I don't mean any harm; I was simply resting here. You can see, my horse isn't even saddled. Are you all right?' Morgan asked hoping he wasn't going to leave this world with a reckless shot from a woman holding a hand cannon.

She stared at him and remained in silence. He could see that her clothes were messed up, like she had been in a fight. She also had a cut on the back of her hand that was bleeding.

Morgan repeated, "Are you ok? You speak English. Would you talk to me? And again, would you please put down that gun. I can help you if you will trust me. Don't shoot me. I'm really a nice guy."

Morgan laughed to himself at the last part of his comment, thinking about how stupid that sounded to a person holding a gun on him. Apparently, it sounded stupid enough for her to draw a smile too.

Her next words were, "who are you?"

"My name is Morgan. I'm just out for a ride. My family and friends are in San Antonio waiting to head West with the next wagon train. I really mean you no harm. That hand is bleeding badly. Is there someone after you? What happened if you don't mind me asking?"

She slowly lowed the gun. Partly because she had time to observe him and he must have appeared to be non-threatening and the other reason he guessed was that the gun was getting too heavy, she wasn't going to be able to hold it up much longer anyway.

"My name is Cocheta. A small group of us were attack by bandits a couple of miles back. One of my friends was shot. I took his gun and ran to hide along the riverbank. The others scattered. The bandits mostly wanted the horses and guns. While trying to round up the horses they lost track of me. I made my way up the riverbank slowly, hiding as much as I could until I met you." She stated with her whole body starting to shake. Tears coming down her face, she appeared to be falling apart after what must have been some extremely intense moments.

Morgan approached her slowly, "Your safe now. Let's have a look at your hand. Are you hurt anywhere else? Please, let me help you."

At that moment she passed out momentarily, hitting the ground. He rushed to her side, moving her around so her head was in his lap as he sat on the ground. It was at that moment that he was able to see her beauty up close. He had been concentrating on the gun, not her looks until now.

"Speak to me, wake up, we need to move on." Morgan couldn't help but stare at her.

He almost wished that she wouldn't wake up right away as he became mesmerized by her looks. She had skin so smooth, with high cheek bones. Her eyes were closed, but when he last saw them, they had an intensity beyond anything he had ever seen. He guessed her to be close to his age. She was much shorter than him, but then they hadn't stood close enough side by side to really tell how much. Her hair was shiny black. So beautiful, she was starting to intimidate him.

Morgan kept reminding myself saying in a whisper, "Please don't say something stupid when she wakes up. She likely already has a low opinion of the high opinion I have of myself...right? After all, I'm a really nice guy." Still sounded stupid. Why was he so concerned what she thinks? I have seen pretty women before. His thoughts immediately changed to describe her as beautiful, not just pretty but incredibly beautiful.

He looked at her hand, taking out his handkerchief. Morgan tied it around her hand, attempting to put pressure on it to reduce the bleeding. Next, he looked her over to see if anything else seemed out of sorts.

Morgan gently laid her head down on the grass, lifted up his saddle, deciding they had better get back to town, just in case those bandits were looking for her, or maybe because they might be headed their direction toward San Antonio for a fun evening.

Having saddled up, Morgan decided that they should follow the path along the river back to San Antonio. It was a little longer, but if the bandits were headed toward San Antonio, they would probably use the main road.

As he turned around, he noticed that Cocheta was moving. Morgan ran over to her, lifting her up on her feet. She wasn't very stable. As he walked her over to his horse, she appeared to be slowly gaining her strength.

"Can you hold on to me if we ride double? We need to go now before it gets dark. Can you?" as he gazed into her eyes.

"I can hold on, if it isn't too rough of a ride." As she tried to sound convincing of her strength.

"Let's get you up here," reaching out after mounting to lift her up behind him.

The moment she moved up against Morgan and put her arms around him to hold on, he felt the warmth of her body. He looked down at her hands, as they embraced. He felt better now that they were taking the longer way back if for no other reason than he had her next to him, all to himself.

As they started back, he was thinking about the questions he wanted to ask her. They would have about an hour to talk if she even felt like it.

"Where are you from?" was his first question.

"I grew up near the Mission Concepcion. My mother and father died a long time ago, so I spent a lot of time at the Mission. That's where I learned how to speak English at an early age." Said Cocheta.

She was now feeling the warmth and safety as she embraced him even tighter. She had many of her own questions but felt best to remain quiet for the most part and answer Morgan's comments first. It was also nice to simply feel good in the moment. She told him later that as she ran from her pursuers, she prayed for God's intervention and He sent you. God answers prayer. She knew that from having a strong belief in God and Jesus, which she had learned from growing up at the Mission Concepcion.

She was pressed up so tight against him that he could feel her heart beating. She held on tight and at times even squeezed even tighter as if to thank him. Even if it was not her heart, Morgan chose to believe it was. He continued to speak with her to take her mind off of her possible pursuers or thinking about what might have happened to her friends.

"Cocheta is a very beautiful name? Does it have a meaning? Now resorting to small talk.

"It means the unknown one. When my parents died, I was only five years old. They were killed during the Battle of Concepcion. My father as a fighter and my mother ... well, she was killed too. Many of our tribe were killed. I am Lipan Apache. A descendant of Chief Flacco who rode with your people many times fighting the Mexicans." Her answer being far more than she had expected to be sharing with a stranger.

Morgan thought that she might be mentioning her Chief having fought with the white man, so that he wouldn't look at her as an Indian in the way most white men did. It seemed like an unusual piece of information to share at a time like this.

"I'm sorry to hear that. Do you have any family?" Morgan replied.

"No." My brother died at an early age of fever. That's why I was taken in by the mission and as I got older, lived nearby. I hope and pray that my friends are ok." Spoken as a pleading statement causing them both to think about what the outcomes could be for those she left behind.

Morgan asked her, "Did you see the men that attacked you. How many were there?

"Four. They came out of nowhere. My one friend had a gun, but as quickly as he tried to pull it, they shot him. The others tried to ride away, but as I looked back, they were being chased."

Morgan knew as she put her head against his back that she was crying. The thought of her in this pain injected anger into his veins. Yet her arms still holding on tight, gave him pause. Morgan wanted to get back to San Antonio to make sure she was safe. He also wanted to see if there was any news of the attack.

Hopefully, some of Hay's men would ride out in the morning to hunt these men down.

They rode now in silence. The horse made the only real noise. Cocheta had quieted down. Either in shock or possibly in a daze, having experienced so much trauma. It was getting later in the day, so Morgan yelled back to her to make sure she was really holding on as he brought the horse to a slight gallop. He didn't want to be riding in the dark, plus he wanted to get her to a doctor.

Morgan kept asking himself what would become of Cocheta when they got back to town. The wagons would be leaving in a couple of days. That would mean he would never see her again. Then he would ask myself, why he even cared. He already had taken the role of protecting her and caring for her, but it was far more than that.

Maybe it was her beauty that captivated him. Men always seemed to see the physical beauty in woman first. Even for the short period of time they had been together, he knew or wanted his feelings for her to be far more than just a fleeting moment. It couldn't be love, they had only just met. He didn't really know anything about her except the little that she had shared. Yet everything he felt seemed to suggest what Sally had described about Pat, when she spoke of her love for him. Morgan closed his thoughts on the matter for the moment with a ...that would be ridiculous. No one really falls in love at first sight.

42

Bad Blood

—⚬—

We followed the trail into town and headed toward the hotel.

As we rode through town past one of the many saloons, Cocheta jolted back away from my back and tried to hold back a scream. Morgan immediately pulled up on the reins stopping in the middle of the street. Cocheta had now let go of him, using one hand to point to a mare tied up alongside of them.

"That horse is my friends. The blanket, saddle, it's his. Please, please, help me," as the terror of a few hours ago rose in her.

"Don't worry yourself about that right now. Your safe. I'm going to take you to the hotel and get a doctor to look you over," said Morgan as uncontrollable rage started to build in his gut.

As he rode up in front of the hotel, some of the men and woman from their group immediately ran up to help, seeing that something was amiss.

"She and her party were attacked by bandits south of town a few miles near the river. I think she is mostly alright." as Morgan dismounted.

Two of the women had helped her off the horse and were already helping her into the hotel. She was again a bit unstable not having had her feet on the ground in the last hour or more.

"Yes, thank you. Take her inside and get her a room. I will get the doctor to come over. Then I'm going over to the Captains Headquarters. I'll be back after I report this." As Morgan walked quickly knowing she was in good hands.

It didn't go unnoticed by the men in the crowd or anyone for that matter as to how beautiful she was or that she was saying thank you in almost perfect English. Didn't see many Indians that spoke English better than most of the people. Let alone the immigrants moving around the wagon trains.

Talk started up again about the bandits, putting a new scare into the women and men when they wondered how many there might be. Although it was said there were only four, they could have been part of a larger group. Most of the men and woman knew how to handle a gun, but they had never shot at someone or been shot at. Everyone was getting nervous at the thought of a threat.

Morgan walked quickly over to find the doctor who picked up his bag and headed for the hotel. He walked with him part way and then excused himself saying he had to see to business with the Mounties.

The doctor was suspicious of his actions when he noticed that he was heading off in the opposite direction from the Mounties Headquarters. When the doctor entered the Hotel, Pat and a couple of the group asked where Morgan was, and doctor told them he was headed down the street away from the Mounties Headquarters. As the women were helping Cocheta they had heard the Indian woman ranting about seeing the horse that belonged to her friend being tied up out front of a saloon as they entered town. Pat and two other men immediately took off to see what trouble Morgan might be getting into.

Morgan spotted the mare still tied up in front of the saloon as. He approached slowly, stepping off to the side of the boardwalk to check his guns and look into the front window of the saloon. He wanted to know who was riding the horse and second if anyone else was with them. Couldn't tell from outside so he decided the best way was to go into the saloon and observe. None of them, if they were in there, would know him. Morgan stepped into the saloon, looked around and headed for the end of the bar. It was always good to have everyone in front of you and the back door where you could see it and use it if necessary.

Before Morgan got to the bar, he heard a table of men yell out to him to join them. It was some of the Roberts clan. He signaled to them and pointed to the bar, as if to say, I'll be over when I get a drink.

There were less than two dozen men in the place that he didn't know. There were a couple outside of the Roberts that he had seen before, the owner of the hardware store, who would hardly be hanging out with bandits, and a drifter, gambler type that had been around since he arrived. Then he noticed two men at the other end of the bar. They seemed to be minding their own business. In other words, they were not paying any attention to Morgan.

It was only a few minutes before Pat entered the front door of the saloon with one member from the Peeples family and another one of the Roberts family. The three of them among shouts from the already exiting table of friends, walked straight over to where Morgan was standing at the end of the bar.

"Are you ok? Thought you were going to the Mounties Office and tell them what happened. Could be, you could have told them about the horse out front and let them handle this." As Pat gave Morgan a mean stare.

Pat had a side to him that meant business. He was a compassionate, loving man, but also good with a gun and ready for a fight if he thought it was necessary.

"Why don't you just join the others over there. If I need you, I'll call you." Trying not to look over at the men at the end of the bar, who appeared to be finishing their drinks. Morgan assumed that they had plenty of time to down a couple drinks before he had arrived, so they might be getting ready to settle up and walk out.

"Why don't you two join the others, I'm going to stay here with Morgan for a bit. We have some business to talk over." Said Pat nodding toward the table full of their friends.

"It must be one of them. They are paying the bartender and getting ready to leave." Said Morgan as he reached down without realizing he had his right hand on his gun.

"If we are going to do this lets slowly follow them outside and see if it is one of them that rode in on that horse?" said Pat.

By this time the men that had come over with Pat had joined the table of Roberts. They quietly told the others what was going on. The room was getting a little too quiet about the time the two suspects walked away from the bar and out the front door.

"Come on..." Morgan said as they started for the door.

"Slow down," said Pat as the table of friends also started to get up.

Morgan walked out the door first with Pat in tow. The two men were walking to the left towards the horse. There was another horse next to the mare. The moment the first man stepped off the boardwalk toward the horse, Morgan yelled, "Hey you, that your horse?"

That's when all hell broke loose. Both men turned. Seeing Morgan with a hand on his gun already, they both decided to draw down on him.

They pulled their gun's, and each fired at Morgan, hitting him once in the side, almost hitting Pat, who had hardly cleared the doorway stepping into the gun fire.

They both ran for the ally when Morgan started to return gun-fire, hitting one of the men in the shoulder. Pat held his fire not having a clean shot. As Pat and Morgan ran for the entrance to the alley, the rest of the group came running out of the saloon, drawing guns and filling the street. It was all guns and no targets. Then they saw Pat and Morgan run into the alley. The crowd of men started to run after Morgan and Pat to pursue them too.

The alley was dark and smelled of rotten food thrown out from the kitchens in the surrounding buildings. There were staircases and water barrels in dark corners, too dark to see an ambush. There wasn't enough time for them to get to the end of the alley without being seen by Morgan and Pat as quickly as they came around the corner, so they had to be hiding.

As they both moved, each to a side of the alley to take advantage of the dark shadows and have a bit of shelter, the first man fired from behind a water barrel. Another round grazed Morgan in the left shoulder causing him to fall to the ground. The man tried his best to put another couple of rounds into Morgan as he laid on the ground. Seeing men running across the entrance of the alley with guns drawn he was distracted as he fired a couple more rounds toward Morgan as he got to his feet.

Anger had taken over any common sense at this point and Morgan remembered being overtaken with hate, determined to kill this man. The second man came out of hiding and ran for the back exit of the alley hoping that no one was waiting for him. In the moment, Morgan started walking toward the first man. The one that was going to get on the horse out front. The one that likely shot Cocheta's friend. The one that had shot him twice although Morgan might not have even realized it given the level of anger and rage that had engulfed him.

On his feet with a revolver in hand, Morgan took aim and fired, hitting the man in the right leg, which brought him to his knees. As the man tried to raise his gun to fire another round at him, Morgan fired again hitting him square in the chest.

By now, even with a bullet in his left shoulder and a wound in his side, Morgan had pulled his other revolver too. The bandit likely received a deadly shot when hit in the chest, but blinded by hate Morgan continued to fire, round after round until both guns where empty. He fired as he advanced, ending up standing right over him for the last round.

Pat had run up to Morgan almost in shock having watched him openly walk against this man, firing every round he had into him. They heard gunfire from the back street where they assumed the other bandit was facing some of their friends or possibly some Mounties by now. Everyone was running up to see what happened. Pat noticed that Morgan was standing strong knowing he had seen him get shot at least once. Morgan's adrenalin filled veins erased the bulk of the pain of having two bullets in him. If it were not for the fact that he had empty both revolvers, twelve rounds, putting eight of them into this guy, Pat envisioned he would be reloading regardless of his wounds. Pat could tell by the look in Morgan's eyes that he was running on pure hate.

Pat placed a hand on Morgan's shoulder to draw his attention away from the body on the ground.

"Morgan, steady. Calm down, it's all over. The guys will get the other one. Holster up so we can get you over to the hotel. Hopefully the doctor is still there. You need some work. Do you know you have two holes in you?" said Pat holding on to his arm, expecting him to collapse at some point, as he led me away.

As Pat was walking with Morgan out of the alley it seemed the whole town had come to life. It wasn't that late, so everyone was moving into the street to see what all the shooting was about. There were some Mounties at the office who were now on sight having run out the door the minute the gunfire started. All three that showed up recognized Pat and Morgan. They said they would get our story after Pat had seen that Morgan was cared for, excepting that they were the good guys in all this.

The other bandit was alive. A little beat up, but better alive than dead. A mixture of towns folk and Roberts clan brought him to a halt after shooting him a couple of times followed by a bit of a beating before, they turned him over to the Mounties. They decided not to hang him as they didn't want to get into any trouble with the law creating delays in joining the wagon train. That would have been the only option knowing that most decent folks only wanted to confront bandits one time if at all. The only way to assure not dealing with them again is make sure they are dead.

"Pat, Pat, Oh Pat, are you all right? Morgan, you've been shot." Screamed Sally as she ran up on Pat walking Morgan over to the hotel.

"Sally, is the doctor still in the hotel?" asked Pat.

"Yes, he's in the restaurant after tending to Cocheta, "stated Sally. Even though the excitement was all over, she was breaking down at the thought that Pat and Morgan could have been killed. Stillwater was never like this. Though every location has its good side and bad side.

The doctor was leaving the hotel when Pat and Morgan were coming in.

"Figured with all the shooting that someone probably hit someone. Any others?" as the doctor stooped over to take a quick look at his side wound.

"Yes, there's one more who has been shot and kicked around a little. He was part of the gang that attacked Cocheta and her friends," said Pat.

"Well let's get you upstairs to a bed. After I look you over, I'll attend to the other. No need to hurry myself over the likes of him.

Might move my office into this here hotel given all the business I got over here today." Trying to lighten up the situation.

Morgan asked, "How is Cocheta Doc? Is she alright?"

"I'd say she is just fine. Looks like you're the one that will need some looking after, if you know what I mean," with a grin on his face.

The side wound was not bad, because the bullet went right on through. The doc had to dig a little to get the bullet out of the shoulder.

"That shoulder is going to hurt for a while. I would not put any use to it for a couple of weeks. Just to make sure you take it easy, so you get healed," was the doc's final advice.

Morgan remembered falling asleep right after the doctor left having given him something to relax. All he could see as he drifted off was the image of the man he shot lying on the ground in a pool of blood. Shot and killed by him. He would periodically have flashbacks of that vision for months to come.

43

What Do You Believe?

T he cool of the night seemed to calm things down as people in the street or in the saloons were talking about the shooting and how they either were a part off or observed. Some of the men had run around the building, down to the back of the alley exit to cut off the second man trying to escape while Morgan was facing off with the other.

The bandit looked a mess by the time they handed him over to the Mounties and the town Sheriff. The Sheriff was usually beholding to the Mounties whose presence demanded order in San Antonio.

The man once in custody and with a little coaxing told where the other two men were camped outside of town with the horses, they had stolen from Cocheta's friends. The Mounties with the Sheriff would ride out in the morning and round them up. Once the justice of the peace held court and proclaimed them guilty, there would likely be a proper hanging of all three.

Pat had personally gone over to the jail to speak to the bandit about what had happened to Cocheta's friends.

"Hey mister, we were just looking to get some horses to sell. The man you killed is the one that shot the Indian boy. The boy was reaching for a gun. We ran down the rest, took the horses and let them run off. We didn't mean to shoot anyone." Said the stranger, like it wasn't the same rope that hung a horse thief as the killer.

Pat continued with the Sheriff listening in now, "So your friend killed the boy?"

"No, no, no, the boy got shot, but he ran off like a wounded buck. I don't think he was hurt bad. Honest," Said the man starting to realize that his very existence was coming to an end.

Honest. That word didn't have a whole lot of credibility coming out of a person that just did what he had done.

Pat continued to ask a couple of questions and then the Sheriff took over. Pat left the conversation to head back to the hotel to see how everyone was doing.

Cocheta had heard the shots from the gun fight. Once she heard from one of the women that Morgan was involved, she feared the worst for him. She started to cry thinking he might have been seriously hurt or killed. All she was told was that he had been shot.

She immediately got out of bed, even with two women trying to hold her down and attempting to convince her to stay put. She would have nothing to do with it. She stood up, still wobbly and not being able to stop her, the two women escorted her to Morgan's room.

The door to his room was open and men were going in and out from the Roberts and Peeples clans to check on him. The doctor had cleaned the side wound and was now bandaging up his shoulder.

"Got it," said the doctor as Cocheta entered the room. She moved slowly to his side, kneeling next to the bed and taking his hand in hers.

Noticing the concern on her face the doctor told her, "He'll be fine. Just a flesh wound to the side. He will need to take a break for a while as it heals. But he's ok."

Tears were running down Cocheta's face as she held Morgan's hand not saying a word to anyone. Her total attention was on him until Pat came into the room.

"Just talked to the one they caught over at the jail," as he looked now straight at Cocheta, noticing her holding Morgan's hand and the tears. What a scene. It was clear that something of a kinship had developed between the two of them.

Her attention now turned toward Pat, "Did he say what happened to my friends. Are they alive?'

"Better than that if what he is saying is true. The boy got shot and ran off with the others. They were just after the horses. He said that the man Morgan killed was the one that shot your friend and the others ran off after surrendering their horses," said Pat.

The room was getting crowded as Sally entered with extra blankets, she had gotten from the hotel manager. She laid them down and hugged Pat. She was hurting for her brother, at the same time thanking God that Pat had not been shot or worse under her breath. Sally also noticed the affection that Cocheta was showing toward him. It didn't escape anyone in the room.

It got even more strange and even uncomfortable for some of the men, as Cocheta started to pray for him, "God, thank you for protecting both Morgan and Pat. Thank you also for protecting my friends. I pray that they are all well and continue to receive your gift of protection."

Many in the room kept asking themselves, who was this woman. She looked Indian, spoke like an English professor and seemed to have a direct path to God. She was shining as she raised her head from prayer as if she knew everything was going to be fine.

The doctor bandaged Morgan's wounds and packed up his bag. As he walked toward the door with some last words of advice regarding his care, Sally took the lead to ask everyone to let them, meaning Morgan and Cocheta, get some privacy. With her hand on Pat's back she started by pushing him and waving the others to leave. As she looked back, Cocheta gave her a smile and a wink. Sally laughed under her breath and chalked up Cocheta's gestor as rather strange coming from an Indian woman.

When the last one out closed the door, Morgan gave out a sigh and squeezed Cocheta's hand while looking her in those incredible eyes. Holding her hand, he slowly pulled her hand to his chest forcing her to slowly get on her feet leaning over him. The two of them were as if in a trance, not speaking, just staring at each other. Their feelings and concerns for each other due to the day's events had grown.

Slowly she leaned down, meaning to kiss Morgan on the cheek, when at the last moment he turned his head and met her lips with his. They both felt something they had never felt before. It was magical to have someone else that you feel so strongly about that every part of your body tingled when they touched you.

Morgan was still in considerable pain as he moved himself over in hopes that Cocheta would welcome the invitation to lay down next to him. She felt excited and yet uncomfortable as she continued to hold his hand as she laid down next to him. She felt like her heart was about to burst which confused her yet indicated to her how much she had a desire for this man. He had an equal desire for her.

This was the first time they were alone since their arrival on horseback earlier. From that point it seemed that they both lost track of time as events unfolded. They both had enough excitement for the evening and resting next to each other put a perfect ending to the day.

"I'm sorry if my praying may have embarrassed you in front of your friends. Growing up at the Mission led me to the Lord at a very early age. It had become a big part of me. I'm sorry if that does not agree with you." Spoken with a wavering voice.

Morgan had forgotten about the pain in his shoulder as he laid there with his eyes closed having just listened to Cocheta tell him that she was a Christian. She sounded like his Sister. If only she knew what he had grown up with in the Church. He thought if she questioned why she and her friends were attacked and himself shot, he might mention that if there was a God protecting us, He didn't do a great job. In a separate thought, the circumstances that had Morgan's life at risk, given the result being Cocheta laying at his side could easily be deemed a miracle. Morgan was more than grateful for her company and even though she laid on top of the blankets, next to him, he felt her warmth. Morgan didn't have to look at her to remember how incredible she looked. He was trying to put his feelings in check knowing that in another day or two he would be heading West and they would never see each other again. The sadness of that truth caused tears to swell up, that he hid as he turned his head away from her.

"Are you going to speak to me? If not, I should go back to my room." Said Cocheta.

"Please don't go. I don't want you to go and yet I'm leaving to join a wagon train head West in a couple of days. I already can't explain my feelings for you. I'm confused. You're saying a prayer didn't bother or embarrass me at all. It made me feel more for you. Maybe because in that, you remind me of my Sister and her faith." said Morgan in a low voice.

"I should ask you directly, do you believe in God? If not, how come your Sister does and you don't?" said an inquisitive Cocheta.

"I did at one time believe and had a strong faith, but with a number of things that happened to me and my family, I lost my faith wondering how God could have let certain evil things happen. How could He allow me to be hurt like this? Sis keeps trying to talk to me, but so many things are still so fresh in my mind." As Morgan reached out for her. he was very uncomfortable talking about God, as he thought about his dad and all. That led Morgan to wondering what might have happened to his mother and dad along with Mr. Johnson. A host of other people started to come to mind that he had met on his journey to San Antonio, wondering what they were doing and what some of them thought of him.

Morgan felt Cocheta turn on her side so she could look at him while she spoke.

"Do you think that bad things don't happen to good people and if it does, that it is God's fault? If you look at the bad things that have happened and what might have resulted from them, maybe you can see that sometimes you have to go thru bad times and events to get to the good ones. God has a plan for everyone, but we also have ability to choose not to follow that plan which can put us in harm's way. I believe there is a reason behind every-thing, even if we don't understand it." Said Cocheta now making direct eye contact with Morgan.

Again, they starred at each other. They both wondered if this would be the last time, they would be together, able to speak in privacy, then never to see each other again.

"Are you headed back to the Mission? Can you stay in San Antonio until we leave? The Mounties will likely have the other two bandits in custody tomorrow, and you could identify them. They will also send someone on to the Mission to see if your friends had arrived and if they are ok. Stay here until we at least know that your safe to head back." Morgan was afraid or embarrassed to say why he really wanted her to stay. He wanted every minute he could spend with her.

"Is my safety the real reason you want me to stay until you head out. I have friends back in the Mission town, but no family. I have no one that speaks for me," said Cocheta.

Morgan decided that if he didn't say something now, he may forever regret it. He found himself with incredibly strong emotions for Cocheta and he wanted her to know it, even if they parted and never saw each other again. The memory of having met her and what he felt would never go away.

"Cocheta, I, I don't know how to say this because I have never felt this way or spoke this way about a woman. There is something about you that I find, well, that I really like and even though we may never see each other again, I just wanted you to know that I have a certain love for you, there I said it, "stated Morgan in a deep quiet tone, embarrassment in his voice.

Cocheta would tell him later how she was experiencing disbelief that someone she just met was proclaiming love for her. Someone besides her friends or Jesus. A man. A man that was all man yet had a compassion and softness about him that made him even stronger in her eyes. She had felt a closeness from the moment she climbed up on the horse and leaned against him. Their conversations reeled her into becoming not just fond of him, but in a place where she was falling in love. Falling in love with Morgan, a man she had only known for one day and one kiss. She was going to question her sanity, but not right now. Right now, she was going to enjoy and bask in the moment. Morgan found himself telling her what he had never told any woman before.

44

Wilderness Love and Partnership

Pat was up early in the morning, wondering how Morgan was doing. He decided to check on him and let him know that the Mounties and Sheriff had already left to hunt down the two men that Cocheta had described for them. Walking over to Morgan's room, Pat was anxious to ask him how it went with Cocheta after everyone had left. He knew there was something developing between them.

Instead of knocking on the door, Pat tried the doorknob thinking that if it was unlocked and Morgan was still sleeping, he would walk away and let him get some rest. Slowly he turned the knob. The door was unlocked. Pat slowly opened the door to experience an interesting surprise. Cocheta had fallen asleep next to Morgan. They were both asleep, or so Cocheta left him to believe. She had awoken at the turn of the knob. She didn't move hoping that whoever was checking in would go away and leave them alone for a few more precious moments.

Pat was stunned, but he couldn't take the smile off his face as he quietly closed the door and went to join Sally in the restaurant.

"Well, you wouldn't believe what I just saw. Morgan and Cocheta still holding hands asleep. Her on the bed and him in the bed. There is something happening between them that I want to think is very special. They looked ... well, they just looked content?" Pat spoke with confusion in his voice.

Sally added, "I felt something very special when she knelt and prayed for you and him. She is so different, and I believe would be so good for him. We should check on things at the stable and get ready for tomorrow's trip to Castroville."

"We will get all of the final items we need for the trip in Castroville where they are set to supply what everyone needs heading West. Horses, wagons, food and a good woman." Said Pat.

"I hope not in that order," said Sally as Pat pulled her close for a long passionate kiss.

"I could move you up just behind the horses!" Pat said laughing as Sally took a friendly swipe at his broad shoulder.

Cocheta and Morgan both laid still as if they were asleep, each fearing not to wake the other. Yet, both of them had been awake for some time just wanting to enjoy lying next to each other.

When Morgan finally whispered, "Are you awake?"

"No, I'm sleeping!" replied Cocheta

They both laughed lightly. A real change from the day before. Cocheta rolled from her side facing Morgan, onto her back. The sun was shining in the window already. Even with shorter winter days coming it seemed they had slept in. Cocheta sat up on the edge of the bed.

"I should get back to my room." Cocheta said as she stood up looking over Morgan.

"Please promise me that you will not run off. Let's meet for breakfast in the restaurant downstairs in a half hour. Ok?" Morgan had a pleading in his voice she could not say no to, although she thought the longer, she stayed around this man the more she would become attached. That only meant more pain in the pending separation.

"Ok, I'll meet you downstairs." As she headed for the door.

Morgan watched her leave and close the door. That moment brought on a separation that created a sadness. As he sat up, he was reminded of his wounds by all the pain. Morgan walked over to the mirror to see what Cocheta saw when she looked at him a few moments ago. Morgan was a mess. His mind flushed with thoughts of what had happened, the gun fight, her friends, the kiss last night. There was also the trip to Castroville to prepare for. He had to get cleaned up and not only talk to Cocheta but find Pat and Sally.

Morgan opened the window in his room to let some fresh air in. As he turned around, he looked at the bed and found it hard to believe that this incredible woman had cared enough to stay with him all night. His thoughts continued to run wild.

He heard a commotion out front and looked out the window to see the Sheriff and the Mounties returning with two men and a string of horses in tow. They stopped momentarily to see if Cocheta was around to identify them. In a few moments a Mounty escorted Cocheta out in front of the hotel.

She had a blanket wrapped around her shoulders and her hair although black and beautiful looked like she hadn't got a brush to it yet. It only took a moment for her to identify the men as the ones that had attacked her party. Turning back into the hotel, she momentarily looked up at Morgan in the window and smiled.

Sally took over and brought her back into the hotel and took her to her room to help her with her hair. She was luckily the same size, so Sally insisted that she get into some clean clothes and they would then meet Morgan and Pat downstairs for breakfast.

Cocheta's heart seemed to miss a beat when she had looked up at Morgan. She couldn't wait to see him at breakfast even though they would not be alone. He could tell that she had so much she wanted to talk to him about but was afraid they would never have the privacy to share what was not only in her mind, but in her heart.

The two women were in Sally's room. Sally was making a fuss over Cocheta's hair, while also complementing her on how beautiful she was.

"I have been told how beautiful I am many times? That's all most men see in me. White men look at me and see an Indian woman. They reject the thought of being with an Indian woman. I wonder if Morgan is like that down deep?" as she looked up at Sally, knowing that Sally would be honest with her.

Sally laughed, "Maybe you didn't see how he looks at you. He is looking a lot deeper at you than just your outer beauty. I certainly see how you look at him. And... Well, Pat looked in this morning to check on Morgan to find the two of you looking very close?"

Sally hurried to make Cocheta look the best she could in the time she had. They didn't want to be late in meeting the others. Plus, both women had commented on how hungry they were.

As they entered the restaurant area of the hotel, Cocheta took a moment to look around. The first look around was to see if Morgan had arrived. He and Pat had gone over to the jail to learn what they could about what happened to Cocheta's friends from the two bandits that were just brought in.

The second look around the room was to admire the beauty of the surroundings. Even though it was nothing compared to the restaurants back East, it was extreme luxury to Cocheta who had never seen anything like it. If she had, she would have likely been asked to leave. Because of her friendship with Pat, Sally and Morgan and the fact that she was the talk of the town, near no one was going to be so bold as to treat her like a lot of her Indian friends were treated in such an environment.

The two women sat down at a table, followed shortly by Morgan and Pat joining them. Uncomfortable was the best way to describe the atmosphere around the table as the four of them said hello to each other. Cocheta didn't even look Morgan in the eyes even though she wanted to embrace him. Her mind was flashing back to the kiss they had and the warmth, and comfort of lying next to him through the night.

"Pat and I were just over at the jail and spoke to the two that were brought in this morning. I believe that your friends are ok. We will know later this morning how the boy is. One of the Rangers rode onto your village to check and get a report from him and your friends," said Morgan looking more at Pat and Sally than Cocheta.

"Thank you," said Cocheta looking at him eye to eye, this time with a slight smile.

It was as if the two could only really talk to each other when they were alone. Pat and Sally picked up on the discomfort of having the four of them at the table. They went along with their breakfast and excused themselves as soon as they were done eating, hoping that Morgan and Cocheta would open up to each other after they left.

The first comments came from Morgan, "I need to speak with you. I don't know how to say this, but I don't want to see you go. I guess it is better to say that I don't want to leave without you. I know I sound crazy, but I know you feel something for me, at least I hope so. If I'm wrong, I'll just be more embarrassed than I already am trying to tell you that I would like to have you stay with me. There I said it."

Morgan continued to be embarrassed and confused, but he knew if he didn't say something, he would soon be watching her fade in the distance. Crazy? Maybe. He had a feeling that the two of them would be a perfect pair. He was looking at one of the most interesting women he had ever met. The trip West would be an adventure that a woman like Cocheta could handle. His emotions were starting to show. He was prepared for the rejection which was the only sensible thing a woman only knowing a man for one day would do. He remembered and kept repeating, a quote from some British poet that Mr. Johnson, back at the store used to quote all the time stating, "Better to have tried and lost than not have tried at all." He was trying, even if his method was totally unconventional.

Cocheta did not have to say a word for Morgan to figure out that he was on the right trail. As she looked at him without speaking a word, her appearance changed, making her look like a different person. Her eyes lit up and teared up, looking like crystal sparkling under water. She started to display a broad smile with an expression with so much emotion that she tried to cover her face with her hands so not to show her embarrassment at the same time.

Morgan reached over, grabbed her hands and moved them away from her face. He wanted to experience this magical moment and make sure she understood his request.

"I want you to go West with me. I want you to be my partner. I know this sounds crazy, but I know now that you have some feelings for me. Please say something before I lose my mind." Blurted out Morgan.

Trying to hold back breaking into sobbing tears, Cocheta said, "I don't think you are crazy. I knew last night when I kissed you that you were special. I never did anything like that before. No man has ever spoken to me the way you have. I can also see through your Sister what kind of man you are. I don't know what to say beyond that. I want to go with you. I want to believe that we could be forever. I just need to think, please. Not long, but a little.

Please." Said Cocheta with tears settling back. The smile would remain with thoughts of disbelief. She had to find Sally.

45

Frontier Romance

~⊚

Pat and Sally had gone over to the stable to check on the horses for the next day's journey. The excitement of themselves with the Roberts and Pebble clan and well… Morgan and Cocheta? As they walked toward the stable, they laughed and recalled how quickly their relationship had happened. Now it seemed that they might be watching the very same thing happen to Morgan.

Cocheta went to her room, explaining to Morgan that she would like to speak with his sister if he knows where she is. Knowing that it had to do with their relationship and her making up her mind he immediately checked the desk to learn that Pat and Sally had left. He went into a fast walk to track them down.

Cocheta was in her room admiring her newly obtained clothes in the mirror and thinking of her and Morgan as a pair when there was a knock at the door. It was Sally.

"Oh, Sally. Please come in. I really need to talk to you. Have you heard what Morgan said to me at breakfast?" Seeing her nod her head as a yes, she continued. "I don't know these feelings. I need to ask you for your help. You know him, even if you don't know me. Please talk to me." Cocheta pleaded.

"I think I do know a lot about you. I learned a lot when you knelt and prayed for Morgan in front of all those people in the room. I don't think as a proclaimed Christian that I could have done that. You are a strong woman. You are a good woman. One that I would be proud to see alongside my brother." Said Sally.

"Pat and I only meet a few weeks ago and we both knew almost immediately that we were meant for each other. The trail ahead won't be easy. We all know that, but Pat and I believe we will be stronger dealing with it together. Pat is searching for the Almighty. He hasn't had much of any influence in his life. I think he is ready to accept Christ with help. There is nothing stronger than a marriage of three strands. That's what I pray about. Have you prayed about you and Morgan?" asked Sally

Given the shortness of time before the wagons would leave, the trail ahead, the uncertainty of life itself day to day, tremendous pressure was blanketing Cocheta over her decision.

"Tell me about Morgan. Your childhoods, upbringing. Please. Anything. I know you're his Sister so I should first ask if you would even approve of us as a couple. It would be very important to me." Searching for words.

"Cocheta, our past is not as important as you and Morgan's future. I would not only approve but be grateful to have a woman in his life like you and like a sister to me. Pat and I were just talking about how the two of you seem to have something special. You just have to give it a chance. I can tell you that he obviously cares for you a great deal. I think he could even be in love with you already. You would be great for him. I think he needs you, and that might be why you are here. A gift from God," Said Sally thinking she might have disclosed more of her thoughts than she should have. However, time was short, and decisions had to be made. Important ones.

While Sally and Cocheta were having their meeting in the hotel room, Morgan and Pat were looking over the horses and wagons. Morgan wasn't apparently opening up to Pat, so Pat took the opportunity to move straight into the subject of Cocheta.

"Well, do you love her?" said Pat.

"What? Love who. What are you talking about?" replied Morgan

"I peeked in this morning to see how you were and saw the two of you laying there. Quite a sight. Looked like the two of you were getting along really well for one day. Most people would say there was already something very special going on between the two of you. Whether brought on by the tragedies of the day that threw you two together or otherwise, who cares. If I were to make a quick comment about the two of you, I would say you might be perfect for each other." Said Pat while he was checking the rigging.

"It would be crazy to think that two people could have a meaningful relationship in one day. Simply crazy." Said Morgan.

"It wasn't all that crazy for Sally and me. We might not have said anything to each other right away because we had time knowing we were heading in the same direction and would see each other the next day and the next. We could just have well said our ...I love you's the day after we met. That's how intense it was, the feelings I felt for Sally and she said she felt for me. It's not crazy. If it is, so what. Sally and I are enjoying it and actually thinking of getting married in Castroville if we can find a pastor to perform the wedding." Said Pat not meaning to tell their secret about getting married just yet.

"What? That's fantastic. Your right!" yelled Morgan smiling ear to ear.

"Slow down. What's fantastic and what part about what am I so right about? Marrying Sally? With your approval of course," said Pat.

"Of course, you have my approval. Not only are you right about what you and Sally are doing but your right about giving in to my feeling about Cocheta and stop thinking about how crazy it is and start thinking about how I feel. I have to go find her and congratulate Sally if it's not a secret?" Morgan threw the rigging aside, looking up at Pat.

"No need for secrets." Said Pat.

Morgan headed back to the hotel to find Cocheta. He was gaining confidence with every step knowing that wanting her was the right thing. He just had to convince her now. He didn't realize that Sally had helped Cocheta move in his direction with that idea.

Cocheta and Sally were outside the hotel thinking about heading to the stables when they saw Morgan heading their way. Sally told Cocheta to talk to him from her heart. She was going to go over to the local dress shop for the last look at civilized woman's clothing before becoming a pioneer.

Morgan jumped the steps of the hotel to stand in front of Cocheta. Before she could get a word out, he gestured for her to sit down in the bench in front of the hotel. He didn't care who was around, walking by or the dust from the street. This was the right time and right place to say what he had to get out.

"More than anything, I want you to go with me tomorrow. I have incredible feelings for you. I think I even love you. Not that you can't take care of yourself, but I want to take care of you and have you in my life. I know the trail is not the easiest life, but who knows what might be ahead of us. I wouldn't be making this trip if not to look for the things in life I want and believe I can find. That's to include a wife and family. Did I just say that? I guess I did, and I'm tired of thinking it is crazy to think about you and me as a pair." Morgan said intending to continue as long as it took to convince her to join him.

Cocheta, remembering her conversation with his Sister, put out her fingers over his mouth to stop his conversation which was moving into babble if he kept on speaking and said, "Stop, please stop."

"I don't think it is crazy either anymore. I don't have much to look back at. I would rather look forward at what might be. What might be of you and me. You have a great sister and I believe we should give this a chance, but I want you to know that it is important to have God in our lives. I won't compromise. There will be three of us in our wagon if you agree. I prayed for help and God gave me you." Said Cocheta

"That's strange. As I sat on the riverbank yesterday trying to sort out my thoughts about God and the conversations with Sally, I prayed for help. Maybe God also put you in my life to help me." Said Morgan, hardly believing he was just spewing out his most inner thoughts.

It took a few seconds to understand that Cocheta had said yes. The thought of what was happening seemed like a miracle, so why wouldn't he agree to God being in their life. He would have to find out what his Sister and Cocheta had spoken about. But there was not time for that right now.

"I can't believe it! I can't believe it! What do we do now?" stated Morgan

The obvious didn't need to be stated as the two drew together for their second long and passionate kiss. This was a kiss, not based on never seeing each other again in the future but one of many sealing their future together.

Word moved quickly about Morgan and Cocheta around the group that were headed West. By evening, everyone had decided it was time to celebrate the addition of Cocheta to the caravan heading to Castroville. By the time everyone joined together at the restaurant, by invitation of Morgan and Cocheta, the word was not only out about Morgan and Cocheta, but the plans had expanded to having a double wedding in Castroville to memorialize the beginning of both couples' new lives together.

Sally following Morgan's direction, had taken Cocheta over to get outfitted with what she would need for the trip. In addition to the day's excitement, news came that her friends were all safe and the Indian boy that had been shot, was going to be fine. This gave Cocheta comfort although leaving without saying a proper good-bye would bother her. She would write letters to all of them of her adventures and especially describing Morgan and how her life had just changed.

Morgan had arranged to reserve the majority of the restaurant area for dinner to celebrate with everyone in the wagons moving west invited. There were a couple of families and a few men that up to then were strangers. Everyone enjoying a rare moment of celebration engaged in the evening like one big happy family. The food and drink kept coming with one toast after another. Morgan and Cocheta sat next to each other at a corner table with Pat and Sally fully enjoying the evening. Morgan continued to reflect on how miracles do happen.

As the celebration started to quiet down, some of the men headed over to the saloons to carry on into the early hours. The rest knew that heading out in the morning for Castroville would be the event to make heading West real. Although the official start would be leaving Castroville, Morgan and Cocheta saw leaving San Antonio as their official start in heading West.

They spent a lot of time talking at the table after most of their friends new and old had left. They spoke for over four hours, learning and telling each other about themselves. They shared their first thoughts of what the journey would be like. Where were they headed and where would they settle? There was an excitement in not knowing. Some people would have never considered doing what they saw as exciting. Dangers put aside, they tried to speak of the positive outcomes of the journey ahead.

46

San Antonio to Castroville

The "Old Spanish Trail" ran from Florida to California, followed by thousands moving West.

There was a tremendous amount of activity with so many people preparing their teams, tying down their supplies and getting ready to head out to Castroville. Word had moved around that they should leave mid-morning. A rough gathering of wagons was in no special ordered, on the grounds out back of the stable. There was a wide patch of prairie where most of those that had stayed overnight or longer had camped. Morgan, Sally, Pat and now Cocheta had stayed in the hotel.

The four of them were now packing their gear. Soon they would be looking back at the last real hotel they may ever see. At least for some time to come. Morgan and Cocheta had gotten up with Pat and Sally for a real early breakfast. They had checked over most of their gear the day before knowing that future meals would be around a campfire, without waiters or menus.

"I keep telling myself that I'm ready for this," Morgan admitted to those at the table.

"Does that mean down deep you really don't think so?" replied Sally.

Cocheta was silent, hardly believing that she would be moving out to places no one or very few people, with the exception of Indians had ever seen. She reached over to hold Morgan's hand under the edge of the table.

"Let's be honest with each other. Everyone in this group and those in the wagon train are likely feeling the same way," said Morgan.

His comment took the sting out of being scared or afraid of the future. Life was about to change, and everyone knew it. At least they had a slight edge having heard stories about previous pioneers.

"I guess it is time." Said Pat looking at everyone at the table.

They all rose grabbing what they needed to carry over to the stables. Most everything had already been loaded. They just needed to hitch up the horses. Mid-morning had arrived.

As they walked around to the rear of the stable the entirety of the group, wagons, horses, and all of their friends were scattered all over, looking ready to move out.

Within the hour, one by one in no special order the wagons headed out. Mr. Geo Roberts took the lead. It seemed appropriate to have the patriarch of the family up front. The rest fell into a column, which as impressive as it looked now, would pale next to the wagon train with 50 to 100 wagons. That didn't include the cattle and assorted livestock that would have to survive the trip.

Pat and Sally's wagon was directly in front of Morgan and Cocheta. Even though they had big wagons, both couples were traveling light. They had extra horses, but no livestock since they were not planning on being ranchers. They didn't even have a dog. Separating themselves by looks even further was Pat and Morgan who looked more like gunslingers driving wagons than true Pioneers. Then again, men looking for gold took on all sorts of descriptions. Some of the farmers and future rangers would abandon their dreams with new ones of gold. No one was immune to gold fever. It seemed to spread quickly to those not already infected when on a long journey like the one they were getting ready to embark on

It was a clear day. The sky was clear although this late in the season usually brought on unexpected showers with some great lighting displays. The lighting was fun to watch, if you didn't have horses and cattle being scared to death. Today that wasn't going to be a concern. The temperatures this time of year would vary twenty to thirty degrees in a twenty-four-hour period. It might be cold at night, but nothing would compare to what Sally and Morgan experienced growing up in Minnesota. They would joke about being able to withstand the hardships of weather to mine gold in Alaska if they had too.

The two wagons were near the back of the column. They were thankful that it was a short trip given the dust they had to endure being in the rear of even a small group of wagons. The horses if on dry desert ground could kick up a lot of dust. Just another issue to get used to. Dirt was going to be part of their diet on this trip.

The trip to Castroville was the closest experience to actually being on the trail for Morgan and Cocheta. Yet, it was only a short time before they arrived at Castroville. It was shorter than they had expected arriving midafternoon with lots of time to spare before sunset.

Geo headed to the out skirts of where all the wagons had assembled in preparation for the long road ahead. They proceeded to create their own little encampment to hold the livestock. They were close to Fort Hondo which for now gave them a feeling of safety.

It took a couple of hours to set up camp. Speed would come with repetition. The only person that really knew anything about living in the outdoors among the four of them was Cocheta as she grew up in the shadow of the Mission. The four of them joked about their naivety, knowing that survival in the long term depended on them knowing what to do. The comfort was in their friends that they had made that knew what to do when they didn't. There was an education to everything.

As the two women prepared something for Pat and Morgan to eat, the men headed over to see if they could find the wagon master. It appeared from looking around that there were more than enough wagons to form a good size wagon train. The wait wouldn't be too long before heading out.

There were a couple of saloons, mostly tent style with a host of card games and ways to lose your money. The gamblers often left farmers with nothing bringing them to the end of their trail right here in Castroville. Although Morgan was tempted more for the game than the need for money, he didn't want to get into a game with anyone from the wagon train and risk a good relationship if he walked out with their money. Pat and Morgan would just look in to see if they recognized anyone, ask around for the wagon train master and move on.

They never did find him. A couple of men mentioned that his name was Henry Cooper and that he usually made his rounds in the morning to greet new arrivals and to answer any questions they might have. On the other side of the coin, he wanted to weed out those that he saw would either be trouble or so unexperienced, that they would slow down the wagon train or become a liability to the rest. Most of these people had little idea of the risks or hardships. Half would probably turn around just to hear about what he had seen in his time on this trail.

The trail that was being taken had a couple of different names. Some called it the Immigrant Trail and others called it the Old Spanish Trail. It went on through Fort Clark, Coon's Rancho or Franklin, Yuma and on to San Diego. Most of the miners were heading up to Sacramento where some big gold strikes had taken place. The stories were embellished to where people were walking through the shallow streams picking up nuggets until their back was sore. Not that fortunes weren't being made, but the stories outpaced the reality soon after the first discoveries.

After a long walk through the numerous small saloons Pat and Morgan returned to satisfy their hunger and see what the women called dinner. They were hoping that one of them knew how to cook and they learned from the other. The availability of certain foods would certainly influence the menus. They thought that Sally and Cocheta might find it too embarrassing to ask other women in the train for help cooking. That was something every woman was expected to know.

It had been a long day since breakfast. Pat and Morgan could smell something in the air as they approached the camp. From their walk thru the small town they knew that they would be able to get a cooked meal at a couple of the so-called saloons they looked in on if the ladies failed. Then they were struck with the scent of food, not just something cooking, but something good cooking. Neither man could determine what it was they smelled but their hunger had taken hold.

There was a big pot over the fire. It smelled delicious. The fire crackled and sparked from the dry wood as the meal held its secrets inside the big pot, except for the smell which drifted to every set of nostrils within one-hundred feet.

"We passed up the saloon food when we smelled this pot stewing. You can smell this all the way into town. The woman laughed, knowing the smell was good, but who would know yet if their beef stew was any good. The two of them had cut up some of the vegetables that were fresh alone with a slab of beef. Cocheta knew how to live off the land. Morgan remembered the old saying that you eat what you kill, although his family didn't have to kill the cow that the beef came from in Stillwater. Beef stew with one or two additional wild creatures added in the pot would satisfy anyone anytime. Toss in some potatoes and vegetables and they would have a real presentable meal.

Even though stew was a simple task the women took pride that their men didn't feel the desire to sneak something to eat from a table in town.

The sun was setting earlier and earlier day after day. Some of their other friends came over to share a drink around the campfire and speculate about the trip. Some had heard that the wagon train was heading out the next week. They were all getting anxious to get on the trail.

"Spoke to a couple of the Mounties I had met back in San Antonio," said Morgan. "I asked them about the settlers that were attacked that they rode out to help. The story was told with far more detail."

Morgan had also had a long conversation with Captain Jack after arriving in Castroville before he joined Pat to come back for dinner. He found Captain Jack speaking with an Indian that was hired on to scout for the wagon train at a campfire among the wagons. Settlers looked on in an uncomfortable manner, given what they had heard about the Indians. As settlers and miners, most couldn't tell one tribal Indian from another. This led to many innocent killings.

Morgan hesitated to approach but didn't know when he would have an opportunity to talk or set a time to talk with Captain Jack, so he interrupted their conversation.

"Sorry to interrupt your meeting. I just wanted to ask if we could talk later sometime today." Stated Morgan trying not to stare at the Indian sitting at the Captains side.

"We met in my office in San Antonio. I see your still traveling well-armed. Let me introduce a very good friend of mine, Chief Flacco. He and I have fought many battles together. Heard you had your own little battle back in San Antonio. Glad to see you made it. Join us if you wish. We were just talking about you or rather Cocheta. You know that Cocheta has been a friend of the Chief's here since childhood. Heard you two are getting married too. That true?" said the Captain as the Old Chief Flacco stared at him in a rather unapproving manner. His son was known as the Younger Chief was unfortunately killed years earlier by unknown murderers.

Morgan chose to be direct, "Yes that is true, and we would be honored if the two of you would attend the wedding tomorrow at noon. If it puts the Chief's mind at rest, please tell him that I will take good care of her. I love her very much."

"Why don't' you tell him yourself. He speaks pretty good English. Sorry to say I don't speak his language anywhere as good as he speaks mine." Sporting a broad smile as the two laughed out loud.

"I am sorry chief. Honored to meet you. I heard some of the stories about you and Captain Jack from the Mounties back in San Antonio." Said Morgan taking the invite to join by sitting down. He had no idea of the stories he would hear firsthand about Captain Jack and Chief Flacco over the next couple of hours. At one-point Chief Flacco opened a cloth he had been carrying to display a headband, beautiful in the design on the beads used which held a grouping of Golden Eagle feathers. The Golden Eagle was extremely favored by the Apache. The Chief offered it as a wedding gift. Morgan was speechless in receiving such a gift. By the time he left, he felt a true friendship with the two legends.

When Morgan found Cocheta and told her that he had just spent a couple of hours with Chief Flacco, she was truly excited. She proceeded to tell him even more stories about the two men. During their conversation it was decided that they would ask the Chief if he would stand with Cocheta in the wedding since she didn't have anyone to give her away. That is, if the Chief would agree. She went to sleep in the wagon with the wonderful thoughts of the next day.

Morgan had made sure that the women were out of earshot as he told the men what the Ranger had described. He suspected that the others were not sleeping so well tonight either. Morgan covered up in his bed roll with different thoughts. He was thinking of the Mounties description of what the Indians had done to the settlers they found. He would attempt to put such visions out of his mind before going to sleep.

The rest of the Mounties that had gone back to inform those in San Antonio didn't see any reason to get detailed. It would only scare everyone. The attack on the settlers was rare being so close to the Fort and both towns. The real threat would be when the train gets out and days away from Castroville. The safety at that point will be the numbers and weapons those in the wagon train had.

Morgan spent a lot of time cleaning his guns. He would continue to wear both pistols and make sure his rifle was always within reach.

47

Morgan Meets Waltz and Weiss

Long Way from Germany, both Jacob Waltz (who would later be known as the Dutchman of the famed Dutchman Mine) and his partner Weisner felt they were finally making progress towards their quest for gold. Looking back on the trip from Germany seemed like an eternity ago. Now they were moving toward the final leg, even if the goal was over a thousand miles away. They knew where they were going, and the destination was spinning stories of fortunes being made. Men buying a drink with a pinch of gold not even concerned over weighing it. The spilt dust falling to the floor to be swept up with the rest of the dirt and thrown out the door.

"It seems like it has been a long trip here Jake," spoke Jacob, who seldom said anything. He was getting anxious to put Castroville behind them. Henry Cooper, the wagon train master, had signed them up later that morning after returning from Fort Hood. He had spoken to the commander to see if they could get an escort of soldiers for a couple of days on the trail when leaving Castroville.

Waltz continued in their own language which several people could speak that had joined the wagon train as they were also immigrants from Germany, "It is good I guess to hear that some soldiers will be with us for the first couple of days. Doesn't mean much if they are watching us. The Comancheros will just wait until the soldiers are gone and then depending on their numbers, they will either start stealing a horse or cow at a time during the night or outright attack us if they feel they outnumber us enough to kill us and take everything at one time."

"Is that what you have been quietly thinking about all the time you have been sitting there not saying anything? We may not even see any Indians on the trail. With our numbers and guns, they will think twice before attacking a train this size. There has to be 50 to 70 wagons lining up here."

Just as the two men were finishing their conversation, Morgan following the Roberts and Peeples clan, slowly entered the prairie area set aside the town for those forming up the wagon train. They drove their wagons in view of Waltz and Wiess. As Morgan's wagon moved past the two men standing near their wagon, they commented on how out of sorts Morgan and Cocheta appeared.

"Well, there's an Indian and we haven't even left yet. I wonder who this group is and where they are from? As Waltz pointed out Cocheta less than 50 feet away sitting next to Morgan.

"Isn't that a sight," replied Jake. It was rare to see a white man with an Indian woman.

"Looks like their fixing to join us." Was Waltz's last words for the evening. He would spend the rest of the evening staring into their fire and drinking a cup of coffee that looked like it was made from mud instead of coffee grounds.

It was mid-morning when three more relatives of the Roberts rode in. They were riding light hoping to catch up with the group and purchase a wagon and supplies in Castroville. Aside from their arrival the day passed with everyone walking around Castroville. It didn't take long to cover the entire town. People were getting to know each other everywhere you went. They were all eager to get on the trail, but also wanted to have the friendships that would help them cope over the next couple of months. The wagon train would cover 15 to 25 miles a day depending on the terrane. Most of the way would be dry prairie. Water was going to be important and everyone had water barrels to be topped off at every stop that had water whether they needed it or not.

Morgan's wagon was parked within view of Waltz and Jake's. Morgan in a gesture of friendship walked over to meet Waltz and Jake when he saw them simply sitting near their fire talking.

"Hello, hope I'm not intruding." Said Morgan as he approached the two men.

Waltz, known to be a quiet man that kept to himself, looked up and nodded. That looked like it was going to be the total of his participation for the evening.

"Have some coffee?" said Jake in his harsh German accent. "We have plenty to spare."

Morgan accepted the invitation as Pat walked up behind him. Jake held out a cup toward Pat to indicate whether he would like a cup.

Pat replied, "Don't mind if I do. Mighty friendly of you. Thank you. Nice to know everyone a little before the group moves out, don't you think?"

Waltz once again looked up but said nothing. He nodded in his usually way and went back to thinking about whatever it was that he had been thinking about earlier.

Jake poured two cups of coffee and handed them to Pat and Morgan. As they sat down near the fire on a couple of crates set there partly for that purpose, Morgan spoke up, "Where do come from. Pretty heavy accent, I'd guess overseas."

"You'd be guessing right. Waltz and I came over from Germany several years ago. Figured we could starve to death here just as easy as there. Then we worked on a plantation and mined for gold in the Carolina's. After that we decided to follow up the stories about gold out West like everyone else on this little stretch of prairie fixing to get rich."

"We just got here a couple of days ago so we haven't met too many people and as you can see my partner here is not quick to pick friends. Just his way. Don't make anything out of it. Just his way. Always been like that. Since we were kids," said Jake reflecting back on all the years they had known each other.

In reply Morgan stated, "I'm from Minnesota along with my sister."

"Your sister in the wagon with you when you came in?" said Jake.

Both Pat and Morgan burst out laughing knowing that Jake was trying to make sense out of Cocheta being his Sister although stranger things happened out in the wild West.

"No, no, no, Cocheta, the woman that was with me is not my sister. My sister Sally is with Pat here," realizing what confusion Jake was experiencing.

"I'm sorry. Couldn't make out how the Indian woman fit in I guess." Leading the conversation to where Jake was trying to get his other foot in his mouth.

"She is my wife to be," said Morgan wondering if this friendship was about to end. "We plan on getting married tomorrow. Pat and my Sister, Sally are also getting married at the same time."

Morgan and Pat were both waiting with utmost attention to what Jake's next words would be. Hoping that he would carefully choose his words.

While Jake carried a revolver, it didn't escape his attention that Morgan carried two guns inside holsters and a small revolver in an under the arm holster. Jake couldn't figure out why Morgan carried so many guns unless he was a gunfighter. Again, if someone carried two or more guns usually meant the man knew how to use them and had a poor disposition. He didn't want to offend Morgan or Pat over the carrying on of an Indian woman.

"Sorry again. Mighty pretty woman you have their Morgan. Tomorrow heh? Right here in camp?" with a sheepish look.

"Your invited along with you Mr. Waltz. Preacher coming over from Fort Hondo in the morning to get things started. One last day to get married, celebrate and then we are headed West the next morning I hear." Morgan now sounding very proud with Pat smiling right next to him also wearing one of his new revolvers that Jake had never seen before.

"Would like that very much. What do you say Jacob? asked Jake, staring at his partner.

"Sure, why not?" in a rather course tone, Waltz sounding like Waltz, is the way they all took his response.

Morgan and Jake continued to have conversation. It was obvious that all of them had gold fever. As Jacob listened, Morgan spoke of the hills north of the Salt River while Jake spoke of the gold rich areas just West of Sacramento. From what Jake relayed to Morgan most of the miners on the wagon train were indeed headed to Sacramento.

By the time that Morgan and Pat got back to the wagons, both women had turned in, leaving the campfire burning low. The two men decided to talk amongst themselves a bit before turning in for the night.

"Hard to believe that we are both getting married tomorrow. What are you thinking about Morgan?" Pat asked.

"I was thinking about how lucky the both of us are. It's like we already struck gold with the two women we are about to marry. I may not know Cocheta all that well, but I can guarantee you that my Sally is a real gem. You're more than just a little lucky. In the meantime, I rather enjoy the mysteries that are left to be discovered about Cocheta. I feel really blessed." Replied Morgan, wondering why he said he was blessed? It was a strange word that he never used.

Morgan had a lot of things on his mind and his faith and belief in God was one. He wondered about having killed a man. He had emptied his guns into that man. It could be described as a lot more than just killing him. He had stolen from Mr. Johnson and men on the riverboat, outright and in card games. Mr. Johnson bothered him the most because he liked him. Mr. Johnson was a better example of a man than his own father and he had stolen from the only man that had cared about him and thought of him as a real friend.

The more Morgan thought the deeper he looked into the fire to see nothing except the flames of hell that he would experience someday. If he truly believed in God, it was hard to believe He had the grace and forgiveness to excuse what Morgan had done in his brief life already. Why would God have anything to do with him after all the sins he had committed. He was so deep in thought, that he didn't even hear or notice Pat saying goodnight and heading off to his bedroll.

That night Morgan had his reoccurring dream once more, except this time the hand that reached into the water to save him, pulled him to the surface. He was feeling the realness of the dream almost expecting to be soaked as he awoke in the middle of the night. He was a bit sweaty, but it was only a dream. Yet as he lay reviewing what he could remember, he saw an image of light that he could only compare to the supernatural. That's when it hit him that his dream was that of God reaching out for him. Every time he had dreamed this dream he felt uncomfortable the following day, but now he was at peace as he fell back to sleep.

48

For Better or Worse

❧

Everyone was waking up to a gentle breeze which was moving smoke around the wagons and making a morning haze on one end of the prairie reserved for the members of the wagon train. The air was brisk as usual with the temperature have dropped considerable during the night. Mornings were always cold. It was a race to get fully dressed and warm up with a couple cups of hot coffee.

The event of the day was the double wedding that was going to be performed. To add to the unusual event of a double wedding was the addition of a white man marrying an Indian woman. This made the day a unique day. Nearly everyone in Castroville from the wagon train to the store and saloon owners were looking to observe whether invited or not.

An area near the end of town near a clump of trees and upwind of the occasional smoke from the campfires was chosen for the great event. There was a hill on one side where people would be able to sit like in a theater.

The preacher rode into town and was greeted by Pat, Morgan, Sally and Cocheta. They sat around the campfire near Morgan's wagons.

"Well what a blessed event and very special event this is going to be." Said the Preacher taking a second glance at Cocheta. He had never married up a mixed couple. He was searching scripture to put his mind at rest.

Everyone noticed Morgan being a little reserved when he greeted the Preacher. With the peace of his dream from the night before he still was nervous approaching the Preacher. Sally knew why but wasn't about to bring up that their dad was pastor which would lead to questions neither Morgan nor Sally wanted to answer.

Sally walked behind Morgan and whispered, "Be nice. This is our day to enjoy and celebrate. Don't let anything get in the way of that. You hear me?"

The last part of her comment startled Morgan enough to cause him to turn his head toward Sally and give her a questioning look.

"Love you Sis. Don't worry. This is our day," he confirmed. Morgan put the thoughts of his dad into a dark corner of his mind.

"I trust that we're going to have a big turnout today. People were talking about the wedding clear over at the Ft. Hondo. Lucky for you it's just a little too far for people to ride for the day or there would be a whole bunch of them here. So, we're going to do this by the trees at the edge of town? Sounds great." Stated the Preacher with confidence and vigor.

He went on speaking, "Are their going to be rings to exchange?"

Glances went from Morgan to Pat, then Pat to Sally until Morgan took the role of spokesperson.

"We didn't have time nor the proper place to purchase rings so you can leave that part out. Is that ok?" asked Morgan in an attempt to settle everyone down.

"Certainly. I will skip the ring exchange. We will concentrate on the vows. I always add a few words which would only be proper since you requested a pastor instead of a justice of the peace. God always has his place in a good marriage.," said the Preacher announcing in his own way that everyone was going to hear a sermon whether they wanted to or not.

At that moment the normal sounds around the encampment went silent except for the gasps of some of the women. The small group turned around to observe Chief Flacco accompanied by Captain Jack and several of Flacco's braves approaching. Captain Jack had decided to join the event to make sure no one mistook the Chief and his men as hostile natives.

Cocheta lit up at the sight of the Chief. She was on her feet running to meet both Chief Flacco and the Captain since she had seen the Captain on several occasions when he was riding with the Chief and his Mounties through their village.

She hugged the Chief saying, "I'm so glad you're here. Thank you. Thank you. So good to see you Captain." She wasn't aware of the dozens of people watching in confusion.

Captain Jack gave her a hug stating, "You know that the Chief has agreed to stand with you. Give you away, like in traditional weddings? I couldn't miss that."

Tears were pouring down her face as she tried to hide her face from the Chief. It was not proper for her to show such weakness.

As Cocheta was wiping the tears from her face, the Chief walked up from behind and put his arm around her stating, "tears of joy. What a wonderful day. You and Morgan will make a wonderful pair." She felt the honor of having the Chief a part of her wedding. Cocheta took the sign of the Chief attending and taking a part in her wedding as a true blessing from above. She knew now that this was meant to be.

Morgan rose to shake hands with the Chief and greet the men that were with him. As he shook their hands, he couldn't help but notice the awe-struck bystanders who couldn't believe that they had a group of Indians in their camp shaking hands and laughing with the Captain and some of his men who had wondered over.

After causal conversation, the entire group started to head for the area that had been chosen for the wedding. Morgan was walking hand in hand with Cocheta as were Pat and Sally. As they walked through town a mass of people joined them. Store owners put up closed signs on their doors not wanting to miss the event.

The pastor put everyone into their proper place to include Chief Flacco and the Captain behind Morgan and Cocheta. Morgan would have had Pat has his best man, but since Pat was also getting married, he took the liberty to ask Captain Jack to stand in for both himself and Pat as a best man. The Captain was honored to do so. He proceeded with the short sermon that no one was going to escape, making sure it was stated before the event. That way, no one was going to leave before the wedding ceremony took place.

To everyone's pleasure the sermon was short, quoting verses from Corinthians about God's love. The vows seemed longer as Morgan, Cocheta, Pat and Sally individually repeated what the preacher said word for word. At the end the preacher took a deep breath and yelled out so everyone around could hear him, "I now pronounce you, both couples, husband and wife."

The couples engaged in kisses while everyone around was yelling and clapping. After a few minutes the celebration started to move closer to the town where the men could use the event to enjoy a few drinks. Everyone was going to remember this day.

Pat and Sally moved off with a group made up of the Roberts and Peeble families. The women were all commenting on how great the ceremony had been. Morgan and Cocheta in a different manor, walked over to Chief Flacco first. In shaking hands with the Chief, Morgan felt a bonding. Morgan felt good that he seemed to have the approval of the Chief since Cocheta didn't have her father. He felt that their wedding was proper with the Chief involved and his sister on his other side, although Sally was giving Pat all her attention.

The day moved into full celebration as the saloons opened up, men woman and children were all celebrating around the wagons. There was little else to do except tend to the livestock, so when an occasion to celebrate came along, so did everyone within earshot.

After saying good-bye to the preacher, the Captain and Chief Flacco, the two couples turn in early to have some intimate time to themselves. Their wagons had been decorated with what was available so they would remember their wedding night.

The celebration in general slowed down quickly after the brides and grooms left. Everyone knew that the next day they would be heading out in search of their dreams. Tonight, Morgan, Cocheta, Pat and Sally were beginning to experience their own dreams.

49

Move'm Out...Headin West

∿◎

"**M**ove'm out ... Headin West", yelled Mr. Cooper, the Wagon Master. The wagons had all been assigned their position in the column. The Roberts families, Peeples along with Morgan's wagons and Waltz and Weisner moved together near the front of the column. Slowly, too slow to suit Mr. Cooper, the column started to move forward. The toughest to manage were those wagons that were accompanied by livestock. Whether a couple of cows, string of horses or small herd of cattle, they all seemed to be like anchors dragging in the desert sand.

The soldiers would meet up with the column later in the day at Maryville. No one was thinking about any threats other than being responsible for too large of a gap between their wagon and the next. The first day was slower than the Wagon Master or anyone would have expected. Maryville was only seven miles away, yet they arrived late enough in the day that the Wagon Master decided to circle them up for the night. Creating barriers with the wagons for protection and corralling the animals was another task that seemed to take to near dark.

With the first day closing, fires started up one after another in anticipation of cooking some dinner and relaxing with a cup of hot coffee. Many in the group had carried a few pieces of firewood to get started. Others spread out to pick up what they could find. As it was better to camp in an open area so one could spot any enemy from a distance, it also made it a chore to collect firewood for some warmth during the night.

The soldiers from Fort Hood rode in as the wagons were trying to get positioned for the night. They had some comic relief watching the green horns try and try again to make a perfect formation. It was funny to watch now, but the soldiers, scouts and wagon master knew that in a couple of weeks the train would make this maneuver with precision, even if they had to do it under attack.

Some of the men went into the town to see if they could get some supplies they had forgotten to pick up in San Antonio. At least that was the excuse they used with their women folk to check out the town's saloons. The four newlyweds decided to sit around a common fire and enjoy reflecting on the last 24 hours. The impact of being married and sharing their first night together became apparent. Lives had changed. Responsibilities seemed to surround the women as much as the men, both groups realizing the need to take care of each other.

The cool air of the night had everyone moving closer to their fires. The conversation about the trail was different now that they were moving toward their dream. They all realized that every day now would be more miles behind with fewer ahead.

Pat asked Morgan, "Do you know for sure where you are going? We never spent much time talking about the information regarding the gold finds that you got from Mr. Wakefield the banker. I heard that any place north of Salt River is hostile territory. Even small groups of prospectors have stayed away. Is that really where you might leave the wagon train? Just the two of you?"

"That has always been the plan. We will have to see what it is like and what we hear the area is like when we get to Salt River," replied Morgan.

"Sally and I sure wish you would go with us to Sacramento. I know you feel a commitment to Mr. Wakefield to search out the information he gave you, but we are talking about your lives here. Plus, it would just be better if we traveled together." Said Pat.

Morgan laughingly replied, "Well then it is settled. If we are going to travel together, then we are all turning north when we get to Salt River."

"You're crazy. My business is to sell guns, not shoot them," said Pat as they both started laughing.

The women remained silent. The two of them had spent enough time together to bond. The double wedding and Morgan and Sally being brother and sister put an extra emphasis to their bonding. Although not a matter of any deep discussion was the brother and sisters background. It was getting harder and harder for the two of them to avoid talking about their past. Pat had overheard talk of Morgan's past during the conversation that Sally, and Morgan were having, yet he and Morgan had never sat face to face to discuss each other's history. It was also considered rude to dig too far into one's past, since many people moving West were moving away from their past and didn't want to be reminded of it.

Morgan and Cocheta climbed into their wagon for the night. The Prairie Schooner had lots of room. Even so, it was still cramped when it came to the two of them laying down side by side sharing room with the assorted supplies they had for the trip.

As they lay next to each other, Morgan listened to Cocheta make soft talking, less than whispering sounds.

"What's wrong. Are you talking in your sleep?" said Morgan.

"I'm praying. Don't you pray before you go to sleep?" said Cocheta.

"I have at times." Was all Morgan said in response?

In a persistent manor, Cocheta asked, "What do you mean at times. I thought you were or might want to be a God-fearing man?"

"What would make you think that? I mean, I believe in God and all, I've still been having a rough time with all that over the last year or so." Said Morgan trying not to go any further. It was apparent that the conversation was taking the lead over their physical passion for one another tonight.

"I just thought, having talked openly about God and faith with Sally that you might have some of the same thoughts." Cocheta stated realizing he did not want to pursue this conversation.

Already knowing from a couple of days how she is when she locks onto something in a conversation, Morgan begged to pick another time to talk about his life over the last year or so. Again, he cut her off knowing she was going to ask what happened. He could not speak of any doubt about God without speaking of why he thought that way. That would bring up what happened before the trip.

He tried to avoid the subject and at the same time he found something very attractive about her directness. Also, her boldness to display her faith. She was not afraid to stop and pray at any time in front of or with anyone.

"I will explain, but just not tonight. Ok?" Morgan said in an especially pleading voice.

"Ok" was all that Cocheta said. She knew that this was a very sensitive subject. She would learn what the circumstances were in due time. Although that wasn't going to stop her from asking Sally about what might have happened to have caused Morgan to be so shaken in his faith.

Cocheta knew that for as much of a man as Morgan appeared to be, that he also had a soft heart. She knew he was good man, or she would never have fallen for him so quickly. Convinced that the story behind his actions would make sense, she also believed that he wasn't totally separated from whatever faith he had before whatever it was that happened in the last year or so. Right now, she was just going to enjoy the comfort and feeling of falling asleep in his arms.

The nights were getting a little longer every day, and it seemed like the sun was rising early with many in the camp awake, preparing for the day's journey before the sun even broke over the horizon. It looked like it was going to be another clear day. The rainy season hadn't started yet, so every day they spent on the trail was going to be better than moving thru mud and swollen steams and river crossings.

After a few days the entire wagon train developed a routine of sorts. The weather had remained clear and dry. Water was plentiful at various locations along the trail, so the experience of having to ration it was not upon them yet. Maybe they would be lucky and avoid that difficulty all together.

About four days in the soldiers decided to leave the wagons and head back to the fort. There had been no signs of any Comancheros. Army scouts had searched the hills and watched for anyone following the wagon train during the four days on the trail. If they were going to have problems, it would not come here but further down the trail.

The wagon master, Mr. Cooper, had a couple of his own scouts who were very skilled at spotting trouble. The scouts were of Indian decent, which at times drew harsh comments from some of the miners regarding the degree one could trust them. It soon became apparent that the wagon master knew his business and those who worked for him did too.

50

Wolves and Coyotes

very night as the fires burned down, a chorus of howls brought the night to life. Sleep was different for different people. It all depended on how long it took to get used to the night sounds. The wolves and coyotes seemed to go on the better part of the night. There was never the threat that the wolves or coyotes would attack the camp, but they could wake the dead making a kill of another creature in dark of night. Coyotes made a lot of noise, but they were not a big threat to the cattle, where a pack of wolves could take down a steer in minutes. It was common to see one or the other in the distance in areas that didn't have a lot of cover.

There wasn't much likelihood that even wolves would attack a herd of steer. They might pick off a straggler that got separated during the day or one that wondered off to far at night. Threat or not the sound of the howling with time became a settling sound to Morgan. Cocheta always referred to it as the wolves and or coyotes were singing to them during tonight.

On the night of the fifth day, the sounds of the animals fighting dominated the night sounds. It was clear that there was fighting going on and that a decision was likely being made as to what male was going to be the alpha of the pack and who was going to be chosen to leave, start his own or be killed.

Although it only took minutes to decide, it seemed to those listening from their bedrolls that it took hours. The screeching, snarling sounds were horrific to hear. One might imagine what it would be like to be attacked by a pack of wolves. It had happened and was among the stories one would hear about the dangers of the wild west.

The sound of whining was followed by a silence as if mother nature herself had demanded it. A solution had been found and life or death could now go on. The rest of the night was filled with dreams of struggle.

In the morning, Cocheta was up first. She had told Sally she was going off to get some firewood. Camp was less than 100 yards from the tree line. Morgan woke up concerned when he discovered she was gone, and he as he looked towards the woods in the distance, he didn't see any sign of her.

Speaking to Sally, "You shouldn't have let her go by herself."

"Aren't you being a bit protective. She knows more about the wild than you?" replied Sally.

He quickly saddled his horse to ride out to find her and to help, hopefully to just carry some wood back. It only took a couple of minutes and he was in the saddle at a lope off towards the woods. Morgan repeatedly yelled her name. He was also prepared for any surprises carrying his arsenal of weapons on him and his horse.

"Cocheta, where are you? Cocheta!" Morgan continued to yell as he entered the woods.

"Over here Morgan," responded Cocheta in a calm voice.

As Morgan rode a few yards further he spotted Cocheta on her knees with her back facing him. When he was close enough to see what she was doing, he saw three small dogs. Morgan saw three newly born pups on the ground. She was holding one of the three.

Morgan dismounted noting that his horse was a little uneasy. The horse shying gave him pause. That's when he realized that they were not dogs, but wolves. There was a small litter or what was left of a litter of wolves. There weren't any other signs that other members of the pack were around. It was unlikely they would see them if they were close by. None the less it was apparent that these little ones had been abandoned to the natural survival of the wild.

"They are so helpless. They can hardly walk. They won't be able to feed themselves. We can't just leave them here like this." Said Cocheta.

"I don't think anyone on the wagon train is going to take a liking to us harboring a wolf pack in our wagon. What will we do with them as they grow? They are wild animals. Cocheta, listen. I know you have a soft heart but taking these backs to the train is not going to be welcomed." Morgan said pleading with Cocheta.

Discovering how much his words of wisdom meant to her, Cocheta gathered the three pups into her arms and headed back toward camp.

"Please bring back some wood, would you Morgan?" said Cocheta.

Morgan was reflecting on his first experience of being outvoted without a vote in his marriage. Probably the first event of many to come. He knew down deep that she wanted to protect those pups, just like he felt he had to protect her. As he gathered some wood and rode back, he convinced himself that they were cute and that once they could fend for themselves, they would send them back to the wild.

As Morgan tied his horse and walked over to the camp for some breakfast he noticed that Pat and Sally had joined the, "aren't they adorable" club, each holding one, with the care of handling a small baby. Last night might have been a loss for the little ones, but today looked like they had been dealt four aces.

"We need to set up a box under the seat in the wagon that they can be in for the trail. You, pointing at Morgan, might also buy some milk from one of the families with goats." Commanded Cocheta.

Cocheta's motherly instincts were on display as she was planning all the preparation to raise these three new members of the family.

Pat and Sally laughed at the display of Cocheta's commands as they held the precious little ones. After the excitement toned down, Sally and Pat decided to make breakfast for everyone so that Morgan could head out on his quest for some goat's milk.

While Morgan was gone, some of the Roberts and Peeples parties happened by and took notice of all the commotion, wandering over to see what was getting so much attention.

"Cute, but you would have been better to have left them for the coyotes. They're going to be trouble. Like having three kids. More food, water and attention." Stated Ab.

"They're wild you know. Never be friendly. Ab's right. Nothing but trouble. You women, meaning no disrespect, are too soft hearted and motherly. Not to mention without children. You pick up these wild critters like their adopted kids. You'll be sorry." With Geo's last words said, the two turned to walk on.

Cocheta had to have the last word, "We are all part of Gods living creatures Mr. Roberts. These animals will adapt and be a blessing in return someday for the compassion we will have shown them."

The two men didn't turn around to acknowledge her statements. They just walked on shaking their heads. As more and more people in the wagon train heard about the wolf pups, near anyone thought it a good idea. Maybe it didn't seem like much now, but they all knew that the hardships ahead and survival would be a real challenge without adding to it with wild pets. It would be difficult enough to simply get everyone to their destination. Some believed with good cause that a number of those here would not make it. It was simply a fact. Taking on wild pets was viewed as crazy.

Ignoring the advice that continued to be freely given by passer byes, the two women found some rope to tie a sort of leash that had one of the pups tied to the next. They wouldn't run too far as small as they were all tied together. Their rope would have to be checked frequently for chew marks. If they had to go hunting for pups, the wagon master would put a quick halt to their possession with the ultimate authority everyone had signed over to him in his position.

Morgan soon returned with a small jar of milk. Having walked half of the wagons before he found out who had some goats, he finally found a source. The family with the goats weren't too happy about their milk being used to feed wolves. All they could think about was the completion of nature's circle where the wolves grow up and eat the goats. Morgan fed the sheepherders need for cash as the incentive to close the deal.

It was now Morgan's turn to play with the pups. They were only a week or two old and already starting to grow some teeth. In another two weeks it would be hard to play with those sharp little teeth poking holes in everything they could get a hold of. Boots, harnesses, and fingers especially.

All three had unusual dark colored coats. One was all black setting him apart from the other two that retained lighter shades of dark. They would soon be growing out that second undercoat which made their fur so thick. It was going to be a warm if not hot trail most of the way so the little creatures wouldn't likely see anyone wearing one of the many wolf fur coats the pioneers and trader wore because of their warmth.

"The cooking is getting mighty good out here on the trail." Pat said as a kind of complement.

"You'd eat anything not moving after a day on this dusty trail. But I'll still take your comment as a complement." said Sally as she and Cocheta laughed.

"Morgan, the trail so far has been easy. I hope this continues." Said Pat. The comment really meant that Pat was thinking about the hardships ahead. He could feel that it was going to get ugly at some time in the future. His thoughts were being shared by everyone, but no one wanted to talk about it.

Pat's words were still ringing in everyone's head when they woke up in the morning to a threatening overcast of dark clouds. The clouds heading in from the West were following a drop in the temperature.

'Looks like we are in for a cold wet day today." Said Pat, acting as their local weatherman.

No one had any idea how understated that comment was about to be in a few hours. The storm front was moving at a steady pace and didn't appear extremely threatening at first, causing the decision to be made to break camp and move out. As the wagons started to move out, the expectation was some gentle rains on and off. What wasn't noticeable was a major storm moving in from the other side of the mountains that would hit midafternoon.

51

Black Sky Overhead

Morgan had purchased eight horses for the two wagons that he had loaded for the long trip. This was instead of having some heavy oxen pulling or several mules like the supply trains that moved from city to city. He felt that with each wagon capable of holding up to 5000 pounds that four horses on a steady pull should be able to do just fine. Besides, they hadn't loaded up their wagons to the hilt. They simply didn't have enough to fill the entire capacity of the Prairie Schooners. In the event of something happening with one wagon getting stuck, he could take the second team to help the first for the extra pulling power. In addition, it only made sense to have a couple of extra horses when they reach their destination.

The wagons were loaded down with the usual list of items with some extras which Morgan having the funds decided would be better with than without.

"Those scouts are riding hard and fast. Something's going on." Said Ab who was on horseback and had ridden up towards the front of the wagons.

As they rode straight up to wagon master, those that saw them, sensed concern.

"Over the ridge. You can see for miles. There is a big storm coming. And I mean big. Never saw clouds that mean. Seem to be moving fast even though the wind hasn't hit us yet. Don't know if you can see the gulch ahead about three quarters of a mile out laying low." Said the first scout to ride in. The others were following as fast as they could ride.

"How wide and does in look threatening?" asked Mr. Cooper, the wagon master.

The scout replied, "What you really mean is should we be on this side or the other. We best make a run to cross it or we might be stuck on this side for who knows how long."

The wagon master looked over the terrain ahead and past it to the mountain pass ahead. The ground was dry, but that would change real fast with a hard rain and the runoff into the gulches that it created. The thought of having to cross a gulch after a downpour, the mud, the wait for the water go down was too much to risk.

The wagon master yelled out to one of the scouts to ride back and signal the rear scouts and make sure there weren't any Indians or Comancheros than might be watching from a distance. They would love to attack the wagon train in the middle of a run like this where they would not have time to circle and defend themselves.

He sent the scout that just rode in to mark the trail through the gulch while he and the other riders rode back informing the rest of the wagons that a bad storm was coming and we were going to make an organized run to get on the other side of the gulch before it hit.

Morgan was reflecting on Pats words about how peaceful the trail had been. Panic was setting in as Morgan looked forward and back on the wagons from their position near the middle. It was good that they were already moving, but they would have to get over the next mile and circle up on the other side of the gulch before the downpour.

Men on horseback were moving small herds to the rear to cross last as the wagons picked up their speed. Drivers were told to look ahead for the scouts that were marking the crossing, prepared to help wagons over the banks of the gulch. The banks were only a few feet high but enough to break up a wagon wheel if they weren't careful coming over it.

From a distant observer the wagon train might have looked like a slow-moving land rush. Dust was rising into clouds of their own making. Some of the cattle were getting mixed together, but that was something that would get worked out later. To see cattle moving with sheep and goats looked like a preparation for Noah's Ark. They would all get sorted out later after the wagons circled.

Cocheta was driving the wagon with Pat right behind her with Sally at his side in the other wagon.

The first wagons were approaching the gulch. The total wagon train was moving slightly to the left of the position the scout had picked out to cross which gave the rest of the wagons a deceptive view as the first wagons, horses and all went over the edge and disappeared into the gully. Then the next and then the first crisis happened with a wagon tipping over that was not lined up properly and approached too fast. With a wagon on its side the horses in harness were screeching while the scouts and men on horseback, jumped off their mounts to cut the harnesses and roped the horses to lead them out of the way. They moved the pathway over a several yards while men worked on getting ties on the wagon to get it turned upside, somehow hitch up some horses or oxen and get it moved or dragged up the other bank. If for no other reason than to recover what was in the wagon if the wagon couldn't be repaired.

There was also one of the men who had broken his leg jumping from the wagon. He ended up having one of the horses stepping on his leg. Two men were desperately dragging him up the other bank trying to ignore his screaming in pain. Pain was better than losing his life in the waters when they hit.

One by one, over the bank and up the other side. After a few went over the embankment, they actually had cut into the bank making it easier for the rest.

Morgan still on horseback held the halter of the lead horse to help Cocheta down the bank and up the other side without any accidents. The pathway to circling up was laid out as the wagons continued. With only a couple of wagons left the storm came over the mountain to do its worst.

The livestock was moved inside the circle that was formed by the wagons as they came out of the gulch. Men on horseback tended to the livestock in case they got spooked from lightening. The rain started with a full down pour. No sprinkle leading in, just a downpour like someone turned on a faucet. The wind hit hard. The pass thru the mountains was right in line with where the wagon train circled up. When the wind picked up it was like standing in front of a wind tunnel. It came through twice a strong as if it were on the open plain.

The wagon master ordered the scouts and available men on horseback with ropes to upright and pull the tipped wagon up the opposite bank. There was damage, but nothing that couldn't be repaired including the broken leg the driver ended up with. It was looked at and decided to be a clean break. Splints and a few weeks would see him walking again, maybe without a limp.

The rain was so heavy and the wind so strong that it tore the canvas off some of the rigs, causing considerable damage to their supplies. The trail ahead was going to be the hardest part. The supplies were going to be needed. Some believed in sharing, while others believed that each held their own. It was survival of the fittest, pure and simple.

With everyone under tarps or in their wagons, the storm went on for a good three to four hours before the wind slowed down. Then the rain started to slow down, and that's when everyone became grateful that they were on the West side of the gulch. Within thirty minutes of the heavy rain, the gulch turned into a roaring river. It would have swallowed up any wagon or animal in its path.

The water was cutting into the bank creating new pathways as the water moved like a saw, cutting deeper into the main base and moving the banks out further on the outside turns.

Mr. Cooper had picked ground far enough away and just high enough having quickly studied the surrounding area to avoid what seemed was impossible. Looking at the rushing waters, the intense sound of it, the smell of lighting and seeing animals scared to death, made one start to understand how this could have been a real disaster in so many ways.

The women had gone over to help with some of the other wagons where their tarps had been blown lose to get an idea how bad the shortage of supplies might be. It was also crazy to think that they would desperately be needing water in a few days, when they nearly all drowned today.

The wagon master asked that everyone that could, excluding those tending livestock, meet to report any damage to goods, livestock and equipment not already known to him. At the same time following the meeting, Cocheta asked that they all bow their heads as she would lead them in prayer. At that point about half of the men that were mostly miners respectfully walked off for lack of interest. They were the same ones that were opposed to sharing, even if it meant life or death for some of their fellow travelers.

"Lord, we want to thank you for your guiding hand and walking this path with us. For showing us your mercy today in guiding our wagon master and his scouts, leading us to safety. We are beholding to you. May God continue to Bless this group. Amen,"

52

Leaving the Wagon Train

Everyone on the wagon train seemed to collect themselves quickly. The Mr. Cooper decided to hold over one more day to let everyone get some rest before enduring what he knew was the tough part of the journey. The weeks ahead would be dry and hot and where there was water there would be mud so thick in areas that the horses would need help pulling the wagons through.

Once the wagon train was on the move again, one day started to blend into the next. Everyone was thankful that there hadn't been any attacks. That was still thought to be the size of the train and how it easily displayed a vast number of armed men and even some of the women. The women that wore pants and had holsters were hard to tell from the men. Most didn't mess with their hair. They cut it short making it near impossible to tell a woman from a man from a hundred yards off.

The people didn't mix very much. Although they were friendly the Roberts had so many in their clan it was hard enough for them to keep track of themselves. They considered Morgan, Cocheta, Pat and Sally as family even before they had started on the trail. Geo's cousins, Cyrus, Charles, Return, Daniel, Mose and Gideon were always quiet on the trail, but in the evening, their campfires were always filled with laughter.

Jacob Waltz and his partner Jake Weisner always kept to themselves except for an occasional visit. The visits were usually by Jake who probably got tired of listening to Waltz's silence day after day. Jake enjoyed some social contact with the others. Then there was a group of miners that seemed to hang together since they were all miners. They spoke of nothing but the gold they were going to get rich over. In the evening, if you were walking past their camp area you would hear them telling the same stories about huge gold strikes over and over. It seemed that they would never tire hearing them.

The wagons had moved on now for a couple of weeks. They went through what was loosely called a fort, Fort Clark. It was a location that a Lieutenant Whiting founded near a spring that would eventually build into a real fort. The makeshift garrison had two companies of troops. Company C and E. Again, they had all felt comfort for a while knowing that there were troops within a day's ride, but once they moved beyond, they were once again open prey.

As the sun took its toll the reality set in about the stories of those that died due to lack of water. They went past one location where the bones of the animals and what was left of the wagons were both bleaching in the sun. The bones had been bleached white by the sun. The reality of survival had taken lives. So far, their trip had been well planned and without any attacks, serious illnesses, or other calamities, everyone remained hopeful they would make it to their destination.

Over a period of four to five weeks they had moved thru Del Rio, Fort Stockton, Van Horn, arriving soon at the Coon's Rancho. Depending on who you were speaking with Coon's Ranch was also referred to as Franklin (El Paso in 1855). Franklin was a destination point. Planning for telegraph, stagecoach lines, and railroad were all in the making to connect Houston to San Antonio and on to El Paso. It was hard to imagine how that would change anything except to bring more miners. The problem with that is that sooner or later the gold and silver would run out leaving ghost town after ghost town.

A great deal of anxiety had built up over the days approaching their arrival in Franklin. Franklin was about halfway to Salt River (Phoenix) where everyone knew they would have to face the separation with Morgan and Cocheta leaving the wagon train and heading North while the rest continued to move West. Time and again Pat and Sally had taken turns trying to get Morgan and Cocheta to come with them to Sacramento. They described how great life would be for the four of them. The answer would always be the same. It seemed that Morgan and Cocheta had both confirmed their commitment to each other to head North and make a life for themselves in what they hoped and prayed would be not only gold country, but fertile soil to raise cattle.

In addition, Morgan felt a very personal obligation to check out the maps that Mr. Wakefield had entrusted to him as a business partner. Morgan couldn't explain to Pat and Sally why it was so important to fulfill his commitment to check out Mr. Wakefield's information at risk of their lives. Morgan knew that there was little he hadn't done in the line of sins, but the fact that Mr. Wakefield would trust him to information in the form of detailed maps where there were some gold finds and attempts to stakes claims was a promise to be honored. Morgan wasn't going to add Mr. Wakefield to the list of people he deceived or took unfair advantage of. For some reason Mr. Wakefield had seen enough honesty and integrity in Morgan to make him a partner and he was intent on honoring the old banker and his wife.

The wolves had continued to grow. Over the last few weeks, they went from pups that could hardly walk to bouncing little trouble makers, chewing everything they could get their teeth into including a couple neighbors in the evening. One of the men referred to them as Tanzanian Devils as he left everyone wondering what that was. By the size of their paws it was evident that they had a long way to go yet, but they were getting uncomfortable traveling in the wagon so they had been tied to a long rope so they could walk behind Morgan and Cocheta's wagon on the trail some of the time. Since Pat and Sally had their wagon directly behind Morgan's, they could signal if there was a problem like them getting tired or tangled up in their rope. This worked surprisingly well.

Since leaving Franklin the trail was dry and water was being protected. Morgan had taken on extra capacity, hauling two additional water barrels along with additional food. He was already helping some of the settlers out with water and figured he might have to help with water up ahead also. As soon as they would get over one range of mountains and threw a pass, they would see another in the distance. They learned very quickly that seeing the mountains in the distance, didn't mean they were close. As they continued toward the mountains it almost appeared at times that they were moving away as fast as they were approaching them, leaving them to wonder if they would ever arrive.

To their surprise they met several families along the trail at different locations that had turned around and were headed back East. It was a dangerous move. Most of those they came across had headed back traveling in small numbers. Some were just a single family. That made them easy prey to hostile Indians or bandits. If they met up with the wagon train near dusk, they would settle in for the evening always drawing attention from those on the wagon train that wanted to know what they had experienced up ahead and why they were returning home. The stories were heart breaking. They usually involved a close family member dying or getting killed. One husband and wife had lost both of their children to fever. They had buried them along the trail, never to see their graves again. The misery was just too much for many. Most were settlers that didn't contemplate what they were getting into when they decided to pack up and hit the trail for months on end. They weren't ready for the hardships. The miners seemed to be a tougher group that had experienced previous lack of comforts. They were accustomed to living in a tent and fighting to protect their claims. They all knew how to shoot and had better survival instincts.

Small towns, Deming, Lordsburg, Douglas, Tucson, Florence and finally Salt River (Phoenix). They were only miles away from Salt River and would arrive tomorrow. A new pathway to the northern territory had a point at Lordsburg where explorers and military had turned north in a form of a shortcut, but Morgan wanted everyone to spend every moment he could with Sally, and Pat in part thinking he may never see them again.

He had spent all night thinking about whether he and Cocheta should continue West with the rest. Then he would weigh in on how few friends that he trusted to include one old banker and his wife who brought him in on a partnership of possible riches beyond belief. He could hear the old man's voice and his wife laughing making his decision one of honor more than money.

Not being foolish, he had pulled out the maps that Mr. Wakefield had given him and a document explaining what a couple of explorers had found in an area north of Salt River. He read the statements about the gold over and over. Then he would study the map. At one point a few days ago, he had walked over to talk with Mr. Cooper and a couple of his Indian scouts to see if they knew anything about the region. All they could add was that explorers and miners had been known to go up into that area. No idea where the ones that found gold found it as it was usually a well-kept secret. Many were known to have kept their secret in death at the hands of the Apaches.

There were certain people that seemed to move through Indian country and others that fell victim at the first encounter. There were so many various tribes that it seemed it would be difficult to avoid them all. It was the thought of what would happen when they eventually met up with them that consumed Morgan. One man can only fight off so many before falling.

The wagon train was going to hold up for a couple of days at Salt River. There was a small trading post and area that attracted the friendly Yavapai Apaches who farmed maze and hunted in the nearby hills.

It was an uneventful day as the wagon train moved into Salt River. The river was named Salt due to deposits of salt that the river flowed over. One could taste the salty mixture in certain regions of the river. As the wagons circled up as a matter of habit now in addition to protection, there was little conversation. As Morgan and Pat stood around after unhitching the horses and feeding them, they did little speaking to each other. Sally and Cocheta were cooking and putting up a pot of coffee for the evening. They didn't seem to be speaking either. The task for the two of them to prepare dinner had also become a habit. Each observed the other and wondered as their trails separated what the future would be like. What little companionship they had among themselves would be gone.

Pat was as usual, the first to speak when things got awkward.

"Hey Morgan, have you had any other thoughts than to head North from here when the wagons pull out?

"I've given it a lot of thought, especially over the last couple of days and I really have little choice. I gave my word to the partnership with Mr. Wakefield and his wife. I believe that it is meant for me to go." Replied Morgan.

"Now that doesn't make sense over life and death. I'm sure he is not expecting you to sacrifice your life so you can feel that you kept your part of the agreement. What about Cocheta? And what about Sally. You are her only living relative... that matters. She is looking at this separation as if she will never see or hear from you again. That may end up the case. Does that seem fair?" said Pat with more questions forming in his head as fast as he was speaking them.

"I have a certain peace with going North and so does Cocheta. We have spent a lot of time talking about this. If we don't find anything, we will continue Northwest through the mountains as we have been told there is a route West and meet up with you." Giving hope to possibility of seeing each other after the Northern Territory.

"No need to talk more about this. My gift to you is the small crate of ammunition I left over by the back of your wagon. It may be a while before you get to a place to stock up again." Said Pat with as hopeful a tone as he could muster.

"Thank you, Pat., You're a hell of a man and I'm proud to have you as part of the family and there to take care of Sally. I know she is in the best of care. I have to have another conversation with the scouts and one of the Yavapai that know the Northern Territory." Said Morgan with little else to say he walked off knowing that the wagon train might leave in two days' time.

Morgan always drew attention as one of the pups, all of which had grown quite a bit over the last few weeks seemed to have picked up enough loyalty to follow him around without running away. Morgan had been untying him more and more, trusting him to learn to come when he was called. They decided to name the three Dalaa, Naki and Taagi. The names were simply 1,2,3 in

Apache language. It was Cocheta's idea. A formal name would make them more attached and they knew that someday soon they would run off into the wild when they could take care of themselves.

"Thank you for meeting with me." Said Morgan as he stood in front of the wagon master with Dalaa at his side. Morgan was introduced to two Indians. One was an Apache scout that had been with the wagon train and the other was a Yavapai Apache from the territory who went by the name Itsa, which translated to Hawk in English. He had scouted small groups before and knew the surrounding mountains. Between the three that Morgan was asking questions of he got a pretty good interruption in the answers.

"My wife Cocheta and myself will be leaving the wagon train tomorrow to head North. I have some maps which lead to a high valley about a week's ride north of here. Maybe two to three weeks by wagon if there is a way thru the mountains. Can you give me any help, which I'll gladly pay for, to get to the high-country North of here?" Stated Morgan with everyone looking at him as if he had a death wish.

"You know that many an explorer have never returned going thru that region. If you think all those guns you wear give you passage, you should know that many a group of well-armed miners went into the surrounding mountains and from there straight to hell. The Peralta's from Mexico had dozens of men and they were all well-armed. From time to time miners crazy enough to go into the mountains find their bones. Gold too, but nothing they will ever spend. Granted they went West of here into the mountains, but the Apache consider a lot of these mountains to be sacred. You don't know what you are doing." Said Mr. Cooper, after exchanging words with the Indians present.

The meeting went on for some time, resolved that for a reasonable sum that Itsa would guild Morgan and Cocheta to the highlands. Morgan offered him two of his best horses if he rode with them and got them to the high country according to the map. It looked like there was no question that they were leaving the next day. The Indian insisted that if he was going to guide them that he wanted to leave the next day. They would be leaving one day sooner than when the wagon train was pulling out.

53

To the High Desert

The last evening was unbearable knowing that they were going to be saying their goodbyes the next morning. Everything had been said that could be said in an attempt to stop Morgan and Cocheta from leaving. Sleep was at minimum that night. The next morning, chores started up as usual except that Morgan was the only one in the wagon train hitching up his team, preparing to leave.

"I love you; don't you ever forget that. And don't you go and get yourselves killed." Said Sally with tears flowing down her checks.

Pat attempted to comfort her, but it was useless. Sally felt she was about to lose the last member of her family. She held onto Morgan until he had to push her away. Goodbyes were not only with Pat and Sally, but the Peeples and Roberts families. Even Waltz and Weisner both came over to say goodbye and wish them the best. They had made a few, but very close friends. Some without even knowing it.

The Indian rode up pulling a pack mule. He had conveyed to them with what little English he knew that there was no telling if the Apache's to the North will be hostile or look at them as explorers simply moving through. It would very unlikely that they would finish their destination without someone knowing they were there. The hills and forests north had eyes all over.

Pat had a hard time as men always do, telling in one way or another how much he cared for Morgan. Pat thought of him as he would a brother. He promised Morgan that he would take of his Sister, which was comforting to Morgan, already feeling like he was abandoning her. This trip had turned into a mission and he had to see it out.

There was one last thing that Sally wanted to do that she had already spoke to Cocheta about. "I want you two (Pat and Morgan) to join Sally and I for a short prayer."

Cocheta decided to speak even as her tears would make it difficult. Sally was silently crying holding onto both Pat and Morgan. A few of the others that had come over to say goodbye joined the small group noting they were going to pray. They all took a knee as Cocheta started off, again not caring who else was watching or what they thought.

"Lord, we ask for your guidance for all here. As we go our separate ways, we pray that both groups will have your protection as we have had since we started this trip. Be with Morgan and I as we move Northward into hostile country that our enemies might see us as their friends. Help us to spread your word in the same way it reached us. Your grace and mercy be with us. Amen." As Cocheta kept her head down adding a few lines that no one could hear.

The time had arrived. The wagon, horses, their guide and the wolves started to move out. People waving, the wolves barking and the ladies all crying, the separation was emotional as the wagon moved on into the distance. They stopped to look back at the first rise knowing that once over the small hill they would be out of sight, making the separation seem permanent.

Dalaa ran alongside the wagon without a tie as his liter mates, Nahi and Taagi, remained tied up due to lack of trust. They didn't want the pups running off to end up being eaten by coyotes. The dogs were confused wondering why they were headed away from the wagon train and all the attention they were given in the evenings as people would pet them and give them snacks. It was their job to simply follow wherever their masters were going.

They were still in the valley after riding all day. They had made great time with level land for the most part, but the valley was wide and the distance to the foothills was still a day's ride. After that they would be relying heavily on their Indian guide.

Cocheta had changed into her Indian clothes to look more aligned if and when they might come across any of the northern tribes. The first day up without the wagon train and more precise, without Pat and Sally was a shock. Both Morgan and Cocheta had a simple breakfast while they spoke of missing their brethren already. Itsa, their Indian guide just sat a bit off from the couple, not speaking, probably because he knew very little English.

It would be a warm day although they knew it would get cooler as they went up to the high country. The wolves were all loose now. They hung together, not letting each other out of sight, especially Dalaa who it seems had become the Alpha of the pack. Yes, they seemed to be moving more like a pack everyday rather than a bunch of puppies. They were growing with their bodies catching up to their huge paws. All three slept within a few feet of Morgan and Cocheta throughout the night. Morgan felt it ok to leave them untied. They were big enough to survive on their own and the intent was never to turn them into pets. As long as they were with them it was a comfort. They would be the first to warn them if intruders were to approach during the night.

Itsa had explained that there was a very small area that the wagon should be able to get through if the terrain had not changed. If not, they would have to take what they could pack on the horses and abandon the wagon. That was something they would hope to avoid.

As they started out that morning, Itsa decided to ride ahead to examine the terrane. It had been nearly a year since he had gone up into the high country and he wanted to ensure that the wagon could move ahead on the trail before they might run up a valley to a narrow pass or worse yet a dead end. There were markings left by explorers and Indians alike, but they weren't always visible and most travelers taking this trail would be traveling horseback with pack mules.

"The Lord is with us," said Cocheta out of the blue. "Look at the beautiful day He has created. I feel Him looking over us."

Even this simple statement still made Morgan uncomfortable. With the real possibility of hostiles attacking at any time he didn't want to be discussing God right now. The look on his face spoke clearly to Cocheta that there might be a better time to speak of this.

In her mind there wasn't any better time. Before getting up she had quietly thanked God for the safe passage over the hundreds of miles of barren land they had traveled. Cocheta felt they had to have had the good Lord protecting them, given the stories of those that didn't make it, or the extreme hardships that many travelers had experienced that they seemed to have avoided. Avoided? No! It was clear to Cocheta that there was a reason that the Lord had brought them this far. God had something planned for them and it didn't seem right that it would be to die in the wilderness. A calm came over her as she handled the wagon and spoke to the horses as Morgan rode alongside horseback.

It had been a couple of hours since Itsa had ridden off. Cocheta was well experienced in handling the team pulling the wagon as

Morgan rode ahead of her on horseback periodically riding to the rear to watch for any danger that might approach from behind.

The landscape seemed the same as it had been for the last several hundred miles. How nice it would be to experience the thick forests of home. Smell the fresh air with that distinct forest smell. Morgan was daydreaming when a motion ahead caught his attention. It was Itsa riding at a slight gallop coming into view. No need to be alarmed, as he wasn't riding like he was being chased. Cocheta pulled up and stopped the wagon as they watched Itsa approach.

Following his arrival, he indicated to Morgan that there was a wide enough trail that they should be able to get the wagon another day's ride before exploring more road ahead. He also mentioned that he knew that he had been seen and followed once he reached the foothills. Itsa didn't know how many, but they only observed, which for now was a good thing.

Cocheta reacted more to the announcement than Morgan. She knew many stories and had seen what the Comancheros did to people. The Apache's in the high country and the mountains that framed them to the East were known to have treated their visitors in the same fashion. Better to be dead when they arrive than to let them capture you. Cocheta was now starting the think about what it would be like to have moved to Sacramento with Pat and Sally. Then she whispered to herself, "God has this. It is in your hands Lord." As she snapped the reins to move the team forward.

They were right at the base of the foothills when they decided to make camp for the night. The horses seemed restless. They acted like this sometimes when the wolves were running around. Morgan didn't tie them anymore since they seemed to know where their food was coming from. They hadn't learned to hunt, so he felt they wouldn't wander far if at all.

Morgan wasn't hungry as the sunset exploded over the sky. From their vantage point the sky to the West seemed to go on forever. The color changed from bright orange, yellow and then as dark set in a royal purple. What a display. It almost gave relief from thinking about who was watching them.

If they were being watched, they were seen as having a string of horses, supplies, and guns. Just about everything that a young warrior would receive praise for returning to their village with. This would be far more than just stealing a horse from a nearby tribe which was almost a sport for the young men.

Just before turning in for the night Cocheta showed concern that the wolves hadn't returned yet. Morgan was now feeling like he shouldn't have untied them. They had little chance of surviving in the wild with everything from wolf packs, mountain lions, coyotes, not to mention getting bit for messing with a restless rattler. Both Morgan and Cocheta had become attached to the pack. They would miss their evening play times and cuddling them with their thick fur. Their hope was they would eventually return when they were hungry.

The evening had the usual sounds. Every so often one would wonder if the sound was that of a coyote howling or the sound of a rabbit being killed by a coyote or a wolf. Then of course it could be Indians copying the sounds to signal each other throughout the night. There seemed to be more sounds than normal tonight or maybe everyone was a little edgy knowing there was a real threat out there in the dark. Itsa assured Morgan and Cocheta that hostiles seldom attacked at night, but he would stand watch.

The sun hadn't broken over the mountains to the East which Itsa had explained were very sacred to the Indians in the region. The air was already starting to warm up when first light streamed across the valley with another hue of color to introduce the day.

Cocheta was already up and quietly off by the wagon on her knees praying for safe passage for the day ahead.

It was at that moment that Dalaa came running up to Morgan wagging his tail. They had returned during the night. The other two were close behind, still stretching from having just gotten up. Nahi was dragging some kind of critter that Taagi kept attempting to grab. It was like a game of keep away until they reached Morgan on his knees lighting the campfire for the morning meal.

"What do we have here", as Morgan reached out to grab Nahi, who wasn't about to part with his prize. "What? What do you have there?" smiling as it became apparent that it was what was left of a rabbit. Mostly just the pelt. That's when he noticed that all three had telltale signs of having had a messy dinner during the night. All of them had blood stains around their faces and paws. They seemed to wear them like a badge of honor.

Morgan couldn't believe that they had killed a rabbit. I guess the instinct to hunt was strong in a wolf at a very early age. They had taken it upon themselves to show their prize to Cocheta and Itsa as they joined around the campfire for first coffee.

"They already had breakfast," said Morgan as they all laughed and watched them play with the rabbit pelt.

Following breakfast, the usual ritual of hitching up and moving out had them heading up the trail. Literally heading up as the horses started to feel the difference from pulling the wagon on a flat terrain and pulling it up a hill. At times you didn't notice the incline so much and then at other times it took all the team had to move ahead.

Itsa once again left Morgan and Cocheta to ride ahead to make sure they weren't going to end up in some dead-end gulch. Which, if attacked with no way out could literally be a "dead end". They lost sight of Itsa quickly. The trail started to have twists and turns and the rock formations gave thought to the many hiding places that Indians could attack them from. The pack seemed be enjoying the day following along, although Morgan had learned to keep an eye on them. They could sense things, see and hear, that a person never could. He had seen how they would react to the slightest movement. The three if they decided to hang around would be great watch dogs giving them a great advantage preceding a conflict.

It was late morning and Itsa hadn't returned yet. As Morgan wondered why Itsa hadn't returned yet he noticed Dalaa having stopped and was staring up into the hills. He turned and looked quick enough to see something move and then it was gone. Morgan got off his horse to phrase Dalaa giving him an opportunity to stretch and look around without seeming to conspicuous. Dalaa had hardly started to enjoy the attention when the other two were right on him wanting their share of attention. Morgan pulled some jerky out of his saddlebag and threw each a chunk to enjoy.

For the brief time that they had stopped, Morgan checked his guns, He had a Winchester rifle, his Navy Colts and a smaller handgun in an underarm holster. His colts were draped on a double holster laid over the horn of the saddle so he could reach them quickly. He kept a second belt across his chest for addition ammunition. If they were going to have trouble, he wasn't going down without a fight. He was at times made fun of along the trail carrying an arsenal of weapons, but no one would be laughing or making fun of him now. He kept remembering the stories of Captain Coffee riding into combat with a revolver in each hand firing round after round. The mere amount of constant firepower alone confusing his enemy and throwing them off balance. Some in hasty retreat.

54

Hostile Neighbors

Three more days passed with Itsa riding ahead and marking the trail with cairns or small piles of rocks. The vast majority of the time, Cocheta and Morgan would be traveling alone while Itsa rode ahead to find a way thru the mountains with the wagon. It was the third day that Itsa had returned later in the morning, looking more concerned than usual. He motioned for us to halt as he got off his horse to speak with us.

He proceeded to inform us that he had seen the Apache's. This time they were not hiding but in full view of him, riding parallel observing his every move. At one point, two of the Apache braves rode close enough to yell to Itsa, seeing that he had a rifle which made them easy targets, they remained distant. They wanted to know who is this Wolfman who travels with an Indian couple. Itsa conveyed to the young braves that he was showing them how to get through the mountains and that the Indian woman and wolves were not his, but the white mans. He went on to explain that they did not seek to interfere with their tribe. The white man had also traveled many moons to get to here and intended to take his wife and wolves to the high country to live in peace.

The Apache Indians had seen travelers before and on occasion they had seen what they called bluecoats. Rare, but on a couple occasions a patrol from a larger company of soldiers would venture out and be spotted by the Indians. Itsa went on to tell how these tribes were very superstitious. This led to them having watched Morgan who they referred to as Ba'cho or Wolf because he was being followed by and admired by the wolves. White men were known to shoot or trap wolves the same as the Indians, but the Indians had great respect for them. Wolves were a serious subject of many Indian myths. The white man just wanted to sell their furs for money.

Morgan and Cocheta found it interesting that there every move was being watched. That the Indians seemed to be mystified that the wolves were not tied or being forced to follow but acted as part of the couple day after day. They also noticed that Morgan and Cocheta would feed them on occasion, showing in their minds great respect for the wolves. A close peaceful existence between man and wolf was not normal, causing them to see this couple with an Indian guide almost supernatural. It might even bring evil spirits to rise if something bad happened to this couple. They continued to refer to Morgan as Ba'cho.

The real shock came when listening to Itsa's description of the meeting, Morgan declared that he wanted to meet with them.

"I feel it is very important before we proceed much further that I meet some of the members of this tribe. What they seem to believe can be used to our advantage for safe travel if they don't see us as a threat." Morgan said with Cocheta nodding her head in agreement.

"I believe that this is a message from God. This is the answer to my prayers for safe travel." Said Cocheta noticing that Morgan was not real quick to acknowledge her statement.

They moved on for the day, never seeing the faces of the eyes that keep watching them. When they had stopped for the evening, they set up the wagon as a barrier on one side with a rock wall and overhanging cliff above on the other. The pack were free and late into the evening Morgan spotted Dalaa standing up, smelling the air and with a couple of soft yelps. Signaling the other two, they headed back down the hill and out of sight. There was no doubt that they were on the hunt and Dalaa was their leader.

Morgan moved to the back of the wagon, reaching in from the rear he removed a rather flat box. He opened the box and removed the headband that he had received as a wedding gift from the Old Chief Flacco. Again, he took in the beauty of the craftsmanship of the bead work. The feathers, which he folder the cloth around very carefully to properly protect them were from a Golden Eagle. He tied the head band to size and decided to wear it in honor of the Chief and to show respect for the Apache's watching them should they notice.

The first to notice was Itsa. He asked Cocheta where Morgan had received the remarkable headband. Cocheta explained that it had been a gift from the Elder Chief Flacco to Morgan on their wedding day. She went on briefly to explain that she was a Lipan Apache and knew the Elder Chief Flacco having come from San Antonio region of Texas. Itsa had heard stories growing up of the great Chiefs. The Young and Elder Chief Flacco's were spoken of many times. Itsa was in awe. The image of this couple had just taken on a completely different status.

He asked if they could speak more of the great Chief some-time. To hear some of the stories from someone that knew the Chief would be incredible. He now reviewed what he knew and how he would tell this important information to the Apache's if he could get another meeting with them. Surely this would impress them and help influence a peaceful nature between them.

The following day Itsa was up early and headed off in hopes that he would not only find an open trail ahead, but the Indians that he had spoken to a few days ago. He knew they were out there, but he had not spotted them to be able to signal a meeting. As he rode off, as usual, Morgan and Cocheta knew it would be a couple of hours before he returned.

The trail was getting rougher and Morgan was curious to ride on up a way to see what was over the next rise. If it looked like a rough road, he might plan on setting up camp midafternoon and not drive the horses too much. He was also looking for a stream that Itsa said he couldn't miss coming up the marked trail.

Morgan felt conflicted leaving Cocheta alone for any amount of time even with the pack. He told her to fire one shot if there was serious trouble and two if she just wanted him to come back. She took the rifle that was under the seat of the wagon and leaned it up against her leg as she started moving ahead with the team. Morgan commanded the pack to stay, having Cocheta tease them with some beef jerky so they wouldn't follow him as he quickly rode off.

Cocheta kept moving thru the rocky terrain spotting marker after marker. The trail where the wagon could pass was clear even without the cairns marking the way. A couple of times in the past 100 yards or so Cocheta had to look around the side of the canvas to try and see where the pack had gone. Each time she saw that they had stopped and were looking back over the trail. They had spotted something. Were the Indians following now?

Morgan hadn't been gone more than an hour when four horsemen appeared riding in fast toward the wagon from the rear. Cocheta pulled up on the reins. Looking all around the rough hills expecting to have an ambush, she instead determined that it was just the four riders in the rear approaching. Their fast-paced approach made Cocheta nervous. The pack started barking and running back and forth as if to indicate danger.

The four riders were soldiers who were supposed to be out on patrol but decided to follow the wagon they had been told broke off the train with a city type guy, and an Indian couple. The opportunity to grab some horses and guns looked easy. The small group of three would disappear subject to an Indian ambush. They had decided to follow them waiting for the right opportunity to attack. While observing through their telescope from a long distance, they saw the guide leave every morning to head up the trail. Now it seemed perfect when they also saw the man leave. They assumed he was headed up the trail to meet up with the Indian. They would easily overcome the woman, kill everyone when they returned and blame it on the hostile Indians.

They rode straight at her. There was a lot of confusion with the horses rearing from all the barking and commotion that the pack were making. The pack didn't run out but instead positioned like they were going to protect Cocheta and the wagon.

It soon became visible to Cocheta that the men riding in were soldiers. Why were they riding hard and fast? Deciding to trust the pack and her instincts she picked up the rifle and seeing them only a couple hundred yards away, she fired one round in the air. The shot echoed up and off the rocks forming the pass ahead as the soldiers came straight on. Cocheta had expected that they would have rode in slowly, especially after the shot if they were friendly. She had heard about Comancheros along with other bandits wearing soldier uniforms so they could get closer before drawing down on their victims.

Morgan pulled up on the reins as the sound of the shot echoed past him. He guessed that he was about a mile away. He only rode away from Cocheta at a gallop so the pack wouldn't chase him. They would rather enjoy their jerky and stay then with Cocheta. Once out of sight he slowed down not to put strain on his horse. Now he was stopped and waiting for the second shot.

"Come on Cocheta. Second shot... now. You just miss me?" although he knew it was too soon after leaving that it was anything less than trouble. He had already turned his horse around to hear the second round. Either way he was heading back only to be determined at what pace.

No second shot put him and his horse into a full run. He had to be careful given a great deal of the terrain was rocky. He couldn't allow his horse to have an accident as his mind flooded with anxiety as to what crises Cocheta might be experiencing. Why didn't he stay with her as more and more thoughts went through his head?

As the soldiers moved closer, they pulled their pistols and started firing. One of the men fired at and hit one of the pack, who started yelping while the other two wolves took to attacking their horses causing one of the horses to rear up nearly dumping its rider.

Cocheta was now taking aim and firing her rifle as the men started to come up on the sides of the wagon. Just at that moment a couple of arrows flew by just missing one of the soldiers. They first two soldiers came to a screeching halt as the other two slowed and turned to look around and see what was happening.

Realizing that there were arrows coming out of the hillside above them they rode to the opposite embankment and took cover.

Morgan was a mass of solid adrenalin coming over the last rise toward the wagon after hearing all the shooting. He had no idea what to expect with the number of shots being fired. As he rode full speed ahead toward the commotion, he first looked for and saw Cocheta crouched down on the opposite side of the wagon from the assailants. Soldiers? They looked like soldiers. Why were they firing at Cocheta?

That was enough thinking! Morgan rode within feet of the men who were still disoriented over where the arrows were coming from. Then suddenly there was this man on horseback with a colt in each hand firing round after round. The first soldier fell as a direct head shot took half of his head off splattering on the man trying to fire back from his other side. He only got two reckless rounds off before he got hit from Morgan's repeated firing, once in the lower chest and one direct to the heart. He was already dead as he fired off his final round aimed at the sky.

The other two jumped out thinking they would overpower Morgan and spook his horse. Instead, Nahi and Taagi decided to attack drawing the soldier's attention as their horses broke free and ran from the wolves at their hooves. This gave Morgan long enough to close in and pump several rounds into the last two leaving them dead like their other two friends. The dogs walked around them sniffed them and stopped barking realizing the threat had been dealt with.

Morgan jumped from his horse and ran to see if Cocheta was all right. She came around the back of the wagon and flew into his arms still holding on to her rifle. As Morgan hugged and held her tight, he noticed something that at first put a chill up his spine and put him on guard. There were arrows stuck in the wagon. He pulled her to the ground and grabbed her rifle from her. Hostile Indians? The soldiers weren't using arrows. As he looked up the hill in the direction from where the arrows would have come from, he noticed movement behind several rocks. The dogs became quiet. Why weren't they barking. That's when he found Dalaa on the ground. He grabbed the dog's leg as it lay under the wagon and pulled it out to see that he had only received a flesh wound. Dalaa was wining as Nahi and Taagi came over as if to console him. But what about the arrows? That's when a real miracle happened.

Having moved back to their horses, mounting up. the Apaches who had been following the wagon started to appear as they came around a high hilltop with boulders and out into the open. There was more than a dozen. They rode proud on their mustangs armed with a couple of rifles, the rest with bows and arrows.

Morgan tossed the light coat he wore revealing his ammunition belt and handgun. He didn't need the coat in the way if he had to reload in a hurry. He stood as tall and stern as he could attempting to show that he had a lot more fight in him. That's when Cocheta screamed at Morgan that they had helped her. She was also yelling at them in Apache to prevent any further conflict.

Cocheta stepped out in front of Morgan to speak with the approaching Apache's. Morgan still held onto the rifle in his hand not sure if he should trust anyone right now. Adrenaline was still flowing thru his veins. He stood on high alert.

The warriors lined up around in front of Cocheta and Morgan. A couple had smiles on their faces as if they were enjoying themselves. Others held their weapons at ready not knowing yet if they should trust Morgan or Cocheta who showed courage firing at the approaching soldiers. However, the one that showed unbelievable courage was this man, who seemed shoot at his enemy faster with more accuracy than anyone they had ever seen.

As they faced off, Cocheta stayed in front of Morgan to speak with the braves. This was not a move nor was it the place for a woman to speak in this manner. Then again, the braves had seen her courage. They knew she was a very unusual Indian woman. They remained quiet and waited to see what she would do or say.

"We are here in peace. We do not want conflict or war with the Apache. I am Apache. I am of the Lipan Apache. We want to pass through to the high country north of here to live in peace with the Apache and nature. She had heard how they were so amazed at the way that the wolves had followed them and freely chose to protect them. This was a sign to the Indians that they were at peace with nature.

In the brief moment that Cocheta had spoken, Morgan put Dalaa onto a blanket, and looked again more carefully at his wounds. The remaining two wolves came over to his side, one sitting as if to protect him the other licking Dalaai's wound.

Cocheta reached back and nudged Morgan, indicating that she had stopped talking and that the braves would more likely want to speak with him than her.

Morgan stood up and addressed the braves speaking thru Cocheta.

"We come here to live in peace. We would someday hunt together and fight side by side as today." Stated Morgan with a stern look.

The braves were quiet. They turned together and spoke among themselves before speaking back to Morgan.

"Why do you wear an Indian head band and the feathers of the golden eagle?" said one of the braves who seemed to have become their spokesperson.

"This is a gift I wear with respect to the Apache. It was given to me by the Elder Chief Flacco as a wedding present the day, I married Cocheta, my Apache wife. Do you know of Chief Flacco? He explained to me the meaning and importance of the Golden Eagles feathers. You know this." And Morgan remained quiet as Cocheta parroted his comments.

This caused some commotion among the braves. Here stood a white man claiming he was friends with one of the great Chiefs. They had all heard stories around the fires of their elders about the Old and Young Chief Flacco's. Father and son. The son had been killed which some say put the Apache at odds to the white man forever because his death saw no revenge for the one that murdered him. The Elder Chief was living his final years grieving his son's death.

The comments flew back and forth, Cocheta understanding some of what they were speaking about but most she was not close enough to hear as they turned into a huddle. What she did know is that they had heard of Chief Flacco and if she was of his tribe then the story of the head band could be true. None would want to dishonor a friend of Chief Flacco. They also commented again how he had ridden in without hesitation and killed four blue coats defending an Apache woman. He traveled with an Indian scout and fought with the courage of an Indian brave.

The young brave that was their spokesperson turned and commented that they respect any friend of Chief Flacco.

With that, Morgan took center stage stating, "I have the right to the possessions of these men having killed them. I make a gift of their belongings to you. The horses, gear and guns. They are all yours with a warning to bury or destroy anything that might make the army think you killed them if they come looking for them. We are friends. We have food to share if you will sit with us."

Cocheta finished translating. They were once again in a huddle quietly speaking about trust and friendship.

"We accept your friendship." Said the brave as they proceeded to dispose of the bodies behind some large out of the way boulders, covering them with rocks. They also buried the military saddles with them.

Morgan looked to Cocheta, "The army will think that they ran off and were tired of serving. It happens frequently out here in the West as I'm told. They won't likely even send anyone to look for them if they even know which direction, they left in.

It didn't take long for Cocheta to have some of the venison over a fire. They decided since the only thing they feared were the Apache's, and they were being invited to dinner they simply unhitched the wagon and made camp.

Dalaa needed a little bandaging and as he laid on the blanket taking in the festivities, his pack mates seemed to be getting a lot of attention. The braves kept reaching out trying to touch the young wolves. Morgan finally picked one up and after the wolf realized that the Indians meant no harm along with being bribed with some parts of their dinner, they allowed the braves to touch and pet them. This was almost a sacred moment to the braves. Unheard of in their lifetime. Legends and myths described Wolfs as supernatural and this is what it felt like to touch one alive and be among them.

Knowing the food was ready, Morgan signaled and indicated to be silent as Cocheta moved forward, lowered her head and started to say a prayer in Apache. The Indians had met and heard stories of these people who speak in this manner with their God. In respect they remained silent observing Cocheta as she continued on expressing thanks for their friendship and that they may live peacefully together. The braves were impressed with the way in which the woman spoke. She spoke Apache as well as she did English. When she said Amen, they recognized Morgan's signal to eat.

Cocheta quietly turned to Morgan to thank him for supporting her and drawing their attention to be silent while she gave thanks. Morgan's only reply was, "I definitely saw a miracle today."

As the meal went on and conversation flew back and forth Morgan started to get concerned that Itsa had not returned by now. It was getting late. He had expected that he would have been back by now.

As he moved along in the dark, Itsa was also concerned as he followed the trail back expecting to meet up with Morgan and Cocheta on the trail much earlier. He wondered why they hadn't made more progress hoping they didn't have a crisis or worst yet, run in hostiles. There wouldn't be much hope for them if they were greatly outnumbered and that wasn't hard to do with only two of them.

As he came over the hill in front of the camp, he saw fours fires. Why so many fires. They lite up quite an area. They left good silhouettes to shoot at with people standing next to them. Why so many fires? The closer he got, the more worried he became finally deciding not to ride in any further but to tie his horse and crawl closer to the camp to see what was going on.

The sight as he glanced thru the brush, he chose to hide behind was unbelievable. He was close enough to make out the two braves he had spoken to. Then he noticed that Morgan and Cocheta were also among the group exchanging conversation with Cocheta as the interpreter.

He no sooner noticed who was in the camp when the wolves broke away from their pampering to acknowledge that something was off in the distance. They didn't make any noise because they knew it was Itsa. He hadn't been careful enough to approach the camp down wind, so they had picked up his sent and knew he wasn't a threat. Unfortunately, the braves didn't know that. As they started to scramble for their weapons, Itsa yelled to identify himself. He walked in toward camp he continued to yell until he was almost among them.

Standing, looking over the participants, left him so confused that when he stopped identifying himself, he really didn't know what to say. Otherwise hostile braves having a meal conversing with Morgan and Cocheta. It seemed that Morgan got the meeting he wanted. That's why they stopped and made camp instead of having moved further up the trail which would have made his journey back to them shorter.

How they got together would have to wait for tomorrow. He was tired. He retreated to a distant tree with his rifle in hand to get some rest. With the Apache's bedding down for the night, tonight's rest for him might be questionable. He wasn't about to put any trust into this group. Maybe tomorrow would shed a new light on how this unusual friendship had developed.

55

Arrival In Paradise

As morning arrived the Apaches were gone. They had left early before the sun was up to go back to their tribe and let them know about this white man and his Apache wife so that others in the tribe who might come across them would treat them with the proper respect. The braves believed that both the man and woman had special powers and seemed to speak directly to their God.

Itsa had been up all night watching the Apache's. He didn't trust them. He had quietly watched, pretending to be asleep as they led their horses away quietly a distance before jumping on them and riding off. Itsa noticed that the pack slept as if trusting the Apache braves not to be mischievous during the night. With little to no sleep he didn't know how long he would last this day. He decided that he would ride along with Morgan and Cocheta as he had scouted out the trail far ahead the day before.

The pack was huddled up around Dalaa. Dalaa had been hit with a bullet in his side. It grazed his side which seemed to have stopped bleeding almost immediately. He was getting up as Itsa watched. You wouldn't have known that he was wounded except that he was experiencing some pain and walked slower than usual. That's ok. It was going to be a slow day.

There was only one way to get the wagon up the mountain to the plains above and Itsa knew it best if they take their time and move carefully. No need to risk losing the team.

When Morgan and Cocheta got up, Morgan decided to tell Itsa what had happened. The real story. Itsa knew that as incredible as it was that he could never tell anyone. They would connect him with the killing of the soldiers, if for no other reason than he was an Apache. Yavapai Apache were peaceful, but they were still blamed over and over for the crimes and misdeeds of the other Apache tribes. He probably would have slept better the night before if he had known how the Apache braves had helped Cocheta.

Still, they weren't about to let their guard down as there were always bandits and renegade Indians that didn't care about anything but themselves and how much they could steal and who they had to kill to get it. However, the trail ahead seemed different this day. The air seemed fresher. The birds seemed to fly higher. As they moved ahead in a rather lazy manner, they found the creek that Itsa had told Morgan about and stopped to take on water and give the horses a rest.

"You mentioned back in Salt River that the Indians treat the mountains as sacred. These mountains we are moving over?" said Morgan addressing Itsa.

Cocheta walked over to help with the communication, knowing that this first question from Morgan was going to lead into more. She could quickly speak Morgan's words in Apache so Itsa didn't have to try and work out what he said.

In reply, "No not these. The mountains East of Salt River. They have been the subject of many stories. The Apache tribes in those mountains, pointing off to the South East knowing that they were not visible from where they were, were hostile toward anyone that came into their sacred land. There have been many Mexicans and other miners attempt to go into the hills there for gold that were killed."

This was the first time in a long time on the trail that the word gold came up. Morgan started to wonder if they might be headed to the wrong place, but the map seemed to be exact so far. Yet he couldn't help asking the question of Itsa.

"So, is there gold in those mountains?" said Morgan as he tried to speak in a disinterested tone.

"There is gold in many places. Indians find it strange that the white man travels in large strings of wagons to the great water West to find gold when it is everywhere. Every Indian knows where there is gold. Yet few white men want to risk their lives to go into the hills to get it. Only a few have found the gold to spend it." Stated Itsa in a matter of fact way.

"Only a few? Like who?" Morgan realizing that he was starting to tip his hand to Itsa. He was reacting to the case of gold fever he thought he had control over.

Cocheta continued to translate moving the conversation along at a near normal pace.

"Some time ago the Mexicans came up from Mexico. They were aware of the area around Salt River from early Missionaries that had come up many, many moons ago. There was a family of Mexicans called the Peralta's. They came in large numbers, many wagons. Two-wheel wagons with oxen pulling them. Many mules were brought to haul the gold back home. They had many men with many guns. Women and some kids to do chores. They came in the cooler time of the year and headed into the mountains. You passed those mountains to the North on the trail you followed from the East just before Salt River.

They spent three maybe four moons looking, finding and digging out the gold. That's when they encountered the Apache. They killed the Apache. The tribe couldn't fight the large number with guns. After a time, they packed up the gold and left, going back to Mexico. That was the first time.

The second time they came for gold they arrived in the same manner with even more men to dig and women to cook. This time the Apache sent out braves to other tribes that were also enemies to the Mexicans. As the men dug out the gold, the Apaches were invisible to them as they watched them day after day, week after week. When they saw that they were starting to prepare to move out they sent braves out to all the surrounding tribes who honored their sacred ground. Warriors came from all over. They also saw the prize of many mules and horses.

When the Mexicans finally set out to head home the Apaches numbers had grown greatly. A place to attack the wagon train had been decided on long before. During the attack one young Mexican boy ran, hid and survived to tell people. He made it to Salt River to tell the people there about it. The Apache had a great victory that day. They killed everyone except for the boy.

There is gold. It is just dangerous to go into the mountains there to get it." Said Itsa finishing his story thru Cocheta. This was more speaking than they had ever heard from Itsa. He took pride in telling the story because the Apache as warriors defeated the well-armed Mexican's.

"That's quite the story. Anything ever found up this way?" asked Morgan, wishing he had just let it end with Itsa's story. Itsa became quiet and didn't speak after that question for the rest of the day. Itsa knew they were not trappers. He almost took their excuse as an insult to his intelligence. Morgan might be a gun fighter among many other things, but he wasn't a trapper. He knew they were after gold. He had a job to do. Then he just wanted to go home.

The next couple of days was the final push to get over the mountains. The final phase was difficult with some steep areas where the wagon had to be lightened coming back to pack horses with their worldly goods and after catching up with the wagon, return everything back to the wagon. A team of six horses strained, but Cocheta claimed it was the grace of God that put them over the top and onto the most beautiful high desert area. This wasn't desert though. It was the most incredible prairie, big enough to raise enough cattle for the whole Eastern Coast if they could get them there. The view to the West went on forever. Even Morgan was romantic enough to want to see the sunset as it moved over the horizon and dropped over the vast mountain range they were looking at.

They set camp for the night wondering if the closest water would be their future home. Water, trees in the distance. That's what they wanted Itsa to believe.

After reviewing the map given to him by Mr. Wakefield, Morgan knew they had further to go. The map showed they had to go north and then West to where they would run into a creek that they would follow to the tall pines. Morgan was getting better at reading distance and knew they were still a good week from their destination. It would be hard to leave the view and rich level land he was looking over. It was also a concern to be traveling on without Itsa knowing this wasn't their final destination.

Morgan had kept the final location a secret from Itsa. Morgan had told Itsa that they were looking for the prairie on the other side of the mountain. As far as they were concerned, they had arrived. The excitement of getting over the top and the incredible prairie they were in helped convince Itsa that this is where they wanted to arrive from their long journey.

Itsa had ridden up and over the mountain to locate water earlier knowing they were going to have to nearly empty the two water barrels, getting rid of weight, to get the wagon moved over the top of the mountain. The good news was it wasn't difficult to find water in this region as creeks seemed to be coming out the surrounding hills from every direction.

Discussing the Apache's around the evening fire, they wondered if they were still being watched. Why hadn't they returned? The result of their conversation led to the Apache's being afraid to confront them after appearing so unusual to them. Supernatural would be a better description. The elders, as a part of their superstitions probably chose to leave them alone and made their decision known to the tribe. This could be the real blessing when they finally reached their destination. They would still be in Apache country and maybe Navajo from the north. Itsa had mentioned the Navajo earlier on the trail and claimed they were unpredictable given the few he had met over the years. All these hostiles were capable and had taken the lives of intruders. Men, women and children. They played no favorites when it was time to kill.

As Morgan began to fall asleep, he wondered what Pat and Sally were doing. Did Henry and Betsy Wakefield know that they were this close to checking out his map. Would they believe they were still alive? He had written the name of the creek on the map with respect to Henry Wakefield.

They broke camp preparing to part company with Itsa who had kept his part of the bargain. He had another agenda. Not knowing if they were hostiles in this valley, which could be Navaho or Apache he just wanted this trip to be over. If he collected what was due him, he could start heading back today. He felt he would be safe the next few days on his return hoping that the Apache's would likely recognize him as a friend if he was spotted. If anyone else spotted him, the horses and mule would be a real temptation. He had been promised more reward from Morgan during the course of the trip but right now his main thought was that he just wanted to get out before anything else happened.

Morgan cut out two horses from the team and paid Itsa $200 in cash. This was a tremendous amount of money for which he dearly expressed his appreciation. They spoke of the trip briefly and their experiences. They had started to communicate fluidly. Both Morgan and Cocheta said they would look for him when they returned to Salt River for supplies. It looked as if Salt River would be growing being on the trail to California. Thousands would be following that route to the gold fields West.

With final good-byes, Itsa rode off South to head over the hills to return home on the other side of the mountains, while Morgan and Cocheta started to look for a location where they could make their camp with a defensive position. Not knowing what to expect it looked like they would have to be on constant watch for danger. The wolves were going to continue to be their best warning of anything trying to sneak up on them.

As they now moved on the relatively level ground, they had to maneuver over the many creeks and some of the creek beds that were dry for the time being. Morgan soon figured out that the creeks they were crossing were all one creek that zig zagged in front of them. He spent time scouting this in hopes that this was the one that lead to the tall pines. The creek continued to move West and the map said that they had to cross it. This had to be it.

Traveling the flatland was far more preferable to the rocks and steep hills they had to move the wagon through and over earlier on the mountain. At times thinking back Morgan couldn't believe what they had accomplished in the last couple of weeks. Then he would hear the echo of Cocheta's words. "God's grace pulled us over the mountains." He was beginning to believe that she was right. How many miracles would make God real?

More and more, the conversations he was having on the trail were reminding him of the Biblical part of his youth. At first Morgan would ride his mount during the day, but by mid-day he was tying up his horse to the wagon and climbing into the seat next to Cocheta which would give them hours at a time to talk.

As he studied the map, they continued to follow the creek. The map marked two large hills to the north at one point where the creek was running West instead of North. They would know when they had gone to far as the creek would turn south and end where small tributaries feed into it. Another indication of having gone too far was if they ran into a prairie of giant rocks, looking like they had been pushed out of the ground the size of big houses and bigger. This formation lay northwest of the creek as it turned south. The map had other markers. Morgan could only hope they would discover the correct location in the next couple of days.

According to Mr. Wakefield, the man that left him this information was the only one to return leaving two of his fellow miner's assumed dead. They went up stream one day never to return. After two days of no return, having expected them back the same day he went upstream to see if he could find them. There was nothing but a clearing where the horses and mules along with other horse tracks moved off to the Northeast. There were no bodies or signs of them being attacked. But somehow, he knew that this was the work of Indians. Quiet and unsuspecting. All he could think about now was getting out of this area before he disappeared never to be heard of again.

He had gone back to camp, packed up the gold they had found and what the remaining two mules and his horse and one extra could carry. He decided to head out Northwest to the gold fields in California. He had made it to the gold fields where he filed two additional claims and leaving them in good hands decided to return to Ohio where he used the producing claims as part of the collateral for a business he started in Cairo, Illinois.

The business didn't work out, so Mr. Wakefield was forced to foreclose on the collateral. The man had thrown in the maps of his find in this wilderness territory along with the maps of the trail.

Morgan had replayed that conversation with Mr. Wakefield a hundred times, each time hoping and praying it was true.

Again, there would be a creek. They were to follow the creek which would lead them to an area of the two hills and vast open valley of grass with a multitude of elk. It sounded like entering heaven except for the part where the men were likely killed. Morgan thought for a moment and wondered if the man that survived hadn't taken advantage of the situation having killed his friends after they found gold. He had moved some sizeable deposits back to Ohio. He wondered if they were all from the claims in California or the find indicated on the map.

56

I Wonder

‿❀꒰

It had been weeks since Morgan and Cocheta had left the wagon train. Mr. Cooper, the wagon master, had tried to talk them out of going as did everyone else. He would look to the North every so often the first few days after leaving Salt River, but after that he had the wagon train to think of. He had to leave them behind in his thoughts with the decision they had made. He wasn't about to tell their relatives or friends that maybe Itsa is still alive, being able to move faster and avoid the Apache, but he didn't give any chance that Morgan and Cocheta were alive. He would find out if any of them ever returned when he came back thru Salt River in a few months having delivered this group to their destination.

Sally was curling up at night feeling safe with Pat at her side, while she cried herself to sleep wondering if her brother and his wife were still alive. Whether they made it to the valley or found gold didn't seem to enter the picture. She just wanted to see them alive. She didn't believe that would be the case, but that's why no one would talk about them. It was because they probably all believed that they were dead by now. She had even had thoughts about how they would have died. Hopefully not slowly in the hands of the Apache's. They had heard so many stories and some of the men had already seen the results of their torture.

Pat knew he didn't have the ability to stop Sally from crying. She would be in the wagon seat with him during the day, when she would suddenly break out sobbing. Only time and as she said, "God will fix this. It is in His hands." Pat too was beginning to think more about God and where he stood. The wilderness they had chosen took lives like a kid reaching into a bowl of candy. One after another. If it wasn't Indians, it was fever. One small child almost died from a snake bite but somehow managed survived. It was being spoke about as a miracle that the wagon train hadn't lost a single person... So far. It was the "so far" that kept coming up that started to make Pat think more and more about his belief in God or lack of. He felt special having Sally by his side and to comfort her and himself he had decided that he would speak with her about the subject soon.

***

After breaking out a bottle and before passing it around to their clan, which included the Peeples with the Roberts group, Geo chose to make a special toast in memory of Morgan and Cocheta. Somehow this wasn't a farewell to life but to seeing them again when their trails would meet. Geo and the Roberts clan were sound thinkers. They were determined to think that their friend and his Indian wife were going to survive and likely find gold just where the map that Mr. Wakefield had given them showed it was.

They were very optimistic. Geo knew they had the better deal from the old banker with two claims already producing to check out for him and take over. He had wished though that Morgan who he had taken quite a liking to would have traveled on with them. It seemed that from what they were hearing, there was plenty of gold for everyone willing to dig it out in Sacramento. Geo had gotten to know Waltz and Weisner better over the time on the trail. All the miners were getting anxious to get to work. They were all a tough, hard working group and not taken to riding the trail.

In a conversation with Geo, Weisner had stated, "I sure miss that young couple and them wolfs. They just walked off following them like any other dog. Except... they aren't dogs, they're wolves. Darnedest thing I ever saw. I got to look forward to them visiting me for a handout in the evening. Any other wolf would have taken my hand. Those were some special animals all right. Thinking I might get me a dog when we get to Sacramento."

Geo just laughed, "It sure was something watching those pups grow up on the trail. Wonder how long they will stay with them?" Indicating that the wolves having grown up will take to the wild at some time leaving the young couple to watch out for themselves.

***

Back in Cairo, Illinois, Henry, and Betsy Wakefield were entertaining friends for the evening. The conversation among Henry and the men in his social circle spoke about the news. How the country was becoming divided over the economic structures of the northern states and the southern. Two different cultures were beginning to clash. Another subject was the land values rising in the East and how industry was developing. They never left out the trains or communications which now had the telegraph companies stringing line into the wild West of the Mississippi. But the number one subject ever since Henry had handed off his claims to Morgan along with the Roberts and Peeples clans, was the mystery of what was happening out in the wild West.

"OK, enough of the politics of the day. We have been waiting all evening Henry to hear the latest news about your gold explorers. So, have you heard from them since they left? Or did they just disappear with your gold claims. Henry, you're too trusting an individual. Betsy is the one with the common sense. She should of spoke up." As nearly all the men assembled chuckled.

"Yes, I have received word from my explorers. There is something else that I shouldn't divulge but will in the interest of protecting my ability to choose a person of good character." Responded Henry.

"Betsy was consulted, present at the time of this matter and agreed on the decision to trust the men I put in charge of exploring my interest in gold. May I add that after Mr. Morgan Sommer…," at what point Henry was rudely interrupted.

"Mr. Morgan? Who is Mr. Morgan? Henry what is…"

Henry now breaking back into the conversation said, "I will not have my friends insulted. Certainly not without some points of fact as to back the criticism. The Mrs. and I said Mr. Morgan Sommer, commonly known to all of you as James Sommer chose to become my business partner assuming the risk of his very life to fully file his part of the contract, and only then did he approach me with another proposal before he left. The following day before leaving he left in my care a sizable amount of money as a contribution to our partnership to invest in any matter, I so chose on a 50/50 basis, the same arrangement as we have on the claim. Realizing his generosity not expecting any contribution from my side, I agreed to match his funds in like manner to our other agreement making us truly 50/50 partners. We had the agreement drafted which stated beneficiaries in the case of death along with all the other legalities to form a real partnership. He is trusting me to invest the funds in any manner that I chose. That, gentleman is trust. Which is the greater, mine in his or his in mine."

One man spoke out asking, "Henry, who is Morgan? Why were we introduced to this man as James and now he is Morgan? Would you care to explain this peculiarity to us Henry?"

"James Sommer is his real name. He and his Sister, yes Sister, Sally were traveling incognito. That's why they claimed to be engaged. They had run away from their home in Minnesota. Morgan explained it all in a telegram to me feeling he had deceived Betsy and me. I believe it takes a real man to confess his errors. The rest of the families, the Roberts and Peeples have been notified and they have all excepted Morgan and his wife under any name they chose," replied Henry.

Silence had hung over the room since Henry displaying an edgy tone to his guests, started to talk. His comments left the men in the room speechless.

"Gentlemen, Gentlemen, let's make the explorations of these folks from our safe and comfortable positions, a positive entertaining and learning experience that we can participate vicariously in, not a point of separation or ridicule. After all, it is my money, and my gold we are talking about, not yours. Although if any of you wish to invest in the new company that Morgan and I have formed to take advantage of our future investments, please feel free to speak with me later or anytime this week. After that, the opportunity will be closed." Henry slowed down and said the last sentence very slowly as he looked over the faces of the men in the room. These were the wealthiest of the wealthy in this region and he could see that he was going to have a few of them visiting his office before the end of the week."

"Now on to what I have learned so far. I received a telegram from our Mr. Goodhue having arrived in New Orleans and another when he arrived in Houston. Yes. He and his sister made it to Houston.

The men were sitting now with pipes and cigars filling the room with smoke. The men were quietly making applauding statements but not to interrupt Henry, but to show their admiration of the suspense.

Henry continued, "The Young lady met a gentleman on one leg of their river journey and love be what it may, fell for the man who is on his way to San Antonio to sell guns from Mr. Samuel Colt himself to the famous Captain John Coffee and his US Mounted Rifles. The man that turned the tide on the Mexican war."

The concentration of the audience had one spectator burning his fingers not watching how far his cigar had burned down. Betsy had come into the room to open a window or two wondering what was being said that had the men mesmerized. Having seen the amount of smoke flowing into the area that the women were socializing, she at first thought that the men had unknowingly started something on fire beyond their tobacco.

As soon as Betsy had opened the windows to let in some fresh air before everyone became fixated, Henry looked intently at the men and said, "Shall I continue?"

It was rare to hear all these men agree to anything, yet, in unison, they all said yes in one long undertone. In the other room the women wondered as they heard all the men slowly say, "Yeaaaeeeesssss!"

Henry had them in the palm of his hand and he always enjoyed a good story, especially if he was the storyteller.

"Morgan has had to tell his friends about Sally being his Sister before one of them took to challenging her new boyfriend thinking that he was moving in on Morgan's wife to be. This Pat seems to be a kindly gentleman that has fallen for Sally.

We read about the fire in St. Louis. Well, Morgan and Sally passed by the great fire that very night. He didn't write a great deal of detail but imagine the sight of over 20 to 30 riverboats on fire in the harbor area not to include half the city in the background. What a sight to be seen! It must have looked like Dante's inferno."

There were gasps and shaking heads as Henry continued with the stories taking some liberties along the way. If the story he told would have been in a letter, it would have been the thickness of a good book as he enjoyed telling them chapter after chapter.

"That's enough for tonight men. Our women are likely wondering of our whereabouts. Best we join them before we break for the night." Said Henry with a broad smile on his face. As he stood up the men were slapping him on the back and nearly begging to be informed of any future developments as they happen.

**

Back in Stillwater Mr. Johnson was sweeping off the front walkway of his store. He had not slept well thinking that Morgan had attempted to kill his dad, a preacher no less. He had wrestled in his mind over and over and still could not believe that Morgan stole money and supplies from him. The one man that was really enjoying his friendship.

The tragedy of that morning was a horrible memory, then compounding that with the break in of his store and theft of his money. The thought of Morgan having attacked his dad, leaving him for dead and stealing the offerings from the church. It was more than he would ever understand. Morgan would be wanted for murder if his mother wouldn't have returned home early from her trip to find the failing Rev. Sommer, dehydrated and seriously wounded, nailed to his bed. The Reverend confirmed that

Morgan was the one and that Morgan likely drove their daughter to killing herself indicating that they had never suspected, but Morgan might have been abusing his sister. Mr. Johnson's mind was still filling up with mixed thoughts that he wished he could dispense with and get on with life.

***

The Irishman, Mr. Joseph Murphy was in amazement having orders now for hundreds of his new wagon, the Prairie Schooner. He saw the orders stacked up as more were coming in everyday, yet there was one he nailed to the wall. Every time he looked at the order on the wall it put a smile on his face. This order was special because he especially enjoyed getting to know a very special person. One he hoped he would meet again sometime in the future.

***

"Another purchase?" Stated Mr. Overly's attorney. "That's three different land purchases this month. How can you keep this up?"

Houston was quickly becoming a hub of activity and Bill Overly was one of the first to realize that land around this small city would be increasing in value as the city would soon stretch out a couple of miles. Land in large parcels surrounding the community would be desirable for cattle ranches to supply beef back East. The train would be arriving to St. Louis and Kansas City which would allow cattle rangers to move their herds north, then take them by rail to hungry markets out East. Someday the train would be coming into Houston proper. The telegraph was being strung to all the cities bordering the Mississippi and in some areas like Houston it had just arrived.

"I have a sale of another parcel for far more than I purchased it and I'm starting to use the money that my partner Morgan left me to invest. I can't believe that a man I only met for a few days, invested in me, someone he really didn't know. I owe this man my hard work given the opportunities that his investment is going to open up for me. That's how I can make the purchases I just made. You're going to be a very busy attorney just working for me alone if we are successful. Let me restate that, working for Morgan and me" Stated Mr. Overly

The attorney replied laughing, "One can only hope, Mr. Overly, one can only hope."

57

Is It Gold?

W e set up camp with the tremendous anxiety that we were about to find our home. It would be home for a while. While we traveled with Itsa we had continued to let him believe that we were looking for the valley over the mountains where we were going to build our homestead. We never mentioned that we were looking for gold, but we guessed that he knew that's what we were looking for after he had said that gold was everywhere, and Morgan asked him if there was any up in this area. Itsa never had any interest in gold although he knew that some prospectors had moved through this area. He assumed they had left Salt River north to move thru this area since they never returned meaning they either moved through or were killed. More likely they were killed. Still, he couldn't remember anyone ever speaking about any gold finds outside of the mountains that the Mexicans had mined.

"This is the day. Today we are going to settle into our new surroundings." Morgan said while hugging Cocheta.

Looking to the North were the two hills. They were very unusual with few trees growing on them. They were sure that this had to be the two hills that were on the map. Neither one of them could believe that they were about to arrive at their destination.

Especially Morgan. He was mentally following his thoughts all the way back to his home in Stillwater. He forced himself to stop. Too much to do today.

The hills seemed to start growing forests as they moved further up the creek which for names sake, Morgan had named Henry's creek.

After tying up two of the horses Morgan saddled up the other two horses so that he and Cocheta could ride ahead to find the end of the creek and look over the surrounding terrain. They had spotted elk and tracks that the wolves had drawn attention to indicating a rich area to hunt. They wouldn't go hungry and neither would Dalaa, Nahi and Taagi who were growing by the day, feasting on their nightly kills and daily handouts.

In a few miles moving through the thick forest and rolling hills the creek having turned south ended. It was incredible to think they had traveled for months, for this far and had arrived at the very location they were looking for. The creek wasn't a big creek, but it seemed by the shape drawn and position with the turns indicated on the map that they were there. The last miner to see this location was probably the man that handed this map to Mr. Wakefield all the way back in Cairo. They took a break to water and let the horses feed while they sat on the bank of the creek and soaked in the beauty of the wilderness. The trees were tall and majestic. Thick forests surrounded them in every direction. It would be just as difficult to get the wagon back here as it was over the hill as they looked around. Having gotten this far they would figure it out. There was an abundance of tall straight pines to build a cabin. They just had to decide where.

As Morgan put his arm around Cocheta, pulling her to him, he whispered, "God does perform miracles, doesn't He?"

Cocheta with her head on his shoulder just smiled as she continued to take in his words and their surroundings.

They hastened their return realizing that there was a lot of work to be done. They had the basics to cut down some trees and with what Morgan and especially Cocheta knew, build a shelter for the second night. The first night they cleaned out room enough to sleep in the wagon. They also had the tent they had been using on the trail which just seemed like too much work at the end of a hard day and riding around the terrain to return and pitch. They would do that in a good dry location tomorrow. That night Morgan listened to Cocheta say a very long prayer, thanking the good Lord for their safe trip and that the future may hold His desires.

The sun was over the mountains in the East and the wolves were up having once again returned from a night of prowling the countryside. There were no tell-tale signs of how successful their hunt had been the night before, but they were all sleeping in with the rest of the family.

Dalaa was up first acting completely healed now having chewed off the bandage from his previous injures within minutes of being put on. It seemed that Dalaa licking his wounds along with Nahi and Taagi licking on him on occasion had been the best treatment. They had continued to grow quickly still determined to stay close to Morgan and Cocheta. Any time that Morgan and or Cocheta would leave their campsite, the wolves were good to go with them 100% of the time. By now, they had the strength and stamina to run alongside with the horses at a trot for hours.

The next morning as Cocheta prepared breakfast, Morgan took to walking the creek with the pack running around him, in and out of the water. There was a great deal of the creek where you could clearly see the bottom. He had walked a good half mile before he found an area where the creek widened after a turn. It was in the silt at the turn that he first noticed what he thought to be gold. He had asked questions and learned a lot from the miners on the trail, but he himself had never panned for gold. It turned out that the panning might not be all that necessary, although he had learned how to do it. He looked down hoping what he was seeing was not fool's gold.

The small stones had a glint to them of yellow. They were small and in addition he could see the shavings of sand that held some of the same color. It couldn't be this easy.

Hearing Cocheta call him for breakfast he turned around and headed back. He couldn't resist telling Cocheta that he thought he had found gold on his first walk out following the stream.

"I think I found gold about a half mile downstream." Said Morgan.

Cocheta replied sounding doubtful, "That's nice. Let's eat and after breakfast we will go pick it all up so we can go home wherever that will be after we are done here."

"I'm not joking with you. Why would it seem so strange to find gold where no one else has probably ever been? The man that gave the map to Mr. Wakefield didn't care. He was never coming back here again, and I doubt he took the time to tell anyone, knowing that they wouldn't be likely to survive if they did come out here." Morgan said starting to display his anxiety.

"OK, here, lets hurry up and eat so you can show me." Replied Cocheta.

Breakfast went down quickly, the final scraps going to the wolves.

Cocheta was quick to follow Morgan to the turn in the creek where he claimed he saw gold. He had shown her a small nugget with what seemed like gold in it. If it was true, this gold ore held great promise.

Morgan heard Cocheta scream. He turned, drawing one of his revolvers. He wasn't walking or riding anywhere without his guns. Carrying two Navy Colts wasn't all that comfortable, but it felt reassuring in case of attack. Cocheta was picking up a nugget which was larger than the one that he had brought back. Then she reached down for another smaller one just that fast.

Cocheta knew what gold ore or nuggets looked like. Gold and silver were used a lot for payment and many times she had seen nuggets this size used for buying very expensive items. Neither one of them were going to question the reality of miracles. Morgan was thanking God under his breath.

Morgan didn't waste any time. He decided to start that afternoon collecting what they could literally pick up. They noticed the particles of gold glimmering in the sand that they would have to pain stakingly pan through at a later time. Right now, they were going to walk this creek until they had picked up what they saw, knowing that after a couple of hard rains that the creek bed would disclose new treasures as it probably washed some away. This is why they had come. The map was right.

Later in the afternoon he went out with the wolves hunting and managed to shoot an elk which was going to feed everyone including the pack for a while.

Over the next few days, they ended up spending a lot of time hunting for nuggets. It was crazy the way Morgan or Cocheta would see a rock with gold in it, then search out the immediate area to lift out a pocket full of nuggets in an hour or two. They had plenty of creek to walk before they would come back later to pan thru the silt. But they made sure they would remember where the largest deposits were.

They started to accumulate a fair amount of gold nuggets. Thinking that bandits or others might happen by, they decided to move their camp further up the creek, closer to the headwaters in the thick of the forest, so they wouldn't be noticed and if they were, they would look like trappers instead of miners. Morgan had purchased some traps that hung on the side of the wagon, but nothing next to what a real trapper would carry with them. Given time they would acquire some pelts that would make their camp surroundings look more like a trapper's camp.

They had to force themselves for the sake of the horses and their own wellbeing to build a coral to hold the horses and start the process of building a real cabin for shelter. The cabin would require s lot of cutting and assembly. Morgan knew how it was supposed to work but had never experienced building a cabin before. Their determination demonstrated their ability to do whatever they put their minds to doing. Then with Cocheta's blessings from the good Lord, failure was not an option. Every day at the cabin, a couple more logs went up, until it started to take on the appearance of home.

It only took a couple of weeks and they already had more nuggets, mostly small but gold nuggets none the less than they could comfortably carry down to Salt River on horseback. They felt the need to get their findings appraised and verified. They didn't want to attract attention, or file a claim, so they decided to only take a few small nuggets and some of the gold flakes panned out of the silt. If word did get out, they would claim to have found it by a creek north of Salt River before entering the mountains or in the mountains northeast of where they left Itsa.

Morgan and Cocheta would then purchase more traps for beaver and racoon. They would bring along the few pelts that they already had, but claim they found good areas to trap. They had returned to purchase more traps. If no one believed they were passionate about trapping they knew they would at least have meat on the table for dinner as a result of their effort.

Preparing to head down to Salt Creek they moved the wagon to an area and under a ledge that bordered the creek. The ledge hid most of the wagon from two sides. They placed branches to cover the exposed side. They buried the gold they had found thus far about 100 yards from the wagon and camouflaged the location. They then saddled up two horses and packed the other two with the few pelts they had. They couldn't leave them behind unintended. It would only take five to six days by horse back to get down the mountain and into Salt River. They hoped they would not run into the Apache, even if they seemed friendly to them right now.

Everything hidden or buried, Morgan and Cocheta headed East this time making a new trail straight East instead of following the creek back and forth. It was a five-day journey which had they pushed it could be done in four, but there wasn't any rush. The two of them were enjoying each other's company and they still didn't have a good idea of how they would hide their discovery and still get the gold ore looked at. They had to make sure it was real and discover how good of a find was it based on the gold content in the nuggets.

The little settlement was more of an Indian compound than any kind of town. Salt River wasn't that big, so Morgan and Sally were recognized immediately as they rode in. They had only been gone for a couple of months. That they only had a short time to trap would be their excuse for having so few pelts. During their couple day layover, they had bet the one person they knew that could tell them if the gold had any potential, worked at the small trading post. Local Mexicans and even Indians that were getting familiar with the wagon trains full of miners would bring in scrapes of gold every so often. The interest hadn't spread because of the extreme hostile territory. Until the military developed a fort nearby, very little activity would be reported when it came to gold.

Itsa was one of the first to walk over to greet the couple. He enjoyed learning English by talking and having Cocheta translate with the skill that she seemed to have.

Itsa yelled out in English as Morgan and Cocheta approached him, "Hello. Hello, friend. Hello friend."

Cocheta answered in Apache greeting Itsa.

"Hello to you, our friend. You got home safely. Good." As she smiled as the two men shook hands with firm grips.

Itsa spoke, "You have been trapping. That's good. Or not so good, seeing that they only had a small number, mostly beaver which they found along the creek. It was hard not to notice the two large beaver dams that created a small second lake from all the smaller mountains streams that fed into the main stream from further up into the mountains to the South of the headwaters.

Not saying any more than they had to, they simply unpacked the pelts to take them in and see what they might get for them in trade for more traps and a few supplies. This place was not stocked with a lot of goods. Each wagon train knowing it was getting harder and harder to get basic items as they moved West generally bought up most of what was available as it came in on supply wagons pulled in two-wheel carts from Texas somewhere. The immigrant trail which dipped into Mexico for part of the journey went through all the dangers they went through. The Mexican government had been taxing the wagons knowing that they were following a trail that moved through Mexico. The tax was on a per wagon basis. The wagons used were the small two wheelers pulled by oxen until just lately as the Prairie Schooners with huge capacity started to show up.

To Morgan's delight he had seen a supply train of the new Schooner wagons that had come into Salt River. Again, he wondered how Joe Murphy, the Irishman who designed these wagons was doing. Many men had come up to Morgan with envy of his wagon and the one Morgan gave to Pat and Sally. They had never seen a "Prairie Schooner" before. And here was a train of them.

It had only been a couple of months since their wagon train had showed up in Salt River.

The supply train would be moving on to supply another larger trading post West and slightly North of Salt River about a two days ride. Supplies were expensive. With the danger involved, limited capacity to haul, time, distance and then the Mexican tax made it a dangerous occupation. The risk was rewarded with hefty profits for traders and men that owned these wagon supply trains as the number of people moving West were demanding more and more.

58

Everyone's Secrets

I t was time to get some business done and settle their anxiety about the reality of the gold. Morgan approached Ben Collins at the trading post and signaled that he wanted to speak with him out back. Ben was laughing over the small pack of pelts and had a contagious laugh and a loud voice that always had anyone within ear shot of him either laughing but at minimum holding a smile on their face. The look on Morgan's face and the need to speak privately did not escape the festive character as they walked out the back of the store. Morgan had introduced himself to Ben before he and Cocheta had left for the high country. Ben had confirmed that Itsa was reliable and knew the territory as well as anyone.

"Ben, I need to ask you about something and as difficult as it is to ask, I need you to promise you will keep it a secret. I don't know you that well, but from our first meeting I took you to be a good person. What I have to show you, if real, could either be the best thing for the territory or the worst. The responsibility for that could be in our hands. I am going to trust your word and there will be rewards for your secrecy." Said Morgan.

Morgan standing in front of him demanding privacy with guns strapped to every part of his body put a serious backdrop to his request. Ben had heard stories about how Morgan killed a man back in San Antonio, emptying both of his revolvers into the man. Their friendship seemed to go only so far. Disclosing what Morgan was about to show would have dire consequences, especially from a man that could kill without hesitation. Given the look on Morgan's face Ben was thinking about whether he even wanted to know. Yet his curiosity got the best of him as he said, "Well sure Morgan. I won't tell anyone if you don't want me too."

Morgan followed his statement with, "You'll know why when you see what I have. Like I said. I am prepared to give you my word that you will be rewarded for your silence."

With that Morgan reached into his pocket and pulled out two nuggets that he handed over to Ben. Chills ran down Ben's back as he reached out for the nuggets. He could tell immediately that they were real. The question was how much gold content and how many more nuggets like these are there? Ben had seen plenty of gold nuggets. Miners in route one way or the other seldom had cash. Gold was accepted everywhere for goods and services. There wasn't a bank to deal in currency and most preferred payment in gold if they could.

Ben knew that Morgan didn't go up to high country to trap the minute he dropped the pelts on the counter. If he had any talent as a trapper, he had none as a skinner having hacked up the pelts of those animals to the point of nearly destroying the value. He knew he was after gold. It wasn't worth risking your life for anything less. Morgan also appeared to be close friends with the miners on the wagon train, not the settlers or merchants that hoped to feed off the miners once they were settled and set up.

The closer Ben examined the nuggets the more he failed to hold back his excitement.

"How big is the strike Morgan?' was Ben's first question. The look on Ben's' face confirmed without question that the nuggets were real gold. The next question was, "If the strike is of any size, how do you expect to keep it a secret even if I never tell a soul."

Morgan was still entertaining the confirmation on Ben's face. It was gold. He had actually found gold right where Mr. Wakeman had hoped it would be. He couldn't wait to tell Cocheta it was real. She was already pretty sure it was, given what she had seen. She would likely be the only other person he could talk to about this for some time outside of Ben. He couldn't risk sending word back East fearing who might read his communication.

"Trust me, there is gold and a lot of it. I followed a map from miners that abandoned their discovery and ran for their lives from the Apache's. The fear of being killed drove them North and then to California. I don't know if the fear of the Apache's will keep miners away or if the news of this would create an all-out war between the flood of miners it could create and the Apache's. Although they might stay away in fear of the Indians, like what I heard about the mountains East of here. Say, are those story's true Ben? Itsa told me about a Mexican boy that survived an Apache massacre of his family and dozens of men mining gold out of those mountains. Any truth to that?" asked Morgan leading up to a point he wanted to make with Ben.

"Yes, there is a lot of truth. Here is my secret to you. You can't tell anyone, but I have a good idea where the mine is that the Mexican's were last mining." Said Ben

"And how do you know that? Have you been up in those hills?"

"No, not deep into the interior where the mine is but I heard about it and the attack in detail from the Mexican boy that survived. We spent a lot of time talking about it. It was me that helped him. I feed and helped him until he was old enough and able to head back to find what was left of his family in Mexico. He told me the best he could where it was in gratitude for caring for him," Ben commented as they starred at each other.

"Cocheta and I are returning to the Mountains north to continue to put up all the gold we can find, but on occasion we will be coming in to get supplies and find out what is happening in the real world. Would you be able to move the gold East for us without anyone knowing? Maybe, in the future when this pans out, I can help you with your secret. In the meantime, I will trust that we will keep each other's information to ourselves." Reaching out to shake Bens hand. Morgan's hand felt like that of a card shark or gun slinger next to shaking hands with a miner. Ben hoped that Morgan had what it took to survive the wilderness so he and Cocheta might enjoy their treasures someday. If he did survive the Indians to the North, he would make a good partner to go after the Mexican's gold mine.

It only took the day to get some supplies, more traps, and create a bond of secrecy with Ben. It was important that they head out in the morning. There wasn't a proper hotel anywhere, but Ben had a couple of tents for storage. He told Cocheta and Morgan they could stay in one of them over night.

In addition, after thinking over Morgan comments about moving the gold East, Ben commented, "Gold comes through here frequently and there are always shipments moving East under guard. Usually once a month. I will see that it reaches the destination you desire without drawing suspicion.

That night the dream of having real wealth was coming alive. Cocheta was again, thanking God for their good fortune while Morgan listened and pretended to be asleep.

They packed up the horses and headed out the next morning retracing the trail back up to the high country. As they made their way along the trail, Morgan couldn't stop thinking about the story of the Mexican boy and the gold that was so plentiful that dozens of armed Mexicans came hundreds of miles to risk the Apache's. Months they had mined gold out of the mine. How much gold did they find? Morgan was thinking it was starting to sound like Itsa was right when he said there was gold all over the territory.

Not having seen any Apache's on the way down the hill it was a surprise that they spotted them several times on the way back up. They had waved at them with no response. They would just turn their horses and disappear. It seemed that they were following them. The wolves where aware of them each time they were about to appear, but they didn't act as if they were a threat. They just stared at them until they would disappear. Beside the few sightings, the trip went fast and in four days, they were back at their camp along the creek.

Cocheta and Morgan were together all the time which eventually led to a saturation of Biblical conversation. At first Morgan was reluctant to engage, but his love for Cocheta and the will to please her, had him speaking and questioning about what he had or hadn't learned in his early years at home.

Even though his dad was a preacher he had never really learned any more as a child than Bible stories. He had a lot of questions, starting with one major question on his mind, never knowing if today might not be their last.

"So how do we know that we are going to have a chance at heaven?" said Morgan surprising Cocheta. She was usually the one to start the conversation when the subject was about God.

They would speak out loudly to each other as they hunted for nuggets walking the creek over and over. If anyone was near listening, they would be facing Dalaa, Nahi and Taagi in seconds. The pack hung around keeping anyone or anything at a distance. They protected Morgan and Cocheta more than they were aware of.

"I have committed nearly every sin in the book. I don't feel that there is anything I can do to make up for that. How can you think that we are going to be in heaven? I know you will, but I don't see me going up that trail. Without going through my list of sins I think killing and theft alone put me out of the running, so I guess beyond this we will at some time go our separate ways."

"Don't talk like that" said Cocheta, looking at the fateful expression that Morgan had on his face. "I know you believe in God and Jesus as His son. So, the first thing you must do is ask for forgiveness and surrender to Him accepting Him into your heart. You need to accept the grace that He extends to those that genuinely want to follow in His footsteps. He will show his mercy and forgive you for your sins. He will cleanse you of whatever sins you've committed. This is the new beginning you should be looking for. Not moving from one place to another. You think moving West is starting life over. You have it wrong. Accepting Christ is starting over in its purest form."

"I believe you know what I'm saying. We grew up with Christ in our lives. You have always had a good loving heart. The men you killed, it was either them or you; they threatened someone you love. They were bad people. Use the gambling and the times you stole to be a lesson to teach others not to do as you did. Show them that you are now a Christian by how you act. For the days I knew you before we married, I could already tell you had a good heart. One that meant well and could be a warrior for Christ. You only have to accept His Grace and you will receive his mercy. This is what I believe." As Cocheta stopped speaking not knowing what else to say. She wanted him to remember the three points. Forgiveness, Grace and Mercy.

Morgan didn't act in his usual sarcastic or bitter way. Not because he didn't want to hurt Cocheta's feelings, but because he was starting to understand the true meaning of being a Christian and how he admired how Cocheta displayed her faith in front of everyone. She had a strength that came from something supernatural and he once again found himself giving God all the credit. The Apaches saw right away what he didn't.

As Morgan and Cocheta continued to have conversation after conversation from what Cocheta knew and read from the Bible, Morgan came to the truth one day after another very convincing miracle occurred.

They had been collecting nuggets walking and digging around for months now along the creek. From a couple of trips back down the mountain to Salt River, they had met up with the Apache's that had heard about them. On one occasion while they were heading home from Salt River, they came over the top of the mountain to stand face to face with a couple dozen Apache's. Among them were some of the young braves they had met before. This time they were invited to sit with them at their village. The stories that were told had many elders from the tribe wanting to see and speak with these people, especially the man that walked with wolves.

Knowing it would be a huge insult to turn their invitation down, Morgan and Cocheta followed the braves East until they reached a small clearing near a creek. Their teepees were abundant, showing that there had to be well over two hundred Indians to include woman and children. Everyone was coming out to see them. They felt uneasy as they had heard about what this and the neighboring tribes had done in recent months. They had fought against the soldiers and the settlers, killing numbers of both. The military couldn't afford to send troops in large numbers due to rising concerns of a possible split between the states back East. The settlers and miners kept coming and every so often they would pass through the territory that the Apache claimed.

Not only were they all looking at Morgan and Cocheta, but they were looking nervously at the wolves who moved along side in a protective manner. Here was the man who walks with wolves. The wolves were nervous as were some of the woman as they clung to their children. Every so often one or more of the wolves would growl knowing that this wasn't a place without threat.

Morgan always wore his headband while moving through the mountains so the Apache would recognize him with Cocheta. When the Chief first came out to meet them, he looked carefully at the headband, having heard the story of this man and the great Chief Flacco. He invited them into the lodge to sit with the other elders of the tribe.

As Morgan and Cocheta walked their horses over to the lodge entering with the Chief, the wolves which were used to going everywhere, side by side with them, entered with them. The room was silent as the elders watched the wolves. They were full grown and threatening in appearance. They ended up laying down in the back edge of the lodge directly behind Morgan and Cocheta. No one questioned them about the wolves or asked that they be put outside. The wolves shared the same food and respect as Morgan and Cocheta did. The wolves escorted and protected this man, which was again, supernatural to the Indians.

Morgan and Cocheta were invited to eat with the elders, but before the two of them ate as they were now seated with the elders of the tribe, Cocheta fearlessly said a prayer. The elders had been told that these people speak directly to their God. This put Cocheta in a different class from what the Apache's usually thought of their women. Next, she was very busy trying to translate between Morgan and questions that were coming from various elders throughout their meal together. After their meal, they were directed to an Indian Teepee that they could use for the nights shelter.

In the morning without their normal breakfast or coffee they were given a sendoff. The elders gave Cocheta a necklace of beads and Morgan an armband with a grouping of feathers. They both wore their gifts to show the respect and relationship they had with this tribe with pride, even if they couldn't prevent them from what they did at times to others invading their lands.

It was this event upon leaving that caused Morgan to accept Christ. The first night back after they went over the mountain to head down to Salt River, Morgan joined Cocheta in praying and accepting God once again. Cocheta in tears of joy could only think about her husband who was lost and found again. He had been quiet throughout the day reflecting on what had happened, thinking back to his youth in Church and remembering what Cocheta had said about simply asking for forgiveness and excepting his grace.

During his prayer, Morgan experienced a relaxed feeling. A relief that made him feel that all his concerns and fears for the moment were gone. As he would hear Cocheta constantly say, "God has this. Just put in His hands."

Before they fell asleep, Cocheta commented, "I believe that God spoke to me to help this tribe find Christ. Somehow His hand will direct me."

That evening the night air, Cocheta tucked at his side and God displaying the heavens above, Morgan had feelings that he had never had. The closeness to Cocheta, the thankfulness for the friends they had made, to include the Apache had to be part of Gods plan. He didn't know what all that would be, but he believed tonight that God was the designer of their future and likely had been all along.

59

It's Getting Crowded

⁓◎

The savage reputation of the Apache continued over the years in an attempt to keep settlers, miners and anyone heading West out of the Northern part of the territory. Morgan and Cocheta lived most of their life in isolation except on occasion when they went into Salt River. They found an easier trail down to a trading post to the Southwest which all the wagon trains would pass through after moving through Salt River for supplies. It was more of a trading post where salt river was more of an Indian community. If they had gold to move they would then take the two-day trip to Salt River to do business with Ben and return up their original trail North.

It was over a decade that Cocheta and Morgan had made their home in the Northern area of what would become Prescott Arizona. They had managed to use slews to take out more gold having spent the first year collecting nuggets, panning gold, and hiding it in case bandits show up. They had made many trips to Ben in Salt River. Ben indeed had been well rewarded for his secrecy. Ben would in turn use the Gold in trade and see that it was shipped back East, eventually ending up in an account at the bank of Mr. Henry and Betsy Wakefield.

Henry was always given instructions from Morgan as to what would be distributed to what accounts. There was the company partnership with Mr. Wakefield and his numerous associates, Mr. Overly for land purchases in Texas and money for miscellaneous debts like Mr. Johnson and charities that Henry took care of anonymously for Morgan and Cocheta. Over the approximate ten years of mining, many a fortune quietly was to these various accounts.

The Indians didn't care about the gold, and although rarely social would enjoy meeting from time to time with Morgan and Cocheta. They would use these occasions to present real gifts of livestock or horses to the tribe. This trading relationship with the Mountain apache's no doubt indicated that in one way or another they were being protected. It was a combination of God and the maybe His use of the Apache's. The Indians of the northern tribes had all heard of this couple and for some reason granted them peace even though there would continue to be raids, killing or simply miners that disappeared due to the hostility the tribes had for the invaders.

There were a few times when young braves that were acting outside of their elders attempted to cause trouble with Morgan and Cocheta. They didn't believe that these people were protected by their God and their wolves. One such time had Morgan facing five young Apaches who were demanding their horses and the mules they had acquired. When Morgan refused the first one of the youngsters raised his rifle to shoot, Morgan planted his feet, drew his pistols, and put two slugs into the boy before anyone else could move.

The wolves heard the shots as they were deep into the woods, came running in full attack mode. The commotion again with the wolves attacking the legs of their horses left them unable to draw down quickly and accurately on Morgan. Morgan held his position and his fire allowing the young braves to be chased off having seen their friend killed in front of them with the wolves and whatever spirits were with them coming out of nowhere to attack them. This whole occurrence only made the Indians more superstitious. They feared them, the wolves and their God. Tribes throughout Northern Arizona heard of this man who stood strong against five young armed braves. The belief that they were supernatural added to their reputation.

Morgan and Cocheta to show respect and keep peace had saddled up and rode off to return the body of the young Apache and meet with the Elders. There was concern about whether they would be attacked riding in, but then again, the Elders had given sanction to them and no one, was to break the word of the Elders. Even other tribes respected such action. The word had been broken and hopefully the Elders would understand.

It was a harrowing ride into the village with some of the woman already morning the loss having heard the story from the young braves that returned. Their version of the story was that all of them had fired their weapons at Morgan, but the bullets did not hit him. Both Morgan and Cocheta showed no fear riding into their camp. They went undisturbed to the lodge tent that they had last meet with the Chief and the Elders of the tribe.

The Elders approached waving the small crowd assembling to stand back and away. Even the Elders held their distance. The conversation was brief and respectful with the understanding that the young braves had broken the word of the elders. One had paid the price and the others would stand before the council after Morgan and Cocheta had left. With that said, a couple of men untied the body and removed it. They both wanted to leave quickly as they didn't want to be there if the Elders decided to change their minds on the issue.

Over the next few months Cocheta had spent a great deal of time in prayer, that they might have a child. She had wanted someday to have children and she was getting to an age that woman already had their families, yet she remained barren. Morgan had attempted to comfort her, but it was to no avail once she started to think about the subject. Morgan would see her look off in the distance with a glaze in her eyes, a sure tell that she was in deep thought over not having children.

Morgan had wanted children as badly as Cocheta, yet often wondered how they would raise a family in the Northern Arizona Territory. The trading areas south of them continued to grow supplying the wagon trains that had their sight on California, settling in whether to ranch or farm. The local areas of growth in farming was Tucson and Salt River. Both locations were starting to look like real towns with little shops, saloons, trading posts, churches, and restaurants. He often asked himself if even moving to Tucson or to a more populated area with a school and church would be better. If not there, maybe they would move back to Texas where the culture had developed since their last time through to be much of what it was like in Stillwater and St. Paul where they came from.

He would dismiss the thoughts as quickly as they came, with the quiet comment to self that they didn't have and may not be blessed with children.

About a year after the occurrence with the young braves, a messenger had come to them from the Elders inviting them to their lodge. It was important to them that Cocheta also attend. The fall weather had started to move in, and the evenings were getting colder and colder and they knew soon that winter would be upon them. Morgan and Cocheta had started out early for the Indian encampment. The cold air showed with the horse's breath appearing like they were smoking from fire in their bellies. They had some of the pelts made into wraps that kept the two of them warm. Draped over their shoulders, they would be warm on the journey back to the tribe's location which as the braves had told them had moved further up the valley to the side of the mountains, but not that much further for the ride ahead.

They had not been to the village since the death of the young brave. They would likely have enemies from the braves that had lost their friend. It was understandable, but the power of God and the Elders is what they would put their trust in.

The constant in their ride were the wolves who freely chose to tag along. They had grown into beautiful beasts. Strong, fast and with a much larger pack over the years. They had been free to roam. They had sought out and expanded by two additional wolves from the wild. Nahi and Taagi had had litters also. Each time they had a litter they had disappeared for a couple of months until their offspring could take care of themselves to a degree, never to be introduced to Morgan and Cocheta. The wild had taken hold of the next generation. These wolves or their offspring would never come in any closer than to let Morgan and Cocheta get a rare glimpse of them. More and more, Dalaa, Nahi and Taagi were spending time away. It seemed that they still had an instinct that told them that if Morgan and Cocheta were on the move, they would eventually show up on the trail to join them.

It was also apparent to the Indians who at times watched the strange couple as they traveled through their lands that the three wolves would travel with them, but they often noticed that there were others likely from their pack which would follow far in the distance never to be noticed by Morgan or Cocheta. This created the stories that became folk lore to the Indians. The story told outside of the tribes to any white men, soldiers, settles or the like would always be thought of as fantasy. The story of Morgan and Cocheta having a pack of wolves that protected them would draw laughs like some of the other superstitions the Indians had. The Indians knew better.

The Elders of the tribe and other tribes around had had many conflicts with the miners coming through and contact with soldiers in an attempt to make and keep peace. It was a difficult task. There were few people who understood the Apache language and spoke English also. Even then, some of the translation was made to fit the circumstances in favor of one side or the other. The Elders wanted to have someone to speak for them that they found honesty in and could trust. That person was Cocheta.

Morgan and Cocheta were welcomed by the Elders once again. No mention to their last visit was made as the two once again entered the lodge with the elders. The conversation was direct, which was always the way in which they seemed to speak. Cocheta felt pride and a special purpose in being asked by the Apache to speak and translate for them in difficult situations. She expressed joy in being asked and said that she would be available anytime they needed her. In addition, she asked that she might pursue teaching those that were interested to learn English. The Elders took more time to address that issue. In the end they felt that they would be willing to do it on a trial basis.

On the return trail Cocheta expressed her excitement because this would give her an opportunity to introduce God. Surely, they would be interested in hearing about the God of Morgan and Cocheta. This dream developed for Cocheta over the next couple of years. Conflict arose and the government would send soldiers who would also seek out Cocheta as a known contact of the Apache to speak for both sides.

60

Another Miracle Another Lesson

organ and Cocheta had given up hope of having a family. The years passed and Cocheta kept working, teaching English and reading the Bible with members of the tribe while Morgan continued to discover additional gold deposits eventually accumulating vast amounts of it. They were both in their early 30's when their lives really changed starting with the announcement from Cocheta that she was going to have a baby. After all their prayers, thinking they went unanswered, they were expecting a two-legged addition to the family. He had answered their prayers.

As exciting as that was there was other shocking news that they had learned from their last trip to the little trading post West of Salt River. Morgan had heard about a group of miners forming up in Yuma that were destined to head up to their part of the country. Gold had been discovered around Yuma and miners were coming back in from California as well as from the East. Morgan wondered how they might have suspected that there was gold North of Yuma, but they must have believed there was to put together an expedition of size. He had heard that anywhere from 30 to 50 men were signing up. That kind of a number would give some level of safety if confronted by the Apache.

The war between the states had started and as a result, nearly all of the troops that were stationed in the Arizona Territory were Union. A vast majority of them were called back East to fight which created a formula for disaster. One, was the depletion of the army in the West. Second was the announcement of new gold strikes in the Arizona territory and third was the Apache knowing that with the troops nearly gone they had to protect their lands. They also had an advantage over the miners trying to move in with sheer numbers. This started the first Indian wars that went on for years.

It was the following spring with Cocheta expecting that the Peeples expedition arrived. Morgan had moved their homestead and staked claims along the creek in addition to hiding the gold that had taken over ten years to accumulate that he hadn't taken to Ben in Salt River to ship back East yet. He thought that they were as prepared as they could be to welcome the group of miners until he rode out to meet up with them on the trail. Those in the expedition had already been informed about Morgan and Cocheta, but they had no idea that the men in the expedition included many of their friends from the original wagon train.

The first to ride forward to meet Morgan was Geo Roberts with Abe Peeples at his side. In a matter of minutes, they were circled by William and Gideon Roberts, Jacob Waltz and his partner Jake Weisner. Most of the men thought they had seen the last of Morgan and Cocheta when they left the wagon train thirteen years ago until word came from Pat and Sally in San Francisco that they had heard from Morgan and Cocheta. The last ten years saw the completion of the telegraph from coast to coast. Eventually, Henry Wakefield, Morgan's banker tracked Pat and Sally down to connect them with Morgan and Cocheta. Now, here they were alive and welcoming them into the unchartered territory. They couldn't wait until they set camp and heard each other's stories.

There were about thirty men, all well-armed and pulling mules packed with the gear. These men were planning on being here a while. Morgan lead the group to his cabin where the expecting Cocheta greeted the new arrivals. She was delighted to see the all the men they had made friends with from on the trail to the Arizona territory. Other members of the party were introduced to Morgan and Cocheta as they greeted them. There was Pauline Weaver who was hired by Ab to lead the expedition. Others included Joe Green and Henry Wickenburg who stood out in Morgan's mind as one intro took place after another until everyone had met everyone.

"It is hard to believe you're here. Any of you," said Morgan as the familiar faces gathered around him and Cocheta. "There is so much to talk about and so much time has passed. We haven't had much of any word about anyone or anything but the war between the states." Morgan gave them directions on where to make their camp near their cabin. They were anxious to get everyone settled in so they could catch up.

As the group pitched tents and settled in for the night, Morgan had so many questions to ask with the first one being, "What can you tell me about Pat and my Sister Sally? Anything at all?"

Cocheta, had taken a seat next to Morgan and listened intently. Geo and the guys seemed to be searching their minds for remnants of their meeting with or what they last heard regarding Pat and Sally.

"The wagon train got through to Sacramento with everyone safe and sound. We were greeted by Captain Coffee who had been put in charge as Sheriff of San Francisco. He had heard of our arrival and rode to meet us. I think he wanted to make sure that Pat and Sally got to San Francisco safely." Said Geo.

Waltz whispered to his partner Wiesner who in turn spoke up, "Seems we ran across Pat when we were in San Francisco for few days after the mining got thin. Thought we had better move on before we started to get thin too. Had enough of that in the old country. Yah, he was doing good. Said Sally was expecting a child."

Cocheta took a deep breath as a tear moved down her cheek. She had heard through their correspondence that Pat and Sally already had a child. Even as an incredibly strong woman she could not hide tears of joy once more. She only wished that she and Sally could be together to share the experience of having newborns.

"I heard from one of the men that rode with Captain Coffee that he was going to be appointed to some big position by the President of the United States. I guess Captain Coffee nearly runs San Francisco. Nice friend to have for Pat and Sally. Don't you worry about them. The trip was the roughest part. By the look of your homestead here you've made a comfortable place, but what about the Indians. We were told over and over not to even try come up this far." Said Ab looking and pointing around as he spoke.

Cocheta spoke up, "It has been a blessing that the Indians have given us permission to live here. We showed no threat and they have looked upon us as somewhat of a mystery because of our pack." Cocheta pointed to the tree line behind their cabin. Some of the men stood in amazement to see three wolves staring at them from afar.

'Are those the pups? The ones you picked up on the trail? Impossible." One comment out of the group as others made gestures.

"They are getting old. Not only did they stay with us, but they have their own packs now. So please tell your men not to shoot any wolves they see around here. They are likely all part of one of their packs. They don't bother our livestock. They do their own hunting in the mountains. The Indian's saw how the three of them followed us around which led the Indians to thinking that we are supernatural. Cocheta teaches some of the younger ones English when she can and reads to them from the Bible." Morgan acting proud of their achievements.

"The Bible? How do they take to that?" Asked Ab with everyone leaning in to hear the answer.

Morgan let Cocheta answer, "Over time some of them have taken a serious interest. Others remain at a distance, afraid of learning or being a part of us praying or speaking to our God."

"Amazing. When we were told that you were alive and living up here where the Apaches are still killing anyone they find moving through their lands, we wondered how that could be. You been here the whole time since you left the wagon train?" asked Geo.

"That's right. It is getting late and there is going to be a lot to discuss tomorrow." Said Morgan as he and Cocheta headed off to their cabin. Many of the men stayed up late that night and they posted sentry's around the parameter not trusting that they would be in any way a part of the agreement that Morgan and Cocheta had with the Apache's.

The next morning Morgan met with the men to explain what he could about the Apache's. Since they had known that he and Cocheta were mining more than trapping, it might be possible for the group to settle into mining around the area without conflict. There was also comments from Morgan about their wolves and the pack. "If you don't bother them, they won't bother you, but it will be hell to pay if anyone hurts them. They are family." Some of the men later spoke among themselves describing Morgan as being a little touched in the head. Maybe the Indians left him alone because they thought he was crazy. They saw him petting and hugging wolves with his Indian wife. This wasn't easy for some of them to dismiss, given the hatred that had built up having lost friends or livestock to Indians along the trail to and from Sacramento. Add to that the wolves which were known to be an enemy to man, made Morgan a difficult person to figure out. Then add that he apparently became taken with the Lord made it difficult to figure out given what they knew of his history. Maybe God was in the works creating a truly remarkable miracle.

Over the next few days Morgan pulled his old friends aside to let them know about the gold he had found up stream near the headwaters. Another location had been further downstream from his claims. With a few tips, most of the men started splitting up to see where they might stake claims. The stream was coming to life with the miner's activity. This activity didn't escape the Indians whose land they had encroached on. They had an understanding with Morgan and Cocheta, but that didn't include any and all the people they might allow in to occupy their valley. It wasn't Morgan's or Cocheta's valley to give away.

Peeples and his group had left Yuma in March of 1863, having no way to know that another expedition, the Walker Expedition of 1863, had left Colorado in June headed of the same area. It was mid-summer when a group of 34 men were spotted moving with their gear across the valley from the north. Captain Joseph Walker and his group were shocked to find a number of miners already in the valley along what Morgan referred to as Henry Creek.

As Walker's group approached, the men that were along the creek with Morgan ran over to greet them. Captain Walker dismounted and approached Morgan with an expression of shock. He looked like someone arriving at their secret fishing hole to find every Tom, Dick and Harry with a line in the water.

"Walker, Captain Walker," as he extended his hand.

"Morgan Sommer. Surprised to see you, especially coming in from the north, through Navajo country. You're likely as surprised to see us here, I suspect," said Morgan.

"We heard about possible gold along Granite Creek. Looks like everyone's working this creek. Any luck?" as Joseph Walker looked up and down the creek for what he could see.

"There is plenty of room here for everyone. Seem to be pulling out anywhere from $20 to $200 a day per man. A couple miners here went over to Granite Creek and said there are some good spots there too," Said Morgan.

Mind if we settle in here for the night. We'll be moving over to check out Granite Creek in the morning then. Any problem with the Indians in these parts? Heard there was a lot of trouble which is why we came armed with no women or children. Looks like you all did the same?" Joseph looking around noticing no women or children in site.

"The Indians know my wife and I and have befriended us. Been in these part for nearly fourteen years. I don't know how they will be reacting with more and more miners coming in but tell your men that we consider them friendly and not to start anything. We've enjoyed the peace and the company of the other miners that came in here a few weeks ahead of you," said Morgan with a stern look.

"No problem. The men will be only too happy to know that the Indians aren't hostile, at least not yet. Talk some more after we make camp," said Captain Walker as he walked over to talk to his men who were already mingling with some of the other miners that had come over to greet them.

Captain Walker moved his men over to Granite Creek the next morning where they staked out some areas. Over the next few weeks most eventually joined the rest of the men on Henry Creek which Walker, having asked permission of Morgan, renamed it as Walker Creek. That was short lived as it was soon renamed Lynx Creek, a name that stuck.

The days ahead would show once again that miners never got along well with the Indians, which in this case were only being held back by people like Morgan, Cocheta and his new friend Pauline Weaver. Weaver was a person that some of the Indians had met or at least heard of. Pauline Weaver was a true "Mountain Man", had explored this area over the years and met up with the Apaches who he had gotten along well with while trapping beaver.

61

A Tribute to God's Messenger

Over the months ahead, more and more skirmishes occurred with the surrounding tribes. Morgan knew that it was getting too risky to raise a family here. As it came time for their baby to be born, Morgan started thinking about moving down to what Henry Wickenburg had renamed as Wickenburg. There he could house the family safely while he would go back and forth to work his claims in the high country. He knew he could trust Walker and Roberts to protect his claims from any claim jumpers between trips. He was still in the planning stage of the move when Cocheta presented her surprise.

It was now winter when the blessed event occurred and Cocheta gave birth to a healthy baby boy. They decided to name the boy Levi, Levi James Sommer! On the day of the birth, several of the men comforted Morgan. A couple of women that had weathered the trip to the high country to stay with their men were at Cocheta's side during the birth.

When the good news hit, the men let out to whooping and hollering' to where the Apaches could have heard them across the valley. Under watchful eyes the Apache's knew from Cocheta's frequent trips to the mountains to read and teach that she was to have her baby soon. A couple of the Apache woman had offered to care for her if she stayed in their camp. Cocheta felt that she wanted to be sure she and Morgan were together and at their cabin.

Over the next few weeks following Levi's birth, Cocheta fell ill. Having just had a baby put her in a weak state. She didn't seem to have the strength to fight the fever off and day after day, Morgan watched her slowly slip away. It was only about six weeks after Levi's birth that she passed away. Morgan spent a great deal of his time praying. He prayed for the kind of strength that Cocheta had shown over the years. As sad and torn as he was, he was thankful for Levi. He could see her in his eyes. With Levi, the memory of Cocheta would be living and breathing. Morgan was grateful that she had led him to the Lord to face this tragedy. He thought of how she would tell him in response to her passing that the Lord had a plan that they didn't know about. A bigger picture that would explain her passing if they knew the details. Morgan was blessed to have so many of his friends around to simply comfort him and Levi.

It was a difficult time for everyone around the creek. This included the four-legged part of the family. Dalaa and Nahi seemed to take a position in front of the cabin door where knowing she had passed, refused to allow anyone but Morgan entrance. Morgan had to restrain the two wolves to allow anyone else access.

Dalaa and Nahi left that night to join the howls that came from the packs in the nearby hills. It was an ere event for the miners to witness. The activity of the wolves did not escape the Apache's that heard the echoes of their howling throughout the night. Morgan never again saw Taagi again. Dalaa and Nahi would come by during the day. They would lay next to Cocheta's grave for hours. Then they would follow Morgan around for a while and then disappear into the hills. Morgan was busy with the help of the couple of women that were among the miner's wives taking care of Levi. It was apparent that it was going to be impossible to raise Levi in this wilderness especially knowing that the number of conflicts between the Indians and miners was increasing by the day.

It was the third day when Morgan heard a huge commotion outside. Morgan grabbed his holster, heavy with the two Navy Colts and ran out the door. Men were forming up with their guns ready to fight. As they looked over the prairie, north and east the number of Apache's which Morgan identified as they got closer, from different tribes seemed to cover the entire floor of the valley. The miners wouldn't have a chance as they looked over the oncoming enemy with a look of defeat. The mere image of the cloud stirred up by hundreds of horses pounding the dry soil as they advanced made their hopes for survival vanish. Where did they come from? With guns drawn they knew they didn't have a prayer against such a vast number. It looked like all the Northern Tribes of the territory decided to go to war.

Morgan yelled, "Put down your guns! Put down your guns!" as the field of horses rode forward with hundreds of braves. They were moving very slowly, not how an Indian party would attack. Many were on horses and many more were on foot.

"Put down your guns, they are not coming to war with us. They are not attacking us." Morgan continued to scream.

Morgan walked out a good one hundred yards from the make shift line of defense that the miners were pulling together. To the miners it looked like Morgan had a death wish, but he knew some of these Indians and they all knew of him and Cocheta.

One of the young braves who he had first met in conflict had taken an interest in learning some English from Cocheta. Morgan identified him as he rode out ahead of the procession moving toward him.

Greeting Morgan and dismounting, he told Morgan that they had heard of the Cocheta's death. They also had been aware of the child. Morgan was speechless as he listened to the Indian brave speak of his admiration of Cocheta in broken English he had learned from Cocheta. They had come to show their respect for her. There would be no killing today. No blood shed. It was very difficult for Morgan to hold back his tears, to be strong in the face of these men and women. The women were walking following the men. Even if some of them didn't understand or like them, they were here to show their respect.

Morgan walked back toward the area where Cocheta's grave was with the Apache brave. The miners were told by Morgan to put down their weapons as there would be no blood shed today. In amazement they complied although keeping them within reach.

The number to include the Elders that could make the trip was unfathomable. Morgan was in awe. The miners took in the spectacle thinking they would never have come up here in the first place had they known there were so many warriors, some with bows and arrows and many with guns. They immediately understood the value of having had Morgan and especially Cocheta among them.

"Thank God for Cocheta," continued to be whispered throughout the ranks as the procession of hundreds of Apache's moved past her grave, leaving small gifts until they piled up into two long mounds on either side of her grave.

Morgan acknowledged the Elders as they moved forward. He was thinking that this was going to be the last time he might see them. Thoughts of leaving with Levi and heading toward San Francisco were developing as his next move.

He decided in having the brave that stood with him explain to the Elders his gratitude for their gifts and having enriched Cocheta's life. How important it was to her to be reminded of her people and giving some of their tribe an opportunity to learn English and hear about God which was so important to her. In addition, he informed them that he would be taking their new-born West of the mountains to family. He might not see them again before leaving on this journey.

In a gesture of friendship, the elders instructed the brave acting as interrupter to take some braves and escort Morgan and his child through the high country and to a safe outpost for their journey West through the mountains.

The day went down permanently in the minds of the miners to tell their children and grandchildren about the day the Indian nation numbering hundreds came to pay their respect to a friend of theirs. As some of the miners knowing now that Morgan was leaving, decided themselves to move on. At least to an area that would be safer than the high country. Henry creek as Morgan had named it never got registered and Morgan really didn't mind Captain Walker renaming it Walker creek before it became registered as Lynx creek. Some of miners joined together over the next year and stayed, eventually creating the city of Prescott, Arizona. Unfortunately, the day of respect was to be the last peaceful day between the Apache's and the White man for years to come.

Two days later Morgan set off northwest with an Apache escort of two dozen young braves. He was hoping to connect with a wagon train moving West. His arrival would certainly surprise his Sister Sally and Pat. He could envision Levi growing up with his cousin and getting an education in a big city.

62

A Final Goodbye

Morgan having fallen asleep in front of the fireplace with his pipe in hand woke up in a daze. He noticed that the fire had burned down during the time he either had thoughts of or dreamed of his journey over a lifetime. Not only had the fireplace fire burned down but also his pipe, thinking it lucky he didn't put the house on fire. He felt more asleep than awake, so he closed his eyes one last time rather than try and move. He was so comfortable; he just felt the need to go back and dream a little more. He felt like he had been with Cocheta once again and he so badly wanted to experience that again. This time he would finish his dream and finish it he did.

It was later than usual that Levi decided to get up. He had gone to bed early but had a difficult time going to sleep thinking about his dad, the adventures he had heard, but especially the ones he knew he hadn't heard about. He was thinking about how dad took all his mail to this day from the post office direct. He would walk down every day and pick up his mail. Levi guessed it might be more for the exercise than the secretive way his dad handled his affairs. He always kept his desk locked with the little key on a chain around his neck. This was another of his idiosyncrasies. Today might be the day or tonight that his dad was going to hopefully divulge some if not all his secrets. Was he really going to have an open conversation and answer all of Levi's questions? He could hardly wait after all the years. Would he speak about his early years and his personal mysteries? He had been waiting years for this day as his dad never broke a promise. He was going to discuss and answer any and maybe all questions Levi could think of about his past that he so secretly hid.

Even though he wasn't planning on disturbing him if he wanted to wait to this evening, Levi was still to excited to sleep. It was like Christmas morning. He got up, cleaned up and then woke up Wesley so he could get ready for breakfast. It was Saturday so there wasn't any need to hurry there being no school or church to get ready for.

Levi dressed while his wife, Adella, was just managing to get out of bed. Before anyone else he bolted down the steps with a little more energy for his age than usual. As he came down the steps, he noticed his dad's pipe on the floor near the entrance to the hallway from the front living room. He reached down to pick up the pipe and as he looked up the momentary question of why the dad's pipe on the floor was answered.

Levi could tell as he saw his dad sitting in his favorite chair, that he had left. Left to be with God and the feature of his favorite stories, Cocheta. He appeared as if he had drifted off with a slight smile on his face, as if he was experiencing a happy moment. There was nothing he could do but to sit on the couch quietly to observe. No one to call, no need to yell. Just a quiet moment to reflect. When all was said and done, one thought remained in the front of his mind surrounded by all the love he had for his dad, would he ever know what made him the man he was?

The End

POSTSCRIPT

Lost and Found Again

~№

A Story of God's "Grace, Mercy and Forgiveness" (A Christian Historical Novel)

The **Battle of the Alamo** was the result of resistance being shown by Texans toward the Mexican government. Santa Anna had spent most of 1835 putting down resistance in pockets of Mexico which preceded the march to San Antonio to put an end to the Texan rebellion in the spring of 1836. With William Barrett Travis in command, a small volunteer group which included James Bowie and previous U.S. Congressman David "Davy" Crockett choose to occupy the Alamo Mission. The company of men from Tennessee that were with Davy Crockett were joined by Juan Seguin's company of Hispanic Texan volunteers. Even though Sam Houston had called for them to abandon the city, some 200 men, outnumbered by nearly 2000 soldiers of Santa Anna's army decided to stand to the opposition. From February to March the forces of Santa Anna continued to arrive putting a siege on San Antonio. On March 6th of 1836 with 2000 of his 7000 plus soldiers having arrived, Santa Anna raised the red flag indicating no quarter (no prisoners). At 5:30 am the attack was ordered after days of artillery bombardment. A few women remained at the Alamo and were allowed to live so they could tell the story of Santa Anna's defeat through numbers that were exaggerated to Santa Anna's benefit. Even though Santa Anna stated they had only lost a few men against the Texans, the count as told by witnesses say that nearly 400 out of 1500 were killed or wounded by the brave 200 that defended the Alamo to the death. The cry, "Remember the Alamo" would be heard on the battlefield only a few weeks later when Sam Houston and his greatly outnumbered army defeated Santa Anna, bringing a successful end to the Texas Revolution.

The Lipan Apache were first referred to in documents by the Spanish in 1718. The word Lipan means "Warriors of the Mountains". They were in constant conflict with the Spanish when they invaded and tried to colonize Texas. In 1836, the United States government recommended the enlistment of the Lipan Apache Band as raiders to attack Mexican settlements. The Lipan's fought with the Texans in such raids for a decade (1836-1846). They settled in a territory east and southeast of San Antonio.

Antoine's is a restaurant founded, owned, and managed **by Antonine Alciatore** who was born of a wealthy New York family. The family built a farming business growing cotton in the South. The year was 1840 that Antonine opened Antoine's. Family contacts in New York with the Rockefeller family lead to Antonine creating a dish called "Oysters Rockefeller." Antoine's dad once worked with William Rockefeller Sr. and thought the name would add to the elegance of the dish. Antoine's is one of the oldest family owned restaurants in the United States. Four generations of Alciatore's owned and ran the restaurant up to 1972. The pictures against one wall display prominent people that have eaten there include names like George Washington and several more U.S. Presidents, Pope John Paul II, and many more distinguished guests.

Miss Burbank: the fictious, prestigious name that Morgan gave to Sally to disguise her identity.

Mr. J. C. Burbank was born in Ludlow, Windsor county, Vermont, in 1822. He moved to St. Paul in 1850. Mr. Burbank was the founder of a freight line that operated on the Upper Mississippi, in partnership with the American Express Company. He quickly expanded his business interests becoming the senior member of J.C. & H.C. Burbank. The company operated on the largest grocery distribution businesses in the state. He was also one of the main forces behind the organization of the St. Paul Fire and Marine insurance company becoming the President and Financial advisor.

Cairo, Illinois was built on a peninsula much like the port in Cairo, Egypt which is where it got its name from. In 1836-37 a large levee was built which encircled the city. The city of Cairo and the Canal Company built the levee to help establish the town by eliminating the threat of flooding. The levee collapsed in 1840 causing many of the settlers that had occupied the town to leave. In 1846, an area comprised of 10,000 acres was purchased by trustees of the Cairo City Property Trust. This was financed by investors that intended to make it the terminus of the Illinois Central Railroad. Unfortunately, the railroad did not arrive until 1855. In 1862 General Ulysses S. Grant occupied the city and constructed Fort Defiance to protect the Union supply base and provide a training center for the remainder of the Civil War.

California Gold Rush started with James Marshall discovering gold at Sutter's mill in Coloma, California on January 24, 1848. From that date forward, one headline after another brought miners from countries all over the world. The Non-native population of San Francisco grew from 1000 people to over 100,000 in less than 18 months. By 1852 most of the easy gold discoveries were mined out. Mining with new methods to process and flush out thinner discoveries changed the industry and made mining a more expensive process. Settlement however continued in California with the population ending up over 380,000 by the end of the 1950's

Castroville, Texas was founded in 1842 by Henri Castro, (1786–1865). Mr. Castro was a Portuguese Jew who left Spain due to the Spanish Inquisition and moved to France. In 1806 he joined Napoleon's honor guard. With the fall of Napoleon, he immigrated to America. In 1842 received agreements for land from the government to establish a colony for 600 families. In the year of 1844, the population of Castroville rose with the arrival of 2134 settlers. Mr. Castro enticed many colonists from France to come to America and join in building this community. By the time of the 1849 Gold Rush, Castroville was well known as a staging area for the assembly of wagon trains located about 25 miles west of San Antonio. Fort Hondo was about seven miles west of Castroville which provided protection. The style and architecture of Castroville was described in 1850 as European. Narrow lanes and thatched roofs. The interior of the inn was described as European rather than frontier.

Fort Clark stood on property owned by Samuel Maverick. In 1849, surveyors creating the pathway for the San Antonio to El Paso Road saw the Las Moras Springs as a strategic location to build a fort. Thus, the fort became a part of a chain of army posts that created a line along the Texas border. The purpose of the fort was to protect the military road to Coon's Ranch later becoming Franklin then renamed El Paso.

The Colt Dragoon Revolver was developed from the **.44 Walker Colt** revolver of 1847. The Dragoon was the result of the problems that the .44 Walker Colt was displaying. Even though the Walker Colt might have been the most powerful handgun produced, often called a hand cannon, it had problems in combat given the weight and exploding barrels at times because they were easily overloaded with powder. They used Pickett bullets which on occasion were loaded backwards causing irreparable damage. Their weight was nearly five pounds which lead to them being carried in pommel holsters on the saddle. The Colt Dragoon was welcomed with a shorter barrel (7.5 inches instead of the walker 9 inches). In the early stages the Colt Dragoon Revolvers were issued for the U.S. Army's Mounted Rifles who served in the Mexican American War.

The 1851 Navy Colt was first referred to as the **Colt Revolving Belt Pistol of Naval Caliber** which was .36 caliber. It was designed by Samuel Colt sometime between 1847 and 1850. One major feature was its six cylinders. Lighter and easier to carry, it became extremely popular. Originally called the Ranger model the Navy title for some reason took precedence and stuck. Over 200,000 of these firearms were produced not including production runs in London, England. The 1851 Navy was produced until 1878 when it was finally replaced by the "Peacemaker" which had metal shell casings. Men of name that across history that used the 1851 Navy included Wild Bill Hickok, Robert E. Lee, Quantrill's Raiders, John Coffee "Jack" Hays, Ned Kelly, John Henry "Doc" Holiday along with the vast majority of Texas Rangers.

Battle of Concepcion was fought at the site of the Mission Concepcion. The battle took place on October 28th, 1835. Mexican troops under Colonel Domingo Ugartechea fought Texian insurgents who were led by legendary knife fighter James Bowie and Hames Fanin. The battle only lasted 30 minutes but stands out in history as the first major engagement of the Texas Revolution.

Mission Concepcion (Mision Nuestra Senora de la Purisima Concepcion de Acuua) was established by Franciscan friars in 1716. Maintained for over 300 years it is today located at 897 Mission Road in San Antonio. This was one of several historic missions built around San Antonio.

Mr. Antonine Dubuclet, Jr. (1810 – December 18, 1887) was one of the wealthiest African Americans in the United States before the civil war. He was born near Baton Rouge the son of Antoine Dubuclet, Sr., and Marie Felecite gray. Both his parents were free blacks. Dubuclet, Sr. was part owner of the Cedar Grove plantation, which he inherited from his parents. It was known to be a very successful sugar plantation with business associates in Chicago and New York. The plantation had over seventy slaves. With his father's death, Dubuclet, Jr. took his portion of the plantation, divided with his brothers, married a wealthy free black woman by the name of Claire Pollard and proceeded to acquire land on the West side of the Mississippi as well as the East and adding to his ownership of slaves to over 100 which made him the wealthiest slave owner in State of Louisiana. Claire died in 1852 leaving him with nine children who were all sent to France to be educated. Two of his sons became Medical Doctors. He remarried in the early 1860's to Mary Ann Welsh and then took up politics as a Republican becoming the first Black Republican state treasurer of Louisiana from 1868 to 1878.

Chief Flacco, was referred to as the Young Chief Flacco. He led a band of Lipan Apache's whose territory covered most of the area surrounding San Antonio on the West and Southwest sides. Chief Flacco was a close friend of Captain John "Jack" Coffee Hayes and the U.S. Mounted Rifles (Texas Rangers). Captain Hays was quoted describing the Chief as "Tall and erect, with well-shaped limbs. He gave an impression of bounding elasticity. His circlet of eagle feathers was set back on his forehead so that it revealed his black eyes and gave to his bearing a fierce alertness coupled with strength and agility. Flacco's general appearance was suggestive of the hawk and the panther." The Chief was honored with the rank of Captain for the battles he fought alongside Captain Hayes. The Texas Ranger also credited Flacco with saving his life on several occasions in battles against the Comanches. In addition to Captain Hayes, Chief Flacco had a close friendship with Stephen F. Austin and with the first American settlers who had homesteaded in eastern Texas. In 1829, Chief Flacco joined the military campaign against the Waco and Wichita Indians. The Chief was a notable figure around the Austin area and was invited to dine with government leaders. Sentiment changed in the 1840's toward the Chief as the Lipan Apaches were blamed for conflicts created by other hostile tribes. Even with friends like Captain Hayes and Sam Houston, in the end, the Chief was rewarded with the murder of his son and was evicted from his homeland. A sad ending for a true patriot.

Galina, Illinois in 1850 had a population of nearly 14,000. The river port was on the Fevre, or Bean River about six miles upriver from its junction with the Mississippi. For someplace that they had never heard of, it seemed to be a growing and active community. The riverboats came up from St. Louis as well as down from Fort Snelling for more commercial reasons transferring goods.

Since the 1830's the city was the center of lead mining. In fact, the name Galena, in Latin, means "lead ore." At one time in the mid 1840's, 85% of the entire nations lead came from Galena. In the 1850's the city was to be the terminal for the Illinois Central Railroad, but moved to Dubuque, Iowa at the last moment. While the riverboats still dominated, Galena was one of the busiest ports moving barges and riverboats loaded with lead to New Orleans, St. Louis as well as Immigrants to the open frontier lands of Minnesota.

Mr. Jim Goodhue, Jr.: the fictious prestigious name that Morgan used to disguise his identity.

Mr. James M. Goodhue (1810-1852) was a lawyer first by trade who came from New Hampshire. After a short period, practicing as a lawyer he found his passion as a newspaper man., Mr. Goodhue moved his family to Minnesota in 1849, when Minnesota became a territory from Wisconsin where he had been the editor of a small newspaper. He created the first newspaper in Minnesota naming it the Minnesota Pioneer. The Minnesota Pioneer eventually became the St. Paul Pioneer Press. He was a strong advocate for Minnesota and wrote favorably about the West. Goodhue County was named in his honor just before he died in 1852. Some people say that he died of exhaustion after falling off a river ferry, nearly drowning.

Captain Richard C. Gray had a long career which covered the golden era of the riverboat. Even though history shows he was the Owner and Captain of the "Pennsylvania" from 1847 to 1850, he supervised the building of the "Minnesota". There is an endless list of riverboats that he either owned, was Captain, or supervised the building. His name was synonymous with riverboat from the 1840's to the 1870's. In 1857 he founded and was part owner of the Northern Line Packet Company also referred to as Gray's Iron Line.

Captain John "Jake" Coffee Hays was born at Little Cedar Lick, Tennessee. In 1836, at the age of 19, Jack decided to move to the Republic of Texas. He was appointed to a company of the US Mounted Rifles, later renamed the Texas Rangers by Sam Houston, who knew his family from years past. Jack had presented a letter of recommendation to Houston from President Andrew Jackson, his great uncle. Hays lead a life that legends are made of. He led the US Mounted Rifles against the Comanche in Texas. His friend and companion, Apache Chief Flacco rode with Hays in nearly every battle. During the Mexican American War (1846-1848), Hays commanded the First Regiment of Texas Rangers at the Battle of Monterrey. Jack was in many military campaigns. He was the first to use the Navy Colt Paterson five shot revolver. He was known to have introduced Samuel Walker to Samuel Colt which led to the design of the legendary Colt Walker six shot revolver. He married Susan Calvert in 1847. In 1849, Hays was appointed by the United States government as the US Indian agent for the Gila River county in New Mexico and Arizona. Later that year he led a party of Gold Miners to California. Following that he was elected sheriff of San Francisco County in 1850 and later in 1853 was appointed US surveyor-general for California by the President of the United States. He amassed a fortune through real estate and ranching enterprises. Jack Hays died in California on April 21, 1883, and his remains were interred at Mountain View Cemetery in Oakland.

Houston, Texas was created with the purchase of land by John and Augustus Allen from John Austin's widow for $5000. The date was August 26, 1836. The Allen brothers were fans of San Houston which the development was named after. January of 1837 saw the arrival of the first steamship. At that time the colony had twelve residents. Four months later Houston had grown to 1500 with over 100 houses. It was officially granted incorporation on June 5, 1937. In 1840 the town was divided into four wards. In 1842 Congress approved the funding to dig out the Buffalo Bayou creating a proper bay for shipping. The 1850's saw the addition of a rail system to connect the harbor area to Dallas, Fort Worth, San Antonio and El Paso. On December 29, 1845, the U.S. Congress annexed Texas to become the 28th state. The population kept doubling every decade in addition to thousands more settlers moving through Texas on their way West.

The **"Minnesota"** riverboat was built in 1849 and was owned by The Northern Line Packet Company. Captain Richard C. Gray not only became the Captain of the Minnesota, but he also assisted in the construction. The Northern Line Packet Company operated on the Upper Mississippi River from Galena to St. Paul. It fell to the fate of fire in 1862 which many of the paddle boats experienced.

The **"Big Missouri"** was the largest steamboat on the river prior to 1848. It operated between St. Louis and New Orleans most of the time. It was launched in 1845 from Cincinnati. It was a side-wheeler, 304 feet long and weighed in at 886 tons. The luxury of the Big Missouri was only enjoyed by its many travelers for three years. It was destroyed by fire near St. Louis in 1851

Joseph Murphy was 5 years old when his family left Ireland in the year 1810. They ventured to a Celtic Community which contained some friends and relatives in the United States. His family came to America to escape the Potato famine in Ireland like so many others. Many of the people from his country were handicapped being poor and illiterate. Mr. Murphy had an expert knowledge of wood which led him to setting up his own business in 1825. Documents found of Mr. Murphy's showed his skill through his comments regarding types of wood to use for various parts and when to cut that kind of wood. He was a natural at business matters, designing and building wagons. His "Murphy Wagon" held up to 5000 pounds of freight and was a common sight on the Santa Fe and Old Immigrant Trails West. His prize was the "prairie schooners" as they called them. They were strong and solid in their design and carried excessive loads. In total, Mr. Murphy, a tough Irish businessman, built and sold over 200,000 wagons in his time. The Murphy Wagon Company on Broadway Street in St. Louis was the most legendary American wagon manufacturer of them all including competitors like Espenschied Wagon Company and Studebaker of South Bend, Indiana. He has been referred to as a true transportation icon.

New Orleans dates to 400 AC. French explorers arrived in the 1690's. The French city of New Orleans was named in honor of the then Regent of France, Philip II, Duke of Orleans. In 1805 the population count was 8500. There were 3551 whites, 1556 free blacks and 3105 slaves. The population doubled in the 1830's. By the 1840's New Orleans became the wealthiest and third most populated city in the United States. In 1849 a levee broke upriver from New Orleans causing the worst flood the city had seen to date, leaving 12,000 people homeless.

The "Nominee" Riverboat was a 212-ton sidewheeler that advertised weekly trips to St. Paul, Minnesota from Galena, Illinois. The passage for such a voyage was around six dollars. The Nominee had a Captain Orrin Smith at the helm who was described as a Christian gentleman, with a sense of humor. Being a religious man, he refused to operate his steamboat on Sundays. This in no way reflected poorly of Captain Smith, as he was a formidable businessman. He was also an excellent Captain who held the record for having made the round trip from Galena to St. Paul, with proper stops, in a record time of fifty-five hours and forty-nine minutes in year 1852.

The Old Spanish Trail was created part in part by the Spanish years before the Gold Rush of the 1800's. The trail went the full length of the current United States starting in Jacksonville, Tallahassee, Pensacola, Mobile, Gulfport, New Orleans, Lafayette, Houston, San Antonio, Fort Stockton, El Paso, Las Cruces, Lordsburg, Nogales, Tucson, Phoenix, Gila Bend, Yuma to San Diego. The total distance was nearly 2400 miles, coast to coast. In 1850 the Western frontier wilderness began at Castroville/Ft. Hood area just beyond San Antonio. It was a rugged trail that had by that time marked itself with the bones of men and horses alike.

Olbers Ship mastered by **H.W. Exter** operated from Bremen, Germany to New Orleans. The passage was roughly six weeks. The Olbers Ship moved many immigrants of German descent and surrounding countries in Europe to the United States. The Port of Bremen in Germany collected numbers of people looking to escape the famine of the late 1830's. At a time when labor was getting paid $1.00 per week, the cost of passage to America was between $75 and $100. Many of the men sought out agreements to work the fare off as indentured servants. This was the ship that Jacob Waltz and Jake Weisner boarded on October 1st, 1839, arriving in New Orleans on November 17th, approximately six weeks. It isn't known for fact that they were indentured servants but others from their village did sign such agreements. The Master of the ship, H.W. Exter was known to be an excellent Master at sea having crossed the Atlantic many times in his years of service. He often bragged about how fit and stout the Olbers was, much like a proud father describing his child.

Abraham Peeples (1826-1892) was a cousin of George Roberts. From the time they met up in Jones County, Mississippi they were best friends. In 1848 Abraham Peeples and George Roberts moved to Cairo. Soon after they headed out with all their family members to Castroville, Texas to join a wagon train to the gold fields of California (see George Roberts above). Abraham and Geo eventually moved to Yuma when the gold ran out in California for them. Abraham then formed an expedition in 1863 to explore the northern Arizona Territory for Gold. Peeples hired Pauline Weaver to lead the expedition (Weaver's Valley). Peeples ended up home-steading about thirty-five miles southwest of Prescott. He made several claims and satisfied his desire for gold.

Peeples Expedition of 1863 was organized by Abraham "Abe" Peeples. After experiencing the shine coming off the gold strikes of California, several miners left California and joined up with Abraham Peeples to head up into the Arizona Territory to search for gold. Peeples hired mountain man/explorer Pauline Weaver to lead the expedition. They left with 30 men, supplies for three months in search of gold. They were all experienced miners and heavily armed knowing the stories told of what was happening to settlers that went up into the northern region. The army was scarce with most having been sent back to fight in the civil war. This left the settlers and miners to fight for themselves. Some of the famous miners in attendance were Jacob "The Dutchman"" Jake" Waltz (Lost Dutchman Mine), Jacob Weisner (Partner of

Waltz), Abraham Peeples (Peeples Valley), Henry Wickenburg (City of Wickenburg, Vulture Mine), Gideon Roberts, George "Geo" Roberts, William Roberts and Joseph Green. They left in March of 1863. In route a mule broke loose and one of the men chased it up onto a rise. There on the ground were gold nuggets. The men dug them out of the ground with their knives. Over $100,000 worth of gold nuggets were packed up in a couple of days. This was the beginning of the stories about "Rich Mountain". Henry Wickenburg would find an outcropping of quartz which turned into the Vulture Gold Mine. Largest mine in the southwest. Abraham Peeples would settle his family in what is today called Peeples Valley also having discovered gold. Gideon Roberts found gold along Walnut Creek which was later name the Hassayampa River. The men of the Peeples expedition changed the northern territory. The gold claims along the Lynx Creek turned into company names instead of individuals. 1800 feet here, 1600 there so that by late 1864 Lynx Creek was covered with mining company claims. Some already big enough to be run by absentee owners.

Prescott, Arizona was named after the historian and author, William Hickling Prescott. Richard McCormick who was the secretary of the territory at the time chose the name. In 1863 President Abraham Lincoln signed a bill that separated New Mexico from Arizona. Lincoln then chose Prescott as the capital of the newly established territory instead of Tucson, which at the time was populated with Confederate sympathizers. The discovery of gold by the Peeples expedition and Walker expedition was important to the Union with the Civil War in progress. John Gurley from Ohio was appointed territorial governor of Arizona, but died in August of 1863, never having traveled to the territory. In his place was John Goodwin of Maine. It was December 29th of 1863 when the oath of office was administered, and Governor Goodwin was officially appointed. Over the next few months and into the fall of 1864, construction of many buildings of Fort Whipple and the Territorial Governor's Mansion was completed. In 1867 the capital was moved after the Civil War to Tucson in 1867 until 1877 when the title went back to Prescott. Phoenix was finally named the capital in 1889. In 1875, due to Indian problems, the Yavapai who had occupied the area were forcibly moved southeast of the territory where they lived alongside the Apache for over 20 years. When they eventually returned to the Prescott area they were confined to a small area (which became their reservation in 1935) near Fort Whipple, where they lived in poverty.

George (Geo) Roberts (1828-1884) was born in Virginia. Geo and his cousin, Abraham Peeples became best of friends having met in Jones County, Mississippi. In 1848 Geo Roberts, Peeples and family members moved to Cairo, Illinois where they joined up with Peeples brother. Abraham's brother was in charge of a trading post or station as they called them. Geo had his cousins, Charles, Cyrus and Return were with him in Cairo when they all heard about the gold rush. Gold fever took hold and they all headed for Castroville, Texas to join up with a wagon train headed West. They arranged for three other family members from Beaumont, Texas; Daniel, Mose and Gideon Roberts to join them in Castroville to take on the adventure. The Roberts and Peeples families stayed together until they reached Sacramento, California, settling for a while to mine gold in "Grass Valley". In 1863 they had all joined up in Yuma, Arizona to join an expedition that ventured into the Arizona Territory. Abraham Peeples organized the expedition. He hired Pauline Weaver a notorious mountain man to guide the group. Henry Wickenburg (Discovered the Vulture Mine and had the city of Wickenburg named after him) and Jacob Waltz (the Dutchman of the Dutchman Mine) were also part of the expedition.

The Grand St. Charles Hotel in New Orleans, Louisiana was located on St. Charles Avenue. It was one of the greatest hotels in the United States opening in 1837. Described by author Richard Campanella as, "one of the most splendid structures in the nation and a landmark of the New Orleans skyline. It was of an original Grecian Palace-style design capped by a tall white cupola, second only in size to the dome of the Capital at Washington. The Parlor was rumored to have hosted more political events than any room of any building in the United States apart from the Capital in Washington DC. The entrance of the hotel led into a beautiful domed rotunda referred to as "The Exchange". This room was known by many of the wealthiest who visited for the slave auctions that went on every weekday from noon to 3pm.

St. Louis, Missouri was the archway to the West in the 1800's. The location on the Mississippi River and the Eastern connection through the Ohio waterway connected Philadelphia and dozens of Eastern cities to St. Louis. The Mississippi's connection to the Gulf of Mexico brought travelers and shipping from the portions of the United States East Coast and the world. For a while it seemed that everything was connected in St. Louis. Vast numbers of settlers launched their new lives to the Western frontier from St. Louis. In the mid 1800's steamboats and riverboats of all kinds were lined up three abreast at a time for a mile along the levee. In addition to the waterways, St. Louis was only sixty miles North of iron resources that turned St. Louis into a leader in the foundry industry. Stoves, tools, iron pipes and plows were all made from the pig iron. In the Spring of 1849, St. Louis had a breakout of cholera that spread in epidemic proportions killing nearly 5000 people. In the same year, 1849, a large fire broke out on a steamboat docked at the levee that spread to 23 additional boats, then to the center of the city destroying a large section of St. Louis. The result was the loss of businesses, and thousands of homes.

Salt River later renamed Phoenix was a location where the Salt River flowed through. The Salt River at one-point flows over a deposit of salt which gave the water a salty taste. The Salt River which flows the length of 300 miles includes the Black River and East Fork Rivers, the tributaries that are the headwaters. The name Salt River comes from the fact that the river flows over large salt deposit in the area where the White and Black Rivers merge. Over early decades the Salt River was used to irrigate large regions which are todays Phoenix. This made Phoenix a major grower of cotton and various produce. In 1867, Jack Swilling of Wickenburg discovered the potential of the "Valley of the Sun" with its rich soil. He addressed the only item missing, water, by starting the "Swilling Irrigation Canal Company". The first season to produce crops using the newly constructed irrigation system was in March of 1868. Phoenix was officially recognized on May 4 of the same year. In June of 1868, Jack Swilling established a post office with himself as postmaster. From there came the four mills to embolden the agricultural base.

San Antonio, Texas was founded by the Spanish in 1718. The Spaniards built a mission and a trading post. In 1821 The mission was the Mision de San Antonio de Valero, later known as "The Alamo".

Anglo-American settlers came from the United States gaining control in 1836 for the Republic of Texas. In 1845 Texas was annexed by the U.S.A. becoming a state as a result of the Mexican War between the United States and Mexico in 1848. By the end of the war the population of San Antonio was reduced to a third (800 families). It was reduced further with a Cholera epidemic in 1849. In 1850, San Antonio became the largest city in Texas with 8,235 people. The civil war mostly supported the Union not having been greatly involved in the secessionist movement. The population supported the Republican Party for decades as the Populist Party which favored a multiracial political base in the late 1800's. After regaining power in the state legislature, white Democrats passed a poll tax (1901). It effectively disenfranchised minorities and poor whites. The Republican Party lost its edge with the ethnic minorities and lowers classes of San Antonio and Texas as a whole, unable to vote.

City of Stillwater, Minnesota was originally named "Dacotah" by Joseph Renshaw Brown. Mr. Brown in 1840 was a retired soldier operating as an Indian trader. He built a small warehouse in what is now the north part of Stillwater which became the county seat of St. Croix County. Members of Brown's family populated the area, making it a favorite place for travelers to stop over. 1844 saw the beginning of the lumber business with the opening of the first mill. By 1846 Stillwater had 10 families and 20 single men. It changed quickly when in 1848 with a population of 600. In 1848, Sawyer House, became the second hotel built in the area. Eventually the Sawyer House was replaced on the same sight by the Lowell Inn which exists today. The Lowell Inn was nicknamed the Midwestern Mount Vernon. It has 13 pillars on the front of the building that represent the 13 colonies.

The Texas Rangers were formed in 1823 by Stephen F. Austin (Austin, Texas) to assist the Mexican military who patrolled the area but were spread too thin to really protect the settlers, especially Austin's colony. Some of the men were paid directly out of Austin's personal finances as others were volunteers, protecting the settlers which included their own families. In 1874 they were officially called the Texas Rangers. Prior to that date they were referred to by many names. The most popular title in the mid 1800's was the U.S. Mounted Rifles. Other names came and went as volunteers were formed to address various conflicts. They were also called the mounted gunmen, mounted volunteers, minutemen, national militia and scouts to name the most prominent. For their services, the men that got paid verses the volunteers, generally received $1.25 a day plus $5.00 a month for supplies. Officers were paid $50 to $100 per month. Mexico having secured the territory from the Spanish, lost it during the U.S. Mexican War (1846-1848). The Rangers developed a reputation as fighters as they participated in several significant battles. Lieutenant Colonel John "Jack" Coffee Hays was the most famous Texas Ranger in his time. He was a brutal and fearless fighter and won battles even being vastly outnumbered. Today the Texas Rangers are Texas' official police force.

Walker Expedition of 1863 was made up of a group of 34 miners from various parts of the United States and Canada left Colorado to come into the Arizona Territory from the north. Captain Joseph Walker Jr. led the group into the Prescott area in June of 1863. Mr. Wheelhouse of the Walker group renamed Haviyamp River to the Spanish name which was Hassayampa River. Walker creek, first referred to after Joseph Walker, was quickly renamed Lynx Creek. The Walker group meet up with the Peeples group in the Prescott area surrounding Granite Creek and Lynx Creek which started a serious gold rush into the northern region. Lynx Creek was a major gold find with clams filed over a 13-mile length. The

Walker group continued to find gold throughout the Bradshaw Mountains north of the city of Walker (named after Captain Walker) and along the Lynx Creek.

Jacob Waltz (The Dutchman Mine) and **Jacob "Jake" Weisner** left Germany October 1, 1839. Their home village of Horb had been subject to famine even as an industrialized city. In Germany at that time it was mandatory that men in their 20's like Jacob and Jake would likely have to serve in the military which aside from the dangers, paid less than what they were already starving on. Arriving in New Orleans October 1, 1839 the two men learned to prospect for gold in the Carolina's eventually ending up in the wagon train that also had the Roberts and Peeples clans. The trail led to Sacramento then back to Yuma where another grouping of men was formed to strike out for the Northern Arizona Territory in 1863 under incredible threat presented by the Apache. A few years later Waltz and Wisner would show up in Salt River, soon to be named Phoenix. After prospecting in the what is today called the Superstition Mountains, they found gold. The assay office in Phoenix could easily tell what gold came from what mine. The nuggets that were from the Dutchman mine never matched up with any of the other known mines in Arizona. Some stories say a descendant of Don Miguel Peralta, that was the only survivor of the last known Peralta expedition into the Superstition Mountains told Waltz where the mine was returning a favor for having saved his life. The Apache's killed all the members of the expedition, with one having hidden and escaped the massacre. The Peralta family from Mexico City had already discovered the gold and in a previous successful expedition brought back a fortune to Mexico. The Peralta's never disclosed where the mine was but did file a claim covering 26 square miles of the Superstitions. Jacob Waltz became known as the "Dutchman". No one knows what really happened to Weisner. Some speculate that the Apaches killed him when he was at the mine location by himself. Regardless in 1891 Jacob Waltz died leaving a box of nuggets under his bed. He tried to disclose the location to a couple friends while on his death bed. The site, never having been discovered has become one of the top 10 mysteries of all time. A young Apache girl speaking in her later years, remembered going with members of her tribe to close and disguise the opening of the mine. She claimed they even planted trees in front of it. It took weeks to finish the task. They did a very good job as thousands of Dutchman hunters over decades have never found the mine.

Pauline Weaver was born in Tennessee the son of a white father and Cherokee mother. He arrived in Arizona around 1820. He became known as an expert mountain man having explored the greater part of what is today the State of Arizona. During the mid-1800's he trapped beaver along the many streams that flowed through the norther territory. He was friendly with the Yavapai and Tonto Apaches having been credited for consistently negotiating peace with the Indians that were around the Prescott area in the 1860's. In 1863 he was hired by Abraham Peeples to lead a group of miners on an expedition up to the Prescott area. Weaver guided the Peeples party up the Hassayampa River. On their route toward Prescott they found "Rich Hill" where the golds nuggets were said to laying on the ground. Other deposits were found where Peeples settled, today called Peeples Valley. Weaver has been referred to in some history books as the first citizen of Prescott, Arizona.

Fort Whipple was a U.S. Army post that protected the Arizona Territory. It was founded by Edward Banker Willis in 1863 in Del Rio Springs. It was moved to its current location on Granite Creek on May 18, 1864 to a location on the Granite Creek, where the soldiers could better protect the miners in the area. The post was named after Amiel Weeks Whipple, a Civil War Union General.

Johannes Henricus "Henry" Wickenburg was born in Essen, Prussia (now part of Germany), in 1819. He arrived in New York City in 1847. Within two years after arriving he heard of the goldrush and headed for California. There is documentation that he became a naturalized citizen in 1853. 1862 finds him driving wagons in Tucson. He met up with mountain man and guide, Pauline Weaver, another historic figure. When Pauline Weaver was hired to guide the Peeples party into the northern Arizona territory to look for gold, Henry joined the Peeples Expedition of 1863. It is said that is was on that expedition that he discovered an outcropping of quartz streaked with rich veins of gold. As the story goes, at the time of the discovery there was a vulture circling overhead, thus he named the mine the Vulture Mine. The mine eventually produced over 340,000 ounces of gold and 260,000 ounces of silver. The town of Wickenburg grew so fast that it was almost voted the territorial capital of Arizona in 1866. Henry Wickenburg sold his mine to a man called Doc Jones. A medical doctor from Virginia that history says didn't really practice medicine. Jones agreed to pay Henry $80,000. He paid him $20,000 at the time of signing. Unfortunately, Jones never paid Henry the balance. Although he once owned the richest gold mine in Arizona, Henry had lost everything in his aging years. At the age of 85, not being able to take care of himself he walked out one morning and sat down next to a favorite tree where he proceeded to commit suicide.

The Wolf has various special meanings in Native cultures. In most cultures the Wolf was considered a medicine. They were viewed with significant similarities to the Indians. They hunted and worked as a pack for the greater good. Both the wolf and the Indian hunted to feed their entire pack/tribe. Most Native American tribes considered the wolf as the older and wiser brother of the coyote. Hunter tribes would study and follow the wolf as a guide in many ways. They tried to learn their skills and admired their courage, loyalty and strength. Some tribes credited the wolf for teaching them how to hunt and credited them with the livelihood of the tribe.

CPSIA information can be obtained
at www.ICGtesting.com
Printed in the USA
FSHW020437281120
76244FS